The Attunement

Gary B. Haley

Other Titles in the Attune Trilogy

The Attuned

The Attunist

The Attunement

Third Edition

ISBN:
9780984724642

Publisher:
Have Coffee Will Publish
(www.HaveCoffeeWillPublish.com)

Editors:
Have Coffee Will Edit
(www.HaveCoffeeWillEdit.com)

Ines Kirkpatrick
English professor, library director, and world-class editor.

Rhonda Lee Carver
Editor extraordinaire and award-winning author.

Pre-Release Proofreaders:
Jane Whitmeyer and Megan McCauley
Accomplished proofreaders for multiple (grateful) authors.

Many thanks to some stealthy editors, too… I am grateful.

Printed in the USA

Foreword

While it's true I am listed as the author of this novel, I feel compelled to let readers know that everything I've written after this foreword is based on several weeks of interviews.

The mysterious and cautious couple who experienced the following events approached me at a book signing and Q&A session in New York to ask if I'd be interested in helping them tell their story. I told them I'd have to hear more, of course, before I could even think about answering. However, at a quiet corner table in the café of a busy bookstore, I *lost* interest after hearing only a little of what they had to say.

Their claims were simply beyond belief. You would not have believed them, either. I tried to shy away and take my leave, but the man was well prepared for any doubts with proof that they were telling the truth. She asked him not to prove their claims to me. She just wanted to leave and spare me the abuse that was the nature of the proof. He assured us it was for the best, and then absolutely showed me how serious they were.

It was disturbing.

I had not experienced genuine fear in a long time, but I have to admit that his unique abilities truly frightened me. I don't scare easily, but for just a moment I felt very much like a child watching a horror movie. The fear didn't last long. I quickly realized that if he meant me any harm, I would not have lived long enough to have known it, but that kind of fright lodges in your chest, with the after-effects lingering a good long while.

Despite the fright, before the remainder of my scheduled lunch had passed, I had already decided I would not only help tell their story, I would do my best to write their adventures in a way that might encourage a large number of people to read it.

When I asked them why they had chosen to ask a total stranger to tell their story, the man laughed and stated with unreserved confidence that there were *four* reasons. First, he said he had read my book, *The Scrapbook Lecture*, and not only enjoyed it, but learned a great deal from it, too. He liked the way I had integrated history and entertainment, and he admired the dedication it took to save and compile twenty-eight years of research.

Second, he had learned from one of my websites that I had read nearly everything written by Edgar Rice Burroughs. (If you are familiar enough with Burroughs's work, you probably already understand why this was significant to him.)

Third, and more obvious, no traceable connections existed between their lives and mine. No amount of investigation into my life would uncover a link that could be used to discover his identity.

The last reason, he assured me, was the most important to him. He said the reason he had read *The Scrapbook Lecture* was because he had recognized my picture on the back of the book, even though it had been months since he had seen me. I had no idea what he was talking about until he explained. He reminded me that I had once stopped to help him by giving his car a jump when his battery was dead.

He noticed I was trying to see his face through his sunglasses, so he removed them, and the man did indeed look familiar. I had seen him one of the times I had driven to Dallas for research. He added that I had left a lasting impression on him, both in person, by stopping to help and taking the time to share my pay-it-forward story, and also as an author, in the way that I had made history easy to understand and remember. I was flattered, humbled, and glad I had stopped to help him.

In full disclosure, when I saw him there with his hood up, I almost drove right past him because I was tired, and the road trip I was on at the time was taking much longer than I had anticipated. (Big D traffic. Even on a Sunday.) I simply could not leave him stranded in downtown Dallas.

I felt as though I needed to know more about the couple's story, so I agreed to their terms and interviewed them many times over the next few weeks. Who wouldn't? However, after many conversations, just when I thought I had nearly enough to tell their story, they disappeared without a word. It's not like I knew where they lived or had any other way to get in touch with them. They always called, e-mailed, or contacted me in one way or another, but then suddenly, all contact ceased one day.

That was about eighteen months before I wrote this foreword. I couldn't help thinking that, more than likely, something bad had happened to them. I only spent a few weeks with them, but I had gotten to know them well enough to call them friends, which is an expression I use sparingly.

Good people, those two. They did more for our fellow humans than anyone since, well, John F. Kennedy. Anything could have happened to them, though. They likely had a large number of very dangerous enemies planning revenge against them, and he was on the most wanted list of several law enforcement agencies, including *her* employer, the FBI.

I hope they are both okay, of course, but I didn't just sit around and wait on them. I spent a lot of time converting the interviews into the adventure story it was, but after many months of no contact, I decided to move forward with publishing, as he had insisted I should do if we lost contact.

Although there are many odd things about his story, what may be the oddest is the fact that my new friend, the main character of this "novel," *never revealed his name to me.* He divulged no telltale facts that one might use to learn his identity, such as where he grew up, what college he attended, or even which sports teams he followed. The only bits of information he shared about his past were something about being an IT consultant, having a beloved cabin somewhere in the Rocky Mountains, and he was probably not from Chicago. Not a lot to work with.

The woman with him had called him "Babe" once, but she never said his name in my presence. I have occasionally wondered whether or not she knew his name. Still, I became close enough to my new friends over the weeks to extend his wishes into the storyline, making him as much a mystery to readers as he was to me. I will take a moment to quote as accurately as I can recall from the conversation we had on the day they first made contact:

"I just want to tell my story to someone who can record it in good faith, under the conditions that I need to protect extended family and friends from some terribly bad people. I need to share this with someone before one of these bad situations I keep getting myself into kills me. No one will believe all of what I have to say, but still, I would like to document everything that has happened, and everything significant we have done over the past several months.

"Revealing my name or any other identifying information is not an option. You'll see why as I tell you my story. Of course, I'll have to change enough of the facts and places and so forth to throw people off and direct suspicions into dead ends. Some things I will describe precisely as they happened, while other things are complete fiction, except for one key element, which will be the point of sharing it in the first place.

"Any of the details I intend to share that can be traced back to me are so unbelievable that a judge or jury would never believe it possible, so I think I'm okay in talking about those details."

As a result of all the changed facts and details, and the nature of this story's phenomenon, publishers refused to print the story unless it was labeled fiction. Please forgive me for this, however, as you read, try to think about stories you may have seen on the news or even noticed on the covers of those rags with the sensational headlines at the grocery store checkout lines.

You might make some connections, although you should know that I will neither confirm nor deny any links between the events in the news and the stories my new friends revealed during their interviews. Mostly because I'm not certain, myself.

So! What would *you* do if you found you had the power to temporarily immobilize people? What would you do if you could purposefully kill with merely a focused thought? Would you avoid being around people altogether so that you wouldn't have to face the possibility of harming others?

Or would there be dead people everywhere?

Would you, perhaps, clean up your town? Or make considerable improvements in your personal life? Maybe even become a public guardian? (For a loud group of ungrateful people who blame you for all that is wrong with their world because you have the means to fix it, yet you don't.)

What would you do? I'll tell you what my new friend did, as he told me.

Introduction

Pleased to wake up and find the first snow of the season beginning to accumulate, I knew a nice, warm fire and a hot cup of tea would make the morning perfect. I added kindling and fresh firewood atop the night's cooling embers and, after some enthusiastic poking and bellowing, the tips of leaping orange flames reached up into the chimney.

As the new aspen logs began to burn and crackle, the fire's soothing warmth began radiating through the chain curtains. I sat sideways on the hearth, lost in thought, and warmed my hands until the mountain chill in my bones subsided.

The whistling copper tea kettle in the next room coaxed me away from the native stone fireplace and into the kitchen. While the tea steeped, I pulled a heavy jacket over my sweats and then stepped out onto my back porch to enjoy a steaming Sunday morning cup of tea.

Sinking into a plush lounge chair, I wrapped my hands around the hot cup and carefully shifted my position until I was comfortable. Witnessing nature redecorate the beautiful scenery behind my home was a treat I always enjoyed. My back yard slowly changed from a predominantly autumn yellow and golden orange to a white winter blanket pierced by tall, intermittent evergreens. I filled my lungs with cold, clean, rustic mountain air, which heightened my senses and pacified my restlessness.

A few quiet minutes to relax in the dawn's early light might be exactly what I needed to help get into the right frame of mind. Making what could easily be a lifestyle-altering decision is not something to take lightly. I struggled with all the nuances of trying to decide whether I should accept the offer of a new job.

What if this decision changed my life into something I could no longer appreciate? I wondered if the snowy weather or changing seasons would interject some kind of unconscious influence into an already difficult decision.

Settling down further into the comfortable cushions, I sipped my tea and tried to focus. However, with the natural silence that comes from the nearest neighbors being nearly a mile and a half away, it was easy to become lost in thought. Within seconds, the beauty of the forest had me distracted again.

Snowflakes the size of dimes floated down silently as I watched the grass and groundcover slowly disappear under the falling snow. A leap of free association somewhere in my mind found a comparison between the disappearing foliage and the dwindling interest in my career of fourteen years. It was a little like watching a time-lapse video of the past couple of years as my efforts and expectations at the office slowly became shrouded and suppressed by bureaucracy and ulterior motives.

Occasional streams of bright morning sunlight found their way through the clouds and the trees, sparkling in the snow as if they represented promising new beginnings. Right on cue though, when my mind drifted back to the insane politics involved in getting anything accomplished at the office, the clouds peppering the eastern horizon would close ranks enough to dampen the sunlight and intensify the snowy chill.

For the past few months, I had been trying to convince myself that my job was not so bad, or at least believe my situation could be far worse. Yes, I appreciated the stability and reliability of the corporate world, as well as the opportunities for promotion and advancement inherent in most large companies. I was also involved in several projects I would like to see through to completion and had many other job-related, yet personal, goals to fulfill as well.

The cool, crisp air on my face and the back of my neck became uncomfortable when I thought about leaving the defense industry. The corporate world I could live without, but contributing to our nation's defense gave my life purpose.

Condensation from my breath mixed with steam from the hot tea as I brought the cup to my lips in an attempt to clear my mind again. The morning was quite chilly, but when you appreciate the calm serenity of a quiet snowfall, the picturesque view impresses you to the point of not caring about the temperature. I gazed out through the falling snow and into the woods while savoring bold, soothing, bergamot.

Refocusing, I considered my new opportunities for a moment. I would be working for a research facility that had a prestigious reputation and was consistently responsible for displacing well-established paradigms. Several contracts were currently in the works with separate, independent teams assigned to each project.

Their business model was structured in a way that allowed each team to govern themselves, with unique company policies that relied heavily upon the integrity and ethics of individuals. This typically paid off in the form of very loyal and energetic employees. I was intrigued. The concepts they endorsed were obviously working for them and certainly sounded like something I could support.

If I accepted the position, my workload would include supporting a team of researchers with whatever information-technology assistance they required. Mostly software engineering and database solutions, but could also be any type of IT support, or something else entirely.

I had to admit that I loved the possibility of never having to attend another one of those weekly meetings where I had to witness the incompetent ceaselessly derail progress with counterproductive, hidden agendas. It was comforting to imagine deadlines that were not stressfully impossible, and the thought of someone appreciating my efforts appealed to me. Was I faced with a genuine opportunity? Or was I falling victim to a classic case of the grass being greener?

A sudden movement in the trees behind my spent vegetable garden attracted my attention. Two squirrels were scampering through the snowy branches. Were they trying to find shelter from the cold or merely playing in the changing conditions of their simple world? Small clumps of snow fell from the bouncing branches as they jumped from tree to tree like little daredevils and were soon far away.

When the squirrels were out of sight, my eyes scanned the snowy scene in search of something else on which they might focus. Taking in my surroundings, I noticed how beautiful my back yard had become.

A blanket of white illuminated a scattered group of bright pink, late-blooming perennials. They poked up through the snow, contrasting pleasantly with the gray and light brown bark of the trees and the dark greens of pine needles. Soothing, peaceful snowflakes and the distinctive smell of smoke from the fireplace put me into a dreamlike trance as I delved deeper into the possibilities of a major career change.

Beginnings

I remember that morning on my back porch with vivid clarity. The memories were burned into my memory through the very act of making such a tough decision after many days of stress and tormenting uncertainty. As I sat overlooking my beloved, picturesque back yard that day, watching the snow fall, I decided on a life of research along with the possibility of contributing something worthwhile to humanity. I chose this new life over a life of—what? I still don't know.

A month earlier, I had become fed up with the politics and frustrations at work and decided to get a feel of the turbulent job market outside of the defense industry. I put together a resume, which took two evenings and a weekend, and posted it on a couple of career-oriented Internet sites. I was taken totally by surprise when I got a call a little over an hour later.

The party on the other end of the line had made strange requests but explained that they did not want me to draw unnecessary attention to myself during the interview process. I was also told they would be willing to travel to my home for the interview. I guessed the allure of the Rocky Mountains might have had something to do with that, but I didn't mind.

He said he and a colleague were willing to meet with me the following evening, after hours, so I would not have to miss a minute of work. He pointed out that I could always repost my resume if I did not accept their offer, but for the time being, he suggested that I immediately remove it from the website, or sites, *if* I was interested in a career in research.

I assured him that I was interested.

The interview was tough, mostly focusing on my claims of being able to write screaming fast SQL and get incompatible information systems to communicate with one another. The two men that showed up were also interested in the depth of my computer experience in the research and development field of the defense industry, which was extensive. We talked our way through a large pizza and beyond. I answered many questions but asked nearly as many. I wanted them to feel as though they were being interviewed as well. Because they were.

"Our IT director, Bob, was particularly impressed with your 'blog."

"What, that old thing? The name seems a little contrived now, but back when I first put TheSQLWhisperer.com together, it was kind of cool."

"As it turns out, Bob reads your 'blog regularly and has passed on a couple of your tips to one of our DBAs."

"Excellent!" It was good to know that people used some of the SQL examples I took the time to make generic and post online. "So, how'd that work out for you guys?"

"Well, we're here."

A few minutes before ten o'clock, they assured me that this union would be a rare opportunity for all involved and that adequate compensation would not be a problem. The more casually dressed of the two made me a generous offer on the spot that had caused me to make a face they interpreted as disappointment, although it most certainly was not. The defense industry isn't known for generous salaries unless your job title starts with "Chief" and ends with "Officer."

He repeated "Okay," several times as he withdrew the offer, which was about 35 percent more than I was currently making. He took out a piece of paper from his shirt pocket, held it out away from his squinting eyes, and spouted out a figure that would raise my salary by over 40 percent.

The more nicely dressed of the two added that they would be willing to pay for my moving expenses, as well as set me up in a high-rise condo that he was sure would meet my needs. He quickly included a disclaimer that I would have to make the payments on the condo, of course, but they would find something suitable, make the arrangements *and* provide the down payment.

I suddenly became wary. Why? Why were they trying so hard to recruit me? I am good at what I do, but there must be hundreds of people qualified for this position.

"Why me?" I came straight out and asked them. "Why do you want me? You probably have your choice of hundreds of applicants."

"We're sure," started the more casually dressed of the two, glancing at his coworker, and the older one interjected, "Quite sure."

"Yes, we are *quite* sure that your particular skill set is exactly what we're looking for."

I had to laugh at that. "So, you're *sure* then?"

"Quite. We have found that skill sets such as yours are actually somewhat rare."

How could anyone say no to that? I felt sure I would accept but told them I would consider their kind offer for a few days and get back to them. Making a life-altering decision that late in the evening after a mere four-hour conversation was not a good idea. I struggled with that decision for days, but have never regretted making it.

Plans

Despite the early snow falling in the Colorado Rocky Mountains, the temperature was still stifling deep in the *heat* of Texas. What little shade existed in the prison yard was occupied by groups of people who were not easily displaced, so if prisoners wanted to have a private conversation with a couple of fellow inmates, they had to go for a walk in the yard. In the direct sunlight.

A car thief with a nasty scar running through his right eyebrow looked over his shoulder. Seeing that they are out of earshot of rival gang members and guards, he picked up where they had left off earlier. "Best time to move is a half hour or so before the evening shift change."

His orange coveralls faded more than the others, the wrinkled rapist asked, "Spell it out, yo?"

"Hacks'll be tired and more likely to hesitate."

"Gotcha."

A few steps later, the one who had been silent so far added, "We'll just need a few seconds if we do this right. When ya think you can finish those bones?"

Suddenly mad enough to risk getting another scar on his face, their fellow gang member raised his voice. "Hey! It takes time to cut the corners off bricks with nothin' but a dime. We'll be diggin' for weeks!"

"Easy now. Save the rage for the wage. Just remember, the sooner you're done, the sooner those chromers'll catch cold."

Insignificant

Three weeks later I had fulfilled my two weeks' notice and had taken a scouting "vacation" to New York. As I looked through each room of my cherished log cabin, I felt it was no longer home. Furnishings were covered with white sheets and anything of any value, like antiques and electronics, had been packed up and were on their way to New York. I made one last cup of tea in a paper cup and stepped out onto my back porch again to soak in enough of the Rocky Mountains to last a good long while.

Also on my mind was the thought that I was an extremely lucky individual to have landed such a prestigious job at Elucidate Research Laboratories (ERL). I had no idea what to expect or what I would be doing, as ERL was secretive and protective of its research.

All employees were on a need-to-know basis, particularly the new hires. Even many of the ERL investors had no idea where their money was going until the final product or technology was delivered. Their clients tolerated the blind investments because they were rarely disappointed in the returns.

Savoring that last cup of tea, I tried to focus on the future. I wondered what surprises were in store for me. I hoped I could live up to my full potential. Had I known my life would change in ways that would prevent me from ever returning to the way it was, I might have hesitated. Yes, I still would have made the same decision, but I'm sure I would have hesitated. It's just that, thinking back, a simple thing like a career change now seems to be relatively insignificant.

Intimidating

The following Monday morning, several hundred miles from the Rocky Mountains, FBI Agent Carla Bright scraped ice from her windshield in the parking lot of her new, modest apartment in Burke, Virginia. She was determined not to be late on the first day of her new promotion, despite one of the earliest and most severe freezing rainstorms she could remember. This was her first assignment in the DC area, so it made her wonder if the local weather around her new neighborhood was always so severe in the fall.

A cold, bitter wind blew snow and ice fragments around in a blistering whirlwind between her face and the windshield, but that just made her scrape even faster.

She stopped scraping for a moment as she listened to the weather and traffic reports coming from the radio inside her car. The storm was only getting worse with more snow and freezing rain on the way, and her planned route of I-395 was no longer a good choice, as it was backed up behind an ice-related incident near the Little River Turnpike.

"Better take I-66," she thought out loud as she continued scraping. The warmth from the defroster finally began to melt some of the ice as well, but she felt as though her ears were already suffering from frostbite as she moved to the rear windshield.

Her mind wandered back over the past six years of service with assignments in Pittsburgh and two field offices outside Boston and Philadelphia where she had constantly been assigned cases that were either old, had precious few leads, or both.

Those were hard times. Most of the routine investigations seemed to drag on forever, although one evolved into a dangerous situation, resulting in a nasty scar on her back. But as she was so fond of saying, "on the Bright side," the experience had certainly refined her skills, tolerance, and patience, possibly even earning her this promotion.

Carla had worked the cases to the best of her ability but had only solved fifteen percent of them. In her eyes, she had been failing miserably and attributed the good reviews and nice pay raise every year to the fact that she was the only woman in the group. Those good ol' boys were simply covering their collective asses to prevent a class action lawsuit based on gender bias.

She had often felt like the token female assigned there to satisfy equal rights laws. She grew even more suspicious when her highly opinionated supervisor recommended her for a position in Washington, DC. She wondered if he had been assigning her the cold cases because they were less dangerous, or because his old-school ways made him believe that cold cases were more akin to "women's work." Was her promotion simply a way to get her out of his office?

Wisely, she had kept these thoughts and opinions to herself and remained focused on doing whatever job she was assigned. This was for the best, too, because when she went to the interview in DC, she realized the truth. The agent in charge had explained to her that she had first been given cold cases because that is what *all* the new people in their department were assigned. It was something of an initiation they had all been forced to endure, but also served to discover and illustrate the capabilities of the new agent.

Back in Pittsburgh, she had solved an eleven-year-old murder case within weeks. The department head was so impressed that he assigned her two more cold cases to see if her success was a fluke, or if she really was that talented. Carla tackled those as if she had something to prove and solved one of them before two months had passed.

She did not have the best of luck with the other, or the next few, but it did not matter. She had already earned her reputation. Several agents, both new and seasoned, had already investigated the cases and had turned up nothing. Carla didn't just uncover a new clue or lead; she had *solved* the cases and made arrests.

Many people had sought the new position she had landed in Washington, DC. Most investigators were also aware that if the White House needed additional FBI personnel quickly, they invariably looked to that office, as they were just a ten-minute drive away. Carla was appreciative of her new opportunities but did not yet realize how fortunate she was.

Through semi-ice-free windows, Carla made her way around stalled cars and trucks through slow, bumper-to-bumper traffic and now heavy snowfall. She was relieved to arrive at her new assignment on time, despite all the obstacles, and report for duty well before the appointed hour.

Carla's first day on the job had not been what she expected. Even though the office was small enough to find restrooms, the break room, and office supplies without help, she still got the nickel tour and met four colleagues who managed to overcome the traffic challenges.

"This is The Coffee Can. If you want to drink coffee, pitch some change in here." Her new lead, Agent Goodman shook a few coins around in the bottom. "When we run low, we take turns bringing in a big can of Folgers or a couple of bags of dark roast. The good stuff, please. The darker the roast, the better. We often need a jumpstart around here in the mornings. And you know the drill. Your mother doesn't work here, so you'll have to clean up after yourself."

The half-hearted attempt at humor was lost as the sentence turned bitter near the end. His old age was not an excuse to bring up Carla's mother, who had recently passed away. She was surprised that the seasoned FBI agent lacked the social finesse to leave someone's mother out of an introductory conversation.

Agent Goodman was not unfriendly, but he seemed anxious to finish the tour. Carla wondered if he just needed to get back to work, or if he was irritated about having to show her around because of inclement weather.

Carla had no way of knowing that the man was intimidated by her presence. The regional director had warned Agent Goodman that she probably had as much upward potential as anyone in the agency, but no one bothered to share that praise with her.

They talked as they walked, stopping occasionally for introductions or brief instructions for a finicky old printer. Carla suppressed the urge to ask him if he thought she was the new admin.

"Here's your office," he said with an arm extended through a door. She stepped in and looked around, but when she did not react how he thought she should have, he added, trying hard to hide how intimidated he felt, "Welcome home! Feel free to hang pictures or decorate in any way you like."

His fake smile rubbed her the wrong way. Before she could respond, he needlessly added, "No candles or loud radio, please."

Her odd new lead suddenly began to appear quite proud of himself, as though he had given his first tour of the place. "Oh, and, uuuh," he pointed to a folder on her desk, "there is your first assignment." When she picked up the folder, he hurried off, but over his shoulder tossed a slightly sarcastic, "Good luck!"

Her new office was bigger than she had imagined, and the high-back leather chair certainly looked comfortable, so she tried it on. "Nice." Carla settled in, logged onto the network, and began working on her new case, reading files and reports until late that evening.

Speculation

"I think that being able to record the act of solving a logic problem, or reasoning in general, will change the very way mathematicians and engineers work."

All four of his colleagues nodded thoughtfully while enjoying sandwiches in a crowded New York deli. Squeezed around a table for four, they took turns speculating about how others might be able to use the results of their research, if only they could process the enormous amount of data they were accumulating faster.

"Could be, but I think the quick cash will be made in keyboardless, touch-free phones and computers."

"Doubtless."

"Mmm hmmm."

"Can you imagine people who have lost the ability to speak because of a stroke being able to communicate effectively again?"

The co-workers were lost in the same thoughts for a moment.

"I am betting that the Pentagon will suddenly see a need for more sophisticated navigation equip–" His mobile phone interrupted the lively, lunchtime conversation, and the only Middle Eastern man in the group excused himself to answer his phone. The others resumed their discussion and didn't notice the sick expression that invaded their coworker's face. The only thing he heard was a gruff voice speaking Arabic.

"Anah alwaqt." *It is time.*

Cheating

Seven and a half hours after the first card had been played, the Texas Hold 'Em tournament was down to two people. One was an older, not-so-gentlemanly man with silver hair and the other was a younger, blonde-headed man in an old cowboy hat.

After having the short stack for most of the tournament's final table, the young man had somehow limped through under the radar and now faced a mean card shark. However, during the dozen or so hands since the second runner-up had gone bust, he had caught up to the elderly man and was now the chip leader by a small margin.

"All in."

"*All in?!* You only looked at one of your cards, son!"

"It was all I needed to know," the younger man explained with a smile and a shrug.

Furious, the old man looked at his cards, allowing a blank expression to haunt his face for a full second. As he flipped his cards over, the poker expert stared into his opponent's eyes and boomed, "All in" loudly and confidently. The queen of spades and the queen of diamonds bounced onto the table.

Tilting his head down so his eyes became hidden under the brim of his old, worn-out cowboy hat, the younger gambler revealed the jack and six of spades.

Laughing, the older man taunted the crowd favorite. "That's it? *THAT'S* all you needed to know? You can't even make a straight out of that, son."

The dealer burned a card and flopped down another queen and the ten and seven of spades. A high-tension silence fell over the spectators while the dealer gave everyone time to fully realize the situation. With a grand prize of two hundred and fifty thousand dollars at stake, the game had become worthy of poker network television. Three queens in one hand and a possible flush in the other.

Burning another card, the dealer then turned the three of spades. Spectators howled and the older gambler's nostrils flared.

Lifting his head slowly and dramatically, so his eyes became visible to his opponent again, the cowboy's expression had still not changed. He showed no signs of stress or anxiety. The older man was actually sweating.

"You haven't won yet. If the river is another queen, a ten, a seven, a three, or *any* other spade, *I* win. I'm working on a full house and a four-of-a-kind here, and *I* have the high spade if we both get a flush." An old, crooked finger tapped the queen of spades in front of him enough times to become annoying. Still, the cowboy remained stoic.

The silence had turned to a bit of a murmur as the dealer burned another card. When the river hit the table, the crowd stood and cheered at the king of clubs, and the younger gambler smiled and nodded.

Above the noise of the crowd, you could hear the old man being a poor loser. He was shouting something about wanting a rematch as the conditions weren't fair. "*Two* opponents dropped out because they were sick! That changed the dynamics of the entire game! What are the chances of that happening, anyway? *Two* people getting sick?" Pointing, he crossed the line as he shouted, "He *has* to be cheating somehow! *No one* is that lucky."

Standing calmly, still smiling, the younger man shrugged and walked off to collect his earnings.

Peers

My first assignment at ERL *did* turn out to be completely life-altering. I would like to think that it resulted in a long-lasting, positive effect for many other decent people, despite the need to use the common rationalization that favorable results often justify the means. The small team I joined consisted of one woman and four men—all brilliant scientists. Between them, they held a myriad of doctorates, honors, awards, and other notables.

Working with them was an honor, but to be considered an equal among them was overwhelming. All five were dedicated to their work, but, fortunately for me, none of them knew a thing about programming languages or computer interfaces. They even thought that spreadsheets made suitable databases. For them, right-clicking a mouse to find the options and properties of an object was a sophisticated maneuver.

The project itself, with the adequately ambiguous name of Express, dove deep into a study on interpreting the brain waves produced by conscious human thoughts. They were separating and identifying meaningful patterns from the millions of waves being produced, and attempting to translate them into usable computer commands. Though still in its infancy, the ultimate goal was a thought-controlled computer interface.

As I had predicted, moving to New York required serious lifestyle adjustments. I had been to a couple of conferences in the Big Apple a few years earlier, but staying in a hotel for a few days and living there turned out to be two different things. The 7th Avenue condominium ERL had arranged for me was in the heart of the Theater District and probably the envy of many, but the concept of not needing a car remained alien, at first.

On the lower floor of the same building where I lived was pretty much everything one needed as far as food and supplies go. There was a deli, a small grocery store that specialized in organic foods, a hair salon, and a pizza place that delivered. Across a side street was a bookstore with a coffee shop, and I was within easy walking distance of Times Square and Central Park. I could also catch the subway right around the corner and emerge directly in front of the building where I worked.

I adapted to big-city life and rarely missed my car. What I couldn't get used to though, was the cigarette smoke, which I often encountered. Sadly, many of the New Yorkers I encountered did not seem to care who they poisoned with their secondhand smoke.

And when they finish their smoke, what do they do? They toss the chemical-filled filter onto the street or sidewalk. When it rains, what happens to the chemicals that seep from all those cigarette butts? Where do the toxins go? Right into our groundwater. I wanted to tell them our planet is not their ashtray, but if they were reasonable people, they wouldn't be smoking in the first place.

Getting used to the overall indifference to crime, gang activity, and secondhand smoke was difficult. The streets were busy all day and the sidewalks were fluid with pedestrians wearing business attire or touristy clothes, but they ignored the graffiti and gang tags on nearly all permanent structures. If someone's property had been defaced in my hometown, it would have been dealt with the very next morning in the form of a sandblaster or a fresh coat of paint. Here in New York, the gangs were the ones painting over each other's tags.

One evening, as I sat on my balcony overlooking the once-prestigious 7th Avenue, I watched a gang of punks with metal-studded faces walk down the middle of the sidewalk as if they owned it. People coming from the other direction would suddenly remember a bestseller they had been wanting and duck into the bookstore or step into an entryway while the punks passed by.

The few that chose to walk around or through the gang were pushed out of the way, accosted verbally, or spit upon. Where were the cops? If most of the people on the streets knew enough to get out of the way of the hoodlums, without a doubt, the police knew a problem existed. Where were they? I had heard that New York had been cleaned up considerably, which made me wonder what the streets had been like *before* the cleanup.

Watching gang activity became a fairly common part of my routine in the evenings. After a while, I noticed members of each gang wore one predominant color and that the colors they were "flying" were invariably in a direct correlation with either the direction from which they came or went.

After realizing this, it did not take long to deduce that two or more gangs were going onto each other's turf to leave tags taunting their rivals. Nearly every evening they were spraying or drawing messages to each other, but then, more often than not, the rival gang would have sprayed over them again before morning.

It all seemed so pointless. When I was young, wasting my time with such foolishness would have never occurred to me. I was always too busy with school, sports, cars, part-time jobs, or girls, most likely. Yet I was sure that starting any conversation with anything like, "Son, when I was your age," would be a counterproductive effort.

Still, the gang activity bothered me. Particularly when I witnessed them harassing people they thought might be in their way or trespassing in their territory. I desperately wanted to do something, but what could one man do? The idea of solving this problem stayed with me much of the time, but I did not allow things to trouble me enough to interfere with my new job, which I thoroughly enjoyed.

My lab became my home away from home. There was plenty of space for us to spread out and be out of each other's way, but still within range of a raised voice. We each had a cubbyhole nestled between file cabinets, bookshelves, and medical research equipment.

There were also a couple of other places partitioned out to where we could retreat if we had inspirations to pursue, or if someone got on someone else's nerves. Our desks and PCs were arranged so that you could see someone approaching. No one was able to walk up behind you and read that personal e-mail you were in the middle of writing.

These people did not miss a single trick. However, we spent most of our time in the central part of the lab where a state-of-the-art digital electroencephalograph was mounted next to a particularly nice recliner. It seemed a bit intimidating at first, but being wired to the EEG turned out to be no big deal.

My teammates were great, too. All five of them were dedicated to their goals, yet they still found time to make it fun. For instance, they had made a game of trying every restaurant in the area, which were abundant. On days they decided to go out to lunch as a team, they debated with each other to decide what type of food fit the mood for the day and then which one of those restaurants to try. On my first day, they had quite a debate on whether they should start over from the beginning on my behalf or forge on with the next restaurant.

"Dr. Gordon?" Doing his best to sound official was Dr. David Lloyd, a forty-six-year-old of English and German descent with salt and pepper hair. The hint of a mischievous smile made it obvious that something was up, even to someone who had just met him. "Shall we start from the beginning of our list, or deprive our new colleague of the fine dining we've been privileged?"

Dr. Gregory Gordon, our director, took his cue and fell right in as though they had all rehearsed it. With a thoughtful glance around the room, he said, "I wouldn't be opposed to experiencing some of the finer establishments again, but I feel we'd be more satisfied as a group if we continued to try new places without backtracking." As he spoke, he continued looking around the room as if he were searching for the right words.

With Dr. Gordon being the team's eldest member at seventy-one, and our point of contact for interteam communication, others followed his lead. Hurrying over to join the conversation was forty-two-year-old Dr. Carol Bertram who could only be described as typically American with ancestries originating from many sources. At first, she seemed like Miss All-Business, but she turned out to be good-natured when she was not fully engrossed in her work.

While looking up at the tall Dr. Gordon, she began detailing the importance of how we should do things as a team, including trying all the new places together.

Dr. Adham Al-shamrani, a thirty-eight-year-old man with a heavy accent, put in his two cents about how long it had been since they had enjoyed Middle Eastern cuisine of any kind. As a distraction tactic, someone reminded him that they had gone to a Greek restaurant less than a week ago. "That is not the same thing, and you know it. Just give me an authentic chickpea or some falafel or something with tahini in it, and I will be good for days."

Finally, Dr. Andrew Livingston, a fifty-two-year-old man of African descent with a clean-shaven head and perfect English, joined the conversation. However, I did not have a clue what he said, for they were all talking at the same time. I had to smile and watch for a moment. They were all carrying on their own, individual conversations toward the center of the gathering as though others were listening. With each one of them intent on being heard, they began getting louder and louder as their opinions became stronger with each point made.

I could make out little bits of their conversation. "What are you saying? We should start over every time we get a new member?" "…besides, you know you love baklawa…" and "I beg your pardon sir, but we *must* maintain continuity as a team…"

They went on and on. Made me laugh! After watching a full minute of banter, I settled it with a loud whistle and the suggestion of moving on to the new restaurants, as either way would be like starting over for me no matter where I started. There were nods of approval, hand shrugs that could only be interpreted as "of course," and an arm was waved in my direction with their palm up, as if to introduce me to the crowd. Then they all turned together and started off like a school of fish, with me in tow wondering what had just happened.

As we walked out of the lab and down the hall, they began complimenting each other's arguments and unique debate techniques. I could not stop laughing. Yes, these were fun-loving people. Science geeks, for sure, which is not too different from the typical IT geek. I was pleased and felt reassured that I had made a good career decision.

Unfulfilled

The case that Carla had been assigned was so cold and insignificant that she could not bring herself to waste her time. A little over five years earlier, someone had used public computers and free hotspots to log onto the Internet and set up untraceable e-mail accounts on unsuspecting free portals so that they could send threats and demands to various politicians and figureheads.

The e-mails stopped abruptly after about three years, and no one had ever followed through with any of the threats. Two of the people who were threatened had even forgotten the incident.

None of the threats developed into actions, so it seemed like a serious waste of resources to her. Being new, she didn't want to make waves in this new unit. She went to the head of the department and explained that she was quite capable of working multiple cases at once. The department head was pleased and not at all irritated, as she had anticipated. He immediately assigned her four more cases, but they were four more *cold* cases.

Barely able to contain her disappointment, she took her new workload and did her best to solve them with the personal goal in mind that the sooner she solved all the workable cases, the sooner she could move on to more rewarding work.

Meanwhile, she learned her way around the capitol. She found a quaint, cozy restaurant and oyster bar with outrageously delicious entrees. Even the healthier options were good *and* reasonably priced. An independently owned coffee house and bakery next door made life even better. Away from the counter a couple of small reading rooms adorned with comfy chairs and four large bookshelves stuffed full of interesting and eclectic titles enticed Carla back many times.

A few blocks from her apartment a fresh market sold whole foods and many of the products and services that health-conscious consumers craved, including chair massage. The employees there soon began greeting her by name. The fitness center in her building had large screen TVs on the walls, so she watched the early morning news while she worked out.

She stayed busy all the time and was almost always in a good mood yet, despite all these creature comfort niceties, her life seemed to be becoming increasingly unfulfilling. She suspected that the monotonous work of the stagnant case load might be responsible for her discontent, but could never quite pinpoint the cause enough to figure out how to get out of the funk.

The lack of companionship didn't help, but Carla had tried dating from time to time, and there always seemed to be a little something wrong with every effort. Having access to police and criminal records of potential boyfriends eliminated many of them before she wasted her time finding out firsthand that they were trouble. Most people would be surprised at how many guys have a police record. Bar fights, DUIs, warrants for unpaid moving violations... she did not understand why the only ones that ever seemed interested in her were the "bad boys."

Sometimes she had been attracted to them, too, which disgusted her. Carla had not allowed those relationships to continue for long. She could *not* put her career in jeopardy. Again.

Bonuses

Things started happening relatively fast at my new job. My computer knowledge was desperately needed to help finish up another project, so they briefed me on the contractual specifics and I joined that team as well. I also helped the team with some simple reports and spreadsheet functions and formatting. This led to linking the formulas directly to the data sources via several efficient Stored Procedures, which sped up data access considerably.

I have to admit that I was genuinely surprised at the general lack of basic computer skills needed to operate proficiently, so I took it upon myself to start sponsoring what became known as "Lunch-n-Learn" sessions.

Once or twice a week, people would bring a sack lunch and gather around my laptop in the break room for an hour or so to ask questions and learn tricks and tips to make their job easier. Everyone was invited, so it turned out to be quite a high-profile endeavor. Within weeks, I found myself on several other projects, doing things like setting up new databases to help track tests, writing queries for existing systems, developing macros and functions for spreadsheets, and organizing data cubes.

The lack of IT support in the company was startling, even to me, and I am well aware of this widespread issue. More businesses than not suffer from a serious lack of proper IT support. I did my best to meet their abundant needs, and as a result, nearly every team benefited in some way.

When the next quarterly report was published, it noted the increased efficiency throughout the company and praised everyone who had sacrificed personal time to learn better ways to do business.

Within minutes of the report being made public, our stock gained nearly 3 percent and began an upward climb that lasted weeks. As a result, the bonuses from completed projects reflected these significant improvements in the form of bigger checks, which helped me more than most because, by then, I was a member of over half of all the research teams. Contracts were being completed every three to five weeks, every one of which meant another bonus equivalent to about a month's salary.

Life was good.

Hint

Assisting my original team with the Express project continued to be my main role at ERL, and I took that responsibility to heart. We re-engineered the lab's electroencephalograph to export its data to the best relational database and hardware money could buy. I wrote a parsimonious graphing control that displayed each identifiable wave in real-time and allowed any number of waves, or any combination of waves to be viewed or hidden at any time.

We took turns wearing the leads attached to our scalps to get a wider range of data, and on the off chance that one of us would be better at focusing in a way that allowed us to separate the elusive patterns.

Within a few months, we had collected about eight hundred gigabytes of useful data, which the pattern-recognition software analyzed twenty-four hours a day. However, we were nowhere near being able to associate specific thoughts with discernible wave patterns. Deviations from the standard "10-20" electrode placement system did not seem to help, nor did studying waves below 8 hertz, so we concentrated mostly on the established 8 to 80 hertz waves, but captured everything else up to about 150 hertz as well.

After many weeks of unsuccessful attempts to associate unknown patterns with unknown frequencies, we changed our strategy. We tried finding patterns by the process of elimination. I wrote a simple program that randomly displayed a short list of common computer commands on the screen while saving the exact time each word was being displayed. Whoever's turn it was to be "in the hot seat" would repeat the flashing words in their head as they appeared on the screen.

These new tactics produced better results—albeit painfully monotonous. Dr. Carol Bertram came up with the idea of adding concepts to the list instead of just computer commands. We decided that task swapping and highlighting a string of text could be represented by thinking about switching to the next task in a list of tasks, and picturing the cursor moving over a line of text, leaving the characters highlighted.

Not only did adding these simple concepts to the list of concentrations help to alleviate the monotony, they also served to add a new dimension for the pattern-recognition software.

One day, while taking a turn in the hot seat, I settled in and tried to get as comfortable as possible with the leads more or less glued to my head. I did my best to focus, but random thoughts drifted by occasionally and distracted. Dr. Lloyd, who insisted I call him Dave, monitored my output and, as always, seemed intent on discovering something new.

His look of concentration and the way he traced the tip of his pen over the graphs on the computer screen triggered a memory. It reminded me of a sleazy criminal attorney pointing at crude notes he had written on a large paper pad supported by a stand in the middle of a courtroom.

The screen flashed COPY, and I repeated it in my head as clearly as possible without mouthing the words.

My mind kept wandering back to the courtroom and that deceitful lawyer, who tried his best to make his client seem like a decent person, and at the same time, make his client's innocent victims seem like very bad people. I vividly remember becoming angrier and angrier the more the man spoke.

The screen flashed SAVE, and I repeated it in my head.

Counsel had effectively described his client's illegal activities in a way that made it seem like the victims were the ones who were at fault for being in the wrong place at the wrong time. He didn't bother to inform the jury that the victims were always either at home or work during the encounters. I drilled down into the memory and relived the countless hours spent thinking of ways I could have spoken up and shown the judge and jury how wrong he was.

ENTER. *Enter.* Was my wandering mind affecting the outcome of the EEG? I knew I should try to focus more on the task at hand, but my mind refused to sit still. I remembered wanting to stand up and shout at the judge who sat there listening to the truth being twisted into something obscene. I wondered how the sorry excuse for an attorney, or rather, the sorry excuse for a *human*, slept at night.

Many times afterward, I wished I had jumped up from that witness chair and interrupted the court's inept proceedings with a detailed explanation of how the events actually took place. I still wish I could have revealed his nightly activities to all and, with hatred and loathing, blast the courtroom with enough facts for the jury to make an informed decision.

This particular stalker needed to stay in prison as long as his victims continued to have nightmares about him. I also wish I would have gotten in someone's face and screamed with piercing clarity that *lawyers* should also swear to tell the truth. They were the only ones speaking in the proceedings that did not have to swear an oath to tell the truth, and they took full advantage of that.

What should be disturbing to decent people everywhere, is that all lawyers vow to *not* tell the whole truth. Even if their client has admitted guilt, they purposefully withhold that information to intentionally mislead juries and judges.

MENU. *Menu.*

"Hmm." Absentmindedly messing up the top of his already disheveled salt and pepper hair, Dave asked, "Will you look at that?" But it was more of a statement than a question. "For a moment this whole set of waves was completely out of range." I peered over and saw that there were gaps in the waves where they extended above the screen. "I thought something had gone wrong somewhere, but then it came back into range. What were you doing differently a few seconds ago?"

What could I say? "Ummm, actually, my mind wandered a bit. I'm terribly sorry!" I was starting to feel inadequate as a test subject.

"That's okay! Some of the best discoveries in history were made serendipitously. Others were the side effects of unrelated research."

I smiled because I could tell he had repeated that line enough times to spout it out perfectly while still concentrating on some other task. He was not even looking at me. He focused on the set of graphs on the computer screen.

"Just do it again!"

He waved the others over and sent a screenshot to the printer. As they walked up, he pulled the last couple of inches of paper out of the printer as though what he had to show them could not wait the extra second to finish printing. Everyone looked on as we explained what had happened, and they all seemed to agree with Dave to "do it again."

Dr. Livingston, now just Andy despite his perfect, proper English, sat in front of the PC and, with a few clicks of a mouse and a small amount of strategic pecking on the keyboard, adjusted the graph to display higher frequencies. I attempted to get back to the state of mind I had been in before, but I found it distracting to have everyone standing around waiting and staring.

Closing my eyes, I cleared my mind so I could relive my experiences that day in court, but in doing so, I could not seem to catch the mood and anger I had felt before. I thought maybe I was rushing things so I tried slowing down and starting the memories from the beginning to build the emotions. Nothing. I unsuccessfully attempted several different means of repeating what had happened.

We turned off the utility that repeated the computer commands on the screen for a while, and then turned them back on. Andy reset the parameters for a while but then adjusted them back higher. I tried verbally telling my colleagues the entire story, sparing no details. Still, after a grueling hour and a half, we had nothing to show for it. I did my best to duplicate the anger I had felt earlier, but I was simply unable to reproduce the neural signals.

"Perhaps *anger* was not responsible for the variation," suggested a thoughtful Dr. Gordon. The old man's calm demeanor had a way of getting your attention. After a perfectly timed pause, he elaborated on how the peak was likely caused by intense focus.

He went on, "I've known beta waves to reach and exceed 80 hertz during intense mental activities, but I've never even *heard* of anything like this before." A slight indication with his head and eyebrows brought everyone's attention back to the printout. "These peaks appear as though they could easily have reached 180 to 200 hertz. Quite extraordinary, really. Could you try focusing on something you know well? Like a repetitive process. Or maybe a line of logic."

I considered this for a moment and said out loud, "Pawn to king four."

With a sly smile, Dr. Al-shamrani, now simply "Al" as Andy had dubbed him, answered with confidence, "I'll take that challenge! d6."

Something about the sparkle in Al's eyes told me I could be in for a good game of chess. I forged on with "Queen to king's knight four—Qg4." After a while, each move became increasingly complicated (and I was down by a knight). I stared at the grid on the computer screen to help me imagine where the pieces would be, but having the game in my head forced me to focus intensely, which finally produced results.

A wide-eyed Dr. Bertram, now Carol, softly said, "Okay, those are not your typical beta waves! What frequency range are we displaying now?"

Andy used his golf-announcer whisper to answer, "Eight to 150 hertz."

"And the peaks are still completely out of range." Carol seemed mesmerized and used a hushed tone as well.

All the whispering distracted me, so I put forth an exhausting, superhuman effort to concentrate on the chess board in my mind.

Dave added, "I'm not aware of anyone ever recording frequencies this high coming from a human brain." He started to trace the tip of his pen over the graph again, but as soon as his hand got close to the monitor, he dropped his pen onto the keyboard. The heavy Cross pen clattered down between the table and the computer, bouncing off every obstacle it could find all the way to the floor. The source of our fascination disappeared as I lost my concentration. People sounded off with disappointment and irritation.

"Sorry! Sorry. I don't know what happened!" Everyone looked at Dave with mixed reactions as he rubbed his hand and apologized profusely. Everyone but Dr. Gordon, that is. He saw me massaging the tension out of my eyes and suggested that we start fresh Monday morning. "Everyone take the weekend to relax and let's all come back with fresh minds and rested bodies to consider what we've seen here today." No one argued, and we all forgot about Dave shattering the moment.

As Al helped me pull the leads from my scalp, he raised his eyebrows, pursed his lower lip, and with an approving nod said with his bouncing Middle Eastern accent, "That was an invigoratingly good game of chess we had started!" I grinned and suggested that we finish it sometime. He was quick to propose continuing our game during our lunch hour two or three times a week. I agreed, and we began swapping stories of childhood chess teams and math meets while we shut down for the weekend.

Klutz

What is a single man in New York supposed to do after unexpectedly getting off work a couple of hours early on a Friday afternoon? I was in the Big Apple! There were probably thousands of things to do, yet I hadn't a clue, even though the early-spring weather was beautiful. I wanted to be outside somewhere with trees and fresh air, not pavement and traffic noise. I missed the picturesque views from my old log cabin in the Rocky Mountains.

I was still fairly new to New York, but because of an extremely busy work schedule, I had not been able to get out much to see the city. One of the landmarks on my to-do list bubbled to the top. Central Park, which led to the most enlightening experience of my life, despite the trouble I ran into while leaving the park.

The park was a lot bigger than I had realized, even after riding past it in taxicabs a few times. Lakes, ponds, baseball diamonds, a zoo, paved trails for walking, dirt and gravel paths for horseback riding, and every kind of person imaginable.

Some of the most interesting things I saw in the park were beautiful bridges that had been there long enough for concrete stalactites to form from rainwater and the mortar between the rocks. A close inspection of the large lava-flow boulders protruding from the ground revealed long scrapes that were likely caused by glaciers thousands of years ago. I tried to imagine ice packed twice as high as the tallest buildings, and mammoths a few miles to the south. It must have been a fascinating sight.

With my head full of wonder, I moved on to see other parts of the park. Admittedly, I was a little disappointed when I learned there were no strawberries in Strawberry Fields, despite the memorial being five acres, but IMAGINE made me think long and hard about the stolen genius of John Lennon. He wasn't just a *musical* genius; what he had to say encouraged people to stop and think, too.

Around the word "IMAGINE" on the mosaic built into the sidewalk, someone had attentively placed red and yellow roses along the perimeter of the outermost circle and along some of the natural straight lines of the design inside the circle to form a large peace symbol. A handful of rose petals were scattered about inside the mosaic as well, but someone was very careful not to cover any of the letters of Lennon's most famous song.

I sat on a nearby park bench to soak in the sunshine, maybe make a little vitamin D. As I took in the pleasant day and did a little people-watching, a small gust of wind blew some of the roses out of place, which distorted the circle and the peace symbol. No less than eight people came to life and hurried over to straighten them up. All the roses were replaced exactly as they were before, with the stems facing away from the setting sun. They were all carefully placed and spaced so perfectly that I took a closer look and counted forty roses.

Hmmm, I thought. *Wasn't he forty when he died?* Interesting. The people in New York still missed him wandering through Central Park after nearly three decades. I wished I could have a positive impact on humanity like that, but what I do best –writing code and SQL– typically only helps businesses.

Still lost in thought, I began considering the past few months. I found it difficult to believe it was already spring again. The comforting warmth encouraged thoughts about all that had transpired in the short time I had been in my new environment. Not just a new job, but an entirely new career as well. One in which I already seemed to be successful.

Not only had I joined a well-established team, but I had also quickly become a valued member. I had received a promotion sooner than I ever thought possible, and to top it all off, we may have just discovered something significant about the human brain.

One thing about my life bothered me, though. I had no one special in my life. Sharing personal accomplishments with someone would certainly be nice. I hated to admit this to myself, but I was lonely.

I had not had a "significant other" since a failed marriage several years earlier. Several months had slipped by before I recovered emotionally, although recovering financially took a couple of years. I found out too late that my ex was far more interested in spending money than saving for the future. She milked my 401K dry and then ran up the bills of several credit cards, charging tens of thousands of dollars for things I never saw. While I foolishly tried to work on our relationship, she took all she could and left.

As a result, I generally tried to avoid relationships altogether. Staying immersed in work helped to keep relationships off my mind. However, on this day, as I glanced around the park, I noticed dozens of women and wondered what life would be like with some of them. Most were with a companion, but many others were alone. A few were on rollerblades, some were walking a dog or two, and a few others had a book or were busy on their phone.

What was stopping me from walking up to one of these ladies and striking up a conversation? Nothing, really, yet I just sat there and watched them read or skate by. I wondered what one might say to one of these lovely ladies that did not sound like some kind of pick-up line. No idea. I was a lonely guy and was probably destined to stay that way for a while.

Out of the blue, for the first time in years, I thought about the good parts of being married. The vacations, the companionship, the partnership, the sex. Ah, yes! The sex. When a marriage is good, the sex is usually great. But then again, even when a marriage is a bit shaky, the sex is usually pretty good then, too. I caught myself smiling when I remembered being young and spending entire weekends naked.

I sat lost in thought for a good while before a spectacular woman caught my eye. Her unique beauty held my attention like no one had for quite some time. A long, blue and white skirt made of a thin, silky material rested low on her hips. A bare midriff revealed toned, flowing muscles, and a cute little belly button.

As she approached, I tried not to stare but I could not help myself. I found her so sexually attractive that merely watching her walk aroused me. As she passed by, I was justifiably excited by the small part of her exposed breast bouncing slightly with each step. Unable to stop myself, I stared rudely. Mesmerized. Once she passed by, I saw that the top she wore was completely backless except for three thin ties.

A steady breeze pressed her skirt against her slight form and revealed the absolute perfection of her behind. The spring in her step caused her muscular cheeks to move in a way that held me captive. Then I found myself focusing intensely on a fantasy. The farther she moved away from me the more passionate my thoughts became and, for a moment, I was doing things to her that were probably physically impossible in reality.

The girl stumbled and fell, catching herself with her hands, but her knees hit the ground hard. I rushed to her as she rolled over to sit with her knees up so she could examine the raw abrasions on her skin. There were tears in her eyes, probably more from embarrassment than the injuries on both knees and a palm.

"Are you okay?"

Whimpering an approval of sorts and said, "Sometimes I can be such a klutz." She couldn't even bring herself to make eye contact at first, but finally started laughing.

I held out a hand in an offer to help her up, which she accepted after a moment of hesitation. I easily pulled her to her feet and she allowed her body to come to rest next to mine with our right thighs touching and her hand still in mine.

Our faces were inches apart as we looked into each other's eyes. Blue eyes! Skin as beautiful and perfect as any I had ever seen. Her scent teased my nostrils and lit me into flames. Bits of blonde hair moved with the warm breeze. Perfect lips formed a smile that could bring about the world peace Lennon sang about.

Several seconds passed, and I felt like one of us should say something, but all I could think of was, "Uh, hello!"

Her smile broadened but took on a whole new meaning. She repeated my witty "Uh" as she held up her left hand and used her thumb to wiggle her wedding ring so that the respectable diamond glistened in the sunlight.

Slipping her hand from mine, the woman whispered a heartfelt thanks, and then her thigh was no longer touching mine. I had already grown accustomed to it. As she walked away, it was not her luscious behind I watched, but *her*, instead.

When I realized I was still standing there dazed, I shook it off and headed in the opposite direction, wondering why I was alone.

Where can I find a girl like her?

Over the years I had become far too comfortable with being alone. Maybe it was time for a change. It had been a long time since I experienced the sensations that this complete stranger made me feel. Could the time be right to start pursuing another relationship?

But then the thought of overwhelming stress and chaos in my life again caused a squinty-eyed, curled-upper-lip expression to invade my face.

Okay, maybe I'm not quite ready.

Adequate

Carla finished her last report with a final Ctrl+s and leaned back in her chair as the tension in her neck and shoulders slowly relaxed. She cringed as she moved her legs around for the first time in what had been hours.

Both knees popped, as did her ankles. Noticing the time, she shook her head in disgust. She closed the lid on her laptop and, noticing everyone else had already gone home, she turned off the overhead lights on the way out. It was Friday night. All her co-workers were home for the weekend, eating something delicious or, more likely, had already finished dinner. As Carla passed through the atrium, she tossed a friendly, "Good night, John Doy! Last one out on floor five."

"Again?" Jonathan Doyen did not look at all surprised, but he loved the nickname she had given him. It seemed to be catching on.

"Afraid so!"

"People 'round here might think you work second shift."

She tried to make her laugh sound genuine before stepping out into the evening air. On the way home, Carla stopped by the grocery store and picked up the makings of a fresh and healthy salad, so that she could "afford" to have a whole pint of ice cream over the weekend. Pleasantly surprised, a rare treat caught her attention. Homemade Vanilla Blue Bell.

Standing at her kitchen counter, she ate most of her salad as she prepared it, washing and chopping each piece meticulously, and tossing what was left with a citrus-infused balsamic vinaigrette and roasted garlic olive oil dressing.

Rush, rush, rush. I even eat my dinner in a hurry.

Carla ate her salad standing at the counter in her kitchen, but clicked on the TV to try and watch the latest episode of a series she had started. She fast-forwarded through some of the commercials but cleaned her mess during others. Rewarding herself, she put two scoops of ice cream in a big bowl and topped them with mandarin orange slices and a sprinkle of cinnamon.

Finally, she plopped down on her favorite end of her nice cushy couch and tried to eat a slice of orange with each bite of Blue Bell while she finished her show.

The show ended like she knew it would, but somehow, she wasn't disappointed. Sometimes, escaping reality helped maintain her sanity. The fantasy lives of television stars made that happen for her, however, only a few minutes of the nightly news made her sigh and get ready for bed.

Her phone did not ring that evening, which made her feel both grateful and lonely, and her only e-mails were from spammers trying to sell questionable pharmaceuticals and penis enlargement products. Apparently, there were lots of great guys on porno and dating sites that wanted to hook up with her.

Hmmm. No breast enlargement spam this time.

She peeked down at her breasts.

What, are they adequate now?

She pushed her chest out so that her breasts looked simply marvelous, relaxed, and noticed they were *still* marvelous.

Yes. Yes, they are.

Still feeling a bit lonely though, she headed for bed earlier than usual, slipped between warm, expensive sheets, and snuggled up to a soft, luxurious body pillow for the night.

Discovery

After an hour or more of absent-minded and aimless wandering through Central Park, I found another wooden bench on a hill overlooking a pond crowned by an extravagant garden. Sitting quietly, I admired the last few minutes of a beautiful orange and purple sunset behind the skyscrapers of Manhattan and the gently swaying treetops.

The sunset became dusk in a hurry. As I stood and turned to head for home, I noticed in the southwest night had already fallen. The temperature had also cooled considerably and the park was strangely deserted. Locals probably knew better than to be this far from a street in the middle of Central Park after dark.

Finding what I thought might be Bridal Path, I quickened my pace toward 7th Avenue, chilled, and wishing I had worn a heavier jacket. Most of the trails were fairly well lit, but some areas were shadowy and provided ample places to hide. I laughed at the thought of muggers in the twenty-first century, but it was a nervous laugh.

As if to answer my concerns, I noticed a man suspiciously leaning against a tree smoking a cigarette.

Ignoring him made no difference. A second man was waiting near the path a short distance ahead. That's when I knew my suspicions were accurate. The infamous Central Park "night shift" appeared to be a reality. I thought they had cleaned up this town.

I made up my mind to show no fear, regardless of what happened. The second man saw me peering into his eyes and turned to look down the road in front of me. With a motion of his head, three others moved out of the shadows. Glancing over my shoulder, I saw the shadow of a man moving in behind me, as well. I considered dashing off into the darkness but they had anticipated that. They surrounded me, closing in quickly and silently.

To make matters even more humiliating, I realized that most of these "men" were mere teenagers. My thoughts flashed back to when I was their age and took martial arts classes. I wished I had continued those lessons or at least stayed in better shape.

I remembered the big fight after the high school football game when a couple of my teammates and I were forced to fight a group of rival fans for fifteen solid minutes before they finally ran from stadium security. For a moment, I also thought of the times I had slugged it out with a bully who lived down the block from me, but I doubted very seriously if those few incidents gave me anywhere near the amount of street-fighting experience as these kids.

Shaking my head again, I cursed myself for having nearly a hundred dollars in my wallet. That's not a whole lot of money, especially when you are talking about your life or a beating, but having that much cash pretty much guaranteed these punks would continue mugging people. I did *not* want to be responsible for that.

My mind was made up. They were not getting *anything* from me.

A reflection of light off metal drew my attention to one of the punks in front of me. He pointed the pistol directly at my chest, holding the gun sideways like his gangster heroes in the movies and in the video games he played.

While he was mouthing off in some kind of street jive, "gangsta" dialect, I thought of telling him he was an idiot for holding his gun in such a ridiculous manner. If he had to pop off more than one round, his aim would be off for the following shots because of the sideways recoil, not to mention the brass coming back and hitting him in the face.

All six of us stood silently, each of us waiting for someone else to make the next move. I stared at the gun and thought of a half dozen things to say and do. I tried to decide if I should deny having any money, or try to snatch the gun from him. I could feign a reach for my wallet with my right hand and reach out with my left hand while turning sideways, in case he managed to get a round off before I could get my hand on his gun.

I stared hard and tried to determine the best way to grab the piece so that a finger or thumb would land in front of the hammer while I jerked the piece from his hand.

Within a fraction of a second of making my move, the moron dropped his gun. His hand went limp and the gun fell to the ground. He howled as he shook his hand in pain while the rest of us stared at the pistol in disbelief. I'm guessing we were all thinking the same thing. *He did not just drop his gun in the middle of a mugging.*

The young hoodlum stared at his hand with terror in his eyes and he began to back up. When the next closest gang member lunged for the gun, I kicked him in the face like a punter kicks a football. Flinging myself to the ground in an effort to retrieve the pistol, I tried to get there first as two gang members made the same dive. I had a split second on them, and a few inches closer.

In midair I realized there was no way I could pick up the weapon in time, so I made a last, split-second decision to swat it away rather than try to use it on them. My fingers scraped through gravel as I whacked the heavy pistol far away from us, into the grass and darkness. I hit the ground and tried to roll, but the two punks landed on top of me. I started swinging and kicking, and they did, too.

Fortunately for me, the very nature of gang life is built on fear and therefore traps mostly cowards. The three still standing turned and ran.

I fought with everything I had, and so did they, but none of us were able to do much damage with everyone all tangled up on the ground. One of them was wearing a dark gray hoodie, so I took advantage of that by pulling the hood down over his face. This gave me a couple of seconds to focus entirely on the other kid, whose breath was bad enough to nearly render me unconscious, but Hoodie Boy managed to get back on top of me and put his hands around my neck.

Refocusing my attention on him, I grabbed his wrists and tried to loosen the grip on my throat, but Hellitosis kept tearing my hands from his gang brother in an attempt to pin my arms to the ground. I struggled for at least twenty seconds to free my neck, but it *seemed* like twenty *minutes.*

My mind raced in a thousand different directions until I realized I was panicking. Were the other gang members going to come back and retrieve the gun? Or return with other gang bangers who were possibly more seasoned or even more violent? I cleared my mind to focus on the lowlife on top of me, and in doing so, threw a piercing glare into his eyes.

The instant our eyes met he collapsed into a heap, half on me and half in the gravel. Thinking someone had knocked him out, I tried to push him off me, but it was difficult as I was out of breath and felt a bit dizzy as the blood rushed back to my brain.

Scrambling to my knees, I franticly searched the area until I saw Hellitosis running for the shadows. I shook my head yet again and tried to catch my breath. Disgusted and exhausted, I shoved the teen over onto his back and peered at him, well aware that he might jump back up at me at any time like they do in the movies, but he did not move a muscle.

Realizing I had been within seconds of dying, I scrambled to my feet and wondered if I should get the hell out of there or call the police. Or maybe even call the paramedics because the guy was still not moving. I eased over in the direction I had swatted the gun, without taking my eyes off Hoodie Boy, and felt around in the grass for the pistol.

When I found it, I pulled the action back and found there was indeed one in the chamber. I kept the weapon trained on the waste of a human being as I approached him. I could not tell if he was breathing. I felt for a pulse but could not locate one.

He certainly seemed to be dead. But why? Had his fellow gang member turned on him? I didn't think so. His gang brother had both his hands on my wrists when the one on top of me collapsed. And it had happened too instantaneously to be a heart attack. He was fine one moment, and lifeless the next.

I suddenly thought of other unexplained events that had taken place that day. Events that now all seemed to be related. Earlier in the day, back in the lab, the EEG had recorded some of my brain wave activity that had soared completely off the charts. While those waves were peaking, Dave attempted to point at the graphs on the computer screen and moved his hand into the same general area that held my focus. He inexplicably lost control of his hand and dropped his pen.

There was also the beautiful woman in the blue and white skirt earlier. I was fixated on her luscious behind when she suddenly fell without reason. Only moments ago, the moron had dropped his gun when I had focused intensely on the weapon and, apparently, on his hand as well. Then, the now-dead gang member collapsed when I looked into his eyes with penetrating hatred.

Could those extended brain waves we had detected earlier be an indication of what was happening now? Could I have caused each of those unexplained incidents to happen? I did not understand how yet, but my instincts were telling me that I was responsible, including the death of a mugger. No one had hit my assailant over the head, or shot him, or helped me in any way. *I* had killed him. He died the instant I looked into his eyes.

Of course, I questioned my reasoning and my sanity. *How* could this be possible? Could everything that happened be coincidence? I had to test it. Neither Dave nor the woman had not shown any immediate side effects like the poor fellow who had been killed. What made the difference? I had focused on my attacker's face, or, perhaps more specifically, his brain. Could that be the difference? Could the high-frequency waves my brain produced somehow be disrupting the neural signals in the synapses of other's nervous system?

My mind raced, trying to put the facts into place. How could the electrical waves produced by a human brain affect the nervous system of another person? They could not! Or could they? It seems to me that the waves would affect the origin, as well, and disrupt its own nervous system. The waves we had witnessed in the lab were probably a mere indication of something more significant.

Movement along the trail! Someone was coming, and there I was with a gun in my hand and a dead body at my feet. Right or wrong, and without hesitation, I ran. I pulled the clip from the gun and shoved it into a pocket. Then I ejected the round from the chamber while I was under a lamppost and managed to catch the cartridge. I stuffed the gun and bullet into another pocket as I approached Columbus Circle. Dusting myself off, I stepped out of the park and made my way to Broadway.

On the way to 7th Avenue, I noticed a mailbox next to the street and decided that was a good place to get rid of the weapon. At least someone responsible would find the gun, and not some other punk. I wiped off my fingerprints using the inside of my jacket, slipped the loose round back into the clip, and dropped it and the pistol into the mailbox.

The hardware made a loud, amplified clatter on the way down that I had not expected. I knew that everyone in the vicinity had heard, but they went on about their business in their indifferent, NYC ways without even glancing in my direction.

On the way back to the condo, I took a roundabout route, just in case any of the young thugs tried to follow me. None had. As I waved my access card in front of the scanner to activate the elevator, I looked at my hand and, still rushing from the adrenaline high, decided that now was as good a time as any to do some testing.

Clenching my fist in front of my face, I stared at my hand and tried to duplicate the anger I felt when I glared into my assailant's eyes. Then I tried to relive the intense focus caused by the logic of a game of chess when Dave had dropped his pen. Fortunately, he didn't lean that salt-n-pepper head of his into the area that held my attention. That would have been disastrous and unforgivable.

Nothing. Concentrating on my fist the same way I had focused on the woman didn't work either, but I had to try. As I stared at my clenched fist, it took on an unrealistic quality, as though my hand belonged to someone else.

An eerie feeling swept over me—much like déjà vu, except that I did not have the feeling I had experienced the moment before. I had an abstract thought and wondered if I were somehow experiencing the *first* half of a déjà vu. The elevator door opened and interrupted my thoughts. I walked out and dropped the matter, dismissing it as silly.

Speculation

After a scalding-hot shower, I went through my mail, checked my e-mail, and put together a hefty sandwich. With a plate and a glass of tap water in hand, I stepped out onto my tiny balcony. I missed my cushy lounge chair back in the Rockies, but I managed to get comfortable anyway and tried to enjoy my sandwich. The fresh, crisp, and calming night air cooled down even more, so I continued my efforts to learn more about controlling this new phenomenon.

I cleared my mind and tried to reproduce the behavior by focusing on my clenched fist. This time I recalled how the gun was pointing at me and the moment my anger returned I felt a tiny pulse going through my hand and my hand involuntarily relaxed. The sensation caused me to lose concentration and I slowly regained control of my hand. I was tingling from my wrist to my fingertips, but I had lost all feeling and control in my hand for an instant.

Trying it again, I was able to duplicate the experience by becoming angry. Using anger for *anything* simply could not be a good thing, so I tried different techniques. Occasionally, I could successfully cause the loss of feeling and control in various parts of my own body without any negative emotions involved, but I needed more practice to become attuned to this new ability.

At nearly one in the morning, I'd had enough. Intense concentration was mentally exhausting. I wanted to sleep, but there were too many theories bouncing around in my mind as I tried to come up with some kind of explanation to help me understand all that had happened. Killing with a mere thought simply did not seem possible.

I compared the phenomenon to other aspects of nature. The first thing that came to mind was infrasound. Those lower frequencies of sound are not detectable by the human ear. We know infrasound exists because instruments can record them, and some animals, like elephants, use them for communication.

Human ears cannot detect these sound waves, yet, when most people are exposed to them, particularly those in the range of 6 to 11 hertz, they often experience terror, confusion, sorrow, and/or a myriad of other negative emotions.

Evolutionarily speaking, it's no surprise to learn that the noise produced by earthquakes, tornadoes, tsunamis, and a few other of nature's scariest events are in that same range. People do not hear these sounds, yet somehow, our bodies detect the infrasonic vibrations in a way that makes our minds interpret them as something threatening or at least worthy of apprehension.

Another comparison might be that of the normally pleasant and relatively quiet human voice of some particularly talented and powerful singers being capable of shattering fine crystal glassware. By voicing the exact natural frequency of the crystal, which is the musical note it produces when lightly struck, but at a far greater volume, forced oscillation resonance shatters the glass.

Comparing the concept of the hair on your body working with your nervous system to act as a kind of radar to detect movements in the air caused by passing or approaching objects might be a bit of a stretch, but many other aspects of anatomy may conflict with general beliefs.

Some species of dolphins are even believed by a few to be capable of telepathy, although this could also be explained by something as simple as electrical signals sent out to notify the others in the group when to make navigational changes. Could that be considered telepathy?

Perhaps the closest thing in nature that might be similar to this new phenomenon I was causing, or experiencing, is a unique organ, or extra sense, sharks and a few other sea creatures possess. This sixth sense is made possible by electrical receptors that detect the electronic fields produced by the nervous systems of all living animal life forms.

A shark can sense its prey over great distances and easily zero in on these electrical impulses, whereas only the most finely tuned, expensive, state-of-the-art pieces of human technology can detect those same impulses when they are very close to the source. Like the EEG technology we used in the lab, the leads must be attached to the scalp to read the electrical waves. A shark can sense these same signals from many yards away.

Surely there were things about the human mind that have not yet been discovered, or not yet understood.

When I finally crawled into bed, too exhausted for further speculation, sleep still eluded me. Mostly because I was simultaneously mortified and relieved about what had happened earlier. I had trouble dealing with the fact that I was responsible for the loss of human life, even if it had been an extenuating circumstance and self-defense.

What if there had been a witness other than the lowlifes who had attempted to mug me? What if I had left behind some piece of evidence traceable back to me? Maybe a DNA sample like a strand of hair or skin under a fingernail.

What if the surviving punks came searching for me, or if we met on the street one day? What if the young man who did not survive the encounter had siblings that counted on him? And what about his parents? How would they take the death of their son?

Mortified or not, I was certainly relieved that I had discovered what I am capable of doing (or more likely, what the human mind is capable of doing) during a time when I was away from the lab. Had I been with my colleagues, I doubt I would have realized the potential of this phenomenon. Continuing with that same line of logic, it was probably safe to say there was no way to understand its full potential, even knowing all that I did.

What if this knowledge were used for personal gain? Exploiting the religious fears of people would be far too easy. Some deranged cult leader could easily assimilate an enormous following. A single person would benefit instead of everyone. Maybe the thing to do would be to tell the whole world about this discovery. At least people could understand what was happening and not think it was some kind of supernatural nonsense.

But what if going public with the information tipped off someone else capable of producing the same brain waves, but had not yet realized it? And what if that person turned out to be abusive or even sadistic? I went on to ask myself if the ability to cause someone to lose control of their body, or even kill them, could ever have a positive benefit in our society. The answer was clear. It was up to me.

Then I wondered if I was being presumptuous by assuming I was the first one to discover humans had such an ability. What if people in the past had been able to do this? Surely some of them would have tried to gain control of armies, or at least the masses. Who might that have been? Genghis Khan? Hitler? Pol Pot?

Could *I* gain control of armies? I thought about that for a moment, but soon realized I would not *want* control of an army. That sounded like a full-time headache, not to mention narcissistic. What *could* I do? I was not about to let this opportunity waste away unexplored, but having goals centered around making a profit seemed unethical.

I have often said that if I ever won the lottery, everyone would win, meaning I would spend the money in ways to benefit many. I would start new businesses and replace harmful products with safer ones, but that's just the kind of guy I am. Extending this attitude to my new reality seemed like the only way to handle the situation.

I must have felt better after resolving to do something positive with my new talents because I promptly fell asleep. However, I had dream after dream as my mind struggled to come to terms with all that had happened.

Discontent

FBI Agent Carla Bright led two of her co-workers and a uniform through the front door of a popular DC bar near several theological "universities." Four other uniformed police officers rushed through the back door and spread out, with one uniform remaining at each door to prevent people from leaving. They all focused on a bartender and two patrons sitting at a table near a blaring jukebox.

While the bartender did a fair job of pretending to be subdued by a couple of uniforms before he could reach the shotgun behind the bar, the two thugs at the table sat silently. One of the two simply had a look of disgust on his face, while the other was upset. The woman they thought was their waitress pointed a gun steadily at the gray-headed, semi-retired criminal, Mitchell Wynn.

The younger of the two patrons knew exactly why he was being busted, but the older man had no idea which crime had finally caught up with him. He was disgusted that he was only able to enjoy his hometown for less than twenty-four hours, after being in Mexico for six years.

Agent Bright and a particularly persistent U.S. Marshal, who had been tracking the man for years, made arresting this hardened fugitive possible. Working from a tip provided by the Marshal, she had managed to lure the criminal back to the DC area by offering reduced sentences to a couple of his old running buddies. In exchange, they contacted him and convinced him that they knew of a job with the potential to return seven figures, but needed his help pulling it off. The two convicts located Wynn within days and had him back in Baltimore looking into the "job" that seemed to be easy money.

They had managed to convince Wynn they could con some of the newer board members of a homeowner's association out of some of the three and a half million dollars they had sitting in several bank accounts. The two told him that four vulnerable junior board members had far greater access to all of that cash than any of them should have, and assured him that any expert con artist could get quite a lot of that money over a period of weeks.

Wynn was hooked and willing to risk coming back to the States because he had already spent most of the money he had either conned out of several wealthy retirees or leveraged from a few other acquaintances by extortion.

All of Carla's efforts to catch this man were successful in a big way, and as luck would have it, Mitchell Wynn just happened to be meeting with his nephew for a drink while he was in town. The young man, apparently following in his criminal uncle's footsteps, was wanted for two murders in Las Vegas. This bust alone earned her a commendation, which she accepted graciously, but Carla Bright did not seek or welcome public recognition. Her only goal was to stop abusive people.

Yet, despite the commendations, respect, and popularity she enjoyed at work, Carla went home to an empty apartment every night and muddled her way through the same nightly routine before going to bed, but always with the same results.

She tossed and turned, wishing she could sleep while her mind churned, constantly trying to fit pieces of dozens of puzzles together enough to see which criminal was responsible for what crime and why. She was continuously tortured by the thought that she wasn't doing enough. Not having anyone with whom she could share her few success stories troubled her.

Even though she knew she was doing more to make the world a better place every year than most people do in a lifetime, she felt unfulfilled and increasingly discontent. She often laid awake at night, wishing she had someone in her life to share the highlights of her day, and her hopes and dreams.

Plans

With only about four hours of sleep, I woke up too early the morning after the attempted mugging, tired and groggy. When I opened my eyes, the first thing I saw was the grass and mud stains on the elbow of the sports jacket I had thrown over a chair.

My mind flashed through all that had happened the previous day. Even though I was overwhelmed, I did not know what else to do but get up and deal with this new reality, assuming my new abilities were permanent. I felt like I needed to make plans based on how to handle the future.

How could I make the world a better place with the limited ability of slightly controlling another person's actions or by committing murder without leaving evidence? At first, the possibilities seemed endless, but the more I thought, the more ideas I had to rule out. What is the right way to force someone to do something? How does one positively coerce another? *Who* do you get to do *what*?

Rolling out of bed, I staggered my way to the tea kettle. On the way there, my shoulder bounced off a doorway and a hip bumped into a kitchen chair, but I forged on undeterred. It was a one-eye-open-one-eye-closed kind of morning. I poured fresh water into my old, copper tea kettle and lit a burner underneath it.

While I waited, my favorite cup reminded me of a bed and breakfast from a small, quaint town where I had once taken a weekend trip with someone I cared about. Good service. Warm weather. A spectacular view overlooking a cove off the main part of the lake, cedar trees, huge live oaks, and dramatic weeping willows. We went water skiing, tried fine restaurants, watched Fourth of July fireworks over the lake one evening, and were amazed by fireflies the other evenings.

A whistling tea kettle extracted my mind from the pleasant memory.

As I steeped my tea, I considered whether I could successfully force a politician to pass laws that would make a difference in everyone's lives. Not likely. I doubted if I could force someone to vote a certain way without compromising my anonymity, besides that, such a law probably does not exist anyway.

I entertained the thought of trying to make CEOs with ridiculously high salaries spread some of their wealth to the people in the company who actually do the work that provides those riches. Not Robin-Hood-style, just fair compensation. When someone has people working for them who are making minimum wage, they have no business paying themselves million-dollar salaries. However, pulling off something like that could easily consume all my time *for decades*.

A chilly morning breeze swept over me as I opened the sliding glass doors to my tiny, sky-high porch. I stepped out onto the terrace and wished for just a moment that I was back on the deck at my place nestled into the foothills between some of the more picturesque Rocky Mountains. I missed the soothing sound of a mountain stream in a pristine, aromatic forest of pines and aspens. The soft crunch of cones and needles underfoot. The wildlife, especially my tiny little buddies scurrying around overhead.

As my mind wandered, I warmed my hands around the steaming cup and tasted a sip. One part of me desperately missed the wilderness I loved so much, and another part of me was grateful I wasn't making that long, hour-plus drive into town every day. Beautiful as it was, snowy days could be tough.

Realizing I was lost in thought again, I refocused on coming up with a plan for the future. Maybe the thing to do would be to bust up the sweatshops all over the planet. I would take great pleasure in closing down factories and other businesses that exploit children and get away with using slave labor. But how would I find these places? How could I get there without giving away my identity? And what would the workers do after the plants closed? I might be forcing them into an even worse situation.

Maybe something a little closer to home would be better. I could hang out in Central Park after dark and wait for my "friends" to come back, but that seemed a lot like revenge, which was not my style at all, *and* I needed to think bigger. Taking out a few small-time muggers seemed so futile.

Perplexed, I knew I could accomplish many great things if I put my mind to the task, but coming up with something viable was difficult. If I were to witness a crime being committed, I would not have any problem using whatever force was necessary to stop it, but being in the right place at the right time would be sheer coincidence. I needed something workable and beneficial to the masses.

After a while, the chilly spring air had cooled down the last bit of my tea, so I stepped inside to make another cup. This time I sank into the lush cushions of my favorite recliner to clear my mind. Softened sunlight from over my right shoulder illuminated the picture on my favorite cup.

The hand-painted image of a sunset behind Comanche Peak brought back memories from a childhood camping trip. The sunlight lit a forest of lush cedar and elm trees on my cup as if it were part of the picture. For a moment, I became lost in the intricate details of the beautiful scene. I even had a nice spot picked out to set up another campsite, but then I glanced up at the clock as I remembered that I had banking business a few blocks away. Showering quickly, I dressed and headed out, not expecting another adventure.

Clearly

Carla had banking business that morning, but what she learned did *not* make her happy. Staying true to her nature, she was first in line to talk to one of the desk jockeys about renewing a five-year certificate of deposit that had matured. "You're telling me that, if I renew this CD, I'll only get a fourth of the interest it has been paying?"

"Yes, ma'am. I assure you that you won't find a higher interest rate anywhere. We have the most competitive rates in the market."

"A *fourth* of what it was five years ago." She had obviously not kept up with the current state of affairs of the banking industry.

"We don't control the prime interest rate, ma'am, we simply offer the best CD rates possible. The FOMC will likely lower the prime rate again soon, too, so a good strategy would be to get into a midrange or long-term investment to lock in the highest interest rate possible. Could be years before they go back up."

Clearly, the Federal Reserve wants Americans to spend their paychecks, not save their money.

Essentially, what amounted to a dozen bankers had met and voted to drive interest rates so low that saving money would be foolish. With the leaders of America's banking system setting examples like that, it's no wonder so many banks had failed in recent history. Why would anyone put large sums of money into investments that guarantee you to lose money?

"Just put the money into my checking account, please."

"Yes, ma'am. I hate to see you miss out on these interest rates, though."

"I appreciate your concern." Carla had almost said something catty about what she thought the banker's real reason for losing yet another account might be, but opted for something more pleasant.

"Um, you want the entire amount in your *checking* account?" The woman seemed shocked that someone would want that much money in a checking account.

"Yes, please. Thanks."

Sleuthing

None of the bank employees had enough sense, forethought, or wits about them to put up those little ropes and a sign asking people to please "Wait Here for the Next Available Teller" so, naturally, I wound up in the slowest line.

Ahead of me was a well-dressed man who was depositing over four thousand dollars in cash. The teller counted the money twice and had someone else count it in the customer's presence as well. During that time, the boisterous fellow bragged about making a lot of money with his new Internet site, as though he felt like he needed to explain away his possession of such a large amount of cash.

I could not help thinking that if he was trying to explain having all that cash, he really ought to come up with a better story. If he had indeed earned the money with an Internet service, I think he would be more likely to have checks, money orders, or credit card statements, but certainly not handfuls of twenties and fifties.

Drug dealer? If so, he was not typical. I doubted if a drug dealer would be depositing his drug money in a bank like that, and I doubt if he would have so many fifty-dollar bills. A drug dealer would also be more likely to just *spend* his money frivolously, and in ways that could not easily be traced. Although the man was dressed nicely, he did not have that flashy, golden, "I have too much money" appearance.

He finally left, laughing loudly at his own comment about a baseball player who was always in the news. I took care of my business and was out of there within a few short minutes.

On the way back home, I stopped at an enticing-looking restaurant for an early lunch. The hostess seated me by the front windows and I ordered the one thing that all but jumped off the menu at me. A shrimp and scallops house specialty, with a variety of vegetables grilled on a cedar plank. Who could resist that? I also ordered a side of sliced avocados sprinkled with real bacon crumbs and organic, plum-sweetened tea.

Life was good to me.

While I waited for my order, I watched people walk by and wondered where they were going. The New York streets seemed as busy on the weekends as they were during the week. As I watched, I entertained myself by trying to guess which ones were tourists and which ones were locals, but then, through the ever-moving crowd, I caught a glimpse of familiarity. I recognized the man who had been in line in front of me at the bank, coming out of another bank across the street and two doors down.

Peering through the taxis and between the passing people, I watched him go to the corner and stop, where he lingered. He would nonchalantly glance at his watch occasionally as though he were waiting to meet someone.

He's looking around to see if anyone is following him. Why? Why was he in the other bank? Who would be following him?

At that moment, ominous dark clouds began rolling in and the bright, midday sun became intermittent. In less than two minutes, the brightest of daylight turned to something more like dusk.

If I were a superstitious man, I'd be thinking this was a sign for me to get involved.

My plate was placed in front of me so I happily indulged myself, as any shrimp lover would, and savored every bite. The man standing on the corner looked at his watch again, shrugged his shoulders with enough animation to assure me that he was indeed acting, and walked away. When he was almost out of my range of vision, he stepped into yet *another* bank.

Curious.

I was thoroughly enjoying my meal, but something told me to look into whatever the man was doing. I ate one more quick bite, left ample money on the table, and made my way to the last bank he had entered. I walked into the place massaging my forehead with a finger and a thumb to hide my face and stood in front of the customer service island pretending to fill out a deposit slip. I had no problem hearing him boasting to the teller again, and neither did anyone else. This time he claimed to make a lot of money selling souvenirs to tourists.

Is this guy some kind of idiot?

The teller went through nearly the same routine as the first bank, counting out nearly five thousand dollars. I began speculating why he was depositing small amounts of money into several different accounts.

Did he believe that as long as he deposited less than five thousand dollars cash per month in each separate account, no flags would be raised by agencies like the DEA and FBI? Maybe he had business accounts set up in multiple banks, into which he occasionally deposited a fairly large sum of money to simulate the income a business might generate. I went on to consider that maybe he was trying to "play the part" of each business at each bank.

What is he up to?

My mind whirred through the possibilities when I heard the same boisterous baseball comment again as he walked away from the teller again.

Money laundering? Money laundering! The guy was money laundering.

Dixon Hill would have been proud.

I patted my body in all the places one might find a wallet, as though I had forgotten it, and hurried out a few steps behind him, realizing too late that I had probably looked a little like the grandfather near the end of *The Princess Bride*.

Still, I followed him to yet another bank where I waited across the street and struck up a conversation with a guy selling roses. As people walked by, sometimes he claimed the roses were from Tyler, Texas, the Rose Capital of the World, and other times he said they were from New Jersey, the Garden State. Some of the tactics the guy used to sell his roses were borderline unethical and obscene at times, but he managed to make an occasional sale.

The man with the nice suit and the dirty money walked out of the bank and scanned everyone as he continued down the street. I turned my back to the street and watched his reflection in a windowpane. He passed by, still suspiciously looking at everyone, including me this time, but he only turned my way once.

We walked into the wind, which had picked up considerably, making a drop in the temperature more noticeable. I buttoned a button on my sports jacket and put my hands in my pockets. We had scarcely gone two blocks when he stopped in his tracks and hesitated for a few seconds. I kept walking so that I would not clue him, or anybody else, into the fact that I was following him. I also wanted to see what made him stop. He appeared to be looking at something up ahead.

The back door of a car a few yards ahead of him opened, and he started walking again. A huge man stepped out of the long, black car, looked directly at the person I had been following, and stood there, apparently holding the door open for him. The big, boisterous fellow seemed sheepish as he cowered before the larger man and climbed into the back seat. A conveniently located bakery and coffee shop provided a decent place to watch without being seen, not to mention get a hot cup of coffee.

While I stood at the window watching, I thought about how easy it was to find and follow this individual. Maybe too easy. Maybe that is another reason why there is so much crime here. New Yorkers had such an indifference to crime and secondhand cigarette smoke that it was relatively easy for one to get away with just about anything.

If this person was indeed a money launderer, then the people he was meeting were his, what? His clients? While I waited and observed, I wondered why anyone would choose a career path where it was best to fear your clients, bosses, and co-workers. They were either making a lot of money or were being coerced.

Drops of rain that were, at first, only visible on the cars and sidewalk soon started falling heavily enough to see through the bakery's storefront window. Moments later the bottom fell out of the clouds. Traffic slowed and people came rushing into the bakery. Every time the door opened, I found myself awash in the fresh, pleasing scent of rain.

The smell took me back to places I have not visited in quite some time. I recalled a time when I was a child, looking through a screen door at a summer thunderstorm, upset that I couldn't go out and play. I remembered exploring a creek teeming with life in a light rain near our campsite when I was barely a teenager.

When I was a senior in high school, our gifted football team played the best game in our school's history in the middle of a downpour. Our team was so far ahead that our coaches stopped the game at halftime, even though the rain had subsided.

An aromatic mix of rain, coffee brewing and bread baking may have triggered memories and caused my mind to drift, but I never lost sight of the long, black car down the street. When the cloudburst had diminished into a light drizzle, the car door opened and out stepped the large fellow. The person I had been trailing stepped out next but was carrying a briefcase that he held over his head to keep the drizzle out of his hair.

A long umbrella emerged from the front passenger side window and jabbed him in the ribs three times as he nodded vigorously. The well-dressed man made no attempt to avoid or deflect the vicious pokes, but graciously accepted the umbrella after the last sadistic jab. He managed a grateful expression until the big fellow pushed him out of the way unnecessarily so that he could climb back into the car. A split second after the door shut, the car sped away, leaving the well-dressed man with his eyes on the ground.

I made my way toward the door to see which way he was headed before stepping out into the rain. Noticing a rack of umbrellas by the door, I saw that only a couple of them were wet. The others had a layer of dust on them, splattered slightly by the recent additions. They had obviously been there for days, so I picked up a compact model and fell in behind the man by a few dozen steps.

Others hurried by in both directions, but the individual I was following walked the pace of a deeply depressed man. I did not want to match his slow pace for fear of drawing attention to myself, but because of my quicker pace, I gained on him and began getting uncomfortably close. What should I do or say if he recognized me from the bank, or from across the street while I spoke to the man selling roses? Time nearly stood still and I became increasingly anxious.

What am I doing?

This guy could be dangerous and, in all likelihood, was probably packing a gun. Was this any way to use my newfound talents? Follow people who might be laundering money? In the rain? AND stealing incidental objects on whims? I began doubting my sanity when I was a mere four steps behind him, but fortunately, he turned right at the next corner. Turning left, I breathed a sigh of relief.

I continued along at the same pace but shook my head. No more stunts. Mind your own business. Go home.

The street on which I had turned was oddly deserted. There were no shops or businesses, only the backsides of a parking garage and a tall building, very little traffic, and no pedestrians.

Or were there? Did I hear footsteps behind me? Yes, and they sounded very much like the man I had been following. I did not dare turn around as I realized that the simple act of following someone might not be over as easily as walking away and focusing on my own business.

As I began to suspect that he had purposefully led me to a more secluded area, headlights with high beams burning appeared from around the corner. The footsteps behind me sped up noticeably. I cursed my carelessness as I looked around and found nowhere else to go.

What do I do now?! Don't panic. Show no fear.

Stopping dead in my tracks, I shook most of the water from the umbrella, folded it, and slipped it into my inside jacket pocket as I turned to face the person behind me. Sure enough, the boisterous fellow I had been following approached with a mobile phone pressed to his ear.

The big, black car skidded over the wet pavement and came to a stop next to me as the back passenger-side door flew open. Out stepped the same huge man, with an especially intimidating air about him.

Ah, New York! Surrounded by thugs, *twice* in as many days.

Out of all the things I could have said, I simply do not know why I chose to say, "If this were a TV show, they'd pause for a commercial right about now, huh?" I just opened my mouth and out popped the foolishness.

Big Boy grabbed me, and with a little help from his friend (not that he needed it) threw me headfirst into the back seat. Big Boy climbed in beside me while the one I had been following went around the car and got in on the other side. I almost made an attempt to scramble out, but did not even have a second to react before feeling a gun against my temple.

As soon as the doors closed with an unsettling finality, the driver took off. I was searched roughly, although they didn't bother with my wallet, and they missed my mobile phone and the umbrella altogether. I could have had a sawed-off shotgun hidden in my jacket. Their lack of concern would give anyone reason to worry.

Practice

The man in the front passenger seat spoke with a thick accent that could have been Colombian as he said, "Paul?"

The boisterous man I had followed was noticeably quieter as he said, "Yes, sir?"

"You *are* the idiot."

"Yes, sir!"

"Miguel?"

With a booming voice, Miguel asked, "Yes, sir?"

Oh, great. Just when you are thankful that a loudmouth has quieted down, another takes his place.

"Find out what dis man want."

With what can only be described as a grinning smirk, Big Boy Miguel turned to me and demanded that I tell him what I wanted, as though I did not hear what his boss had said. Many things ran through my mind, including the truth, which would not be believable. I needed to buy myself time to decide how to get out of this. I wondered if I had it in me to kill them all although I had no idea if I could repeat what had happened in the park the night before.

Was that the night before? It seemed so long ago.

If I *were* able to kill them all, I had no way of knowing if I could take them all out at the same time, so I wondered for a moment about who should be first, and who should die last. If I killed the driver first, an out-of-control vehicle might distract the others. Of course, I might also be inadvertently propelled through the windshield.

Killing the one who appeared to be their leader first might buy a few seconds of indecision from the others. If I started with big Miguel, I would have more time to deal with the others. I did not even consider eliminating the idiot Paul first. I could tell he was a coward at heart. Dealing with him would probably be easiest. I might also get some answers out of him if I played my cards correctly, and that is what I really wanted. More information.

Right or wrong, I needed to see this through. I needed to know if my instincts were dead on, or just deadly.

I decided to see what I could discover first before I attempted to take anyone out. I would play on my assumptions. Without even acknowledging Big Boy Miguel, I directed my question to the man in the front seat, putting myself on his level of authority. "Why are you having this idiot launder your money when you could have a professional working for you?"

Paul fidgeted uncomfortably as the Colombian turned around, glared at him, and then at me. That was all I needed to know. Paul's discomfort and the look from their leader gave them away, and I made a mental note to doubt myself less in the future.

This was turning out to be an excellent opportunity to see just exactly what I was capable of doing with my new talent. I was in a car full of thugs, potential killers, and probable drug dealers, so it hardly mattered if they all wound up dead. As far as I was concerned, a drug dealer, or anyone who supports them, is worth a lot more to society dead than alive or in prison.

Cold rain began falling heavier again as we drove too fast down the busy New York City streets.

Where are we going?

The driver certainly looked like he had a purpose in mind. What should I do? Should I wait to see where they were going? Or end this now while I was still alive and well? What if the passenger in the front seat was *not* the leader and we were en route to whoever was in charge? What if more thugs were waiting at our destination? A sense of urgency swept over me. The driver nearly stopped at a traffic light, but it turned green as he approached.

When the repetitive and irritating squeaking sounds of the windshield wipers began to get on my nerves, I realized I was not being asked any more questions. Apparently, they had heard enough and, most likely, thought I knew too much. As if to confirm my thoughts, the car skidded to a stop, far too dramatically, behind a warehouse facing a tall construction fence.

Behind us was a large concrete pier and to our right stood the retainer wall for the Hudson River, effectively creating a fairly hidden and secure location for who-knows-what. I guessed we were a couple of miles upstream from where the Hudson River empties its foul water into the Upper New York Bay. One more dead body in the bay downstream would not matter to them, or likely even be noticed by anyone.

I was thinking, nearly out loud: This is their plan? Take me out behind a warehouse in the pouring rain to shoot me and dump me in the river?

The boss turned around and, doing his best to maintain high dramatics, gave big Miguel a half nod after staring into his eyes for a moment. Miguel sighed an ominous sigh before returning the other half of the nod. He reached into his jacket and pulled out his pistol again. He checked to make sure there was one in the chamber. There was, and I flashed back to the night before for an instant. I could see the idiot Paul in

51

the rear-view mirror. His face was ashen and expressionless. Was he wondering who was going to be shot first?

By then I could safely assume that, without a doubt, these people meant me harm. They were not bluffing, and they were not making idle threats. They very likely had no regard for human life or the established and accepted rules of our American society. As Big Boy Miguel opened his door and stepped out into a driving rain, I focused on the back of his head. Nothing.

Uh-oh. I wish I'd either drawn up a will or spent more time getting attuned with these talents.

Squinting through the rain, he reached in for me, so I concentrated harder. Before he could get his hands on me, he collapsed, halfway in the car with his knees in the mud. I "hit" him again to make sure he was dead and looked up at the driver and his boss as if I were wondering what had happened to him.

Making a split-second decision to see if I could affect more than one person at a time, I swept a wave of concentration through the heads of both the people in the front seat. The two lost consciousness nearly simultaneously and slumped over. I looked at the idiot Paul who was jerking his head around frantically searching for a sniper or some other reason why everyone was dropping dead. Then he made the mistake of lunging across my legs for the gun Big Boy had dropped in the floorboard. I focused on his neck, and he instantaneously lost all motor control.

At least I'm getting in a little practice.

Turning him loose, I slid out from underneath him while he struggled back to a sitting position. I picked up Big Boy's gun and pointed it at Paul's terrified face. He fumbled for the door handle, apparently ready to bolt and risk getting shot in the back, so I focused on his neck again and, as his body went limp, he fell over. I put my hand on his chest and pushed him back against the seat. His mouth moved frantically, but with no air going in or out of his lungs, he produced no sound.

Still concentrating on the spinal cord at the bottom of his neck, I told him, "Be quiet except to answer my questions, and I'll let you go."

Poor Paul gasped for oxygen as his motor control returned. When he caught his breath, what did he do? He used that air to scream obscenities at me.

I patiently waited for him to gain some composure, even though I needed to do something fast. It was just a matter of time before someone came along and witnessed a dead body hanging halfway out of a car down by the river. Without a doubt, that person would be one of New York's finest. I looked straight into Paul's eyes and said, "I want you to follow my directions precisely. If you don't, you're going to wind up like your buddies here. Do you understand?"

The idiot nodded but was so scared he was now hyperventilating.

"Get out of the car and drag your friend out of the driver's seat. If you try to run, you'll find that you can't move." I focused on his neck again for a moment, and his body went limp during that time. "Just like that. Do you understand?" He gasped for air again and pleaded for me to stop.

Ignoring his words, I repeated, "Do you understand?"

"Yes!"

"Get out of the car and drag the driver out onto the ground. Now."

He got out, leaving the back door wide open, and I watched him closely as the wind and rain swept through the car. The body splashed into the mud, arms flailing, and the driver's jacket fell open to reveal his guns. Three of them, and sure enough, Paul made his last idiotic decision when he reached for one. He landed face first in the mud after bouncing off the car door.

I wrapped a scarf from the leader's neck around my hand to reduce the chance of leaving traceable DNA and fingerprints. While I was collecting their guns and throwing them into the front floorboard, I found a bag of white powder in big Miguel's pocket that I assumed was cocaine or heroin. I dumped it into the mud, leaving just enough for someone to make a positive identification, and stuffed the bag back into his pocket. I kicked the remaining body out into the muck and drove away.

Driving back toward the Theater District, all those traffic lights were now red, so I had time to open the briefcase the idiot had been carrying, and it became my turn to gasp. Inside were *bundles* of fifty and twenty-dollar bills. I slammed the lid and tried to think of the best way to get rid of the car.

When I was back within walking distance of my neighborhood, but far enough away to reduce the chances of being recognized by someone who lived near me, I looked for a place to leave the car. The rain lightened into a fine mist while I drove around a few blocks and happened across a rare payphone within yards of a loading zone.

Perfect! Few people were on the streets, but I needed to hurry as the rain moving on would surely draw out the typical crowd. I whipped that long black car across all three lanes and pulled into the loading zone. Wiping any trace of fingerprints off of everything took too long, but I needed to be thorough. Finally, I kicked the guns under the seat, grabbed the briefcase, and locked the keys in the car.

Still using the scarf, I picked up the payphone, called 911, and whispered so my voiceprint could not be obtained. I told the operator three things; the address where I parked the car, the license plate number, and the name of the warehouse where they had taken me. I placed the handset on top of the phone and walked away, stuffing the scarf I had wrapped around my hand into a pocket so I could dispose of it later.

On the way home, I happened to walk by the bakery and coffee shop I had been in earlier. I patted my chest and felt the obvious lump of the umbrella still in my jacket pocket. Grinning sheepishly, I leaned into the coffee shop without actually stepping inside, and placed it back into the rack.

Home was a welcome sight. I took a hot shower and then went through the briefcase. I estimated seventy-five thousand dollars, although some of the bundles appeared to be short a bill or two. I found an address book in a pocket that only contained three names and phone numbers. There were some personal items in another pocket, too, like his Colombian passport and a couple of old Clint Eastwood westerns on DVD.

What attracted my attention though, besides the cash, of course, was a corner torn from a piece of paper with handwritten information on it. A rendezvous was scheduled in New Jersey the following weekend. A drug deal? I wondered what would happen if I showed up for the meeting. I considered the idea while I fixed myself a simple dinner and surfed the news channels.

Something else I found out of the ordinary: after an hour and four different news channels, I did not hear a single word about four dead men behind a warehouse. A tip leading to four suspected drug dealers being found dead from unknown causes certainly seemed to be newsworthy, but apparently, the prevalent New York indifference to crime is just part of the culture.

Control

Agent Bright spent her entire Saturday afternoon and evening researching online investment tools. The concept was new to her and the companies were surprisingly similar in many ways, yet had radically different interfaces and philosophies.

Carla set up new investment accounts with three of the online traders. This allowed her to try them all while she took advantage of the numerous free trades she received for setting up the accounts. She could diversify nicely, and it wouldn't cost her a dime. Having all her money in one place, no matter how safe an investment it seemed to be, was a mistake she would not make again. Stocks, exchange traded funds, dividends, municipal bonds, and mutual funds. Maybe even startups.

Reading, researching, and filling out forms all day had left Carla mentally exhausted. Fresh eyes in the morning would better serve her during the monumental task of deciding which investments would best meet her needs. She felt good about taking charge of her finances and wondered briefly why she had not done so long ago.

Transportation

Sunday morning found me surfing all the cable news channels and Internet news portals again, looking for a story about a car full of guns and four dead bodies. Not a word was mentioned.

A politician illegally spending nearly seventy dollars per year of campaign money on personal office supplies was *big* news though, as was an ex-porn star trying to make it in the music industry. But the gruesome news of a few more dead bodies in New York was simply too insignificant to mention. What did Mick say about biting the Big Apple?

My mind kept wandering back to the contents of the briefcase, but surprisingly, I was thinking more about the note, than the money. If I could be there for that meeting, it might lead to higher links in drug traffic organizations. I tried to get the idea out of my head, but I couldn't.

Turning on the Sunday morning political shows, I tried to become interested in the mundane and inconsequential political arguments of the day. When I could not, I went downstairs and bought a newspaper, but did not find any news about mysterious deaths. Then I saw the classified ads and had a thought. I could use some of that money to buy a car from an individual and have transportation that would be virtually untraceable. At least for a while, anyway, until the tags expired.

I looked through the ads and found several priced low enough for me to buy with cash without raising suspicion. The lowest asking price was twenty-five hundred dollars, so I counted out that amount and put it into one of my jacket pockets. Another thousand went into one of the other pockets, and five hundred apiece into the two remaining pockets.

So that "they" couldn't track me through Google or Bing maps, I downloaded a detailed map of Manhattan into the navigation software on my phone. I plotted out a course that would take me to the most promising of the used cars in the ads, highest priority first, and used subways and buses to run the route.

The tags on the first car I went to see were too close to expiring to do me any good. The second one looked rough and ill-maintained. The third one was way too overpriced, but the next one I bought on the spot. He was asking thirty-five hundred dollars for a nice, four-year-old car in good shape, with only thirty-eight thousand miles on the odometer.

Few could have resisted the steal. Even if I had been spending my *own* money, I would not have had any problem paying the amount he was asking. I wanted my behavior to seem as much like normal as possible though, so I offered him three thousand dollars.

"Cash," I boasted, pulling wads of bills out of my pockets as if that would seal the deal. He had a sad look about him as he stared hungrily at the cash.

I could tell he was struggling with a tough decision so before he could answer I said, "Okay, how about thirty-two hundred?"

He tilted his head and rolled his eyes as he struggled with the dollar amount. I saw him look up into an upstairs window where a very pregnant woman was watching us with one hand on her big tummy and the other hand over her mouth, as if to suppress a cry, and it broke my heart. I hoped he would stick to his guns and accept nothing less than his original asking price, but he did not.

He nodded an irritated approval as he said "Ah-right," obviously upset. I saw his wife move her hand from her mouth to the side of her face and wipe a tear. I wondered what could make this man sell what appeared to be his only car in an obvious act of desperation, for far less than what it was worth. Lost his job? No health insurance? The economy after a few low IQ administrations in a row?

I *mis*counted the money in an obvious error and handed him forty-two hundred dollars. He looked at me like I was some kind of an idiot, not believing a stranger would offer him help. He opened his mouth to point out the error but I interrupted with, "Do you have a clear title?"

"Yes, but—"

"Well, sign it over and I'll be on my way."

"Uh, sir—"

"I'm in a bit of a hurry." I interrupted again with a slight nod punctuating every two or three syllables.

"Sir—"

"Would you mind? Please, just get and sign the title."

"You really ought to—"

"Thank you!"

Perplexed, he stuffed the money into the front pocket of his jeans and pulled the title and a pen out of a back pocket. He signed the title and handed it to me along with the keys, still unsure, but possibly getting anxious for me to leave before I changed my mind or discovered my mistake.

Jumping into my new car, I drove away before he could complain again. I caught a glimpse of him in the rear-view mirror with his mouth wide open, wondering what had just happened. I was glad that at least some of the drug money might be used for something positive.

I parked the car in a garage a few blocks from my condo and paid a hefty monthly fee in advance. The next morning, I got up and went to work as if nothing had happened. When asked about my weekend, I told them I had a nice walk in the park, found a new restaurant for us to try, and was now thinking about making time to pursue a new hobby.

We picked up right where we left off the previous Friday, but, for some strange reason, we could not duplicate what we had seen before. I had no intention of letting anyone learn more about the phenomenon. If I played my cards correctly, I could live a normal life while cleaning up the neighborhood without ever leaving a trace of evidence behind. If it worked out well, maybe I could expand my efforts to something much more than just my neighborhood or even the entire city. The possibilities of what I could accomplish flooded my mind nonstop, making it hard to concentrate.

During my lunch breaks and several evenings that week, I did Internet searches for anything related to an anonymous caller reporting the mysterious deaths of suspected drug dealers. I found nothing. Odd. However, on Wednesday I happened across a report from the Space Environment Center about a solar flare sweeping over Earth last Friday, so I forwarded the web page to my colleagues as a possible explanation for the extreme readings we had witnessed that day.

When asked how I thought a solar flare could possibly modify brain waves, I explained that I did not think it altered brain waves, but rather things like the computer's power supply, signals to the monitor and data streams, or even the EEG leads attached to my scalp. I added that I had no proof whatsoever, and this was simply a theory, setting the stage for anyone who might have any knowledge of solar flares to take over the argument and convince everyone for me.

"Solar flares *have* been known to cause over-voltages that could *easily* distort sensitive readings like these," Dave added matter-of-factually while running a hand through his salt and pepper hair. I knew I could count on him.

"If solar flares can cause mass communications disruptions, and the *lack* of them can cause ice ages on planet Earth, a disruption or over-voltage like what we all witnessed is certainly feasible enough." Even Carol pitched in to help me out.

Everyone but Dr. Gordon seemed to be buying it. His wise old eyes questioned my motives. I felt certain he knew I was trying to downplay what had happened. He considered the situation for a long moment as our eyes were locked.

Might as well get it out in the open now.

With a tilt of my head, I did my best to fake an interested expression and asked about his hesitation. It was as though he was using the lenses of my eyes to see directly into my mind, but then his focus began darting back and forth, from one of my eyes to the other. I could tell the neurons were firing inside his brilliant mind. The few words he spoke were calculated.

"Don't stop investigating the phenomenon we witnessed Friday afternoon, but don't spend a lot of time pursuing it, either. Our goals are to find a way for the human mind to communicate directly with a computer, so let's spend the majority of our time on that." Of course, there was a resounding unanimous agreement, but thankfully, the odd but quite accurate readings we had all witnessed Friday were largely written off as an anomaly.

Later that day, Al expressed a keen interest in finishing our chess game, so we began dedicating a couple of lunch hours per week to the pursuit. The man seemed to be a good strategist and worthy opponent. I have always prided myself on my chess skills, but I was hard-pressed to win half the time. Still, I managed to stay a game or two ahead of him most of the time, probably because one of my winning tactics includes getting to know how the competition thinks.

Reluctantly, I also have to admit to learning a valuable lesson from playing chess with Al: when you play broken games with someone, like during lunch breaks, it's okay to assume your opponent has loaded the current game configuration into chess game software to see what move a computer would do next. I began to notice that he was the most confident when we sat down to resume a game. Many times, the first move or two were not quite his usual style.

Also, the more time I spent with him, the more prominent his aristocratic, you-are-here-to-serve-my-needs attitude became, but I kept reminding myself to be culturally relativistic and accept him the way he was. Still, that did not stop me from trying to set a good example for him.

Stakeout

When the next weekend finally arrived, I followed the directions on the handwritten note from the briefcase. Just before sunset, I found myself in a burnt-out industrial district in New Jersey, but something did not seem right about the location. The only structure in the area was an old abandoned railroad depot.

A persistent, foul odor hung in the air, even when the wind blew. Airplanes periodically flew so low overhead they were almost deafening. Only the tiny, dilapidated structure of the depot offered any cover. Other than that, the location had nothing but concrete foundations where bustling warehouses once stood, old parking lots, and rusty railroad tracks.

A few small, scraggly trees and clumps of waist-high weeds had pushed their way up through cracks in the cement, but nothing that would hide a vehicle or two from the traffic on the adjacent roads. If people were meeting here, they would certainly be easy enough to spot.

While searching for a place to hide and watch, I realized the area was a perfect place for them to meet. If anyone else approached, they would easily be spotted. Streets headed off in several directions, any one of which could be used for a quick getaway.

Not knowing who or what to expect, or how they would react when the Colombians did not show up for the scheduled meeting, I ruled out hiding in the abandoned depot for a couple of hours until the scheduled rendezvous. Waiting for them in the general area was probably not such a good idea anyway.

Okay, okay! *Of course* it was not a good idea, but maybe it was not even possible. I drove back to a truck-stop-style diner off of the New Jersey Turnpike I had noticed on the way there. The menu contained typical diner food, with only salads for a healthier option. I wound up ordering what was likely the unhealthiest item available, with extra gravy.

The sounds of the kitchen, the loud chatter of the blue-plate special patrons, and the poison from the smokers gathered around the front door abused most of my senses, but the chicken fried steak was delicious. After the dinner rush, the place became quieter, and I was able to think clearly enough to define exactly what it was I wanted to accomplish later at the scheduled rendezvous. I wanted to take out the drug dealers. Not the delivery boys. The dealers.

Wait, how do I know this meeting is even about drugs?

If the meeting was a legitimate business venture, it would be taking place in an office somewhere, not at an abandoned depot, and certainly not in a burnt-out neighborhood on a Sunday evening, arranged by people carrying guns. But how could I confirm that the people I expected to show up were not victims? Follow them? Maybe. How could I accomplish that without tipping them off? I had already proven my sleuthing abilities left something to be desired.

I decided to cruise around the area again to locate a vantage point where I could watch events unfold, even from afar. Night had fallen by the time I finished dinner, but the meeting was still a couple of hours away, so I used that time to explore the area, to try to find a decent vantage point. Those efforts paid off. A quarter mile to the southwest, between two old buildings, provided a fair view of most of the meeting place. I parked, found a smooth jazz station on the radio, and settled in.

During the next hour and a half, at least twenty deafening airplanes flew low overhead, but precious few cars passed by the abandoned depot, all of which appeared as though they had a purpose other than meeting thugs until, finally, an old clunker rolled by slowly. When they passed the area indicated on the hand-drawn map, the car sped up, spewing out a ghastly amount of smoke.

Moments later the car returned, slowing again as they passed the depot. I felt sure the people in the car were the ones the Colombians intended to meet, although they seemed to lack the sophistication of the group I encountered the week before. I was beginning to think that this might be easy.

The meeting time indicated on the map was still ten minutes away, so I waited patiently. If the same car showed up again, should I try to follow them? If they parked, should I approach them, or stay put until they gave up waiting for the Colombians?

My thoughts were interrupted by a sharp clanging noise coming from behind my car, and possibly from within the building to my left. I snapped my head around but could not see anyone or anything. Continuing to scan the building and area to my left, I fumbled for the radio and turned down a Chuck Loeb guitar classic. The restored silence revealed a shuffling sound behind me that stopped a moment after the music went silent.

Hair on the back of my neck stood erect. A wave of goosebumps pushed my shirt away from my body. Reaching for the ignition, I sat poised, ready to start the engine and get the hell out of there, but caught a glimpse of movement behind the car in my peripheral vision. I jerked around but saw nothing through the rear windshield. The side view mirrors revealed deserted streets and closed loading-dock bay doors.

A second before starting the engine, headlights appeared from around a corner. I waited. The old clunker had returned. Glancing around my immediate vicinity reassured me that no one was sneaking up, so I took my hand off the keys. The old car pulled up to the abandoned depot this time, with its headlights shining into what remained of the rickety building. The high beams came on, illuminating the inside of the shack.

Go? Or stay? I did not dare risk turning on the headlights or allowing the brake lights to come on. Driving away with no headlights would likely have the opposite intended effect and draw their attention as well.

Another movement behind me! My heart pounded as my mind and reactions went on high alert. Of course, at that precise moment, a low-flying jet began its approach. My eyes darted about while I tried to watch the old car and identify the movements around me while the glass-rattling roar passed overhead, drowning out all other sounds. Finally, the plane was far enough away to hear noises around me. *Clang!* I jumped so hard I don't know what kept me from severing a nerve in my spinal cord. The noises were coming from the warehouse to my left.

Someone stepped out of the passenger side of the old car at the depot and went into the building. I heard another distinct shuffling behind me and jerked my head back again, quite sure I would see someone approaching. Finally catching the movement behind the car, my eyes focused on leaves and trash being blown along the curb. *Clang!* I spun around. I was going to get whiplash if this kept up, but I finally realized that the wind had simply picked up.

Breathing a sigh of relief, I took my hand off the ignition and turned my attention back to the people in the old car. The individual came back out of the building, wiping a hand on his jeans. They sat in the car a while and then got out to sit on the hood, thumping cigarette butts up and away from the car, very much like two hoodlums waiting on someone.

The driver held a mobile phone to his ear as his head swiveled around in all directions. A moment later they got back into the car and left in the same direction they had initially approached. I cranked up my car and did my best to follow them. I drove without headlights and avoided touching the brakes while I was still in the area of the abandoned industrial park and until they turned onto the service road of I-78, where I blended in with the rest of the traffic.

In Jersey City, they parked across the street from the entrance to a dive of a bar. The passenger got out and strutted in like he had visited the place often. I parked around the corner of the building and devised a simple plan to find out what I needed to know.

Sauntering around the building, I walked toward the door as though I were going in. When I got fairly close, I made sure no one else was around before focusing on the man's neck and approaching his half-opened window. He slumped over, unable to look up at me, and I whispered to him, "Right now you are paralyzed from the neck down. In a moment you'll be able to move again. When you *are* able to move, do *not* cry out."

A barely audible voice coming from the phone in his lap was saying, "Hell-O! *Hell-OOoo!* Are you there?" The voice went on, something about hating cell phones.

I went on, too, "The only noise you're to make is answering my questions." I could see the guy was terrified, so I quickly repeated myself, asked him if he understood, and released him. He gasped for air and cursed me.

"Why were you meeting the Colombians?"

"Whaaa?" He tried to look up at me so I focused on his neck again and watched him slump over.

Still whispering, I hissed, "Again, answer my questions, and make no other sounds. I *know* you hear me. Why were you meeting the Colombians?"

Gasp! "Coke!"

My mind raced into the past and pulled up the memory of my precious high school sweetheart who had died of an overdose. Police found her in the early morning light, between two homes, behind an immaculately sculptured bush. I vividly remember her cold, lifeless face. Foam oozed from her mouth and a white powder lined the delicate crease outside her left nostril.

I wanted the police to finish taking photos and cover her because she was mostly nude. Her shirt was pulled up over her breasts, her short skirt was pulled up around her waist, and her panties were around one ankle. The guys who had given her the snort had raped her dead-or-dying body and left her lying there with her legs spread wide open. I remembered thinking that all drug dealers must die.

"Were you at that depot tonight to buy or sell?"

"*Buy!*" he told me, with contempt in his voice.

"You dealing? Or a pickup man of some kind?"

"What?" He was stalling. Probably hoping his partner would come back out soon and surprise me.

"I want to know if you're selling that crap, or if you were picking it up for the ones who *do* sell it."

Obscenities. A long string of them that he did not get to finish because I had heard all I needed to hear anyway. I looked around again. No witnesses. I focused on his head and he fell over against the top of the window. Just in time, too. He had retrieved a gun from somewhere. It was still in his hand. I seemed to be shaking my head a lot lately.

I reached through the partially open window, picked up the phone, and used it to push the gun off the seat and into the floorboard, out of sight. I walked back toward my car, stopping just around the corner of the building where I waited for the drug dealer's partner and to also make sure there had not been any witnesses.

Standing there in the dark, I glanced around the corner every few seconds. I didn't have to wait long for his partner to return. I thought I heard him say, "Wake up assho'! Let's go," as he climbed into the car. As soon as I heard the door slam shut, I peeked around the corner, focused on his mind, and he collapsed forward into the dashboard.

As I drove away, I dialed 911 on the driver's mobile phone, whispered the name of the bar and the license plate number of their car to the operator, and asked her to repeat it back to me. I removed the SIM card from the phone so that no one could pinpoint its location, but wiped everything clean with a moist towelette anyway. I also disposed of the phone and card in two different locations. After parking my car in the garage, I did my routine wipe-down of it, too.

Despite the day's events, or because of them, I slept soundly that night knowing countless codependent people had fewer people preying on them.

Challenging

That following Monday morning, Carla showed up for the routine departmental meeting a few minutes early and took a seat next to Jesse, one of her lunch buddy co-workers. Martin Derden was a few minutes late, of course, not because he was running late, but because he liked to give people a break in case *they* were running a bit late.

Martin walked around the table in his usual manner, beginning the meeting as if it had already been going on for a while. As he lapped the room, he talked constantly while personally handing everyone a revised copy of the meeting's agenda.

"We have a very interesting multiple murder case in New York City that no one can explain. The NYPD was alerted by an unknown, whispering caller that gave up the name of the warehouse where he had left four dead bodies. He went on to give the address of their car, which he used to leave the crime scene and abandoned next to the phone booth he used to make the call.

"Several loaded handguns had been stuffed under the front seat, and in the trunk were high quality Israeli-made fully automatic weapons with enough ammunition to give even the United States Army cause for concern. One of the victims also had a large sum of money in a jacket pocket, so between the abandoned weapons and the cash left behind, robbery has been all but ruled out.

"And get this," he looked at a report for a moment, made a face of recognition when his scanning eyes found the quote, "'*No* apparent cause of death in any of the victims.' An autopsy showed that one of them, the one with the cash, was probably under extreme duress at the time of his death, but the others all seemed to have unnaturally died of 'natural causes.'"

Some thoughtful looks around the table seemed to be attempting to elicit theories or speculation from colleagues. Someone finally asked, "Some kind of nerve gas, maybe?"

"There were no traceable toxins found in their systems." With a slight tilt of the head and a pair of bounced eyebrows, he added, "None that would have killed them anyway. Two had traces of marijuana and one of those had used cocaine within hours of his death, but other than that, nothing. The one testing positive for cocaine had a small bag with trace amounts of crack cocaine in his pocket. Not enough left in the bag to blow really, so we suspect it was planted there.

"There's more." Heads and faces swiveled back around to face the department head. "One of the victims turned out to be a Colombian we've been pursuing for years on drug and weapons related charges."

Martin Derden went on without missing a beat. Pointing a finger, he announced matter-of-factly, "Agent Bright, you'll need to make arrangements to work out of the main Manhattan office for a while, the regional director wants you on this case immediately. You'll need to be there by this time tomorrow morning." He had moved his finger to point straight down at the precise moment he said "this time" for added emphasis, as though it would make her more likely to be there on time.

"Yes, sir!" She noticed glances from some of her fellow agents, but none were looks of jealousy or envy, nor were they expressions of wonder or amazement. They were more like looks of approval, or maybe even satisfaction. She, on the other hand, was shocked. Perhaps her insecurities were unjustified after all.

"See me in my office after the meeting to get fully briefed." He used his thumb to point over his shoulder.

"Yes, sir!"

Another surprise awaited her in Derden's office. Her signature was needed in several places for a top secret, level three security clearance, which was a requirement for her new promotion. The obligatory raise accompanying the new responsibilities couldn't be called generous, but it was the largest raise she'd ever received.

Sensing some skepticism, Derden assured her that "everyone is noticing how, more often than not, you manage to produce something from virtually nothing, even where others could not. Your new grade of Special Agent gives you the authority to procure whatever federal resources you require to solve this case."

Later that day Carla received yet another surprise in the form of an e-mail:

FROM: "Martin Derden" <dcfieldoffice7depthead@mail.fbi.gov>

SUBJECT: Re: Commendation for Agent Bright

TO: "DC Regional Dir" <dcregionaldirector@mail.fbi.gov>

BCC: "Carla Bright" <cbright@mail.fbi.gov>

Regional Director Lee,

Thank you for your timely response in this matter, and for

extending the gratitude of the Bureau to one of our finest

Agents. I'm sure she will be pleased with the commendation.

Thanks again,

Martin Derden

Department Head, Washington, DC Field Office 7

dcfieldoffice7depthead@mail.fbi.gov

-- "DC Regional Dir" <dcregionaldirector@mail.fbi.gov> wrote:

> FROM: "DC Regional Dir" <dcregionaldirector@mail.fbi.gov>

> SUBJECT: Re: Commendation for Agent Bright

> TO: "Martin Derden" dcfieldoffice7depthead@mail.fbi.gov

>

> Department Head Derden,

>

> Thank you for briefing me on Agent Bright's

> accomplishments. Your recommendation for the a

> commendation is approved and will be awarded to him

> next month. Tell Agent Bright that the Bureau is

> proud of him, and that we are glad to men like him on

> board with us.

>

> DC Reg. Dir. Lee

>

>

> -- "Martin Derden" <dcfieldoffice7depthead@mail.fbi.gov>

> > wrote:

> > FROM: "Martin Derden"

> > <dcfieldoffice7depthead@mail.fbi.gov>

> > SUBJECT: Re: Commendation for Agent Bright

> > TO: "DC Regional Dir" <dcregionaldirector@mail.fbi.gov>

> >

> > DC Regional Director Lee,

> >

> > I am recommending awarding Agent Bright a

> > commendation for

> > outstanding work in solving cold cases. Many of the

> > tasks assigned to

> > this investigator were cases that had been cold for

> > years and were

> > regarded as completely unsolvable. However, Agent

> > Bright has proven to

> > be remarkably resourceful, and therefore deserves to

> > be recognized for

> > these feats.

> >

> > Thank you,

> > Martin Derden

> > Department Head, Washington, DC Field Office 7

> > dcfieldoffice7depthead@mail.fbi.gov

> >

One of the first things Carla noticed, of course, was the subject. A commendation! She also couldn't help but notice how the regional director seemed to have trouble structuring sentences and how he could not have proofread his e-mail at all before hitting the send button, as if the message was insignificant. She expected better from someone in a position of authority over hundreds of people, but at the moment, none of that mattered. A commendation!

For the first time in her career with the FBI, she felt appreciated. She finally even began to get that feeling of actually being a part of the team. Then she read the words intended to praise "him" and her heart sank. The regional director had simply assumed she was male when her department head had failed to be gender specific. Then she began to wonder if Martin had done that on purpose to increase her chances of receiving the commendation.

Although she certainly appreciated her direct supervisor's efforts, the experience ultimately pushed her even further away from feeling like a member of the team. Still, Carla had no intention of letting negative thoughts undermine her efforts to be the best federal agent the FBI had ever seen. The best *Special* Agent the FBI had ever seen.

Martin handed Carla a sealed envelope on his way to lunch and suggested that she go over this additional information as soon as possible before arriving in New York. She opened the sealed envelope, which contained nothing but a USB flash drive and a plane ticket to LaGuardia Airport. She slipped the drive into her computer, typed in her network ID and password, and found several gigabytes of detailed records, pictures, videos, and 911 recordings about her new case.

Several *giga*bytes. Before reaching New York tomorrow morning. She realized she would have to pull another all-nighter.

She began to read about several mysterious murders in and around Manhattan. First on the list was a high school dropout with a violent record going back to age eleven. He was known to be a member of a gang and on probation for two years, but had been found dead in Central Park late one Friday night. There were no known witnesses and the cause of death, which was highlighted and underlined, was *unknown*.

NYPD detectives simply assumed the death was likely drug or gang related. Even though it was obvious there had been a scuffle, no one had attempted to recover any DNA.

Carla was disgusted by the New York police department's complete disregard for protocol and for not doing whatever was necessary to solve a murder case, but moved on. That would have to be a fight for another day.

The second item on the list was the four bodies Martin had discussed earlier in the meeting. The only new information being that they now knew the identities of two of the victims. One had been something of a shady New York businessman that had several run-ins with the law in the past, although no one could ever make any charges stick. Another had been identified as someone who had an open warrant in Florida. The causes of all their deaths were still labeled as unknown.

Two traffic cams on 10th Avenue had caught pictures of the car en route to where it had been abandoned, but unfortunately, there was only enough of the individual's wrist exposed to identify the person as "probably Caucasian."

Last on the list were two unfortunate victims found dead under the same circumstances. An anonymous caller tipped off the Jersey City Police using one of the victim's mobile phones, which was not recovered, and the causes of death for both of them were the same: unknown. No DNA traces were found. No witnesses came forward, and not a single other clue was found, although a New Jersey detective was still looking for a phone taken from one of the victims, which was used to call 911.

Mesmerized, she studied every police report, every coroner's report, all the 911 recordings, and every crime scene photo for the remainder of the day. Around dinnertime, she realized she had not even had lunch yet. Looking at her airline ticket again, she noticed it was a one-way ticket, so she decided to go home and pack like she was going away for a while.

Challenging, she thought on the way home. What was the best way to get to the bottom of this? At the moment, she did not have a clue. Carla packed enough for five days, set her alarm for a quarter-before-early, and flopped around in her bed for two hours before finally drifting off into a troubled sleep. In the morning, she hurriedly packed for an additional two days, just in case.

Embark

Weekends and evenings gave me plenty of time to consider all that had happened since I had become attuned to these new, what? Abilities? I still wasn't sure what to call them. Skills? Gifts? I had no idea and had more pressing things to think about than trying to name them.

Dwelling upon recent events and decisions, I was perplexed about adapting so readily and easily to taking a human life. I had been repeatedly asking myself if *my* actions were just as wrong as the actions of the people I had killed. The reasons to take each of them out always seemed to far outweigh the reasons to remain complacent. Until I had a good reason to stop, I was committed to taking advantage of any and every opportunity to rid the world of individuals who prey on the weak and vulnerable.

I came to realize that, despite getting two dealers off the streets, I had not accomplished much. I wished I had the foresight to recognize that the two thugs I followed to the dive bar in New Jersey that Sunday night probably went there to meet a local drug dealer, or worse, a major distributor.

Looking back, it was painfully obvious that those two amateurs were mere mutt pups for the big dogs. I let a tremendous opportunity get by me when I failed to go inside and take out their contact as well. I needed to be more careful about that in the future. While I put a permanent end to a few middlemen, they were, unfortunately, the easiest to replace and by far the least important in the supply chain. If I wanted to reduce illegal drug use on a large scale, I would either have to eliminate the suppliers or the users, or perhaps both.

Late one afternoon, a special news broadcast caught my attention: a live report about a prison riot at the Texas State Penitentiary at Huntsville. Apparently, inmates that belonged to one particular gang had been planning an assault on a rival gang for weeks. When the opportunity finally presented itself, the more hostile gang attacked everyone who was a member of the other gang, and a few others just for being associated with them. Many prisoners were wounded, some severely, and several other inmates were killed.

Three guards had been killed as well, and three others had been taken hostage, but "only because they had gotten in the way," according to the reporter on the scene. The media was already trying to convince viewers that the prisoners could not be held liable for anything that happened to people who got in the way of their gang wars. In less than an hour, the inmates had completely taken over the prison.

I thought it was peculiar that the inmates made such a colossal effort to attack each other instead of making a combined effort to escape. Were they *that* resolved to being imprisoned? These people had made crude weapons out of whatever resources they

71

could find, devised a plan, however flawed, and then patiently waited for just the right circumstances to carry them out. Had the convicts focused their efforts on escaping, instead of fighting each other, they very likely would have pulled it off, en masse.

An additional report on a competing news channel began showing video clips from the previous year of interviews with some of the very inmates that were now involved in the gang war and riot. The interviews had been recorded for a planned documentary on the lives of hard-core criminals with follow-up interviews scheduled after their release. None of the aired interviews were positive. Some expressed the desire to get out of prison so they could reunite with fellow gang members, while others made it obvious that they had *no* remorse for their crimes.

As the week wore on, there seemed to be no end in sight for the prison siege, which worked the media into a feeding frenzy. The story was also being covered with an urgency induced by very little happening elsewhere. With no other major catastrophe in weeks, and no celebrities behaving badly for the free publicity, *and* with people sick of election news, the national media focused its efforts on the prison riot in Huntsville.

Regularly scheduled shows were frequently interrupted by all-too-familiar newscaster personalities announcing some new tidbit of information. "Breaking News" would be flashing in one of the bottom corners of the screen as they rehashed the same information.

The media ran the prison riot story twenty-four hours a day, and went out of its way to find and interview only the local people who met their stereotypical notion of the average Texan.

None of the interviews were flattering and few of the people knew anything at all about the riot, which was okay because the reporters did not ask them many questions about the inmates taking over. They mostly just wanted to put locals on the air while trying to make them look as ignorant as possible, but I have to admit to being a bit relieved when no one referred to the state as a taco again.

Network news anchors eventually found choice clips in the inmate interviews from the previous year where shackled men in orange jumpsuits repeatedly complained about their lack of basic freedoms. Instead of pointing out that the severity or frequency of abuses against fellow humans is what cost them their freedoms, some of the reporters actually began agreeing with the prisoners.

The inmates were not citizens of some third-world country run by a ruthless dictator denying them basic human rights, but no one seemed to care. I could not believe what I was hearing and seeing. Trusted newscasters were reporting the horrible realities of being incarcerated as though *no one* deserved that kind of treatment. The reports slowly evolved from describing how tensions between gangs rose to the point of them attacking each other, to speculating about how society had dumped on these innocent people enough for them to finally retaliate.

This ugly turn of events made me wish for an Internet site designed to log on and pop up instant messages to the commentators. Every time I thought about the media trying to raise sympathy for the same convicts who freely admitted they were looking forward to getting out of prison so that they could reunite with their gang made me mad enough to kill.

Just let me get my—mind—on them.

Hmmm. Not a bad idea.

I wondered if I could pull that off. How? Flying down there would be out of the question. My involvement would be too easy to trace. An online map indicated a round trip drive to Huntsville would be about 3,265 miles, which was, at the very least, forty-eight hours of drive time, if you pushed yourself hard. More like fifty-two hours after factoring in breaks and traffic. I could easily get by with four hours of sleep per night for a few nights, *and* I could take newly-earned vacation days the following Monday and Tuesday.

The plan was doable! I began weighing my options even though there was a good possibility the ordeal would be over by the time I could get there, and it was not like they had a leader to take out or command structure to disable. They were, no doubt, the kind of mob where every man would be for himself.

The Friday morning news specials reported inmates threatening to kill one of the guards they had taken hostage if their demands were not met immediately.

According to two of the guards who had escaped the riot uninjured, the guards who were now hostages had stayed behind in an attempt to talk the prisoners into ending the gang war before more people were hurt or killed. They could have fled like the other guards, but they stayed because they had gotten to know some of the inmates and wanted to see them rehabilitated, not killed or sentenced to more prison time. That plan had obviously failed.

My decision was made. If the prison was still under the control of the inmates that afternoon, I would sneak out of work a little early and, despite it sounding egotistical, make my way down there to see what I could accomplish.

Well after lunch, the siege was still very much in the news, so I slipped out about 2:15 and headed southwest with plenty of my stolen cash. I left my credit cards on my desk, packed lightly, but included snacks for the road so I could make fewer stops.

By midnight I was in southern Virginia where I stopped at a particularly cozy rest area and got a few hours of sleep. I was on the road again long before sunup and watched the sunrise accentuate the beauty of the Tennessee hills in early spring.

I rolled through Chattanooga, Birmingham, and Jackson, but stopped in Shreveport to stretch my legs and have dinner at one of the casino buffets. I came close to donating a few dollars to the efforts of making the rich richer but remembered hearing someone accurately describe casino gambling as entertainment for those who are bad at math, so I stopped myself.

My second night on the road was spent a few miles outside of Huntsville in a campground within the Sam Houston National Forest. The entire park was maintained well enough to impress me, and there were several nice camping facilities with plenty of open spaces. The weather was pleasant enough to sleep with the windows partially down. Comfortably. In mid-April. A slight breeze blew across me now and then, teasing me with hints of rain and pine trees.

I awoke remarkably refreshed and free from the aches and pains usually associated with sleeping in a car. I stepped out for a stretch and the outhouse, and then got back on the road to the prison.

Due to the swarm of journalists, camera crews, and other support equipment surrounding the high brick and razor-wire topped wall, I had to park on a residential street three or four blocks from the penitentiary. The large crowd had advantages and disadvantages. I could blend right in with them, and my New York license plates would not seem too much out of place. However, with all the cameras and prying eyes, how could I get close enough to the prisoners to take them out?

As I approached the tall brick walls, I walked by someone who was practicing broadcast techniques on an assistant. He asked her the same question over and over, each time a little differently, as though no one had ever asked the question before. Forgive me, but I could not help laughing as he made a fool of himself.

"How does that make you feel?" he asked with feigned sincerity.

The assistant crinkled her nose and shook her head slightly.

"*How* does that make you *feel?*"

She tilted her head back and forth with raised eyebrows, indicating that the performance was only so-so.

"*How* does *that* make you *feel?*"

This time, the assistant gave him an "absolutely not" look. "You sounded a little like William Shatner on a *good* day with that one."

After the horror left his face, he tried again. "*So*, how does that make you *feel?*"

She puckered her chin, pushed her lower lip against her upper lip, and raised her eyebrows again with a slow nod that signaled her approval.

I could not see any more of the ridiculous exchange but heard him trying to duplicate the exact tone and inflection of his latest mastery as I walked away. I had to chuckle to myself and wonder how many other journalists put a higher priority on their acting abilities than they did on the news they were reporting.

There seemed to be quite a bit more acting going on than reporting, but seeing the correspondent's nonsense served to refresh the appreciation I had for my new career. In a moment of distraction, I wondered if I now had an even *newer* career. Was there any way to earn a decent living using my newfound talent? If so, then there was bound to be a considerable amount of deceit involved, or at least hidden agendas.

I wasn't sure how I felt about that. But then again, if I could take enough money from drug traffickers or other criminals, I would no longer have to worry about earning a living.

A reflection of myself in the tinted glass of a high-tech media van caught my attention and nearly caused me to laugh out loud. I was wearing a dark pair of sunglasses purchased at a gas station, along with a Texas A&M cap that looked more like "ATM" than "T A&M." Those Aggies!

In the spirit of my surroundings, I *reckoned* I had accomplished my goal of disguising myself, so I turned my attention back to the plan at hand. Who was I kidding? I had no plan other than to put a stop to the rioting. How? What did I think I was going to accomplish?

Walking through the different camps of journalists, I surveyed the area and the situation. There was really not much to see. No prisoners were visible because of the high brick walls surrounding the prison grounds, and any negotiations that might be taking place were likely happening over a telephone. No progress had been made toward resolving the situation.

The media, however, *had* made progress. They had found a spot to film with the picturesque surroundings of the law enforcement command center on the right and the prison on the left. Each crew took a turn in that magical spot doing live broadcast updates.

When one network found and used a background that was perhaps a bit more interesting than the last, other networks had to use it as well, lest they fall behind in the ratings, even if they had to recap old news. Boasts of "Breaking News" should be limited to important new developments, but the media did nothing but revisit the events that led up to the current situation, for viewers who had just awoken from a coma, I presumed.

One particularly ambitious young reporter felt the need to add a new element to a story that, in her mind, had become stagnant. She seemed to believe that she needed to keep everyone interested in the prison siege and was willing to pull a stunt to recapture drifting interests. She may have been far more interested in how her endeavors were going to affect her career than in actually reporting the news. What she had to say was bewildering to me, and I wondered how many people would jump on the bandwagon with her.

The "journalist" started by saying that good American people all over this great nation were *outraged* by the treatment the inmates had endured for so long, which eventually led to the riot that, unfortunately, took the lives of innocent bystanders.

A lack of new developments made her willing to create a controversy by taking the side of the rioting convicts and lending them her support. Never mind the fact that the riot had started as a war between rival gangs and had nothing to do with protesting prison conditions or demanding fair treatment.

She went on to diminish the efforts of the prison guards, alive or dead, saying they were abusive microcontrollers willing to earn a living by essentially being slave masters of other fellow humans. Yet she failed to mention anything about how underpaid, understaffed, undersupplied, and overworked they all were. The young lady went on, pretending to reflect the views of the American people, but was incredibly out of touch with reality. Rather than simply reporting facts, she insinuated that the proper emotion people should be feeling was sympathy for the rioters.

Or maybe she was trying to assert herself into a leadership role by implying that her different way of thinking was more humane, or perhaps superior. Or was she a spoiled child attempting to appear more mature? I shook my head yet again and walked away, wishing for a way I could report her nonsense to the world.

Yellow police tape formed a partition around one of the entrances to the outer fence of the Texas State Penitentiary at Huntsville where portable tables under a large canopy tent were set up to hold laptops and communication equipment. Several different law enforcement agencies were all standing together, wearing bulletproof vests and other various types of body armor, anxiously awaiting an opportunity to put an end to the situation.

A bright Texas sun had warmed the morning enough to make me break a sweat, so I knew they had to be uncomfortable. Anyone who looked at them knew that these men would never back down or let a single prisoner escape as long as any of them remained standing.

The smell of grease from the deep fry of a nearby diner or pancake house made me simultaneously nauseous and hungry. Hopefully, I would not be in the area long enough to have to sustain myself on deep-fried diner food.

As I was thinking about what I might eat that would be at least halfway healthy, the shadow of a lone hawk circling above swooped by my feet at a startling speed. The magnificent hawk pumped its powerful wings and increased its speed at an impressive rate but circled back around and landed on top of the tall brick wall, probably looking for field mice in its usual spot, but today there was little to do but watch the humans make spectacles of themselves.

Off to the southeast, three buzzards glided effortlessly in the wind, likely circling something dead or dying in the Sam Houston National Forest.

Scanning the camps of news teams, I noticed several people huddled around a television monitor on the inside of a van on the other end of the media command center. Getting closer, I saw they had a layout of the prison on a monitor. The van was also equipped with a camera mounted atop a telescoping pole, which peered over the wall. I eased my way in closer and peeked over someone's shoulder. They were recording a sequence to be aired and were already on their fifth take.

A man in a nice suit was attempting to make it sound as though they had a huge, exclusive story, just for their viewers. He spoke in a low, golf-announcer voice as he summarized the highlights of the ordeal. The monitor in the van switched back to the view of the animated prison layout. A gliding arrow indicated the area where they believed the hostages were being held. I made a mental snapshot of the image and began walking around the fortress of a fence, opposite the area where they thought the hostages were being held.

Escalation

Nothing existed on the outside of the prison walls to indicate what might be on the inside, and there was no way to see over it, so I was not sure what I could do until I saw a two-story home being remodeled. Being the weekend, no one was on the job, but the scaffolding was still up, and thanks to a couple of trees and the neighbor's house, it seemed to be partially hidden from all the commotion and cameras a few hundred feet away. I shrugged and helped myself.

From the roof, I could see much of the prison yard. I could not see inside the cellblocks, of course, but I could see the buildings and the back of the area where the news crew in the van suspected the hostages were being held. I situated myself between an outcropped window and the simple, bright green leaves of a large pecan tree overhanging the roof to prepare myself. *Last chance to back out*, I thought very deliberately, but then said out loud, "Why would I?"

Resolved to making a difference, I did my best to direct the focal point of my new talents into the cellblocks for a few seconds. When I felt sure *some* of the inmates had to have been affected, I relaxed to see if there was any kind of reaction.

Nothing. I heard no cries for help or shouts of fear or rage, and no one came running out of the buildings.

I tried again, focusing more intently this time. I tried to calculate where in the buildings they might be, but avoided the area where the news crew had said the guards were rumored to be held. I swept back and forth, concentrating intensely, but again, I heard nothing and saw no reaction.

Maybe I needed to be closer. Could it be that the deadly focal point became too weak or too widely dispersed to be effective at this range?

I took a short break to rest my mind and clear my thoughts. A mockingbird flittered around in the pecan tree next to me, but became very still when it noticed me high up in its domain. We eyed each other for a short while until it sprang from the branch and flew off in the opposite direction.

Wondering if a more systematic approach would get better results, I became even more intense. Starting on one end, I swept a wave of concentration up and down, back and forth, and in and out, not leaving any areas untouched.

An eternity passed as I covered every cubic foot. My mind grew weary and I was about to give up, despite barely covering a third of one of the buildings. I finally heard what sounded like another screaming riot forming. I stopped as the chilling shrieks and shouts of a few hundred men sent shivers down my spine. The yelling became louder as hundreds began pouring out of the prison into the surrounding yard.

Prisoners ran from the building, fighting each other to push their way out ahead of everyone else. They trampled over each other, stepping on someone if the foothold offered an advantage. Many criminals were experiencing the same terror they had inflicted in their victims. And I was okay with that.

I let the survivors escape into the yard. Some of them began forming a human chain up one of the corners of the tall brick wall. They brought out mattresses and sheets from the cells to throw over the razor wire and began passing them up the living ladder. The guards were still in the watchtowers aiming at the prisoners.

Shots rang out, punctuating the climaxing shouts and screams of the inmates. Some fell, but dozens more were taking their place. The guards fired repeatedly and more prisoners dropped. Still, others took their place, more afraid of the unseen forces within the prison cellblocks than death by high-powered rifles.

Prisoners hurled objects at the guards. This slowed the gunshots enough for some of them to scramble over the wall. I decided to intervene again. Hesitating a moment, I considered the fact that any of these people could have wives or children that might depend on them someday, or could even be wrongly incarcerated. However, all the people who escaped today would likely commit other violent and heinous acts in the future. I put them down in waves as the smell of spent gunpowder lingered in the air, stinging my nostrils.

My original intent was to simply end the siege and get the guards out safely, but they had all brought this upon themselves. I swept over every last prisoner as though they were insects. Soon, no one was moving and I gazed at the atrocity, shocked at what I had done and how easy it was. A nearly deafening, unnatural quiet followed.

Now I know what Manfred Mann meant.

The roaring silence only lasted a few seconds, but it was nearly maddening. Law enforcement officers stared in hushed disbelief. As a rumble rose from the stunned journalists, two guards climbed down from one of the watchtowers and cautiously approached the nearest inmate, weapons pointed and ready to fire.

They found no pulse, of course, and checked a few others. There were a few moments of inactivity as they discussed via radio what to do next. Two other guards climbed from the watchtower and ran into the prison, probably looking for the hostages, hoping they would find them alive.

A flow of guards and other law enforcement officers rushed inside the prison yard and into the building. I did not wait to see what happened next, but climbed down from my rooftop vantage point instead. Around the corner, the media camp had erupted into near-riot conditions of their own. Another media feeding frenzy peaked as they tried to figure out what happened. All they knew so far was there was another loud uprising, shots were fired, and then silence was prevalent.

Tall brick walls separated the hungriest of the media from the things they wished to know. The inaccessibility of information drove them nuts. I took advantage of the chaos and slipped away quietly while people desiring celebrity status speculated wildly via live "breaking news" reports.

In a strip mall up U.S. Highway 190, I sat in a corner booth of something closely resembling a coffee shop, contemplating the drastic measures I had taken to end the prison takeover. The old coffee was as bitter as my thoughts.

Despite my efforts, I could not get my mind off the pile of bodies I had left a few miles away. My gray matter did its best to convince my conscience that the world was better off without those lowlifes in it, but I still had trouble coping. I struggled with it but could think of many reasons to continue taking out the trash, and precious few to stop. Refilling my cup for the road, I added enough cream to mask the bitterness and headed home.

As I sat at a stop sign on a crossroad of the highway, I remembered going through dozens of small towns where I had to endure dozens of traffic lights and stretches of speed limits as low as 30 MPH. The Interstates were a better choice, whenever possible, even if it meant driving a few more miles. Using an online map, I tried to decide which route would be best without keying in my current location. My options included taking a southern route or a couple of northern routes.

As I considered my options, still sitting at the stop sign, a loud horn from an old blue pickup truck startled me. The truck pulled up beside me and instinct nearly prevailed. I came close to stomping on the accelerator but managed to keep a cool head.

The driver shouted something at me. I thought he was angry at first, but he was smiling. What did he want? He had no way of knowing I didn't wish to be in contact with anyone in the area. I needed as few witnesses as possible. Had he noticed me at the prison?

When it was apparent that he was not going away until I answered him, I rolled down my window and heard him say, "Howdy Slick! I said 'Ya look lost.' Need some help?" A disarming young man in a straw cowboy hat leaned forward, talking around the "big hair" of a beautiful smiling blonde woman sitting next to him in the middle of the cab. Actually, she was completely on his side of the seat.

Help? Help with what? Why is he offering to help? And "slick"? What was that about? *Slick?!* Ah! He had noticed my New York plates, and there I was, sitting at a stop sign looking at a map. No threat, just a friendly local.

"Thank you, no. I'm good now, I think."

They both smiled as he waved and shouted, "Awl-righty! Have ya a good'n then!" and gunned it after looking both ways thoroughly. I watched them drive away with him up against the driver's side door and her sitting right up against him. Through the rear windshield, it was hard to tell which one of them was driving.

Interesting. Instead of giving me the finger and going around the lost Yankee blocking traffic, he took the time to stop and genuinely offer help. That settled it for me. I made up my mind to take one of the northern routes for the sole purpose of being able to see more of Texas. I found I-45 and headed north.

Detour

As I rolled through many miles of heavy traffic, the news on every radio station was dominated by what had become known as "the incident in Huntsville." Reporters were still speculating wildly, introducing new theories and ideas, both ludicrous and ingenious, but none anywhere near the truth. I listened carefully for anything to help cover my tracks.

I also drove carefully and stayed under the speed limit to reduce the chances of being stopped by the police or highway patrol. I did not want to leave any traceable record of my visit to Texas or even being away from home over the weekend.

Along the way, I saw the exit signs for Tyler, Texas, and remembered the man on the New York City street selling roses. If I had more time, I would have driven through Tyler just to see all the roses the man had described to so many potential customers. The heavy traffic persisted all the way to Dallas, locked in a perpetual state of rush-hour traffic, even on a Sunday.

In the past, when I imagined how Texas might appear, I invariably pictured wide-open prairies where cowboys herded cattle, but nothing could be further from the truth. The Interstate from Houston to Dallas was like one big metropolis with one town or community after another lining the highway, some of which were trying desperately to retain that small town ambiance progress was stripping from them.

Something peculiar happened about the time I rolled through Corsicana. Prison officials released a statement claiming an equestrian virus from the prison rodeo grounds had mutated and infected the prison population. The viral infection had caused them to act irrationally and had ultimately caused their deaths.

Although difficult to believe at first, the lie soon began to make sense. I'm guessing the unwelcome media encampment dispersed very quickly after the statement. I did not hear anything else about the incident other than they were planning to clean or close the historic rodeo arena.

Eventually, I found myself trying to be impressed by downtown Dallas. True, it was big, but compared with New York, the nickname "Big D" did not seem fitting. The city was certainly cleaner, though, and quieter. I expected to see a hustling-bustling city, busy twenty-four hours a day like New York, but there did not appear to be much pedestrian traffic downtown. A typical spring Sunday afternoon in North Texas?

I drove until I found a couple of interesting places within the concrete, steel, and glass forest. One was a club district called Deep Ellum and the other was an area with an overabundance of restaurants called West End. Quite a few people were hanging out there. Mostly locals, I guessed, but some could have been tourists.

I intended to drive through downtown Dallas and be on my way, but I saw a sign advertising The Sixth Floor Museum at Dealey Plaza and instantly recognized it as part of the JFK memorial. This alone would make the trip through Dallas worthwhile. I followed the signs and parked in a spot directly behind the infamous and inaptly nicknamed "grassy knoll," which was not a knoll at all, but a bluff. And "bluff" is a more appropriate name, given the history since November 22nd, 1963.

A couple of hours in the museum were well spent. All the information provided was sadly interesting, but the thing that humbled me most was walking out and standing on the sidewalk across from Dealey Plaza and looking at the spot where Kennedy was assassinated. I am not an emotional person, but standing there, and knowing what had happened so long ago, quite honestly brought tears to my eyes. Not just in mourning for JFK, but also for the shameful attempt made by fellow Americans to cover up the circumstances surrounding his murder.

Sad. He deserved far, far better.

Chance

When the sun began to hang low over the Trinity River, the western horizon changed into a beautiful glowing orange, and the evening air cooled considerably. That was a good thing, too. Thinking about all the unanswered questions and the serious lack of a thorough investigation America had to endure made me hot under the collar. Besides, I had learned my lesson about hanging out alone in unfamiliar places after dark.

Heading for the parking lot atop the bluff that is better known as "the grassy knoll," I returned to my car. However, I knew I had problems as soon as I opened the door and noticed the dome light did not come on. I tried the ignition but heard only clicks. Too late to do anything about it, I noticed I had left my headlights burning.

"Ds and Fs!" I muttered under my breath as I remembered turning on the headlights while I was on the road. Isn't your car supposed to beep or ding or something when you leave your headlights on? "Well, that's just great," I said out loud. "The conspiracy continues." I cut my eyes around to see if anyone was listening. There did not appear to be.

I popped the hood and got out. There were no jumper cables in the trunk, of course, and no flashlight. No one was in the parking lot attendant's booth, there were no cops around, and I saw no security guards. Meanwhile, the evening grew darker, and despite the heavy traffic earlier, *no* one was around now. As I exhaled a heavy sigh, a flashy little hybrid sports car whipped around the corner of the building.

At first, I thought they were going to drive right by, but the brakes came on, then the reverse lights. The car backed up and the passenger-side window came down, as did the volume of a Led Zeppelin song from the seventies. I could not see inside the car, but I heard a friendly voice ask, "Need a jump?"

"Yes, please!" No wonder thousands of people move to Texas every month. Even people in the big cities were small-town friendly.

He pulled his car around in front of mine and eased up bumper to bumper. I heard the parking brake engage and watched his hood pop open. A blonde-headed man in an oversized T-shirt stepped out and asked, "You have cables?" already on the way to the back of his car, obviously knowing I had none.

"No, I'm afraid I'm completely unprepared. You?" There was no need to ask as he pulled them out from under the floor of the hatchback. He uncoiled them as he walked around his car and handed one end to me.

He used the flashlight feature on his phone to illuminate my battery as he said, "Red on positive?" He could have hooked them up himself, but instead held the light so I could see, letting me handle my end completely. A simple gesture of trust, perhaps?

"Yes. Red, on, positive," I said as I clamped the last connection.

He attached the red clamp to the positive side of his battery but touched the black, negative side to an exposed bolt on the frame of his car rather than to the battery itself. The engine idled down noticeably as it worked harder to charge my battery, and when he removed the edge of the clamp from the bolt, his engine idled back up. Satisfied with the connectivity between the two cars, he clamped the cable to the same bolt and listened to his engine idle down slightly again.

I wondered why he connected the clamp to the frame of the car instead of the battery. The method worked, but why not connect both clamps to the battery? Seems like you might lose a good deal of amperage the way he did it. He must have noticed the questioning look on my face, so, with a courtesy nod, he explained; "Less chance of doing damage to the battery, *and* it reduces the chances of sparks igniting anything flammable."

"Ah!"

"Don't worry, you still get plenty of juice. It just needs a ground. Batteries are typically located in places where fumes can gather—poor design, actually, so I've made a habit of making the last connection out in the open."

"Pretty good idea! Bad experience teach you that?"

"No, an old man who was probably wiser than the two of us put together taught me that."

I like this guy.

With a smile and an imitated Australian accent, he said, "Give i' a shot, mate!" and then reached under the hood and revved the engine with his hand somehow. My car started right up, so I thanked him profusely and tried to pay him, but he would not accept money. Instead, as he neatly coiled his cables, he began to tell me a story.

"You don't owe me anything. Really! I'm sure you'd have done the same for me. However, if you feel indebted, I do know a way for you to pay that debt in a way that would satisfy us both."

I shot him a sideways glance. Where was he going with this? His face was expressionless except for the hint of a smile, which I suspected was present more often than not.

He continued. "You don't have to do anything right now, this is for the future, so don't be thinking anything that would cause you to look at me like that." The funny expression he made trying to imitate me made me laugh, but he went on without missing a beat. This was obviously not the first time he had had this conversation.

"I went to high school in a small town a few miles southwest of Fort Worth. I was working a part-time job after school and weekends, and my co-workers had learned that they could count on me to always be on time." He began describing a not-so-typical job for a high school student, but then realized he was sidetracked, and picked up where he left off.

"So, anyway, on the way to work one day, I broke down in the middle of nowhere, thanks to my preference for taking the more scenic roads to work."

He summarized the trouble he had experienced with a hole in a radiator hose and then told of a man who stopped to help him. Together they used the man's tools to cut the hose off at the leak, pull the slack out of the hose, and reattach it. Easy enough for someone with experience, but he was just a kid at the time. He admitted that the make-run idea would not have occurred to him.

"The guy even had a jug of water in his truck! When we were finished, I offered him the last five dollars I had until payday, but he wouldn't accept it. He said I had to stop and help ten other people instead. Sometime in the future, I had to stop on the side of the road to help people who had broken down.

"He pointed out that someday I'd be married and have kids, so when they were with me, I was exempt. 'In other words,' he said, 'don't endanger your family or other passengers to stop and help a stranger, but when you're able, stop and render aid, especially in the summer when it's over a hundred degrees.' He told me a story similar to this one, only the person who stopped to help him did so in the nineteen sixties, and the person who had helped *that* man was another jobless fellow during the Great Depression."

"Wow," I mused aloud. "Someone in the nineteen thirties just extended a helping hand through several decades."

He had finished rolling up his jumper cables but waited until he finished his story before placing them neatly back in the original bag. Closing the hatchback, he said, "I asked the ol' boy what number he was on. You know, how many people he had stopped to help, and he said he'd lost count around number seven. I got the distinct impression that over the years, he'd stopped and helped a lot more than ten people."

While I listened, I closed both our hoods and he nodded a polite thank you.

"So, I ask the same thing of you. The times you're able to stop and help, do so. I know times are a lot different now than they were in the past, so don't put yourself or anybody else in danger, but when you're able, stop and help.

"Ten times.

"And tell each of them your version of this story, only take some advice; if it's a woman you stop and help, you might want to ask them to help in ways that don't involve stopping on the side of the road or approaching strangers. You know, if they look like the professional mom type, suggest that they help a teacher ten times, or if they're an attorney tell them to help a single parent. Something of that nature."

I shook his hand and thanked him again, assuring him that I would comply with his wishes, but I, like him, could not help asking what number he was on.

"Ummm," he looked out at the first visible stars of the evening as though that would help him remember, then looked back at me with a smile, "…seven, I think."

Of course! I committed to the same notion.

Before I let him go, I asked him about a good restaurant in the area to have dinner.

"Depends. Which way are you headed?"

"Northeast."

"Headed home, are you?" It seems my New York plates attracted more attention than I preferred. "Well, if you can't make it over to Fort Worth, then without a doubt, do *not* leave the Metroplex without eating at one of the Blue Mesa Grills here in Dallas."

"Okay, but do not leave the, *what?*"

"The Metroplex. Fort Worth, Dallas, Arlington, Irving, Grand Prairie, Plano," he said as he pointed in various directions, and then added in the animated voice-over of an announcer, "many, many more!" I had to laugh at him again. "It's all like one big city here, so, years ago, a local celebrity gave us a nickname: The Metroplex."

"I see. And what's in Fort Worth?"

"Some of the best restaurants in Texas, and a lot more. World class museums and art galleries, and a few city blocks downtown called Sundance Square that puts most other downtown areas to shame. There are shops, business offices, the Bass Hall, which is one of the finest auditoriums on the planet, theaters, and plenty of free parking in the evenings. I could go on."

"I'm always reminded of cowboys, cattle drives, outlaws, and the Calvary when I think of Fort Worth."

He might have been a little offended but took it gracefully. "Yeah, well, a century ago, maybe." A slight tilt of his head appeared to be a bit of a concession. "In a few places around town, the city council maintains the Old West look and reputation because it helps tourism, but Cowtown has one of the most successful business centers in America. In fact, most people don't realize it, but Dallas is really nothing but Fort Worth's largest suburb."

I could not tell if he was kidding because he straight-faced it well, but he finally chuckled and I found myself laughing again.

He was right; Fort Worth is a great town. Later that night, while driving back through the *Metroplex*, I noticed two other large, downtown-like areas, one of which appeared to be built around a huge shopping mall. I conceded that maybe Dallas deserves the nickname Big D after all.

The remainder of the trip back to New York was uneventful except for seeing some beautiful countryside, but I did not realize how tense all my stress muscles were from the long drive until I crawled into bed.

I was exhausted but unable to sleep. Quite a lot bothered me. I was responsible for ending dozens of human lives with minimal effort. Yes, they were all criminals who had hurt others enough to land them in prison, but would I be able to keep this kind of power in check, and only use it against other such cruel people? I had no intention of becoming greedy or power-hungry, but what guarantee did I have that I would not change in the future? None. I would have to trust that I would remain true to myself. What other choice did I have?

Throwdown

On the morning of the fifth day of her stay in New York, Carla dropped off her previous four days' worth of dirty clothes at a nearby green dry cleaner. She had come to realize that she was going to be in the Big Apple far longer than the seven days for which she had packed. She might even have to stay in New York for weeks instead of days.

Carla considered moving to an extended-stay hotel with a kitchenette to save a little money on meals and so she could prepare healthier choices for herself. Everything she had eaten in New York had been purchased in a restaurant, or even worse, fast food, so the sodium content was so high it had likely already taken weeks off the end of her life.

There were still several potential witnesses to interview, some of whom even had to be located first, which was no easy task. Many of the people she sought were mere faces on blurry security camera tapes or from relatively low-resolution digital images from Internet traffic cameras and webcams. She spent a lot of time talking to people employed in the areas where the bodies, the Limo, and the old beater of a car were found. Anyone who might have the tiniest bit of information had to be interviewed. This was going to take a while.

On her sixth evening in the Big Apple, she received a call ordering her to be on the next flight available to Huntsville, Texas. Any flight. Commercial, military, special services, it did not matter. She needed to find a way to get to the state penitentiary in Huntsville as soon as possible to help investigate an event related to her case. A local agent would brief her when she arrived.

This presented a problem for Carla on a personal level. She only had two sets of clean clothes left and the rest of her clothes were at the dry cleaners but would not be ready until Monday, so she stopped by a department store on the way back to the hotel. Three new outfits could easily be mixed and worn with some of her other clothes. In the morning, she barely boarded the early flight to Houston on time.

Agent Bright used her flight time to organize the forty-some-odd pages of notes she had printed out from all the e-mails she had received about the case so far. One of the e-mails that someone had called the "summary of the case" had printed out nineteen pages. She wondered what might be in store for her in the Texas prison and considered all sorts of different scenarios, but of course, nothing she envisioned could prepare her for reality.

A Houston-based colleague in a black sedan with government plates was kind enough to pick her up at the airport. He did his best to explain the situation on the way but admitted he knew little more than what he had heard on the news. When she arrived on the scene, she was amazed at the number of different law enforcement agencies being represented. She had not seen so many different kinds of badges in any one place since she attended the international conference on terrorism in Geneva a few years ago.

There were deputies from the sheriff's office, local city police, DEA, CIA, some fellow FBI agents, a Texas Ranger, guards from the prison, and the CDC, which had an air-tight canvas and rubber tent inflated with compressed air around the bodies. There was even an animal control officer there with a clipboard and an animal-restraint rod.

As she and her colleague approached a large group of men discussing the situation, three of them stepped away from the crowd a few steps to greet her. A big man in a cowboy hat and two other FBI agents introduced themselves as Agent Wheeler, Special Agent Lupe, and Ranger Mathews.

"Disease Control is testing the bodies in the tent, in the prison, and the surrounding area for traces of gas, chemicals, hazardous materials, disease, and viral infection. There's talk of something drifting over from the rodeo arena, but no word yet." The Texas Ranger seemed comfortable taking a position of authority, as though he expected her to get all her information from him.

Carla considered her options for only a moment before firmly requesting, "I'd like to go in now and look around before all my evidence is completely obliterated, if you don't mind." She tried to sound polite but did not quite pull it off. Texas prisoners having their very own rodeo arena rubbed her the wrong way.

The Ranger shook his head ever so slightly and made a rugged growling sound everyone knew was meant to signify negativity. His weathered exterior made him look more like a farmer than a law enforcement official. He was wearing blue jeans buckled under a bit of a potbelly, a white shirt with a tie, a jacket that had once been part of a suit, and of course, his big white cowboy hat. "It'd be a good idea to wait till they're finished, ma'am."

Her fellow FBI agents looked at him and nodded, accepting what he said without question, but it simply was not good enough for her. "Ranger Mathews, there are people in there who are probably untrained, or at least ill-trained for crime scenes, stomping around all over potential evidence, and I intend to go in to take a look around." Turning to her stunned co-workers, she asked in her most commanding tone, "Now, where can I find equipment like *that?*" referring to a man wearing what looked like a space suit emerging from the tent.

A smiling Ranger looked at Special Agent Lupe, who took Carla gently by the arm and escorted her out of earshot of the other two. Agent Lupe candidly asked Carla, "Uh, have you never worked in Texas before?"

She wondered if she had detected a bit of attitude from him, but with the thick Spanish accent, she was not sure. "Uh, no. Why? You're not insinuating that we take orders from that farmhand, are you?"

"We are to offer the Rangers every courtesy, and they do the same for us. When we are in Texas, we need to treat the Rangers as partners and equals."

"Surely he does not believe he can actually take over a case from the FBI. This is *not* a TV show." As she was finishing her sentence, she could see how uncomfortable Lupe had become.

"No ma'am, it's not," came a deep voice from behind her. The Ranger had stealthily walked up at just that moment. "I have no intention of taking over this case, *at this time*. If I feel it's necessary, I will, but it would be foolish not to let all these bright young minds investigate *our* evidence to try to figure out what's happened to those inmates. We are all professionals here, waitin' for other professionals to finish testing to see if it's safe to be around those bodies. They'll let us know directly, I imagine. Till then, we'll all just wait patiently."

With that, he took off his hat, ran one of his huge, weathered hands through his hair a couple of times, and then replaced his Stetson with great care, positioning it perfectly.

Everyone watched the Ranger do his hat and hair thing, patiently waiting to see if he was finished speaking. A few seconds passed before everyone realized he had said all he needed to say.

Carla was uncertain, so she decided to play it safe for now and contact her superiors later. Besides, he was right about "waitin'" so she graciously backpaddled. "Of course. My apologies."

The Ranger smiled and nodded, making it obvious that he was not the type to hold a grudge. He looked like he had grown used to conversations like that. She did *not* know the Ranger had made a mental note to contact the FBI director again and ask him if they had recently had another cutback in their training budget.

While waiting for the environmental test results, she noticed for the first time that no reporters were present. She inquired about when the circus might show up and was informed that they had already come and gone, and thanks to one of *her* bosses coercing prison officials into releasing a theory-as-fact press release, they were frightened and would probably not be back.

One impressive thing Carla noticed about the massive crime scene was how well all of the different law enforcement agents worked together under the direction of the single Texas Ranger, who made sure all parties involved shared their knowledge and expertise.

Except for the FBI, of course. Carla shared only the facts relating to the issues at the Texas site. The cases in New York and New Jersey that were similar somehow never managed to surface. Still, every single law enforcement officer present, no matter which organization they represented, spontaneously cheered when the county's sheriff used the PA system in his patrol car to announce that all three of the guards who had been taken hostage and beaten nearly to death were going to survive the ordeal.

The investigation went on for days, and, although a wealth of information was gathered, apparently no one was any closer to anything like a lead than they were the very first day, except the FBI, who came up with a video clip that included four and a half seconds of the only unidentified person on the scene that day. On the right side of the video, the man wore dark sunglasses with a Texas A&M cap and needed a shave.

Whomever it was seemed to catch his reflection in a van's window, which made him do a double take and stop for a moment. Had he adjusted his sunglasses, his hat, or his hair, no one would have paid attention to the man. But he did none of those things, *and* appeared to laugh a little as he moved away, possibly amused by his appearance. The combination of all these things attracted the attention of Agent Wheeler, the young analyst already making a name for himself.

No one recognized the stranger in the reflection. None of the journalists they contacted and questioned even remembered seeing him, but then, they were too focused on their careers to notice things like real news and key evidence that might help solve this baffling mystery.

After several eighteen- and twenty-hour days, a weary and hodgepodge team of investigators stepped away from the area and gave the okay to remove the yellow crime scene tape. Ranger Mathews shook Agent Bright's hand and graciously invited her out to visit his farm one weekend, on the north shore of Lake Sam Rayburn. "The views of the landscapes are spectacular, the sunsets are even better, *and* my wife makes the best meatloaf in Texas."

She theorized for a moment. Was that a shot back at her for the unwarranted comments she made just moments after they had met, or did he simply treat all new law enforcement acquaintances with such high regard? The "wife's meatloaf" comment made it clear he was not making some kind of perverted pass at her for a romantic weekend getaway, so his invitation seemed genuine.

Something about that comment irrationally bothered her. He claimed his wife made the best meatloaf in *Texas*, as though it would be pointless and futile to even consider a meatloaf made in some lesser state somewhere. Arrogance? Or confidence? It was hard to know.

Carla realized she had already hesitated too long and was giving it way too much thought. "Thank you. I appreciate the offer. I have to admit, I'm very tempted to take you up on it. I enjoy a well-prepared meatloaf."

I'd like to challenge that witch to a meatloaf throwdown. Show them both a thing or two.

They parted ways as new friends, either willing to help the other in any professional capacity.

Progress

As far as I know, the prison riot was never discussed among my co-workers at ERL. I suppose they were so far removed from the events, geographically and intellectually, the entire situation and how it was resolved did not interest or concern them.

Over the next couple of weeks, the stories started showing up on the covers of tabloids. I did not know what to think about this new development, other than it was troubling. Why the tabloids? Reasonable deductions would have to include the idea that the tabloids were fed sensational versions of the story.

When the CDC and coroners could not find a trace of anything leading to the mass deaths, did the government step in with an old-fashioned, don't-panic-the-public smokescreen? Were they using reverse psychology, knowing that people typically understand tabloid headlines are twisted accounts of the truth, designed to trick you into reading the nonsense and sensationalism within? (That is to say, to trick you into *buying* a copy.)

People standing in grocery store lines all across the continent were shaking their heads in disgust at ludicrous headlines describing only the most distorted pictures of the events in Huntsville. I could not think of a better way to change truth into fiction.

Yet covering up the mysterious deaths of dozens of inmates did not seem like the kind of thing anyone or any group would attempt to undertake, especially an entity of the United States government. What would make anyone think they could succeed at such a colossal endeavor? I wondered what else might have been suppressed in the past. I suddenly found it interesting that on the same road trip, I had chosen to visit Dealey Plaza, the site of *the* most notorious cover-up in history.

To divert my attention away from my conscience, I went about my daily routines enthusiastically. Yet I was still becoming increasingly burdened by the gravity of the extreme measures I had taken against all those men. My response bothered me so much that my anxiety became apparent to my lab partners and possibly even affected my job performance, which is rare for me, not to mention unacceptable.

Both Dave and Carol independently asked if everything was okay. I fielded the questions with positive assurances, but everyone knew something weighed heavily on my mind.

I struggled with pangs of guilt, which I first attributed to my indiscriminate taking of so many lives, but when I examined my angst more closely, I could not pinpoint the origins of my distress.

Eventually, I began to embrace my extraordinary potential. I came to realize that I could easily change the very course of history for many facets of humanity. I endlessly speculated about the different ways I might exploit these talents *without* anyone's death being involved, but then, as I sipped a dark roast at my favorite coffee shop, it occurred to me that maybe, just *maybe*, I felt guilty because I wasn't doing enough. Idle, by anyone's standards. A slacker!

It was time to make plans, but where should I start? How could I get to the root of the problem? How do you determine who is at the top of the food chain of crime? In my opinion, drugs and gangs tend to feed off each other and are probably responsible for most of the crimes in America. While that sounded like a good place to begin, the fact didn't narrow down my choices. I could think of many other injustices I would love to rectify.

The perpetual violence in the Middle East, the horrific clitoridectomies and other genital mutilations going on in many undeveloped countries, the abuse of power by politicians, the wide separation between minimum wage and multimillion-dollar salaries, the deforestation of our planet, the senseless killing of intelligent beings like whales, dolphins, and elephants…

Lists like that could go on and on, so I considered another angle. I tried to think of illegal activities controlled by single individuals or small groups. Taking out the head of a terrorist organization would solve a considerable number of the world's problems for a few years, or at least a few months, but getting close enough to them to carry out such a feat would be nearly impossible or, more likely, suicidal.

Something else occurred to me. The United States and much of the rest of the free world have tried to infiltrate these extremist groups for decades. Thinking I could do better might be somewhat arrogant.

I thought about using my new abilities to disrupt the nervous system of key people to make them believe their limbs were paralyzed. I could then convince them that some kind of god was amongst them, rewarding or punishing those who cooperated or dissented. For some people, faith, fear, and magic might be all their brainwashed minds could understand, anyway. I kept this idea warm on the back burner.

I thought of dozens of other possibilities, too, but my mind kept going back to the most prevalent issue in my own back yard. Drug abuse and dangerous gangs. Who could I take out to have the most significant impact on deterring drug abuse? The guys selling the drugs on the street corner? Or the users? I was hesitant to start following people again, but not opposed to the idea, even knowing that the individuals at the top, or near the top, of drug and gang organizations might prove to be as hard to approach as those of Middle Eastern terrorist organizations.

The only way to make things happen is to get up and get busy, so I made the ambitious and possibly reckless decision to wade right into the thick of it. I would start with the one element of commonality, which was gang members selling drugs, and work my way up from there.

That very night I peered over the railing of my balcony with binoculars down at the city streets, where I knew gangs to frequent late at night, and started watching the general mannerisms and characteristics of gang members. Three or four times a week, I drove through the city at different times of the day and night and noted the places where the shadiest-looking characters regularly frequented.

In most neighborhoods, the same teens and pre-teens could be seen time after time, while in other places there seemed to be a lot of different people in and out. I paid particularly close attention to these areas. I pinpointed several locations that received a lot of visitors who did not stay long. They were of all different ages and types with some wearing old, ragged jeans and others wearing suits.

One such building seemed to have a lot of nicely dressed people visiting at all hours of the day and night. A few of them were parking in a garage about a half block away. I was unable to see the entrance of the building from the parking garage, so, one warm Friday afternoon, I parked down the street where I could see the garage and the entrance to the overly popular building. I opened a map of the city and peered over it in case the druggies had spotters. Dozens of addicts entered the building only to come back out two or three minutes later.

Several men loitered around the entryway, all wearing the same predominant colors and way too much gold jewelry. Again, this was probably going to be more difficult than I had anticipated.

Foolishly, I had assumed some idiot would be selling drugs on the street corner or out of his car window, but anyone doing that would have been busted long ago. I hesitated and wondered if I should have more faith in the NYPD and DEA, but then a young girl who could not have been more than fourteen or fifteen walked through the gang and into the building with the confidence of a frequent flyer. Nearly half an hour later she stumbled out, disheveled, and hurried away.

I had to find a way to get in there.

Before long, a man wearing a white shirt and tie came out of the parking garage and went into the building. If I could catch him going back into the garage, I might be able to find out what I needed to know from him. I paced myself so I would arrive at the entrance about the same time as the addict. The man in the white shirt emerged from the building and hurried back to his car. I fell into step behind him and followed him through the filthy parking garage.

Walking down the same row of cars, but on the opposite side of the aisle, I could see he was in his late twenties and in good shape. Or maybe he was just skinny, but the lack of fat on his body could be a side effect of doing drugs and/or smoking. A new, black, high-end sedan chirped and blinked its taillights, so I headed in that general direction a few steps behind him.

The SUV he purposefully parked beside offered me the same cover from the street as it had given him. I trotted to his car and jerked his door open seconds after he closed it. Startled, he fumbled around trying to hide a small package in his hand. I pressed the unlock button, opened the back door, slammed his door, and quickly jumped into the back seat of his car.

"What the *hell* do you think you're doing? Get out of my car!"

"Let's talk first."

"Get the *fuck* out of my car!"

I did my best to feign concern and said in a tranquil voice, "Calm yourself."

"Like hell!" He might have been about to take a swing at me over the seat, so I focused on his shoulder, and his arm went limp. He had to be scared, but he did not let it show. He maintained a defiant, smart-ass expression. He had no way of knowing I was responsible for the condition of his arm, and he did not let on that it was limp. Instead, he started negotiating as his other hand slowly started reaching for the door handle. "What do you want? Why are you in my car?"

"I want to know what you bought back there. Coke? Grass?"

"What are you, a throwback from the nineties? Nobody uses or even *says* 'coke' or 'grass' anymore. The going thing is tripcy, now. You know, dex, man!" His attempt at a distraction was admirable, but such a diversion would only work on ignorant drug addicts like himself.

"Just answer my question. What did you buy back there?" When his hand was almost on the door handle, I focused on his left shoulder and watched his arm go limp. His right arm began moving and was probably tingling, as my hand had done when I tested my abilities.

In the rear-view mirror, he had seen me look intensely at his shoulder the moment it went limp and made the connection, but appeared confused. He looked at me with a straight face, without even a hint of fear in his eyes, but when he spoke, he could not mask the terror. Traced in his voice was a hint of a tremble as he asked, "You're doing that, aren't you?"

"You are *not* going to like what comes next if you don't answer my question."

"Crack! Ah-ight? Crack cocaine. Now, let go of me!"

"Tell me what I need to know to get to your dealer."

"Oh! You're some kind of vigilante or something. Gonna clean up the neighborhood, are you? Bring justice to the wor—" His entire body went limp, and his head fell over against the window to his left with a distinct thud. His head then slid forward while his forehead made a squeaking sound against the glass. I caught him before he fell into the steering wheel and blew the horn.

"It's hard to be a smart-ass when you can't feel anything from the neck down, isn't it? You should know something before we go on. You mean absolutely *nothing* to me. You are nothing but a low-life. Now, the rest of this conversation can continue to go poorly, or it can improve dramatically. It's entirely up to you, but trust me, you have yet to see the worst of what I'm capable of doing." I released him and he sucked air like a winded runner.

"Ah-ight, goddamn it!" he gasped. "Just tell me what the fuck you want!" He rubbed his chest and stared at me in disbelief. While he caught his breath, I slipped up and over and into the passenger seat.

"Listen this time. I want you to tell me how to get to the person that sold you drugs."

"They'd kill me! You *have* to understand that."

Focusing on his neck again, his head flopped over backward this time, "*I'm* going to kill you right now if you don't tell me how to get to them. Besides, if you cooperate, there won't be any of them left to come after you. No, let's review quickly before you pass out. You can die right now, for sure, or *maybe* get killed by a drug dealer later."

This time when I released him, he screeched, "Aaaaaah-*iiiiight*! You sci-fi mother *fucker*!" I nearly laughed out loud but managed to keep a straight face while he spilled his guts. "Go up to the third floor and knock quietly on apartment 3B. When you hear a voice, flash some money in front of the peephole. If the mail slot opens, hand him your money. If it doesn't open, he's probably calling the fuckin' goons downstairs."

"How many are usually in there?"

"How the fuck should I know? I've never even *seen* inside."

I paused, collected my thoughts, and told him to "Drive."

"Where?"

"To any of the other places where you buy anything illegal."

He sighed heavily but started his car and took off. The first place he pointed out was a mere four blocks away. We parked down the street while he described how to approach the flat and possibly even get inside. While we were stopped, I made him open his door and dump the tiny bag of crack into the muck on the street. He threw a cussing fit and begged me to let him keep it so he wouldn't go insane. I thought he might break down and cry.

The next place he showed me was a small office building that had been abandoned for years. Several "Danger – Asbestos" signs were self-explanatory. Lovely. And besides being a crack house, there were hordes of homeless people loitering about, and probably living in the building. My *escort* said people can buy practically any kind of drug there, from many different people.

"Just go in and ask anyone. If they're there, chances are they're either using, selling, or both," he said.

There was no need to drive all over Manhattan to show me where to find the last dealer on his list. His contact was a man that spent quite a bit of time in the posh bar, Jazzmen, which I knew to be only a few short blocks from my condo. He described the individual and how best to approach him. I pushed for more details about anything he might have left out or neglected to mention. I scared him with threats and by paralyzing him from the neck down again, but he shared nothing further.

A beautiful sunset tinted New York City in a golden-orange light that gradually faded into darkness as we approached the neighborhood where I had left my car. I had him park in an area where there were fewer pedestrians, fairly close to the parking garage where I had found him.

I had already decided that it was just a matter of time before this sorry excuse for a human threw away everything he and his family had, along with all their futures, so he could continue to get high. To me, it was obvious that he was worth more to his family in insurance money than he was alive, so I killed him without hesitation or remorse. His death may or may not be painful for his family now, but they would most likely be spared years of prolonged suffering later.

With one less drug addict supporting the drug trade, I wiped everything I had touched on the inside of his car with a fast-food napkin from his glove box. I made sure the doors were locked before I wiped the outside door handles, and walked away.

Played

As I breezed by the "goons" at the front door, I made eye contact with the ones who would look at me. I walked in as if I owned the place. When I found apartment 3B, I slipped on my dark sunglasses and knocked softly. I saw the shadows of feet at the bottom of the door and assumed someone was peering through the peephole, but heard the beeping of a mobile phone. I focused through the door, sweeping around trying to catch anyone and everyone there.

Crashing sounds suggested that at least *some* of those efforts were successful, while a woman yelling in panic from within, and footsteps racing up the stairs told me I was not entirely successful. I hate it when a plan falls apart.

Two steps at a time brought me up another half flight of stairs to a landing where I could still see the door to apartment 3B as well as the stairs coming up from the second floor. The gang members who had been waiting outside made their way to the third floor in seconds. When the first ganger came into view, he already had his gun drawn. Two of his gang brothers followed closely but some of them had remained outside by the front steps.

The door to apartment 3B swung open and a half-naked woman stepped out into the hall in a state of panic. Her huge bare breasts bounced and swung freely while she jabbered indecipherably and pointed up the stairs at me. The first ganger pointed his pistol right at my chest at the same time the other two made it to the top of the stairs. As they all beaded down on me, I swept over them and watched them drop. Unfortunately, the woman collapsed with them, falling back into the doorway.

Hurrying down the stairs, I pulled her body the rest of the way back into the apartment. Rushing around before anyone else showed up, I kicked all the guns into the apartment as well, but left their bodies where they fell. A convenient pen allowed me to dial 911 on one of their phones without leaving fingerprints. I took it with me and used it to close the door behind me.

When I stepped outside, I beckoned the last gang members inside by saying, "Uh, I think your friends need you," and pointed up the stairs. A bit confused but feeling the need to help their fellow outlaws, they dashed upstairs. None of them survived, of course, but at least they would not be lying dead on the sidewalk while I was trying to make a clean getaway. I stuffed their guns into the back of my belt and calmly walked away.

I cursed myself on the way to my car. I had wanted to pump the dealer for information. I would not get very far in eliminating the drug and gang problems by taking out the grunts in the organizations. Finding more idiots to sell drugs would not be a problem for them. I made sure no one followed me or was even in the general vicinity when I got in my car and drove away.

Far from being finished for the night, I drove by the second place the druggie had shown me, but there was way too much traffic nearby and far too many people hanging out to even think about approaching them. Determining who was selling drugs would be difficult or impossible, which was intentional. Maybe they could all be considered guilty by association, but indiscriminately killing them all would be unacceptable.

The night was *still* young, so I drove to the asbestos office building the squatters had converted to a crack house. I parked three or four blocks away and had to walk through a dirty, rough neighborhood. I thought it best to pull a toboggan down over my ears and put my trench coat on inside out in an attempt to look homeless, or at least a bit psychotic, as it was nowhere near cold enough for winter attire, even though the evening was cooling off.

Walking to the crack house was not so bad, but crawling through the hole in the fence and entering the building was a bit unnerving. Filthy, drugged-up men stared me down with scornful eyes, no doubt wondering about my intentions. I was obviously out of place. A wave of nausea swept over me from the overpowering stench of urine and the odor produced by a lack of personal hygiene.

Dozens of whispers and hushed conversations mingled together and echoed through empty corridors to become an eerie buzzing. I kept my face down, half buried in my up-turned collar, and tried to stay in the shadows, which was not hard to do in a building with no electricity. Debris and filth lay scattered in every room. Walls were scarred where anything flammable had been stripped off and burned long ago.

People were gathered in small groups around what little light filtered through broken windows. Others were burning candles or had small fires contained in cans. Some people were taking turns sniffing smoke from dirty spoons or pieces of foil held over the flames. It never occurred to me how they smoked the stuff. When I heard the term "smoking crack," I assumed they were using a pipe or rolling it in paper.

Is my ignorance about substance abuse good or bad?

I continued my quest for someone who might know of a major dealer or supplier. People looked at me suspiciously as I ventured past them while others averted their faces to avoid eye contact. Most of them were surrounded by old trash sacks, grocery bags, backpacks, duffle bags, or stolen shopping carts crammed full of what few belongings they were able to retain from a former life.

They had sectioned the place off into many separate living quarters with each individual's area marked as his or her own. Some had big cardboard boxes for houses, while others had upscale versions made of blankets, sticks, and bricks.

Easily, the most horrifying thing for me was *not* the drug users, or the harsh living conditions, but rather the fact that there were *children* with some of them. They sat there in the squalor, wearing dirty and torn clothing, watching their mothers in silence, too afraid to speak or even move.

Throughout the building, people were either enjoying their brief high, or trying to catch a buzz, and I wondered where they got the money to support their choice of dependency. Or is that obvious? Seeing children being forced to live this way wrenched my heart.

How could a country that prides itself on helping starving communities all over the globe ignore situations like this? Shameful. Homeless people with children were living in a building condemned for health risks.

I found a stairwell and began making my way upstairs. The more stairs I climbed, the darker it became, and the worse it smelled. Walking slowly so that my eyes could adjust to the small amount of light trickling in, I carefully stepped around people sleeping on the landings, or cringing in fear of the new face intruding in their space. The doors to each floor had been ripped from their hinges, revealing even more people living in filth.

The higher I went, the rougher and more reclusive the squatters became. No one wanted me in their space and some of them threw trash at me. About halfway up, there were a few doors left attached and I noticed they were made of metal, not wood, so I figured the new tenants had removed those on the lower floors to use as partitions or perhaps a clean place to sleep.

I peered through the tiny, wire-reinforced windows, searching for anyone who might be dealing, until I encountered a window I couldn't see through. It was either covered or spray-painted on the inside. Putting my ear to the door, I heard indistinct murmuring on the other side. I tried the handle but it was locked. People were in there doing something, but I had no idea what. They were not likely drug dealers though, as they would want people to have access to them. I moved on.

The top four floors turned out to be mostly unoccupied, probably because there was little light making its way in from the street. No one I saw seemed like they might be the type to be selling drugs, and I didn't see anyone I would care to ask, so I decided to get the hell out of there.

Turning around to head back to the stairwell, I could not see a thing. There was not enough light to find the doorway, so I reached into my pocket and pulled out my mobile phone. Pushing a button lit up the room enough to see a man had stood up and moved between me and the doorway. Several others were still sitting on the floor looking up at me. The man blocking my way stepped closer to me and demanded that

I tell him who I was. The blast of bacteria breath blowing through a three-toothed snarl nearly rendered me unconscious.

Obviously, the drug user from which I forced information had set me up. I guessed that he hoped I would enter this place and not leave alive. Well played, really. I was glad I killed him.

Again, too late, I realized I was not fully prepared for the situation I had gotten myself into. Several of the squatters had followed me up the stairs as well. I felt a dozen or so pairs of eyes on me, all wanting to know what business I had there. Then the menacing, homeless-hardened man reached for my neck with both hands, and I reacted by focusing on his mind in a way that seemed to be more instinct than anything. He crumpled where he stood, falling into a heap.

Turning my attention to the men in the stairwell, they fell as well, with one of them rolling down a half flight of stairs, bringing three of the other men with him. This created enough noise to draw the attention of everyone else in the building that was not already paying attention. When the noise subsided, I heard stirrings directly behind me and caught movement out of the corner of my eye from two other people emerging from the shadows.

Nature's defense mechanisms took over as the adrenaline flowed freely, probably giving me two or three times my normal strength and agility. All the short hairs on my body stood on end so that the air from passing or approaching objects would send signals to my mechanoreceptors and allow me to react before I fully realized what was happening. This primal reaction saved me.

Ducking from pure instinct saved me. A cinder block flew through the same area my head had occupied a fraction of a second earlier. The brick crashed into the doorframe of the stairwell and shattered. Some of the fragments bounced and echoed down several flights of stairs and struck other squatters, causing them to shout. All the noise disturbed everyone in the building. A chorus of cursing voices and crying children arose from the floors below. The men around me began moving closer in a threatening manner.

And the light on my phone timed out. It was pitch black, but the rustling around me continued, barely audible through the shouting from below.

I swept the entire room and put *their* lights out.

Remaining crouched and perfectly still, but ready to react, I listened for any movement. After a few minutes, the yelling and complaining in the stairwell and the rest of the building died down, so I pushed a button on my phone again and walked out, calm but alert.

For an instant, I thought about killing everyone in the building, but knew I could not with the handful of kids there, nor could I justify eliminating all the addicts and victims in an attempt to stop the drug dealers. They did not deserve to die. They needed help. Treatment of some kind. There might also be pregnant women in the building.

In the darkness of the first-floor landing in the stairwell, I waited for people to settle down and meld back into their pursuits and routines. Fifteen minutes later, I eased my way out of the building.

On the way back to my car, I took off my coat with the intention of turning it back right-side-out, but did not relish the thought of the stench being against the rest of my clothing, so I offered the coat and toboggan to an old homeless lady, who took them cautiously, without question or gratitude. I wanted to go straight home and shower but had one more place to visit first. The Jazzmen club.

Naivety

I hate going to bars. People go there to indulge in *legal* substance abuse. They pour mind-altering, highly addictive, fetus damaging, sensory dulling alcohol down their throats and call it entertainment. But if I wanted to find links to the *illegal* substance abuse trade, I had no other immediate or better choice.

Transitioning from the dark, littered streets where drugs and crime are a way of life into the well-lit streets of the Theatre District was comforting, yet unsettling. The simple experience served as a reminder that we are never far from a life very different from the one to which we are accustomed.

Big, blue, evenly glowing lights arranged on a large sign on the building spelled out *Jazzmen*, which was surrounded by images of musical notes and cocktail glasses. There also seemed to be a lot of activity around the entryway. A man with blue, standing hair and a sports jacket over a T-shirt eagerly opened the door for guests. A couple of college-aged guys were tending to the valet service and a row of taxis lined the curb.

I had to smile at the pair of punny jasmine shrubs on pedestals, but as I went in and smelled the cigar and cigarette smoke funk, my smile turned into more of a grimace. I hoped I would not have to stay in the bar long.

More potted jasmine shrubs adorned the foyer and were decorated with strings of miniature white lights. A jazz band blew sax and trumps around a piano man wearing the traditional dark shades. In the back was a stringy, tall man plucking a large stand-up bass. They were very good and soon had me doing a slightly sideways nod to the beat. I may have even tapped my foot after I sat and ordered bottled water from the barkeep.

Tipping enough to prevent complaints about my not buying alcohol, I scanned the crowd for someone matching the description provided by the drug addict. Was it another lie? Was I being set up again? Had to be careful. I could not risk trying to make contact. I wondered if maybe I should fall back to plan B.

Okay, so I would have to *formulate* a plan B, first.

Absentmindedly, I scooped up several Jazzmen matchbooks out of a bowl and slipped them into my pocket, mostly out of habit from having a fireplace for so many years. As I studied people, looking for a man who appeared to be selling drugs, I noticed there were only men in the bar.

Hmmm, that's odd.

It took me a few seconds.

Oooohhhh. Huh.

Admittedly, "naïve" would be a good word to describe me at times. Live and learn.

A man sitting in a corner booth with a small table could have easily been the drug dealer. He matched the description and was sitting with two bigger men who were possibly bodyguards.

I found a place to sit that allowed me to watch through the mirror behind the bar, and enjoy the fresh air from an overhead vent, which reduced the number of carcinogens I sucked into my lungs. I faced the band but kept an eye on my "suspect," too. Occasionally, other men would walk over and sit in the booth for a few minutes. I never saw any of them accept anything or offer up any cash, but sometimes I saw hands briefly disappear under the table.

The drug dealer stayed until the piano man announced Last Call. I breathed a sigh of relief when he headed for the door. On the way out, with bodyguards in tow, he stopped to chitchat several times, during which there seemed to be a lot of hand-shaking going on. It was probably more hand holding than anything. He seemed to be popular. I took advantage of their lingering and stepped outside ahead of them. And what a relief. Even the filthy, polluted New York air smelled fresh after breathing all that smoke.

Not wanting to lose them by taking too much time retrieving my car, which was parked two blocks away, I climbed into a taxi and told him to start the meter but wait. One of the drug dealer's "escorts" came out and sent the valet after their car, who returned with a stretched Limousine. I memorized the license plate and asked the taxi driver to follow them, but he refused. He may have known who the Limo belonged to. I paid the fare, found my car, and drove home.

And, yes, the following Monday morning, I called the New York Child Protective Service. It took four calls, far too much patience, and forty minutes of on-hold time to get in touch with a human. I described the situation at the abandoned building to an underpaid, uncaring social worker who, after some pressing questions, admitted their field workers refused to enter the building because of the asbestos dangers.

Unbelievable. Is there a number to call to report incompetent government services?

Conflicted

Nearly any job is difficult to do at four in the morning, especially when you have a headache from getting far too little sleep several nights in a row. Examining each minuscule detail found at yet another crime scene was forcing Special Agent Bright to pay particularly close attention and repeat too many tasks, far too often. Her mind was sluggish from the dull ache in her head and neck, but she powered her way through it despite the additional challenges the local police and coroner officers presented.

Dead gang members were scattered all over two flights of stairs and in the hallway, with a couple more in apartment 3B, where the call to 911 had been placed. It seems that most of the gang bangers' guns were cocked and ready to fire, yet all of the weapons recovered were found inside the apartment. An entire gang faction was dead, with no apparent cause of death for any of them.

Nothing seemed to be missing from the apartment, which contained thousands of dollars *and* what might be a few thousand dollars in drugs on a table. Whoever had gathered up the guns and tossed them into the apartment, *and* called 911, could not have missed the drugs and cash. If this had been a rival gang, all of the guns, cash and drugs would have been taken and the topless prostitute would probably not be sprawled on the floor dead. The cause of death for all the gang members would likely be far easier to determine as well.

Before she could finish searching for what might be the tiniest shred of evidence, she received a text message on her phone informing her there was another body in a black, four-door sedan a few blocks from her current location that, in all likelihood, was related to her case. She was to finish up as quickly as possible and process the scene at the other location as well. She agreed, hoping that because the body was in a vehicle, any evidence left behind might have had less of a chance of being disturbed.

Carla slipped her phone back into her pocket and looked over the crime scene. Several people were standing around. Some were waiting on others to finish tasks so that they could do their job. Three of them were actually drinking coffee, standing around the poor dead woman, staring at and talking about her massive breasts. Carla fully expected them to slosh a little coffee out of their cups onto the very piece of DNA that would solve this case, and all the related cases.

Holding his cup at a bit of an angle, instead of evenly, with highly-sugared black coffee on the verge of spilling over the edge onto one of the pistols, a detective asked, "Where are these gang bangers from? What are they, Armenian or something?"

Between loud, irritating slurps of coffee, his colleague answered, "Apparently, they are from Kaliningrad."

Nothing but blank stares.

"Kaliningrad. You know, that exclave piece of Russia that's kinda out there all by itself. Right above Poland."

There was a hint of recollection from a couple of investigators for a moment, then more blank stares.

Carla finally chimed in, "Look it up, fellas. Meanwhile, do you mind?" She waved her hand around to indicate that she needed them to get out of the way.

Doing a thorough job at both crime scenes was an all-day affair, which meant she was on the job thirteen hours before she got a chance to eat her first meal. She did not have enough water during the day, either, so the dull ache in her head had long since evolved into a miserable, pounding dehydration headache. All of these factors made her even more determined to catch the person responsible for all these unnecessary deaths.

Wait, an entire drug-dealing gang and their drugs, AND their guns are now off the streets. How is this a bad thing?

Carla considered this for a moment, told herself it was, in fact, a bad thing, but then wondered again. *Really though, how?*

Reconnaissance

A thorough Internet search of several public data sites revealed nothing on the Limo's license plate number. The following Friday night, I sat in my car a block from the Jazzmen club reading a good book and watching for the Limousine to roll up in the front of the bar.

The wait paid off. When they drove away, I pulled in behind them and followed the car to a bayside neighborhood in New Rochelle. A light rain fell as I drove under impressive sugar maples reaching across both sides of the street to form a living tunnel of branches and leaves.

In the front yards of million-dollar homes also grew lush, green magnolias, magnificent weeping willows dancing perpetual ballets with the wind, and beautiful evergreens, including some gigantic Norway spruce trees drooping with thick, bluish foliage. Sidewalks ran alongside the road, weaving back and forth through tree trunks like suburban stitches.

Most of the homes appeared to be relatively old, but well-maintained, and were nestled into landscaped third- to half-acre lots. Bushes divided many of the property lines, and most of the driveways wound around beside or behind the houses. Without a doubt, it was one of the best-maintained neighborhoods I have ever seen, and it was far too nice for lowlifes who profit from the co-dependencies of others.

They pulled into a driveway, and I made a mental note of which home was theirs, pleased by the cover their trees and bushes offered. Four blocks away, I found a park with a jogging trail entrance and a small parking lot where you could leave your car while you exercised or enjoyed a nature walk on well-kept paths through the woods. Perfect. I drove home, slept a couple of hours, and changed into some sweats.

Close to 8:30 the following morning, I left my car in the small parking lot and took a slow walk under massive maple trees. Native birch and ash woods also bordered two sides of the New Rochelle neighborhood. The cool morning was patched together by diffused sunlight and thick fog, which gave the forest an eerie glow.

Despite the gloomy fog, the nature trail was simply beautiful. The park maintenance crew kept the lower branches and undergrowth trimmed around the path creating, roughly, an eight-by-ten tunnel through the thick woods.

Unseen birds were calling throughout the branches, and occasionally I heard frogs croaking. The smells of the forest were pleasing and refreshing, reminiscent of a part of my life in the not-too-distant past that already seemed to be a lifetime ago. The musty scents of old, decaying trees that had fallen throughout the centuries smelled very much like the thick woods from my past. Early-blooming buds and newly-sprouting shoots of young life had fresh fragrances all their own.

In the gray light of the foggy morning, every shade of forest green known to nature seemed to intermingle and mesh together with the whites, browns, and grays of peeling birch tree bark, a variety of other tree trunks and branches, and last fall's spent blooms and splintered pods.

I hated to leave the tranquility of the park, but as soon as I determined that no one else was in the immediate vicinity, I veered off the trail and made my way through the trees and brush to the road, well away from the parking lot.

A dog barking off in the distance emphasized the quiet of the neighborhood as I walked down the winding sidewalks straight to the drug dealer's house. I rang the bell, pulled an envelope out of my back pocket and began rhythmically slapping it into my palm as I waited. I heard footsteps approaching on a hardwood floor, but when they stopped, the door did not open.

Robins bounced around in the grass as I wondered about which part of my body he might be pointing his gun. I showed no fear as I knocked loudly on the door-frame as if I had not heard the footsteps and assumed the doorbell was not working. I returned to slapping the envelope in my hand, hoping to raise their curiosity enough to open the door.

The seconds dragged on while I tried to look like someone who did not know he was being watched. I smiled at a robin pulling a worm out of the grass and even made a crotch adjustment after a glance over my shoulder toward the street. I hoped they would answer the door. I did not want to try to get into the house the hard way. I made a face, glanced at the time on my phone, and stepped off the porch.

I took two steps and heard the door open. Turning, I offered a jovial greeting to one of the drug dealer's cronies, who wore a purple velvet robe.

"Hello! I'm your neighbor from four-twenty-three." I pointed down the street in the direction from which I had come. "You know, where the biggest magnolia on the block is," as if that was supposed to mean something to him. I doubt if the thug even knew a magnolia tree from a weeping willow.

Extending the envelope toward him, I added, "I was wondering if you might take a look at this." I babbled on about the city wanting to rezone the corners of the neighborhood to allow small businesses and how it would draw a lot of unwanted traffic into the area. I continued to hold out the envelope until he opened the screen door. He took it and I held the door open for him as he pretended to read the bogus legal document I had downloaded off the Internet.

110

He stood there for what seemed like forever, trying to decipher the jumble of cryptic legalese while I went on and on about how convenience stores would pop up on the corners and people would be starting up home businesses.

"Soon we'll be seeing hot dog stands and massage parlors, then, before you know it, a head shop will open and start selling drugs out of their back door." Inside I was laughing, but he was not. I detected the slightest twitch of his eyes and attitude, which helped me to confirm their involvement with drugs.

"Yeah, uh, tanks," he mumbled as he backed up into the house to shut the door in my face.

That was the moment I was looking for. When he was mostly out of sight from the street I dropped him, walked in, and shut the door behind me. Hopefully, from the street or a neighbor's house, it had appeared as though he had let me in. I stood perfectly still in a cluttered foyer, listening intently for anyone else who might be stirring, all the while scanning the parts of the other rooms. I was counting on everyone else in the house still being asleep after being out late selling drugs.

An attempt had been made to decorate the place with expensive furniture, oil paintings, pottery, and knickknacks, but a layer of untidiness blanketed the entire house. Crusty paper plates, dirty ashtrays, and drug paraphernalia covered the top of a coffee table in the living room. Fast food sacks, old newspapers, and pieces of wadded-up, blackened foil were scattered on the kitchen table and one of the chairs. Dirty clothes were piled up outside the closed door of what I assumed was a utility room, and the place badly needed dusting and vacuuming.

Quietly moving through the first floor, I found only tousled, unmade beds in two bedrooms. Music trickled down from upstairs, so when I was satisfied no one else was on the first floor, I took each stair up cautiously. A large window at a landing halfway up caused shadows down the second-story hall, so I tried to stay close to the wall. When I was six steps from the top, I could not crouch any lower or move forward any further without my shadow falling onto the door for anyone in there to see.

Holding my breath, I listened for any sign of movement, but I could not hear anything over the music. I was just about to stand up, dash over, and peek into the bedroom when heavier fog rolled in and significantly reduced the amount of light coming in the window. The decreased light did not last long, but more fog blew by and caused the hallway to become dark again. I crept up and quickly peeked into the room. The drug dealer and the other bodyguard were in bed together, sound asleep.

In the only other room down the hall, I was shocked to see hundreds of bags of drugs and no less than a dozen guns. There were pistols and fully automatic assault rifles, along with what could have been hundreds, or thousands, of rounds of ammunition.

I'm all for well-armed citizens, but *this* kind of nonsense had to stop. Drugs and guns do not mix well.

Back in the occupied bedroom, I focused on the bodyguard's mind immediately, but had a nice, long chat with the drug dealer. Actually, it was not so nice. I will not share the gruesome details of how I extracted the information I wanted from him, but it was not pleasant for him. He writhed around enough to fall off the bed and continued to thrash about on the floor for a while.

He tried to justify his actions by pointing out that he was merely profiting from a readily available resource that had been present long before either one of us had been born. That comment caused him an extended period of excruciating pain, after which I informed him that humans had been torturing each other long before either of us had been born.

Getting him to cooperate at all was difficult, although it was a lot harder for him than it was for me. He was most uncooperative, however, while I was trying to force him to open his safe, but he finally caved. When the heavy door swung open his reluctance to keep me out became obvious. Nearly eight hundred thousand dollars lined the shelves.

The last thing that drug dealer did was flush a small amount of marijuana and many thousands of dollars' worth of crack, heroin, and pills down a toilet. But before I took his life from him, I made sure he knew how much suffering he had caused. And how he was responsible for destroying families. And how he hurt or killed innocent people, including children.

Using the eraser end of a pencil to push buttons, I turned on his laptop and typed the password he had so graciously supplied. I set the telephony software to send a fax at 11:30 p.m. Upon failing, the tool would redial every five minutes until the fax was sent, or until someone stopped it. It would continue to fail, of course, for I simply entered 911 for the phone number. The emergency switchboard operators would get a call every five minutes until the police came to investigate.

A roll of masking tape and some empty plastic bags were useful in strapping the cash to my torso and thighs, which made me look like I had put on fifty to seventy-five pounds after I squeezed back into my sweats. I couldn't think of a better way to get the money out of there without carrying a suitcase or throwing a pillowcase over my shoulder. I left carrying one plastic grocery bag containing every item I had touched while I was in the house, including the note I had handed the guy who had opened the door.

I drove home carefully, being sure to follow all the traffic rules, no matter how trivial. The last thing I needed was to get pulled over by the police for a minor traffic offense. Having that much money on you is a guaranteed way to get arrested. I began stressing over what I would do if I did get stopped, and it did not help my state of mind when I rounded a bend on southbound I-95 and encountered the state police using radar on the people driving in the fast lane.

What would I do if I got pulled over? I did not dare show my driver's license to the police while I was driving a car that could be traced back to so many mysterious deaths. Yet killing a patrolman was completely out of the question as well—my goal was to reduce crime and drug use. Killing someone who shared those goals would be unacceptable. I also knew I would not be able to successfully run from the police, so what choice did that leave me? Quite simply, I could *not* afford to get pulled over for a moving violation.

The parking garage I had been using was a welcome sight. I wiped down the inside of the car, as always, and managed to walk back to my condo without getting mugged.

Safe and secure at home, I bolted the door, closed the drapes, and ripped the bags of money from my body. Two and a half hours later I finished counting over three-quarters of a million dollars.

I can do some serious damage to the drug trade with this kind of money.

But why stop there? Was there some other type of illegal activity I could try to stop? The rest of the weekend was spent trying to think of creative ways to use the drug world's own money against them.

Next

Relaxing on a leisurely Sunday morning, I enjoyed a yin-and-yang breakfast of bacon and whole wheat pancakes. A lively political show on television was both irritating and entertaining. The host repeatedly had to interrupt vicious arguments between his guest politicians and get them back on topic.

There was one individual who refused to get drawn into the arguments and did not get huffy when the other guests attacked his record or history. The well-dressed assistant New York prosecutor defended the way his office handled an international terrorist trial. One of his opponents argued that the state of New York had no business pursuing a federal case, while another guest made a strong argument supporting the USA making the issue international.

Through it all, the prosecutor held his ground. Calm and consistent, he earned the respect of everyone there and, most likely, all the viewers at home. "The federal government has yet to bring charges against this international terrorist. He was arrested for breaking New York state laws and is now standing trial for that. We can't just release him and hope other government entities do something about him."

Everyone knew the assistant prosecutor would achieve his goals, slowly and deliberately.

Only once during the entire show were all the boisterous guests quiet while one person spoke. The demeanor of the independent congressman from the U.S. House of Representatives demanded respect. He used that attention to make an interesting point. "Voters all across this great nation invariably ask themselves, 'Who do I support? Who deserves my vote? Democrats? Republicans? The Tea Party? Green Party?'"

After a perfectly timed pause, he went on, "As people decide how to cast their precious vote, they might try to wonder how each political party would fare if they were the single remaining party. Would they have to change their collective views before America could flourish, or even survive? How would America prosper under the domination of each party?"

Elderly and wise, the U.S. Representative shrugged an acknowledgment. "Some of my very best friends are Democrats, mind you, but bless their hearts, if everyone was a Democrat, America could not possibly survive for long. Wanting workers to share more and more of what they have worked *hard* for would cause a lot of people to stop working to earn those benefits. Someone has to do the work. But now, if only Republicans remained, they would probably do better, but not by much, as few of them want to be the actual workers. Someone has to do the work."

A couple of the other guests were grumbling at this point, but they did not interrupt their friend, who went on. "Libertarians, as we all know, would not even survive as long as the Democrats, and a Tea Party world would last an even shorter period of time. A Green Party America might survive longer than others, but by now people understand my point."

The congressman leaned in for emphasis, "No political party would survive their own agenda. In these admittedly-extreme scenarios, the only surviving America would be the one run by independents. We do not vote along party lines, knowing the vote is wrong. We vote our conscience."

Party-centric guests shifted in their seats and grumbled, but no one challenged him directly. They knew they were outclassed. The host moved on when no one addressed his points. The next set of guests on the political show had a lively debate about what's peace and what's appeasement.

I found the political banter disheartening. The Democrats made excuses by blaming all our problems on the Republicans, while the Republicans made themselves look ridiculous by only taking opposing positions. They went on and on, yet no one mentioned the principal reason for economic distress in America: Consumers. Politicians are not responsible for the economic woes in the United States. Nearly everything we buy has "Made in China" on it. It's no wonder there are as many new Chinese millionaires every day as there are bankrupt Americans.

A sip of tea helped me to refocus on what my next goal should be. If I were to go overseas somewhere, I would need a fake identity, but it is close to impossible to forge today's relatively sophisticated forms of identification, or at least it is for someone with no organized crime contacts. No living contacts, anyway.

If there was some way to come up with an untraceable credit card, I would easily be able to purchase airline tickets from any of several websites, but I'd still have to show my driver's license at the airport. The new passport laws put in place as a result of the terrorist attacks on September 11, 2001, make it difficult to get in and out of the United States through normal channels, but as everyone knows, getting *into* America illegally is easy enough for migrant farm and labor workers to do many times per day, every day.

Maybe the thing to do would be to find a drug addict who resembles me, but is on a self-destruct course, and take his identity. You hear about that sort of thing being done to innocent people all the time, why not take out someone supporting the illegal drug industry, or a dealer, and use his driver's license? I could even use his credit cards, if he has any, or get secured credit cards with all the cash I took.

For the next few weeks, I took no action other than finding and watching new places that appeared to be drug markets. They were easier to find than I had anticipated, which made me wonder why authorities didn't have a better handle on the situation. While I watched, I did my best to formulate new plans to take them all out with less risk to me and innocent bystanders.

I also located several buyers resembling me, who were an unremitting drain on society. Finding some loser who preferred to spend money on his addictions rather than his kids sounded like a good scenario. I could set up a payment plan to automatically deduct child support while I used his name and other information indefinitely. His kids would stand a much better chance at life, his ex-wife wouldn't have to worry about a drug addict being around her kids, and I would have the means of traveling through airports without having to use my own name or identity.

Busybody

All the related crime scenes Carla had investigated seemed to be astonishingly free of evidence. She encountered one dead end after another. It was as though the perpetrator was invisible or forcing his victims to turn on each other somehow. She *knew* evidence existed. She simply had not found it yet, and was considering removing every single item from the next few crime scenes. Storing it all in their evidence warehouse would allow them to examine every single item thoroughly, no matter how large or small.

Today's investigation turned out to be a little different. This time there seemed to be coercion involved, or at least extended interaction between the killer and the victims involved. And there may have been a witness!

A uniform had questioned the neighborhood busybody, who said she had made numerous complaints about the occupants of the home over the past several months. She had predicted and reported that it would all end badly for them. It took the officer a few minutes to get past the previous complaints and get her refocused on the important details of the day, which was quite possibly the description of the individual who had killed them.

"Cars are coming and going at all hours of the night, and they only stay a few minutes at a time. And you know what *that* means!" The neighborhood busybody still had the binoculars around her neck.

"Yes, ma'am, I do. What can you tell us about yesterday? Did you see—"

"*Yesterday?* Sonny boy, this kind of nonsense has been going on for *months*, ever since they first moved in here. This used to be a nice neighborhood, but then scum like those people moved in and, well, you can see how the whole block's gone to pot!"

The officer looked around, but saw only well-maintained homes and streets. He shook it off and tried again to get some useful information from her. "Ma'am, did you see anyone, or notice anything out of the ordinary—"

"*Out* of the *ordinary*? Are you kidding me? They were drug dealers and everyone knew it! Everyone but the po-leece, that is! If I tell you who I saw, are you going to take all the *other* complaints I've made more serious?"

"We take all police reports seriously, ma'am, however, all the residents in the home are dead. I'm not sure what else we can do about any pending complaints, but, ma'am, did you say you saw someone enter the residence yesterday?"

"No! That's not what I said at all!"

The police officer showed considerable patience but needed to get firm with her. "Ma'am, would you like to come down to the station with me to make your statement to the detectives, or would you rather tell me here and now?"

"Don't threaten *me*, sonny! People like me are the best friends you people have."

Carla had seen the officer questioning the woman and joined them. Sensing the witness's belligerence and his frustration, she said, "Thank you, officer, thank you very much, I'll take it from here. Unless, of course, you wish to continue this conversation."

Patient or not, the seasoned officer ripped out the page of notes and handed it to her. "No problem."

"Thank you!" Turning to the woman, she added, "Hello, I'm Special Agent Bright of the FBI. Did you get a good look at someone who might have been involved in these murders?"

"Yes, I did, young lady! Through these," she said, patting her trusty binoculars. "He was not their typical type of visitor. Usually, they are in old beat-up cars with loud music disturbing the entire neighborhood. This guy was a fat man of average height, in blue and gray sweats carrying an old shopping bag, and he lives close enough to walk here, apparently, but I've never seen him before."

"Did you see where he went, or which house he might have gone into?"

"Oh, he doesn't live around here. I know everyone on this street. He walked up the street that-a-way and that's the last I saw of him."

"What color was his hair, did you notice?"

"Hard to say with that hat on."

Carla left the old woman her business card, asked her to call if she remembered anything else, and went to examine the home. There was enough possible evidence in the home to keep several local and FBI labs busy for a while. That didn't interest her, though, as she felt sure all the hairs and possible DNA left on cigarette butts and roaches would turn up dozens of false leads that would distract her from the real perpetrator, who was far too careful and clever to leave behind foolish evidence such as that.

This crime scene was different, so it received her full attention. She focused her efforts on the computer used to automate the calls to 911 and the empty, open safe. Besides three dead bodies, there were many empty bags containing trace amounts of drugs scattered around a toilet, and a disheveled bedroom that suggested a struggle.

Cases involving dead drug dealers and empty safes typically result in open-and-closed investigations. Adding flushed drugs to the mix makes identifying a motive and a suspect more difficult. No apparent cause of death meant the vigilante she had been chasing was very likely involved and was the reason she was called. Carla was a tiny step closer to the killer. She had a general description of him, and now had reason to believe he was working alone.

Alias

I painstakingly researched dozens of habitual drug users. A few had criminal records severe enough for them to be found on the Internet, so I abandoned all efforts with those and kept searching. My persistence paid off. I noticed someone that looked a lot like me trying to bum money from people, so I struck up a conversation with him.

A small amount of prompting caused him to spout loads of good information. He was recently divorced and no longer had any contact with his ex-spouse or kids, for reasons he did not want to admit. His favorite place to smoke his crack was in De Witt Clinton Park, a few steps from the corner where he usually bought it. Hidden behind the shrubbery atop the retainer wall above 12th Avenue, he would get high and watch children climb on playground equipment or play baseball.

He was younger than me by six years but had abused enough substances for him to look older than me. His hair was just a little darker than mine, but other than that, he was a perfect candidate.

With a loose but workable plan in mind, I went to the park and found a shady spot to sit in the grass and wait for him to show up. From my vantage point, I could see both the area where he usually met his dealer and his little hideaway in the bushes.

A foul smell from the Hudson River accosted my nostrils from time to time, and when the lights turned green on 12th Avenue, which doubled as the Joe DiMaggio Highway, the traffic was so obnoxiously loud that it often made me squint. When the lights were red and traffic was stopped, I heard the pleasant sounds of children playing behind me. From over my shoulder came the subtle sounds of a softball game. A fitting sound effect for being right on the Joe DiMaggio Highway.

Being true to his habits, the drug addict saved me multiple trips to the park by showing up right on schedule. I had already committed myself to spending as much time as it took to catch him at just the right moment, alone and too high to think clearly.

It was a Friday evening, and I had anticipated that he would stop off on the way home to spend a portion of his paycheck on crack. He purchased his vile treat and hurried over behind the bushes in the park. From *his* vantage point, he could see people approaching from any direction and still have plenty of time to grind whatever was left into the dirt if the cops showed up. He seemed to feel protected with his back against the fence at the top of the retaining wall.

When the wisps of smoke had stopped for a few minutes, I knew he was high and had no more drugs in his possession, so I stood and walked in his general direction. He sat there for a moment while I approached, but then he started scrambling to his feet in an effort to get away. I hit him with a paralyzing sweep across his upper spine and watched him collapse back down behind the shrubbery. Terrified, he struggled to stand. I turned him loose long enough for him to sit up, but focused on his legs every time he tried to get up again.

We chatted for a while as I explained what was going to happen and how he was going to cooperate. The sunset turned to darkness before I could convince him to do exactly what I told him to do, but when I was sure he would oblige, I escorted him over to W 54th Street, where my car was parked outside Grainger. I buckled him in and used nylon ties (from Grainger, of course) to secure his hands to the seat belts.

"Steve, to me, you are nothing but a drug addict. People willing to buy drugs instead of paying their child support are more of a drain on society than they are worth. Before the night is over, I am going to kill you and take your identity. However, you have the opportunity to do something good before you die. Are you with me so far?"

He understandably looked a bit overwhelmed and had a confused look on his face, probably wondering if he was supposed to answer.

"Good! First, give me all of your drug dealer contacts so I can kill all of them as well."

Steve was not responsive.

"Okay, let's start with something easy. What is your mother's maiden name?"

He became even more confused.

"I may need your mother's maiden name to access bank accounts and credit cards." I looked at him expectantly and added, "Do you understand?"

"Smith?" he asked.

"Smith?" I asked, as well.

Something of a slight nod.

"Your mother's maiden name is Smith?"

Another slight nod.

"Yeah, right. No matter. I bet I can find a copy of your birth certificate at your apartment."

There was a funny look about him that I could not quite identify, but I forged on. "How about dealers, other than the fool on the corner by the park you bought from today? Where can I find them?"

He was still not forthcoming with any information, so I put him out of his family's misery. I took his wallet, which was the only thing he had on him, and dumped his body into a dumpster full of broken-down cardboard boxes. A gallon of gasoline and all that cardboard would create a fire hot enough to destroy identifying features. DNA tests might still work, but without a missing person's report, there would be virtually no way to identify him.

Steven had lived in a rough and tumble neighborhood, in a tiny, dirty apartment. I left a cheap notebook there to make recurring payments for all his bills. His two credit cards were maxed out, but I needed those under control to help straighten out his credit report. I might be able to use them, too. A couple of phony PayPal accounts could be used to fund his overdrawn checking account enough to pay his bills, including his child support.

Searching his apartment, I found a copy of his birth certificate. Sure enough, his mother's maiden name was Smith. I also found the shirt he had been wearing when his last driver's license picture had been taken, and an address book with many of his contacts in it, including his ex-wife and his boss.

The low-flying jets taking off from La Guardia Airport were more than I could put up with, so I locked up and went home.

Early the following Monday morning, I used a burner to call the company printed on the drug addict's last check stub. I identified myself as Steven Andrews to whoever answered the phone and "regretfully" resigned. The woman on the other end of the line did not seem upset. Couldn't blame her. I also logged into the website of the child support enforcement office and made arrangements to have the monthly child support payments deducted from his checking account.

It took three weeks to get his mess stabilized and his credit cards paid off. During that time, I also stayed busy watching and taking out other drug dealers. I relentlessly hit them hard. It was getting to be easy, but even so, I wondered if I was making any impact at all.

What I *really* wanted to do was to get on with tracking down and killing the people who actually believed they could terrorize their fellow humans, simply because they had interpreted their religion in a way that justified hatred and violence. But how could I find them? How could I even get over there?

Experiment

As an experiment, I purchased airline tickets on an Internet site with one of Steve's credit cards. Showing up at the airport wearing the same shirt on his driver's license, I tried to look as much like him as possible. I had grown my hair out a bit and tried my best to make it resemble his picture. I also memorized all the information on the license.

No problem. The security guards at the airport gave the license a good, hard look but barely glanced at me. I walked right onto the plane and had a good weekend trip to Niagara Falls.

As I stood at the base of the falls, I tried to imagine what the first humans who saw them had thought. That could have been fifteen to twenty-five thousand years ago, so the falls would have been further downstream. However, it would have been far more impressive, as three-quarters of the Niagara River water is diverted through a power plant and never goes over the falls. I stared at the magnificent sight with the distinct impression that I was unable to truly comprehend the amount of power nature could produce with so little effort.

Visiting childhood memories of the falls was inevitable. I was very young, but the sight was so magnificent I remember it vividly. I moved up and down the bank, far above the river, trying to find the same spot where I had stood when I was a kid, but could not quite duplicate the memory. I crouched down to about the height of a five-year-old boy and laughed out loud as I matched the scenery to my memory by looking through the designs of the wrought-iron railing.

Niagara Falls is still as astounding to me now as it was then. I made a mental note to make it back again.

Maybe next time I'll bring someone with me.

My homeward-bound plane was as easy to board as the first one. No one questioned my stolen credentials. I was pleased. The flight gave me time to consider the previous few weeks of research I'd done on terrorism. Dealing with that chaos would mean traveling to many foreign destinations. A monumental task I was prepared to undertake if I could simply find the means of getting there and back undetected. I'd need a passport. Taking someone's driver's license was one thing, but getting a passport was on another level.

Stress

Frustration and stress levels were at an all-time high in the office. Superiors, other law enforcement offices, the Pentagon, and even the White House were all applying pressure and demanding results. Carla was sick of people assuming that no one could catch this mysterious killer because investigators were incompetent.

Whoever was responsible for the murders was smart enough, or perhaps devious enough, to carry out the attacks without leaving behind a single clue or piece of evidence that could be used to trace back to him. There wasn't even enough circumstantial evidence or behavioral patterns to make a wild-ass guess as to who might be the vigilante. Making matters worse, in the eyes of those critical of the investigation, the killer was predictable.

Special Agent Bright could not imagine her job getting any more stressful than it had already become over the past few weeks, but then, she would not have to imagine it.

Changes

Jeanna and I had become good workplace friends. With her being the department's administrator, I had worked with her almost daily and had come to know her fairly well. I respected her professionalism, admired her endless supply of energy, and we had learned that we could depend on each other.

One typical sunny morning she and I were in Dr. Gordon's office having our weekly status meeting. I was going over the current state of various projects and classes and Jeanna was taking minutes for the corporate website reports page when one of the VPs poked his head around the corner of the door, looking distraught.

"What are you doing? Haven't you heard?"

Always calm and never ruffled, Dr. Gordon asked, "What are you talking about, Matt?"

Walking into the office, he excitedly informed us about America being under a terrorist alert. "They foiled a major plot in several cities but say there's a good chance that something terrible could still happen here in New York. We have to evacuate the building!"

Jeanna was on her feet before the VP could even finish his warning. She dropped her notepad and pen absentmindedly into the chair behind her and looked at Dr. Gordon, who remained calm but asked, "How bad is it? Have there been attacks?"

"Not yet, but they said to be on high alert and report anything unusual. We have to evacuate! This building was specifically mentioned. We have high-technology research going on here, and that seems to be their target this time."

I watched them have this conversation as though I were watching the dialogue of a play from the front row. It did not seem real. I just sat there, hoping the situation was not as dire as some of the days New York had seen before. I assumed the worst and hoped for something less than terrible, but I sensed our lives were about to change. At that moment, I committed to making decisions that would alter the course of my future, and hopefully the future of society.

"Greg, get to your labs and make sure everyone is out. We have to evacuate!" Matt didn't even finish repeating himself before hurrying away.

The old man breathed a heavy sigh and, turning to Jeanna, said, "Go pick up your son. *Call* me tomorrow before coming in to see where we stand." Without hesitating, she put her hand on my arm, as if to say goodbye, and left.

Dr. Gordon then turned to me. "You have access to more areas than most, if you'd like to help, go down to the lowest lab and start working your way upstairs. Make sure everyone is aware of the situation. I'll start at the top and work my way down. We can meet in the middle somewhere. Always use the east stairwell and we'll find each other."

"Consider it done. I'll see you in a few minutes."

Going through all the labs on each floor took more than a few minutes, and I was hoarse from calling out for friends and colleagues. When I finally met up with Dr. Gordon, I found that the director of HR had joined him, so I reported my findings to them. "Everyone was cleared from every lab on floors thirty-one through thirty-seven, except no one has seen Billy Baughers or Al."

"Al?" asked the HR director.

"Sorry, Dr. Al-shamrani." I clarified. The woman's face changed into an expression I couldn't pinpoint.

Still as calm as ever, Dr. Gordon added, "Mr. Baughers is on vacation this week, but not Dr. Al-shamrani."

The HR director's eyes blazed forcefully. "Are you *sure* you haven't just overlooked him?"

Both of us assured her we hadn't seen the man all morning. "However, we can look again, if you'd like."

"Yes! Please do so. We need to be absolutely sure."

We agreed to enter and search every room on every floor and call out loud enough for anyone to hear. My efforts produced the same results as before but Dr. Gordon found one of his other employees had slipped back in to try to salvage an experiment. It had taken him a couple of days to set up the process and was only an hour or so from having usable results. Dr. Gordon followed the particularly dedicated scientist to the stairwell and made sure he exited.

Reporting our findings to the HR director angered her and she barked additional requests that sounded more like orders. "Check again to make sure he hasn't called in sick or is on vacation."

Her demeanor toward Al gave me a sickening feeling. I had begun to think of him as a friend.

We made our way back to Dr. Gordon's office where he checked his voice mail again, and logged back onto his PC to check e-mail and schedules, but found nothing. When he looked back up at the HR director and shook his head, she put a mobile phone to her ear and reported the news to someone who yelled loud enough for all of us to hear.

"We have to get out of here now. Right now. This building was thought to be singled out as a potential target, and now that threat has been verified."

Hurrying to the stairwell, we opened the door and were taken aback by the huge number of people now trying to exit. Only a few minutes earlier the mass exodus had been flowing but now the line down the stairs was at a complete standstill. When people saw our door open, a few of them tried to push their way through onto our floor. The HR director told them they were not allowed to enter this floor, or any other floor, during an evacuation. They could only go down.

"Please!" a woman on the verge of tears begged. "I have to use the bathroom. We've barely moved for the past thirty minutes!" It hadn't quite been fifteen minutes, but I think we could all empathize.

"I'm getting claustrophobic!" an older man with thick glasses pleaded. "Let me out of here, please!"

A voice from the crowd rose above the others. "Can we try the elevators?"

"Are the elevators working at all?" The shouting grew louder.

Amidst a raucous of other requests and demands, Dr. Gordon tried to ease the door closed. A couple of people with panic in their eyes gave me the impression they intended to push him out of the way, so I stepped into view and did my best to be intimidating. They allowed us to close the door.

We hurried to the other stairwell but found the same situation, perhaps even a bit worse.

"What do we do? Wait it out?" I asked.

Dr. Gordon said evenly, "We try the elevator while we wait for the stairs to clear."

The HR lady hesitated. "Actually, if we can squeeze into the stairwell, it might be better."

We eyed her and asked almost simultaneously, "Yeah?" I added, "How so? Care to share whatever it is you're not sharing?"

She swallowed hard and mumbled to herself, "Everyone will find out soon enough anyway, I guess" and then to us, reluctantly admitted that, "Adham Al-shamrani is a suspect in the foiled terrorist plot today."

The doctor and I were shocked, although some things immediately began making sense: his subtle arrogance and the fact that he could so callously cheat in a game of chess with someone who was supposed to be a trusted coworker. I thought of the pictures of his family, or a family, anyway, on his desk; however, I had never really heard him mention them. He never talked about his personal life and he had also never attended a single computer class I had taught.

Then it occurred to me. The HR director had stated that it would be better to be in the stairwell because it was designed to be a firebreak. If Al had indeed planted explosives, they could very easily be in a place where he could move about freely, like one of the labs. The stairs would be the safest place for us.

I noticed Dr. Gordon doing the first irrational thing I'd ever seen him do. He was rapidly pushing the down button for the elevator, looking back and forth repeatedly at the button and the floor indicator lights above the door.

If the situation hadn't been so serious, it would have been comical. I silently hoped we would all be in a position to laugh about this later. If so, I'd be telling this story to our colleagues, for sure. I had a hard time keeping a straight face, but when the HR director opened the door to the stairwell again, the humor was gone. People were at least moving now, so we abandoned the elevators and squeezed our way into the crowd.

Slowly making our way downstairs gave me plenty of time to think about the man I knew as Al. He had not needed to treat people nicely or fairly. The more I thought about it, the more obvious it became that he had pushed people away so he would stand less of a chance of blowing his cover. Or was the arrogance more of a cultural thing? I had no idea.

His behavior now seemed consistent with someone who believed he would not have to answer for his actions. Cheating in a chess game meant nothing to him and learning new computer tips and tricks was pointless. I had attributed quite a lot of his demeanor to cultural differences and had ignored his rude behavior in the name of relativism. I felt a little foolish.

Obvious to me now, Al simply did not need to put forth any effort to cultivate friendships. He had likely planned to carry out the mass murder of all his "friends" and colleagues today, and probably would have died doing so if America's brightest hadn't foiled his plans.

Making frequent stops and waiting for long periods, we slowly made our way down over thirty floors. More people kept joining the exodus. Leaning over the railing, we could see the lower floors were moving faster than the higher floors. With others still evacuating, it was taking time for the movement to find its way up higher.

One landing had a puddle of urine in a corner, and my heart went out to the poor woman who needed to use the restroom. The more we progressed, the more puddles we encountered. Minutes turned to hours and the smell of sweaty bodies and human waste became stronger.

A few more people fell in line behind us, but not many. At times, the line would move, and other times we stood, or sat, and waited for several minutes at a time.

Urine and rumors seemed to be the only thing flowing freely. The lack of phone reception in the stairwell fueled wild speculation. Thankfully, there was a small amount of air movement, with "fresh" air coming from below.

We all chatted politely for the first couple of hours, but then we grew tired of each other and retreated into our minds. The relative silence gave me more time to think about this new set of circumstances. I found it hard to believe my colleague and lunchtime chess partner was involved in terrorism.

Where was Al from, anyway? That was something else I should know about him but did not. His name was Arabic, but that didn't narrow it down much. We likely didn't know his real name anyway.

Suddenly, I felt great disdain for Middle Eastern "values." They are very different from the American values I respect. The original Americans created something unique and wonderful when they formed our country. Since then, generation after generation of Americans have used their ingenuity and compassion to build a technologically advanced and decent civilization.

In stifling contrast, a large number of people in the Middle East live in third-world conditions and want others to live the same way.

Wisdom told me I was simply angrier than I had been in a while (since September 11, 2001, actually) and that my rage would diminish. I did not like hating anyone, and I did not like myself for hating in such a way. I was *sure* that most of the people in the Middle East were decent. However, I was having serious problems dealing with their latest attempt to crumble America back into the Stone Age with them.

Well after lunchtime, we finally emerged from the stairwell. The amount of time it took to get to the first floor was not very comforting. Had the cause of the evacuation been more severe, like a fire or an explosion, there is no way any of us would have survived.

As people exited the door on the first floor, several police officers were stopping them and questioning them, which explained why it took so long.

When the police took my driver's license, they pulled me aside. Dr. Gordon got the same treatment, but not the HR director. They waved to a group of men in suits at the security desk who headed in our direction.

"You two are from Al-shamrani's lab?"

Dr. Gordon answered with a raised eyebrow. "Well, Dr. Al-shamrani works in *my* lab."

They pulled us aside and one of them identified himself as Homeland Security. He began grilling us about anything we might know concerning our coworker.

"Your friend 'Al' is a very dangerous man, and he is certainly not a doctor. His full name is," he had pulled a satellite phone from his inside jacket pocket and was navigating around while he paused and we all waited, "Abu Azmi Adham Asrar ibn Ibrahim Al-shamrani El-qaatil."

Dr. Gordon and I both had a "Yeah, so?" reaction. We both knew different cultures had different naming conventions. We had assumed there was more to the man's name than Adham Al-shamrani.

"Translated, that means 'son of Azmi, black secrets/mysteries, grandson of Ibrahim, of/from Shamran, the killer.'"

Both of us were feeling sick, but Dr. Gordon stated the obvious. "You could have led with the pertinent information."

An interrogation ensued. From the long stream of questions, I derived that Al was a sleeper in a remote terrorist network whose name I couldn't pronounce or had ever even heard of before. He had not shown up for work that day, nor had anyone seen him since the previous close of business.

Later that day, the news reported that his home had been abandoned hastily during the night. Food was left in the refrigerator and clothes were left in closets and drawers. Although there were pictures of family, none of his neighbors had ever seen anyone but him in his apartment.

They also recovered evidence on his PC at ERL, where he had gathered information from several projects, little of which he was cleared to possess. A checklist of worldwide anonymous buyers had half the contacts completed. Evidence like that simply *had* to have been left behind on purpose as a harassment tactic or intimidation.

Even though the terrorists' plan to cripple America's technology centers had failed, it had a devastating impact on ERL. In the eyes of investors, the most basic security measures at ERL had failed miserably.

An international terrorist had infiltrated his way into some of corporate America's best kept secrets and had likely sold that intellectual property to foreign companies and governments.

The technology that the buyers could develop with the stolen data would directly compete with the investors who had paid to have the technologies developed. Making matters even worse, the profits Al made from embezzlement would likely fund the efforts of other terrorists.

Elucidate Research Laboratories never recovered. Investors pulled their funding over the next five weeks and one project after another ended. Employees somberly packed their belongings into whatever cardboard box they could find and left the building, never to return.

Sadly, being the ones most directly affected by the infiltration, Dr. Gordon's labs were some of the first to close. I stayed around longer than most because I was involved in so many different projects, but it was very difficult watching so many talented people lose their jobs.

In the back of my mind, somewhere in the middle of an unfinished game of chess, I could hear Al laughing at the gullible Americans and how easily we'd been duped.

Most good Americans, particularly those in New York, believe qualities like diversity, cultural relativism, and the willingness to help others who are less fortunate are a few of the things that make the United States strong.

However, terrorists are doing their best to exploit these distinctly Western traits so they can force the rest of the world to be as miserable and dependent upon religion as they are. Their ultimate goal is for their religious leaders to gain control over as many people as possible, and then kill the rest.

How are we supposed to deal with that? I decided on how *I* would deal with it.

With at least three-quarters of a million dollars of untraceable cash hidden in multiple places, I didn't need the job at ERL anymore, nor would I need a job for some time. I could focus on the more important task of doing my best to rid planet Earth of some of the worst of the worst.

Because of all the extra time on my hands, I was able to set up a bogus online wholesale supply company that simulated a slow, steady stream of income from non-existent customers. With the appearance of having an income, I was able to join a consortium of small business owners who had leased an entire floor of an old office building, and turned it into something lucrative.

I also hired Jeanna, from ERL, to be the office manager just hours before she, in desperation, intended to accept a position in retail that only paid a fraction of what she was used to making. I couldn't help myself. I paid her a salary quite a bit more than she made at ERL.

Fortunately, it was also handy to have someone around when I needed research done quickly.

Some cheesy, quick-and-dirty software I wrote would continue to shuffle the same money around from "suppliers" to "customers" using third party online payment tools, arranging deals between wholesalers and manufacturers that simply did not exist.

Money was transferred around frequently, establishing patterns and expectations, and the "business" appeared to be turning a meager but steady profit. Three years could easily pass before I had to worry about doing anything with the business.

However, something unforeseen happened. Jeanna found actual suppliers and real customers willing to use our company. I upped her salary to reflect this good behavior by adding an incentive. She'd get a piece of the profit from each new client she brought in.

The new business model worked. She continued to find new clients and make more money. We would likely never get rich, but the extra income was welcome, and her young son was getting a nice college fund in place.

Tagged

Three months went by quickly while I rearranged my life and worked on a plan to bring terrorism to its knees. The more I thought about it, the more complex those strategies became, with success hinging on finding terrorist training camps.

That research might take months, so I split my time between planning a trip to the Middle East and putting a major dent in drug trafficking in New York. I wanted to take out the major players and not waste my time with street dealers or addicts. I hoped to set them back decades. Getting access to law enforcement data would certainly help with that.

I considered contacting the DEA and telling them a believable lie by claiming to have developed a new weapon. I could tell them I was willing to use it to help them do their job but was unwilling to share the technology. Thinking about what *I* would think if I worked for a government agency and someone approached me with similar information, I was less than confident this idea would work. In a similar position, I would want to track that person down and stop them before they turned on me or my government.

Somehow, I had to find a way to contact and establish a trusting relationship with a law enforcement officer who could arrange for me to get close enough to drug lords to kill them. Someone who had been on the job long enough to have the trust of their superiors, other law enforcement agencies, and people out on the streets. Or maybe I could find a new guy who was eager to make a name and career for himself.

That evening, I put a simple plan together and found it was far too easy to follow through. Putting on shades, gloves, and a sweatshirt with a hood in case webcams or traffic cams were taking pictures, I picked one of the heavier drug traffic areas and watched several people step inside a doorway to exchange something with a guy wearing too much gold jewelry.

Four of the fifteen or so drug users who bought from the dealer presented opportunities for "private conversations" far enough away from the busy doorway to draw little unwanted attention. Those four never supported the drug trade again.

Before I went home for the evening, I also managed to take out the dealer who had been profiting from people's addictions *and* his spotter.

Early the next morning, I drove my untraceable car by each of the sites where these private conversations had taken place. All were taped off with crime scene tape with at least two cops at each site. As I drove by, I made mental notes about everyone.

That night, I took out a few other drug buyers in a different part of town, but couldn't get back to this particular dealer in time to take him out before the police started showing up. Through a couple of windows in, ironically, a corner drug store, I was able to watch authorities come and go while they investigated the deaths. Several of the same cops were at both scenes.

News stations aired the same footage, repeatedly. An NYPD spokesperson gave his official statement about the sudden deaths reported the previous two nights. The cause of all the deaths was blamed on poison-laced drugs.

Clever! Their strategy was evasive, yet it curbed drug use for a short while. It didn't slow me down, though, there were still plenty of hungry addicts out there.

I spent a little time in Newark, New Jersey the next day and found an idiot selling drugs through one of the fences of Mt. Pleasant Cemetery. Several of his customers didn't make it through the night, and he conveniently died right there in the cemetery. This time I slipped matchbooks from Jazzmen into all their pockets so I could easily convince someone I was who I said I was when the time came.

For the third night in a row, I only got about four hours of sleep, yet I'd never felt so alive. I felt like I was making a difference. Back in Newark the next morning, the sunlight illuminated dewy foliage in a way that emphasized the small patches of the first changing leaves of autumn. The trees in the cemetery were peaceful and beautiful, but the adjacent apartment complex was quite a contrast. It was old and in dire need of maintenance.

Dozens of out-of-work residents watched from the parking lot, which made my task of surveying the aftermath of last night's cleanup efforts easy. I just slipped old sweats over my clothes and mixed in with the crowd.

While watching the crime scene investigation, I noticed a woman who I had seen at both the previous crime scenes in New York, and here she was at this crime scene in New Jersey. She had to be the Fed in charge of the investigation. I needed to find her car and tape a burner phone under it, without being seen. It needed to be out of sight, of course, but also placed so it would eventually fall off on its own, hopefully, undetected in heavy traffic where it would be destroyed.

Looking around in the general direction from which she came, several police cars and emergency vehicles were parked in the area, along with cars on the street and in a couple of nearby parking lots. Only one car had federal government plates.

Again, this was going to be easier than I thought. I made my way around the fence of the apartment complex and moved closer to her car, all the while attempting to appear as though I was just trying to get a better look at the commotion.

I put on a toboggan and my sunglasses before coming into view of the police cars in case any of them were video recording. I pulled on one surgical glove as well and slipped both hands into my pockets so no one would notice. When I was near her car, I focused on the knees of someone near the body of the drug dealer. He collapsed and yelled, "*Holy* shhhh!"

Someone approached him quickly to help, and I took out his knees, too. The resulting turmoil distracted people long enough for me to act like I was ducking between two cars, taking cover like everyone else, protecting myself from whatever was going on in the cemetery.

Pulling the phone and a roll of tape from my pockets, I pushed the power button, slid under her car, and slapped the phone onto the top side of the transmission. If they inspected the underside of the car with mirrors when she went back to the federal center, the phone would be less visible there.

Slowly backing away, I watched the commotion in the graveyard like everyone else and made my way back through the crowd in the apartment complex parking lot. Eventually, I eased back to the opposite side of the complex where I walked the few blocks to my car. No one gave me a second glance the entire time despite my dark shades and toboggan.

Every ten minutes for the next day or so, as long as the battery lasted and the duct tape held, I would receive a text message on one of my burner phones. The message would indicate the GPS location of the federal agent's car, along with the direction and speed. Hopefully, I would get the opportunity to approach her, or at least leave a message on her car.

She stayed at the crime scenes for a long time. I busied myself by reading the current headlines and newsfeeds on my phone. The stock market was on another dramatic downward trend, CEOs were getting more bonuses using taxpayer money, and NASA was making interesting discoveries on Mars. New news is old news although it was good to know that rain was in the forecast for the next day.

Finally, a text message indicated the federal agent was on the move and leaving Newark. The next text made it obvious she was heading back to New York.

With no reason to keep her in sight, I stayed about twenty minutes behind her, but soon, the text messages stopped coming. The last one I received said she had made a right off Canal Street onto Broadway. My best guess was that her destination had been the federal building at Federal Plaza, so I drove around the block a couple of times, but I did not see her car. She had probably parked in a parking garage, and the phone could not find a signal.

Taking advantage of the downtime, I stopped by my office and checked on Jeanna, who proudly informed me that she had bagged another client, politely reminding me about the bonus she had earned. I also bought her a thank-you lunch at her favorite salad bar. She had the office running smoothly and there was not a lot to do at the moment, so after our long lunch, I told her to take the rest of the Friday off and enjoy her weekend. She was thrilled, and I could tell she wanted to hug me, but maintained her typical professional behavior.

Early

For the third morning in a row, Special Agent Bright's mobile phone rang long before she was ready or willing to be aroused from a deep slumber.

More mysterious drug-related deaths. This time it was 4:23 a.m. At least she was able to get an additional hour of sleep this morning. Making matters worse, the events had taken place in Newark. Keeping a lid on the frightening details of the deaths was challenging. Now, yet *another* coroner would not be able to find a cause of death and would have to be convinced, or coerced, into attributing the addicts' COD to bad drugs.

The first thing she did, while still sitting half nude on the edge of her bed, was to get as many law enforcement departments, agencies, and officials involved as she could. She needed each of the crime scenes to remain secure. If there were enough different jurisdictions involved, they might all keep each other from contaminating or even tampering with the evidence.

After four frustrating calls, Carla used her thumb to push the little red button with some finality before tossing the mobile phone back onto her nightstand. She breathed a sigh of relief and rubbed her eyes until she realized it was not helping. When she opened her eyes, she focused first on the half-packed, open suitcase on the extended stay's dresser, and a wave of guilt washed over her. She had no business going on vacation with all that was going on.

Okay, it was more of a weekend than a vacation, but still, she should stay nearby in case there were more of these mysterious murders. The next body she investigated might reveal a clue. Or *the* clue that made the difference in the case. At any time, an investigator might recognize someone on traffic or security cam video from more than one crime scene and there she would be, on vacation and out of reach.

Despite being exhausted, Carla drove to a neglected neighborhood in New Jersey where she found that the scenes of all the murders were consistent. At each site, bodies were sprawled as though they had lost consciousness even before they hit the ground, or simply died where they stood.

Yes, the lifestyle they chose had a high mortality rate for twenty-somethings, but that didn't give anyone the right to hasten the likely outcome. What if the man sprawled out on the ground in front of her was the one who would have recovered and made something of himself?

This morning's investigation, however, proved to be different from her previous experiences. One of the veteran local law enforcement officers pulled packet after packet of crack cocaine from the pockets of a dead drug dealer. As he carefully put them into an evidence bag, he suddenly collapsed beside the body, rasping, "*Holy shhhh!*" When a fellow officer rushed over to help him, his knees buckled, too.

Confusion and panic followed. The two officers on the ground shouted at their colleagues to stay away while they regained their footing, and their composure, and scrambled away. When the officers explained what had happened, no one would approach the body. A Hazmat team was there within minutes along with bulky equipment and special dogs, but no sign of chemicals or any other hazardous material, other than the cocaine, was detected by device or canine.

While waiting for the guys in spacesuits to finish, Carla watched several of the different law enforcement officers argue over jurisdiction and attempt to impress one another with the power of their particular organization. She caught herself smiling as she wished her new Texas Ranger friend was there orchestrating the investigation scene. She realized getting representatives from overlapping jurisdictions was a bad idea. No one was in charge. Lesson learned.

Making the best use of her time, Carla examined all of the bodies scattered around the surrounding few blocks. This time, she found each of the dead drug users had identical books of matches on them. The matchbooks were all new and were from a bar in New York called Jazzmen. They had been contacted by the killer! What was the significance of the nightclub? Was the killer trying to tell them something, or were the matchbooks just calling cards?

Special Agent Bright and several crime scene investigators scoured the area around each body, but the only thing they could find resembling a clue were footprints at two of the sites that may have been made by the same shoe. She spent nearly all day being as thorough as possible but could not find anything else that might lead to whoever had caused these latest deaths.

With some of her fellow agents searching images recorded by traffic cams, others were checking with nearby businesses to see if they had security cameras trained on the area. A couple of uniforms were going door to door, too, asking for witnesses to come forward or call a toll-free hotline. The data they collected was compared with information gathered by a New York team at the Jazzmen club, who were interviewing potential witnesses and accessing the images they scrounged from that area as well.

Nothing! No witnesses would come forward and they could find no useful webcams. When she was completely out of options, she released the bodies to the local coroner, headed back to her own office to add what little more she had learned to her notes, and wrote a report for the day's findings. Despite her notorious habit of making thorough reports, on this day she merely outlined what she would finish Monday morning, saved her file, and quietly stepped out of the office a little early.

Pursuit

Not knowing what to expect from the text messages being sent from the underside of the federal agent's car, I settled in for the day and tried to get comfortable. With the remote in one hand and my favorite mug full of hot Earl Grey White in the other, I sat down in my new massage chair to relax.

Shortly after four p.m., I received another text message. The federal agent was on the move again. I threw on fresh clothes, dashed over to the parking garage, and began following her up I-87. She drove north, and after many miles, I considered turning around and going home.

What am I doing?

I thought I would follow her to her place, or find a hangout she frequented so that I could arrange a non-threatening way to approach her. I hadn't bargained on driving so far but, in for a penny, in for a pound.

She went into Adirondack Park, and I stopped getting text messages. Was she staying in the park? Or passing through? Should I keep going, or drive to the last place a text was sent and wait there? Or come up with some other plan? I was about forty-five minutes behind her, so I slowed down as I approached her last known location, hoping she would get back within range of a tower.

Taking a rest-stop break killed some time and presented an opportunity to stretch my legs and think. What if the phone had fallen off or had been damaged? What if she had found the device? What if she was heading back in this direction or already here, at the same rest stop as me looking for someone frequently checking their phone? The best thing to do, I guessed, would be to wait to see which direction she was going. Once I entered the mobile phone dead zone ahead, I wouldn't be able to receive texts, either.

I didn't have to wait long. I received another text about an hour and twenty minutes after the last one. She had driven straight through. I jumped in my car and continued north as well. Before I lost my signal, two more messages indicated she had stopped in Plattsburgh. Was that her destination, or was she just gassing up? Maybe getting dinner?

Driving the speed limit was maddening. I wanted to get through the Land of No Reception but did not dare speed. Getting stopped for something so avoidable would be foolish, so I stayed slightly under the speed limit.

Shortly after topping a large hill, I received several text messages. She had continued north on I-87 until she was a mere two miles from the Canadian border, near

139

Champlain, where she turned west on Highway 11 toward Mooers and Mooers Forks. Another turn to the north somewhere placed her near North Star Road, where the phone began sending coordinates only, with a note saying "Unknown Location."

At 10:30 p.m., I reached the general vicinity of her last known location. I looked around but couldn't find lodging of any kind. There did not appear to be much of *anything* in the area. Still, texts came in every ten minutes. She hadn't moved since before 8:30 p.m. Either that or the phone had fallen off.

Plotting the coordinates from her text messages on a New York state map didn't help. I resorted to simply driving around and searching for any place she may have parked her car, wishing I had thought to buy a GPS device so I could pinpoint her location.

Maybe she had family up here, or a weekend place and her car was sitting in a driveway or a garage. On the brink of giving up for quite some time, I happened to look out through the woods at just the precise moment to catch a glimpse of a distant light shining through the trees. I pulled over to the side of the road and got out of the car to investigate.

A quarter moon low in the sky provided precious little light through the trees, making it difficult to see. After my eyes became more accustomed to the darkness, I saw the glow from the lights deep in the woods. What appeared to be a private drive, complete with rustic mailbox and cattle guard, was the only turnoff on the road, so I ventured up the dirt driveway not knowing what to expect.

The closer I found myself to the source of the light, the more pronounced the glow became. Whatever was illuminating the area seemed more likely to be coming from a large number of dim lights rather than a small number of bright lights. The lights were far from the road, deep in the forest, and spread out over a large area.

After following the dirt driveway for a couple of minutes, the road curved around to the right, leading to the top of a hill, but the glow emanated from my left, so I stepped off the road and stumbled up the side of the small hill. A completely unexpected, yet astonishing scene came into view slowly as I approached the top of the rise. The more I saw, the more progressively shocked and impressed I became by a meticulously detailed replica of a small hamlet from eighteenth-century England. A hidden resort!

This village consisted of three-dozen stone and half-timbered country cottages, complete with thatched roofs, rock chimneys, and wooden shutters on the windows, with each lodge being a little different from the others.

Several other larger structures made up an office, an old country store, and a restaurant. Another elaborately decorated building could have been a gathering hall or clubhouse. In the center of the hamlet crossed two old-style cobblestone roads, illumed by antique, oil-burning lanterns hanging from hooks beside the front door of each dwelling.

A creek flowed through the resort in a roughly horseshoe shape while walking trails weaved their way around trees and structures along the banks. Park benches overlooked gentle waterfalls, enchanting lily ponds, and swimming holes. The creek meandered by all the quaint cottages and passed between several of them. Most of the units had screened-in back porches while a few had wooden docks extending out over a couple of the larger pools.

Someone had put forth a great deal of effort to make this tiny hamlet a charming mixture of history and fantasy. A rock-walled well and several hitching posts lining the cobblestone roads served to lure you back to a simpler time. What a great place to get away from it all for a weekend or a long vacation.

No cars were in sight. There were no parking lots or garages, or maintenance equipment, which added to the surrealism of the resort but didn't help me in my search for the federal agent's car. I needed to move on, but I could not take in enough of the resort. I kept noticing mesmerizing details. Like wooden watering troughs and wrought iron hitching posts for horses.

I stood in the forest gawking until my phone vibrated again with another text message, which startled me slightly. Feeling silly, I made my way back through the trees to the driveway and continued, expecting to find a parking lot. Sure enough, around the curve to the right and over the small hill were a few cars parked in a square gravel lot, including her car.

Thorough searches from two different angles did not reveal any obvious security cameras or webcams covering the parking lot. I trotted over, got down in the gravel, and pulled the phone from under her car.

The tape felt like it would have stayed attached quite a while longer unless she had driven through rain, but still, I felt better with the phone back in my possession. Had it been recovered by the FBI, there was a small chance that a well-funded investigation could track the history of the approximate locations of the phone, *and* the phone receiving the text messages, and triangulate on the buildings in which I worked and lived.

For a moment I thought about how I could determine which cottage the federal agent had booked so I could try to approach her, but then I wondered how long she'd hesitate before arresting me. Not long, I'm sure. I needed to communicate with her on a long-term basis. I couldn't just track her down and leave a note on her car every time I wanted to discuss something.

On the way back to my car, I considered the possibilities. I realized I could easily leave an untraceable disposable phone on or in her car, with a note telling her who I was and what she could expect in the future.

Satisfied with my plan, I drove back into Plattsburgh, the nearest town of any size at all, and found a decent hotel overlooking Cumberland Bay and Lake Champlain. I went to sleep almost immediately, despite the beautiful night view over the lake, and I slept late, too. With half the morning wasted, I went for broke and ordered brunch in bed from room service. I might as well make the best of it and enjoy the weekend and mini-vacation. The view of the lake was certainly an invitation for relaxation.

Even with a bit of a stomachache from too much hotel food, it didn't take long to find an electronics store that sold disposable phones. I purchased two with chargers and a small, powerful flashlight, but had the clerk put all of it into a bag for me—I was careful not to touch any of the merchandise. She didn't ask any questions and didn't appear to think anything was out of the ordinary. I kept a box of surgical gloves in (of course) my glove compartment for just such occasions, which I would use to handle the equipment and put it all together later.

I wrote and printed a short note using the printer in the hotel's guest business center. Back in my hotel room, I used my gloves to trim the paper around the text to eliminate the tracking markers nearly all printers leave around the edges or corners of every page printed. (Sorry, NSA.)

Using one of those untraceable "Thank You" convenience-store bags, I stuffed one of the phones, a charger, and one of the matchbooks from the Jazzmen club into it and tied it shut.

The plan was to take a nap before going back to the hidden hamlet, but I could not sleep, despite a drenching, mid-afternoon thundershower. I channel surfed a while, managed to get a last-minute massage appointment in the spa, and hung out on the second-floor balcony by a warm fire pit. A few other people joined me as the sun began setting behind the hotel. We all sat quietly and gazed out over the lake as dusk began fading into darkness.

While I relaxed, I noticed a random hair stuck in the arm of my chair and thought, *Huh,* with a devious little smile. *That would be a nice distraction to include with the note to the fed.*

After dark, I drove back out near Mooers again and found a better place to leave the car other than the side of the road. It was a longer walk, but at least the car was off the road and less conspicuous. The driveway to the resort was muddy this time from the earlier rain, so to avoid leaving obvious tracks, I walked in the forest parallel to the road.

As the tiny village came into view, I simply had to stop and gawk again. Its charm and appeal drew me in. What was it about the resort that was so appealing? The time period so cleverly replicated, maybe? Perhaps the lighting, made to appear as though the entire village was lit by candlelight and old-fashioned oil lamps? Or maybe it was the lazy, calming creek flowing through the hamlet and over picturesque waterfalls?

A fish surfaced in one of the lily ponds, making a small splash. As the ripples moved toward the rock shores, another fish surfaced and their ripples crossed paths uninterrupted. A large bird that I assumed was an owl glided by swiftly and silently, just outside the perimeter of the lights. I found it all mesmerizing.

I had a hard time tearing myself away from the scenery again, but did so by bargaining with myself. I'd book myself a vacation here. Slowly, I made my way to the end of the driveway.

Her car was *not* in the parking lot. I cursed. Had she only stayed one night? Why did I assume she would be here all weekend? *Why* had I taken the phone off her car?

Moving out of the dim light of the parking lot, on the side opposite the old village resort, I sat on a fallen tree in the woods to consider what to do next. *So close!* Sitting there shaking my head, I reconsidered my limited options. The forest night was soothing enough to calm me and to assure me that, with patience, I would be in contact with her, or *someone* at least, who might be willing to help. I had plenty of time to take care of business.

After what could have been a couple of minutes of silent contemplation, or ten, the eerie sound of a nearby owl calling from the darkness of the woods distracted me from my thoughts. Even knowing how ridiculous the idea was, I couldn't help but notice how sad and melancholy the bird of prey sounded.

Listening closely for the owl to call again, off even further in the woods, I heard another owl answer with a nearly identical call. The hoots were the same pattern, but lower in tone. Immediately the first bird hooted again. The distant owl waited a few seconds as before and returned the song, which was again answered immediately.

As the dialogue continued, I wondered what they were saying to each other. A mating ritual? Establishing or maintaining territory? Comparing notes on potential prey? Warning each other about my presence in their forest? Or were they just letting each other know they were still close by, reassuring one another in the darkness?

A chill overcame me and I shivered as a cool breeze surged by. I turned up my collar and put my hands in my pockets. The earlier rain had cooled the entire area, and the temperature had dropped even more after the sun had set. I breathed in a long, deep breath of the fresh, cool forest air through delighted nostrils and enjoyed the full experience. The pleasing scent of rain on the rotting wood of the forest satisfied me to my core.

The two owls continued their exchange despite the cold air, and just as I made a mental note to look up what kind of owls in the area might have that type and pattern of hoots, headlights appeared. A car was approaching!

My heart pounded, thinking that it might be her. I moved behind the fallen tree I was sitting on and waited for what seemed to be an eternity as the car eased up the rough driveway. I ducked before the headlights could sweep over me, remaining perfectly still while the car pulled into an unmarked parking space. I heard the door open and shut, then I peeked over the fallen tree.

Thankfully, she was back. I breathed a sigh of relief and watched her walk away quickly, turning around for a brief second to set her alarm.

Oh, my. She is spectacular!

The times I had seen her before, she had been wearing the latest technology in body armor, weapons, and radios, which had hidden her exquisite womanly features. Her curves were perfection and her face was the same quality of beauty that artists have carved into the bows of ships and chiseled into stone for hundreds of years. She was truly breathtaking, and when she walked out from under the parking lot light toward the cottages, she moved gracefully and confidently. The glow of the lighting from the village highlighted her silhouette as she stepped up and over the hill and out of sight.

A few seconds later I realized my mouth was open and my heart was still pounding. I gazed off into the night absentmindedly and replayed the last few moments in my mind. I'm not sure how long I stayed there, awestruck by the brief encounter, but I finally snapped out of it and moved over to her car.

I checked the driver's side door, but of course, it was locked. While putting the bag of phone equipment under a windshield wiper, I noticed her building access badge was in one of the cup holders of her console. I glanced around again to make sure no one was coming or in the vicinity, pulled the flashlight from my pocket, and shined it down at the badge, using my body to shield as much of the bright light as possible.

Special Agent Carla Bright. A name! At the very least, I could now make future contact more personal.

With my task complete and my new owl friends resuming their conversation, I hurried back to my own car, which was quite a distance away, parked in the turnout for a small cluster of mailboxes. A smile on my face, I was on top of the world and wanted to make contact with *Special* Agent Bright as soon as possible. I wondered if she would be open to providing information about drug dealers, terrorists, sex offenders, and other extremists after learning about my unique capabilities.

I *should* have been concentrating on my immediate surroundings. When I was fifty or sixty feet from where I parked, I noticed something moving on the passenger side of my car, so I froze. Had they seen or heard me? A partly-cloudy night did not work in my favor. Very little moonlight trickled through at that moment.

Whoever was beside the car had frozen, too. They had likely heard or seen approaching, but I could not see anything. I slowly crouched and wondered how visible I was in the road with no grass or foliage around me. They were wearing all black, and I lost them in the shadows. Fortunately, the fast-moving clouds opened up just enough to let a small amount of moonlight through. Or maybe it was unfortunate. A large black bear was looking straight at me!

The bear calmly stared at me, as if it were waiting to see what I would do. Or not. It took its eyes off me and focused back on my car, smelling the door and the window. The snacks! I had snacks in the car. Peaches, bananas, and mixed nuts.

Okay, what do I know about the situation that I've gotten myself into?

Living in a log cabin in the Rocky Mountains for over a decade, I knew a little something about bears. I had encountered several in the past and had made an effort to keep up on what to do when you come across a bear, and what *not* to do, like run. Chasing things is great fun for them.

Bears typically avoid humans unless snacks are carelessly left in places where they can smell them. They are not afraid of us, they would just rather avoid trouble and go find some berries, or some poor squirrel's nut cache. This one, however, looked back at me, showing no fear or urgency to leave.

Could I stop animals the same way I could stop people? I had no idea. Why did I not know this? Why hadn't I tried this before? I had been given plenty of opportunities in the past, but it never occurred to me to see if my new skill would work on animals. Out of all the dogs, pigeons, and squirrels I had seen, I had never had any reason to stop one. What if the electrical signals that made it all possible were not compatible with other species?

I never thought of myself as one who was the type to be unprepared for so many different things, but I was beginning to wonder. At that moment, in the back of my mind, I could hear a high school football coach raving on with his favorite old worn-out advice, "Failing to plan is planning to fail!" I laughed a little snort at the irony when I remembered he was a huge *Bears* fan.

When I snorted, the bear shook its head and snorted as well, then moved toward me, huffing rapidly in a threatening sort of way. It walked at first, but the pace increased to a bouncing trot. I had no choice but to see if I could stop the bear. I didn't want to kill the marvelous creature, but the aggression had to be checked. A healthy fear of humans would result in a longer life span for the bear. Just like so many other relationships, respect for each other allows for peaceful coexistence.

Focusing on its chest, the bear stumbled but kept coming, maybe even a little faster. I focused on the bear's neck intensely and it collapsed, far too close to me.

My bear friend was angry as hell, but there was not a lot it could do about it. As I held it on the ground, I leaned over and blew bursts of air into its eyes. This seemed to cause more anger than fear though. I moved away a couple of dozen feet toward the car and stopped focusing. It scrambled up but was a little wobbly for a few seconds.

It did not run away as I expected, but instead, turned around, locked eyes with me, and held its ground.

I like this bear!

However, if it did not respect humans, someone would eventually kill the beast with a rifle, or maybe a truck. I dropped the black bear again, approached deliberately, and smacked its snout a few times. Not meanly or maliciously, but enough to make the bear believe that we humans can always have our way. I covered its eyes and patted its nose hoping it would associate the smell of humans with creatures demanding respect.

This time, when released, my bear buddy barely glanced at me as it sulked off into the woods. Good enough. I got back in my car, breathed a sigh of relief, and drove away.

Contact

In Carla's recurring dream of being a college student running late for a final exam, poor weather or car trouble typically caused the stress and the delay. This time, there was no snow involved or traffic jams keeping her from class, but instead, out of all the things she could have dreamt, a lobster on the sidewalk threatened to pinch her ankles. A lobster!

Too afraid of the crustacean to pass by, the alien-looking thing lunged at her feet every time she moved. She kicked furiously, but it would not back off or let her pass. Some unknown figure in the dream remarked that the lobster was "really gettin' after" her, but failed to offer help of any kind as he passed by without being accosted. As Carla awoke, she had to laugh at the absurdity of it all, and for the first time in her life regretted ordering a live Maine lobster for dinner the night before.

Feeling a rare Sunday morning refreshment from a weekend of little to no responsibilities, she lazily donned a swimsuit, stepped outside, and slipped into the heated pool for a morning swim around the rock walls and waterfalls.

Usually, she couldn't get into a pool without pushing herself like she was trying out for the Olympics again, but something about her favorite weekend hideaway encouraged her to relax. The place had seemed like a home away from home since a roommate from college had convinced her to spend a long four-day weekend there nearly a dozen years ago.

Brunch was exactly as another vacationer at a table near her described. "Divine!" This quaint and charming little village was the only place she felt she could heal after a particularly brutal stretch of time on the job. This was *her* sanctuary, so when she spotted a bag on her windshield, she was understandably angry. And *livid* when she saw the book of matches from the Jazzmen club. The individual responsible for all those mysterious deaths had followed her here, to her favorite getaway.

Even as she became increasingly furious, she wondered why she wasn't afraid or feeling violated, or even looking around to see if she could catch someone watching her. As a seasoned FBI agent, she was experienced enough to realize that if this person wanted to do her harm, she would already be as dead as the drug dealers and addicts whose murders she had been investigating. That, and the fact that in his note, he was asking for her help and guidance, of course.

On the bright side, I now know that I am, apparently, only looking for a single person.

147

Subways

On the subway during the busiest part of the Monday morning rush for work, I sent a simple text message to the phone I had left for Special Agent Bright.

```
Are you there?
```

Nothing. No response.

I waited about three minutes and sent another text.

```
Are you really not even going to answer? If not, I will move
on and give someone else this opportunity. This phone I'm
using will be destroyed in a few minutes, and you will have
missed your chance.
```

Within a few seconds, I received an answer.

```
wth do u want & how the hell did u know where I was?
```

Smiling, I could tell she had sent a text message or two in her day. She was obviously used to being the one in charge, too, but *I* needed to be the one in control to avoid distracting tangential conversations. A little redirection, or even a little lie might make things easier for her to handle.

```
During the course of your investigation, you've seen what
this new weapon I've developed is capable of doing. With the
right information and some cooperation, we can bring the drug
trade to its knees and derail terrorism enough to be
insignificant for decades.
```

```
come in, surrender & we can talk about it
```

```
Sorry, can't do that. IQ's too high. We have an opportunity
here to make a colossal difference for generations to come,
so don't waste my time with talk of turning myself in. I
intend to find someone willing to help.
```

While exiting the subway train, I pulled another phone from my pocket and sent another text message.

```
Use this number now, the other phone has been destroyed.
```

I hadn't destroyed it yet. I wanted to make sure I didn't miss anything and, sure enough, on the old phone came her text,

```
I will need to discuss with superiors
```

And then on my new phone came,

OK

I dropped the old phone into a large cup of water I'd gotten from a fast food stop and jumped on a subway going in the opposite direction from which I'd come.

Using the new phone again, I texted,

Yes, I'm sure at least SOME of the people who are helping you trace the origins of my text messages will let your boss know I've contacted you. Are you, or anyone else on your team, willing to help, or not? Or do I need to find another...less capable...organization to help?

I didn't have any particular agency in mind, I just wanted them to imagine a worst-case scenario.

Pausing for just the right amount of time to be convincing, her/their answer was,

OK-lets talk

I knew this was just a tactic to keep me chatting a while longer, but at least the dialog had started.

I need to know where or how to find the right people to take out in order to slow, stop, or eliminate drug traffic into the US, & we need to formulate a plan to get me close enough to the heart of terrorism to take them all out.

At least now they would know my intentions and hopefully realize I was not *their* enemy.

i will have to give that some thought

Her non-committal answer was cleverly positive. Then, most likely at the urging of a teammate, she added,

would u let the pentagon use this weapon instead of forcing us to trust a civilian with military quality weaponry?

No.

could u tell me more about this weapon? its effects r unlike anything we have ever encountered

No, but not because I'm mean or selfish or untrusting, but because of its nature. Right now, I'm the only one capable of using it. It's difficult to understand and even harder to explain. Not even sure *I* understand completely. I'll contact you again soon. Keep your battery charged! Destroying this phone now.

There was no immediate response, so I dropped the new phone into the cup of water as well.

On the way home, I stopped by the grocery store and bought a bottle of household cleaner with a high ammonia content. Replacing the water in the cup with the cleaner would contaminate any DNA I might have left on them. I walked a few blocks and emptied the cup into a subway trashcan, and then threw the cup into a different one a few blocks away.

In a couple of days, I would contact her again to see if we could work together to solve common problems. I still had plenty to do, so I didn't just sit around wringing my hands. I needed to come up with a new way of contacting Special Agent Bright that would throw them off track again. I also needed to find a way to contact her separately, away from her fellow law enforcement agents, so when we spoke or sent each other text messages or e-mail, I could have at least some level of confidence that it was only the two of us in on the conversation.

Two like-minded people can typically keep a private venture between themselves, but as more people get involved, the risk of exposure increases exponentially.

Let them stew on our first contact for a while.

Traced

Many of the people involved in Special Agent Bright's case were in the conference room going over the evidence left on her car when the phone started vibrating. They all looked at each other, shocked, knowing they were probably being contacted by a dangerous and elusive killer. One of the older men who happened to be on the other side of the room broke the silence, "Well, answer it! What did you expect, it's a phone!"

Carla reached across the table, picked it up, and announced, "It's a text! Not a call. He wants to know if I'm here."

A half-dozen conversations began taking place, mostly groups of two or three while others were on their own mobile phones trying to get someone to trace the origin of the text. While they were all trying to decide what to do, another text came in. "Okay people, we need to answer. I'm going to text him back."

"Wait, what? What are you going to tell him?"

"I don't know, but he's threatening to destroy the phone he's using if we don't answer. I need to stall him, and I need to stall him now." Carla furiously worked the keypad on her phone with her thumbs.

Silence overtook the room as they waited for the next text message. She plugged a USB cable into the phone, and in a few seconds, the phone's screen appeared on a large wall monitor behind Carla. The next message popped up almost immediately.

During the course of your investigation, you've seen what this new weapon I've developed is capable of doing. With the right information and some cooperation, we can bring the drug trade to its knees and derail terrorism enough to be insignificant for decades.

Everyone in the room became even quieter. In a few moments, voices rose, breaking the silence and all sounding aghast at this new information. Carla looked around the room, listening to people go on and on about the horror of this new weapon, however, she noticed no one was discussing the potential of using this weapon to fight crime and terrorism. Her thumbs tapped rapidly again at someone's suggestion to tell him to come in and surrender. She knew it was a mistake before she even finished typing, but she hit the send button anyway.

"Okay, this does not leave this room," shouted the senior New York agent. "Anything regarding this new weapon is now highly classified material! Got it?" Everyone nodded or mumbled their acknowledgment.

Special Agent Bright had to suppress a smirk at the smartass message in the next text, but they all worked together to try to figure out how best to stall him and get information at the same time.

"Just tell him you have to consult superiors!" A large man in standard military framed glasses offered. It was all they had, so after a couple of people shrugged, she sent the message.

"Uh oh, I just got another text from a different phone number." She viewed the other text message. "Oh! It's him again, on another phone. What the…?"

"He's going to be hard to catch," were the general sentiments in the room.

The next message angered some and took others by surprise, despite the earlier request for help. "Oh! And he's an asshole, too," remarked one of the youngest in the group quite sarcastically, then he turned to the agent beside him and asked in a quieter voice, "What does he think, he's going to get help from the spooks?"

Before anyone could stop her or even complain, Carla answered,

```
OK-lets talk
```

```
I need to know where or how to find the right people to take
out in order to slow, stop, or eliminate drug traffic into
the US, & we need to formulate a plan to get me close enough
to the heart of terrorism to take them all out.
```

"Oh, is that all" was Carla's first response, but backspaced over it and sent something designed to keep the lines of communication open longer.

```
i will have to give that some thought.
```

Before she could send the message, the ex-Marine suggested, "Ask him if he'll work with the Pentagon to put this new weapon into the hands of the military."

Carla's thumbs pecked the tiny number pad furiously while someone else wondered out loud why they couldn't figure out a way to use the keyboard of the computer to which it was tethered.

They didn't have to wait long for a simple answer.

```
No.
```

"Ask him if he'd at least explain the nature of the weapon. Appeal to his pride or ego."

"Yeah! Tell him we're impressed and we've never seen anything like it before."

She did her best to get all the questions sent, but she knew information would only be allowed to flow in one direction. "He's destroying the phone! If you're going to get a trace it's now or never!"

A phone rang and an exceptionally tall agent pressed it to his ear, "What do you have?" Then he moved the receiver end of the phone away from his mouth slightly and relayed, "He's on a subway!" Turning away from all the eyes upon him, he spoke into the phone again, "Holy crap, are you kidding me?" Focusing back on the people in the conference room, he shouted, "He's on the yellow or green, *heading straight for us!*"

Several of them were on their phones immediately, trying to make arrangements to have people watching the subway exits as quickly as possible. Carla tried to follow some of the one-sided conversations going on simultaneously, but there were too many that were too loud. She sat watching the commotion, wishing she would receive another text.

"The first phone signal is lost, but they are tracking the second number now. Wait, wait! Now he's on the blue, heading back north." Several agents tried to keep the people on the other end of their phones heading in the right direction, and the room continued to grow louder, becoming more chaotic by the second.

"Okay! Hold it, everyone! Stand down. Stand down! HEY!" Everyone became quiet and looked at the senior man in charge. "Stand down. He's gone. We're not dealing with someone who'll be caught easily. We'll get him. Just not today."

Everyone was still quiet enough to hear the individual on the other end of the tall agent's phone say, "The signal's gone. We lost the connection of the second phone!" A pause, then, "Hello? You copy?"

"Copy that. We're standing down."

Special Agent Bright's head was all over the place as anger mixed with frustration and anxiety. She'd never admit it to anyone, but she also felt a longing for more contact with this vigilante. She attributed it to a desire to put him behind bars, but that was merely a place her mind had fled. Her emotions were getting the best of her, maybe even guiding her, which she did not like.

However, she could see that she was not the only one in the room who was unnecessarily emotional. Even some of the men who were supposed to be hardened federal agents were not entirely under control. They were just as frustrated as she was. Surprising her, seeing their emotional chaos caused some of her insecurities to diminish.

Mesmerizing

For the next few days, I spent too much time acting like a stalker. I spent a lot of time at the Civic Deli, a coffee shop on a nearby corner, a couple of different pizza joints, and of course the local Dunkin' Donuts, not to stereotype anyone, but it's there.

Sure enough, early Friday morning, Special Agent Bright showed up at the coffee shop. I *knew* I liked her. I noticed something interesting about her. She seemed to be two completely different people when she was on duty and off. All business and as tough as they get, or just being an average woman with the girl-like qualities that bring out the best in people. She lit up like a teenager when a studly young barista flirted with her. I think she actually giggled. I nearly laughed out loud.

When she left the coffee shop though, she slipped back into her all-business mode, despite those gracefully flowing and mesmerizing movements I had noticed at her vacation spot. It would have been extremely difficult to watch her walk away if it wasn't the absolute highlight of my day.

Phones

Early the following Monday morning, I found a place in Thomas Paine Park where yellow and green foliage on the trees likely shielded me from the federal building's security cameras. While I waited for Special Agent Bright to make a coffee run, I typed several messages into the quick-text feature of yet another clean phone so I could get messages out quickly.

I had gotten into the habit of wearing different clothes, shoes, hats, and sunglasses every time I intended to make contact or take out another criminal of some kind. It was expensive but *so* worth the cost and effort, and after I wore them, I tossed it all into the clothes donation bins. At the moment, I wore a typical "I ♥ NY" hat with sunglasses that were not the dark kind, but instead were lightly shaded, which I thought might make me look less conspicuous.

Special Agent Bright did not go for coffee that day. She failed to make a run on Tuesday, as well. I gave it a rest for a few days so I wouldn't become too much of a recognizable figure in the area, but returned Friday morning. That must be her thing. Friday morning treats.

`You there?`

She checked her phone when she emerged from the coffee shop, stopping when she saw a text from me. She began typing with one hand while she made her way back inside.

`yes`

`I'll cut to the chase. Are we going to help each other?`

`u have to know that we can't help u kill people`

`Right now, there are more hopelessly habitual drug addicts dying than those few who are responsible for their addictions. This just seems wrong to me. If you agree, tell me where the REAL problems are, and I'll make them go away.`

`as you said a few days ago when I asked you to cooperate - no`

`Understood. So! How then can we help each other? We could accomplish things together that would be impossible otherwise. Working together, we could completely disable drug traffic in America.`

`yes, thats very tempting but u know I cant do that`

`Actually, you CAN do that. YOU can prevent the abuse and neglect of countless children and families. That's why you do`

what you do, isn't it? I believe that's why you serve your
society to the best of your abilities. Am I right?

of course, as long as I act within the confines of the law.
Anything else would be against my beliefs.

I watched her texting furiously with one hand while sipping a delicious hot beverage
with the other. It seemed like every time I took a sip, she did, too.

There has to be a way to meet in the middle. There has to be
a way for you, or SOMEone to make good information about bad
people available to the public.

no

Will you be able to sleep at night knowing that you could be
doing SO much more? You could be helping thousands of
families instead of just a handful. Instead, you are
rejecting a once in a lifetime opportunity that could make
THE difference.

A pause in her texting compelled me to peer around a tree. Special Agent Bright was
leaning back in her chair, staring out a window with grimaced lips and vacant eyes. I
might have gotten through to her.

Knowing my next text would reveal that I was nearby, I made my way out of Thomas
Paine Park. I had already seen enough to believe she was interested in helping me by
the way she returned to the crowded coffee house a few minutes earlier. Instead of
dashing back into her office where she and her colleagues could try to track the origin
of the text messages, she had gone in the opposite direction. I told her as much, too,
right before I climbed into a taxi.

If the hesitation I'm sensing means you're considering
working with me, look for the envelope taped to the underside
of the bottom shelf in the display closest to the front door
of the coffee shop you're in.

As the taxi approached the window where Agent Bright had been sitting, it stopped at
the traffic light. She came running outside and scanned the park. She focused on
everyone she saw for a moment, determining if any of them could be me. She did not
look into my taxi or any of the other cars on the road.

When my light changed, we passed by her close enough for me to tell that she was
pissed, although I noticed that she did not immediately call in reinforcements. Instead,
as the taxi made a left onto Lafayette, I saw her go back inside, so I sent Special Agent
Bright one last text message.

Thank you. Destroying this phone now, but I'll be in touch
soon.

Popping the top off my paper cup, I let my phone slip out of the plastic bag I had it in, into the cold coffee I had ignored for too long.

"Do you feel like a leisurely drive through Central Park?"

"Absolutely."

Decoy

When Special Agent Bright heard people wishing they could have a "four-ten" workweek, her reaction was always the same. *She'd* be thrilled to work a *five*-ten workweek. A smaller number of people than you would think hear this and understand it immediately. The rest of them need to hear, "JUST working a five-ten work week would be great." However, her Friday morning java run was a guilty pleasure that had become an enjoyable routine.

She loved to order her favorite hot or slushy frozen beverage of the season, but hot ones especially when the weather was cool or cold, even though spouting out the eight-word name made her feel ridiculous. This morning was no different.

Carla always took a moment to look over the latest books and CDs being promoted while she waited on her coffee. Occasionally she bought a CD when they had some particularly high-quality work of art for sale, like the last two she had purchased: *Lennon*, most recently, and the soundtrack from *A Charlie Brown Christmas* the Friday morning after the last Thanksgiving holiday. Both of which reminded her of her childhood, which brought a smile to her face.

Walking out of the coffee shop was her message to the world that her Friday was starting. Her phone began vibrating before she had taken two steps. When she realized it was *his* phone going off, she stopped in her tracks and pulled it out of her pocket, where it had been for a week.

You there?

Unexpectedly, she felt a surge of relief that quickly changed to confusion. Why would she be relieved that a ruthless vigilante killer finally got back in touch with her? She was excited and sickened at the same time. The respected FBI agent turned around abruptly and headed back into the coffee shop as if she had something to hide. Her shame, perhaps? Or her excitement?

Carla scolded herself for being attracted to the bad boy, yet again, and reminded herself that he was *not* the type of person to be admired, or the kind to which she should be attracted. The riff-raff she had nearly hooked up with in the past would have derailed her career with the FBI before it had even gotten on track had she pursued the relationships.

Yet there it was again, the secret tingle that gave her such thrills. She was irrationally driven to duck back inside, and sit at a table away from the door so she could have a small amount of privacy while she texted him.

Disgusted by the irrational reactions she had to this man, she began texting him with curt, snippy responses to his inquiries, always keeping in mind that her fellow agents were viewing the exchanges and were probably already trying to triangulate in on his location. She tried to respond in ways that would appear as though she were trying to keep him texting long enough for her colleagues to find him. She was also trying to be sufficiently negative so he would *not* use the phone long enough for them to locate his position.

At that moment, she realized she *was* willing to do just about anything to get the worst of the worst off the streets. He was right. Her best efforts accomplished many good things for a lot of people. Still, when she assessed all the crime and abuse still left to alleviate, she knew she could never do enough, no matter how many twelve-hour days she worked.

Yet there was this "bad boy" out there, making an *enormous* difference, and that's why she secretly admired him. By working together, they might be able to disable much of the drug traffic in America, but continuing to do things his way, she argued to herself, would be breaking the laws she held so dearly to her heart and had sworn an oath to uphold.

Experiencing admiration and disgust at the same time could confuse anyone. If she helped him eliminate the worst of the lot, and as a result it prevented only *some* of the horrific child abuse she had learned about and witnessed, it would be so worth the risk to her career. If she managed to take a few of the meanest pimps or most coldhearted drug dealers off the streets and prevent any number of lives and families from being destroyed, the risk *might* be worth it.

His text messages reflected almost exactly what she was thinking. She looked through the advertisements written on the window on the opposite side of the coffee shop, up at the building where she worked, near the spot closest to her office, and thought for a moment what her colleagues might think of her if they knew what she was considering.

The next message she received took her by surprise, although it probably shouldn't have.

```
If the hesitation I'm sensing means you're considering
working with me, look for the envelope taped to the underside
of the bottom shelf in the display closest to the front door
of the coffee shop you're in.
```

Realizing he had been close enough to watch her while they swapped text messages, she cursed a little too loudly for the hippy chicks sitting nearby. She began looking around but quickly concluded he would most likely be texting her from the park across the street, so she hurried outside and began scanning the crowd. *Pissed off!*

Or at least she had to *act* like she was angry. She knew searching the area for him would be futile, however, so she went back inside to see what he had left for her.

159

One last text made her realize that he was watching her closely.

Thank you. Destroying this phone now, but I'll be in touch
soon.

Taped to the bottom shelf of the display were *two* envelopes. They both contained phones, but one was more sophisticated than the other, which had an interesting note in the envelope.

"Keep this phone between you and me and destroy this piece of paper. I'm sure the text on the last phone I gave you is being monitored, so give your colleagues the phone in the other envelope and tell them I told you to keep *that one* between you and me. We will distract them with it while you and I work together to bring the illegal drug market to its knees.

"If this plan works out, then hopefully, we can focus our efforts on terrorism next. (Yes, Special Agent Bright, we'll try to waste as few taxpayer resources as possible, but distracting the rest of your team while we work together will be necessary. Consider it part of the cost of preventing drug dealers from harming kids.)"

Under her breath, but still out loud, she started, "You smug b—" but then stopped and laughed good-naturedly, wondering how someone she'd never even met could know her well enough to add such a wonderfully smartass note. She returned to her seat, picked up her coffee for a sip, and became lost in thought, lamenting over this difficult decision. She had to act quickly, as several of her colleagues came hurrying out of the federal building, scanning Thomas Paine Park for anyone who might need to be questioned.

Opening the other envelope, she pulled out the decoy note. As she read it, she noticed a couple of her fellow FBI agents running to the coffee shop. As they hurried across the street, through slow but heavy traffic, she stuffed the first envelope into her waistline behind her weapon and waved them over when they burst in.

"Get crime scene investigators here to dust this display for prints. Have them look for DNA on these, too." She waited for an agent to snap on gloves and handed her the note and the envelope containing the decoy phone.

Vacation

Jeanna had the office running smoothly and she did not need anything at the moment or in the foreseeable future. Many days had passed and I had not heard from Special Agent Bright, so I had all but written her off as a possible partner and was already working on a plan to contact someone else.

With little else on my agenda for the next few days, and nothing that couldn't wait, I searched the Internet and found the Old English hamlet resort that had impressed me. I made reservations for the rest of the week, including the weekend. I needed a rest, plain and simple.

The next morning, I woke up in the Nottingham Suite, which was easily the most comfortable and quaint room in which I have ever vacationed. Quaint or not, I rolled over and went soundly back to sleep to the soothing sound of a mild thundershower on a thatched roof.

Eventually, I found my way out of a very comfortable bed and had a roaring fire crackling in the fireplace in minutes. A brewing pot of freshly ground specialty coffee smelled so inviting that I welcomed the falling rain.

Outside, everything was soaked, which made it difficult to do anything but relax and enjoy the fire, the rustic furniture, and the antiques in the room. A pleasing view of the woods on the other side of the creek held my attention captive.

Not everything in the room was old-fashioned. An enclosed portion of the back porch contained a state-of-the-art Jacuzzi and I made good use of it when I realized the fireplace was a pass-through design that also kept the enclosed porch warm.

Cool and stormy, a Thursday morning complete with thunder and hail meant I pretty much had the resort to myself. When I noticed it was almost lunchtime, and the rain had diminished to a mild sprinkle, I crawled out of the hot tub to explore the rest of the resort.

I dashed through the shower to the community restaurant, the Cottageshire Café, for a bite to eat. One of the tables surrounding the central fireplace was available, so I sat opposite a couple who were the only other patrons. Best brunch ever! I took my time, savoring every bite and enjoying my fireside table while the rain fell steadily.

Making my way to the business and media center during another slight lull in the downpour, I searched the Internet for anything that might help my quest for criminals, but I was in no real hurry to do anything. Before I left the media center, I did one final search.

"Hmmm," I said out loud. "Great Horned Owls."

By the following evening, the storm had passed after one final, heavy downpour, and quite a few people were showing up at the resort. Several of them had joined me in the large heated pool, which had a beautiful, multi-tiered waterfall tumbling over craggy but smooth boulders. The creek feeding the waterfall looked as natural as it possibly could without actually being formed by the forces of nature, except that the water was pristine.

Downstream, past two other captivating waterfalls, a lily pond contained live fish and several different species of beautiful, pure white lily blooms, both in the water and around the pond.

As we all enjoyed a beautiful sunset, the temperature dropped considerably, which caused an increase in the amount of fog coming off the surface of the warm water. It was thick enough to prevent me from seeing the opposite side of the pool. I heard other people splashing and talking not far away, but the steamy fog rising from the water was too thick to see more than ten or fifteen feet.

I was relaxing in warm water about two feet deep, leaning up against the edge of the pool and my kneecaps sticking up out of the water. Shortly after the other people in the pool settled down a little and became quiet, a floating woman emerged from the fog and drifted lazily in my direction. When she was close enough, I realized she was completely nude.

At first, I thought she would float right by me, and then I *hoped* she would float by. But sure enough, she bumped into my leg, which made her body angle slowly around so that her hip and thigh were closer to me.

What few small waves that were in the pool washed across her tummy and over her chest, making her breasts move quite tantalizingly, as though they were dancing partners in some graceful ballet. The current flowing gently around us held her there against me, with little chance of moving her away without some help.

Not wanting to startle her into causing a big scene by moving unexpectedly, I sat frozen, trying not to gawk at her nude body and hoping she'd swim away. Finally, I cleared my throat and politely said in a soft voice, "Um, hello."

Without even opening her eyes, she whispered, "Push me back out?" I obliged, gently and carefully, so that I did not disturb her. As the woman floated away, she disappeared into the rising fog as if I had dreamt the entire encounter.

She floated by a couple more times over the next half hour, so I guess no one else minded her being nude, or pushing her back out into the pool. I certainly didn't mind.

I love a nice vacation, even if it is just a four-day weekend and a few hours' drive from home.

Displaced

For several days, FBI agents analyzed thousands of images. Most worked twelve- and fourteen-hour days, but none worked more hours than Carla. Her department tapped every resource they could find, but still lacked the manpower to work through all the evidence in a timely manner.

After all the images from their own security cameras had been scoured, they began going through all the files from traffic cams and webcams from businesses in the area that were known to cooperate in such matters and a few others that weren't. Everything they could find that had taken pictures or video of places during the few times they had pinpointed were being thoroughly analyzed and fully documented.

Image after image popped up on a row of monitors in the task room. No fancy Hollywood facial recognition image software here. Agents felt like they were about to go blind from repeatedly studying so many pictures of the same area. Seeing the same background, frame after frame, with multiple variations in the foreground of each photo grew monotonous. Minds were numb. Still, any one of the photos could contain something useful, so they did their best to maintain focus.

Finally, Carla found a series of fuzzy subway images that depicted a man exiting a train, texting on one phone and dropping another into a large cup. A moment later, he stepped on a train going in the opposite direction.

Intense eyes stared at the images for a full minute or more, flipping through the sequence several times. Those same eyes darted back and forth over and around her monitor without her head moving. Then within a short, four-second time span, the images from a few minutes later in the same series were saved over files probably containing photos of the man for which they were all searching.

The worst serial killer *ever* in the history of American crime caught an assist from an FBI agent who hated the scum he was killing even more than the killer himself.

Not a single pang of guilt brushed her conscience. Overwriting the images did not bother her like she thought it would. Carla had personally seen enough evidence at the "crime scenes" to know that this person they had been calling a serial killer had no intentions of harming society. She plainly and simply destroyed potential evidence, hoping her actions would buy him more time before someone stopped him. She had broken the law by undermining the efforts of her own investigative team.

As a competent FBI agent, she also knew future analysts could easily discover that someone had tampered with the image stream and possibly even figure out who was responsible. However, that might take weeks, or even months, during which time she could warn him, provide the intelligence on extremists he had requested, and maybe even help him get away.

The payoff for this better be worth what this could cost me.

She poured through the photos as if she were still searching, but in several other windows, she opened interfaces to all the terrorism and drug-trafficking databases to which she had access and made it appear as though she were comparing pictures of terror suspects to faces in the images they were reviewing. Occasionally, she saw a piece of data that, when compared with other pieces of data she had collected, might lead to finding some of the worst offenders and possibly even the individuals at the top of terror cells or drug distributors.

Unfortunately, nearly all the terrorist information led to remote sites in the Middle East, North Africa, and Eastern Europe. Little of that data could be used to locate anyone within the United States, but she found quite a bit of information that would lead them up the drug trade chain of command.

Carla Bright, a loyal and devoted FBI agent, but an even better human being, copied enormous amounts of terrorist data and New York organized crime intelligence onto a USB flash drive throughout the rest of the day. When she noticed the time, she unplugged the USB and stood up. "Okay, people, it's four o'clock on a Friday afternoon, and we've all reviewed images for days and days, so let's knock off a little early for the weekend."

A chorus of relieved responses, heavy sighs, and chairs creaking was penetrated by one smartass remark about "just getting into the zone." After some obligatory laughter, it didn't take long for the room to clear.

The last of her colleagues to leave stopped in the doorway, turned around, and said to Agent Bright, "You know, I noticed you were saving quite a bit of data to that thumb drive." The glance he gave down at her hand told her she could not deny the fact. Her face became hot and her hands went cold.

Why *didn't I listen to my conscience?*

Then that conflicting notion sprang to life again, and she did something she only did every now and then. She answered herself.

You did *listen to your conscience, that's what got you into this mess!*

Completely exposed, her chest pulsated from the violent beating of her heart.

"Don't work *all* weekend, alright?" Her colleague used a friendly tone—not accusatory. She realized she hadn't done anything wrong by copying the files. That was nothing out of the ordinary, as people took data with them all the time. So why was she getting all worked up?

"I won't, Ken, thanks. Have a good weekend!"

On the way to her office down the hall, she had another little talk with herself.

Is this really what you want to do? You became an agent of the most prestigious investigative effort humans have ever devised so that you could do your part to deter criminal activity, not participate in it.

But I'm not an FBI agent simply to be a part of that organization. I am an FBI agent to increase my chances of stopping injustices committed by criminals. If the FBI is getting in the way of me doing my best to stop the worst of the criminals—

Such hubris! Where do you get off thinking you can do better without the FBI than with them? We have all the resources you need to get to these people.

Then why don't we get to them? And why don't we have this man, who is taking out other criminals by the dozens, or better yet, why don't we have this man working for the FBI?

Perched at her desk like a hawk about to dive for prey, she placed the USB drive carefully and deliberately beside her keyboard. Opening a drawer revealed the second phone he had left for her that day. Has it already been a month? She stared at the phone a while before picking it up and turning it on.

Anticlimactically, the battery was completely dead, so she slipped it and the charger into a jacket pocket with the USB drive and headed north for her monthly weekend getaway.

Traffic was busier than usual getting out of the city because of the heavy rains from a storm that had hovered over the state of New York for days. Nevertheless, she made up some time on the Interstate, especially when she drove out of the storm about half way there. She pulled into her favorite vacation spot by 10:45 p.m.

The drive had given her about five hours to think things through, but she still had not yet fully committed to working with this man, nor had she ruled out anything, either. One thing was for sure, she would need to know more about him and his intentions before she put her career on the line.

Exhausted from the drive, Carla brushed her teeth, washed off what little makeup was left on her face, and took a quick shower. Too tired to unpack, she dropped her towel onto the floor beside the bed and slipped between the fresh sheets of her favorite feather bed. She curled up comfortably, making use of all four thick and plush goose-down pillows.

When morning sunlight crept its way into bed with a completely nude Carla Bright, she woke gently and stretched luxuriously. Not ready to succumb to the new day, she rolled over and closed her eyes again.

In a few minutes, she realized that if the morning sunlight was warming her bare body, then the blinds were wide open and people could see in. Raising her head, she checked. She was fine. Her back porch was also a small, private dock reaching out over the creek.

In the middle of changing positions, while trying to get comfortable again, her eyes popped open as she remembered the life-changing decisions she had to make. Carla considered the possibilities for a moment and wondered if things would change at all. She had devoted her life to undermining the efforts of criminals. Her passion had been protecting innocent or potential victims.

Seems like I may be trying very hard to keep from saying "bring criminals to justice" out loud, or even think it.

If she helped this man, realistically, how would her life change? The two obvious choices at hand were to either continue her work with the FBI, or provide information to someone who could permanently remove hundreds, maybe even *thousands* of abusive criminals. If she continued her normal, business as usual workload, she could still put dozens of people behind bars, at least for a while, which wasn't bad. She would still be pursuing her life goals and passions.

On the other hand, if she and a criminal she should be trying to put in jail helped each other, how much would that change her goals?

Now it sounds like I'm trying to talk myself into something. Is that what I want to do?

Of one thing she was certain. Simply talking to him about what they might accomplish couldn't hurt anything. In fact, she could also use the occasion to perform reconnaissance in case she needed to bring him in.

That was the deciding factor. If it came down to it, whatever she learned could be used against him. Carla wondered what she could say to him in a text that would sound convincing enough to let him know she *might* be interested in working together. She looked at her jacket pocket and remembered the phone's battery was still completely dead, so she reluctantly slid out of bed, retrieved the phone and charger, and plugged it in.

Another long, hot shower with those special dual massage heads she loved so much was something she knew she deserved, so she showered until all the hot water was gone. Carla took her sweet time drying off and getting into casually comfortable old clothes, pampering herself in ways her harsh workdays routinely denied her.

By the time she wandered into the Cottageshire Café, it was a little late for brunch so she ordered her favorite Elevensies Biscuits, which were more like cake than a biscuit, but she was okay with that as they perfectly complemented the bistro's authentic Earl

Grey tea. Steeping her tea bag relaxed her and she knew just when the taste would be perfect by the smell and color.

The cool morning warmed into an unseasonably comfortable afternoon, so the off-duty FBI agent went back to her room to slip into a swimsuit. She unplugged her (his?) phone and dropped it into her robe pocket as she gathered her towel, a hat, and a book she had been wanting to read for a while.

Her favorite spot on the deck was a portion that extended out away from the pool and into a corner of old growth forest. She had taken quite a few naps there over the years and considered the spot her own.

However, this morning, some dreadfully inconsiderate man was in her chair. The nerve! He didn't look like he was going anywhere any time soon, either. With a short sigh, she chose a nearby lounge chair that was still in the warm, midday sunshine, but had to settle on an inferior view of the forest.

Not being in her favorite corner of the deck didn't matter much, for as soon as she stretched out and got comfortable, Carla realized she was still tired from the long drive in the rain the day before. She laid her open book down over one thigh, pulled the unflattering straw hat down over her eyes, and drifted off to sleep again.

Coincidence

A small library of paperbacks graced one wall of the Business and Media Center. Several others with tattered covers were scattered around on a coffee table in front of a plush couch. I picked through the ones on the coffee table until I uncovered one that caught my eye. It was face down so I could see the author's photo on the back, but what interested me was that he looked familiar.

Who IS that guy? Seems like I know him from somewhere.

The author's name did not ring a bell, but I felt strongly that I had met him before. The book itself, *The Scrapbook Lecture*, looked interesting, too, as I am a big fan of narrative fiction, so I took it with me to read poolside.

Settling into a lounge chair as far as I could get from a loud couple swimming in the pool, I admired the beautiful old forest in full, remarkable fall transition for a moment and then opened my new find. I love starting a new book. You never know what to expect, but the anticipation of what is to come is half the fun.

There was an extra-special treat with this book though. On one of the introductory pages, I found the novel was autographed. The note was addressed to a "Hammer" and sounded like the two may have been good friends, along with what looked like a serial number.

I wonder how it wound up here. I bet there's a story behind that.

By the third page, I was into the story and there was no putting it down. I love a trek through time, especially when written from the perspective of being there, experiencing history as events happened.

Reading about a young Joseph Kennedy a few pages later sparked a memory. Another look at the picture on the back cover confirmed my suspicion. He was the guy who had stopped and jumped my dead battery for me at Dealey Plaza back in Dallas. I bet he was there doing more research.

Small world. I found myself absorbed back into the streaming story of history and hearing the author's voice in my head as I read. I was so engrossed in the book that I didn't even get irritated when a woman in a robe sat near me, despite having the entire deck to find a more private spot.

I did my best to ignore her, but between chapters I noticed she was sound asleep, with her robe partially spilled open to reveal two exceptional legs. An old, well-worn straw hat half covered her face as she slept peacefully. I continued reading, unable to stay away from the mounting tension.

When I was nearly a quarter of the way through the novel, the woman near me stirred as she woke and stretched with one of those dramatic, but cute little squeaky growls people make sometimes when they experience a particularly good stretch. Then she pulled a phone out of her pocket.

Oh, great, now she's going to be one of those crazy people who yell into their mobile phones.

I stuck my nose back into my book and did my best to ignore her, which was easy because she began texting, not talking.

My own phone notification vibrated shortly after that.

Ugh! It's my turn now.

My first guess was that Jeanna might be having some kind of issue at the office, but on a Saturday? However, *my* phone wasn't vibrating, it was the one linked to the phone I had given Special Agent Bright. Suddenly my heart was racing. I hesitated a moment before reading the message. Had she decided to help? Or were they trying to zero in on my signal and close in for an arrest?

Strategy

A refreshing nap was just what Carla needed. She pulled the hat off her face, tossed it onto a knee, and stretched herself fully awake. Just a few minutes of soaking in the beautiful day made her realize that it seemed far too warm to be enjoying the fall colors. Brilliant yellows and grounding browns contrasted against bright red undergrowth and leftover leafy greens. The peak colors of autumn had always been calming and soothing for her. She could walk through colorful woods for days and never tire.

Well, if she had that kind of time, she could. Carla closed her eyes and drew in a long, deep breath of refreshment. Peeking over her right shoulder, she could see the man was still in her favorite spot. She was disappointed but did not let it bother her for long. The day was too nice to let anything spoil it. She honestly hoped the man was enjoying the fall colors from his superior vantage point as much as *she* would be appreciating it, but vowed to get there earlier tomorrow morning and considered him no further.

Carla wasn't sure how long she had slept, but she felt great, despite her nagging internal conflict. On one side stood her foolish and impractical desire to join forces with a known killer. She could easily let his new weapon, whatever that might be, work toward getting abusive scum off the streets without ever having to deal with crooked criminal lawyers and the repercussions of unsuccessful trials. The other side of the conflict was simply to continue doing her job and to do everything in her power to put this vigilante killer behind bars.

But then FBI Special Agent Carla Bright thought, on the bright side, what if I can do both? What if I could use him to clean a large portion of the exceptionally evil out of our society, and then use what I learn during that time to get him, and his weapon, off the streets?

Satisfied with her strategy, she pulled his phone out of the pocket of her robe and successfully turned it on for the first time. Only one contact existed on the phone. "Imagine." Several text messages from Imagine were queued up, all asking something along the lines of, "Are you there?" She replied to the newest one, which was nearly three weeks old, typed a quick message, pressed send, and picked up her book.

Date

Messages (1 unread)

Her text message was short, simple, and to the point.

ok! let's talk

I shook my head in disbelief but typed a reply.

Okay, but first please explain the sudden change of heart after a month of no contact at all.

Hesitating a bit before sending the message, I wondered if she was up to no good, or if she had simply come to her senses. Had she become sick of the rat race and dead ends at the FBI? Or did the agency have a trick up its sleeve? Did they plan to pounce on me and take me into custody? I wasn't too worried about that. I was practiced and confident enough in my unique abilities to know I could handle whatever they threw my way, and still allow all of us to walk away unharmed.

I also had enough money stashed away for me to live out my life in hiding, but did I want to deal with all that? Or was the possible payoff for taking this risk worth it?

Yes, I decided, it was. I hadn't waited patiently for an answer all this time, carrying the phone with me twenty-four hours a day and keeping the battery charged for nothing. I needed to see it through.

Send.

With the phone in my lap, I tried to get back into the book I'd been reading. I couldn't help but notice that the woman near me reached for her phone just seconds after I sent my text message. She typed furiously with her thumbs for a few seconds, looked at the message a moment and either added something or made a correction before sending it, and then traded her phone for the book in her lap. Sure enough, the phone in my lap vibrated.

No way.

That was *not* Carla just a few feet away from me. Was it? I picked up my phone quickly and put it inside my book so she couldn't see me texting, just in case it actually was her. I had seen her from afar a couple of times, but at the moment, I could not see enough of her to recognize the still-unfamiliar face.

u r right. We can do so much more working together. fbi is good but not as efficient as our collaboration would b with the info I could provide & ur new weapon

171

It's been a month. What makes you think I'm still interested and haven't already moved on?

u answered. we r talking. not quite a month tho. r u still interested?

Of course I answered you. Foolish not to. Whatever it takes to increase my chances of making a difference. I am interested in hearing what you have in mind, but my confidence in you is something less than optimal.

I was very much interested but wanted to see what she would say to boost my confidence. It was all too obvious now that the woman next to me was Carla, so I was careful to disguise my typing behind my book. Her next reply was not as positive as I'd hoped.

i thought we could at least talk about the possibilities

As did I. Shall we meet, or try to do this through text messages?

text 4 now. i'm out of town for the weekend.u really want to meet?

Yes I do. I'm that confident that we can work together. And, I am out of town, too. Might be a perfect time to meet if you're up to it.

you'd trust me like that? you'd just meet me somewhere?

Yes. Why not? If we're going to work together, maybe even for years, the trust has to start somewhere.

how do I no I can trust u?

Carla was typing faster, using more shortcut words.

You know you can trust me. You've seen the degenerates I target. You and I want the same thing out of life.

if we meet will u show me this weapon?

I considered this for a moment and decided to use it to my advantage.

When we meet I will not be carrying any weapons, however, discussing the nature of this weapon is certainly an option. I'm open to full disclosure, but probably not this weekend. Are you okay with that?

absolutely. fair enough

Pausing, each of us waited for the other to suggest a way to meet. I could see she was not typing anything, but rubbing her eyes instead. A plan hit me. I could suggest we meet *here* tomorrow. If she would agree to that, I could watch her closely to see what she did to prepare. I quickly typed another text message.

```
We could meet back at that quaint vacation resort up north,
away from everyone, where we could both be more comfortable.
That place was nice.
```

I could tell she was momentarily upset at the suggestion, but shrugged it off just as quickly and suggested a time.

```
@ noon?
```

```
Perfect!
```

```
how will I know u?
```

I still had a few books of matches from Jazzmen. I could hand her one of those so she would know who I was.

```
No problem, you will know me when I introduce myself. Where
might I find you?
```

```
i will b n a very public place.by the pool, maybe, or n the
cafe
```

```
The café then! I'll buy lunch, if you'll let me. (-`, See you
then?
```

I could barely see the side of her face, but could tell she smiled, and my heart unexpectedly melted. What the hell was that all about? I hadn't even really met her yet, but there I was sending her goofy smiley faces and talking to her like I was asking her out on a date. She turned her phone sideways and chuckled a little. I guessed she was viewing the smiley face right side up. For a moment I felt like a kid back in high school.

```
c u there!
```

Half expecting the Fed to make a flurry of phone calls to fellow agents, I was pleasantly surprised when she did not. Instead, she stared out into the forest for a moment, then put the phone back in her pocket, and stretched another good long stretch, squeaking somewhat growl-like again until she relaxed suddenly, with her arms flopping back down dramatically. It was hard not to laugh at that, but it did make me smile uncontrollably.

Carla opened the top of her water bottle with her teeth and sucked the water from the upturned bottle for far longer than I would have even thought possible. Then she popped the top closed with her other hand, plopped her straw hat back onto her head and pulled it down over her eyes.

I allowed myself to be absorbed back into the storyline of my book, but after reading another half hour or so, I thought maybe I should go somewhere that would allow me to watch Carla for a while after she woke up. If she was going to call in the cavalry, or even the local authorities to arrest me, I wanted to know as early as possible.

Looking around, I remembered that the media center had a couple of windows facing the pool, so I gathered my belongings and eased away from Carla so I wouldn't wake her.

There was one other person in the media center checking his e-mail and trying hard not to enjoy his weekend. From a recliner by the window, I easily watched Carla while I read. She stirred after a while, noticed I was gone, and moved to the chair where I had been sitting.

Hmmm, I must have been in her favorite spot.

She sat gazing out into the forest with her arms on the railing around the deck and her chin resting on her interlocked fingers. I could tell she was watching the cardinals when they flew by or bounced around in the leaves. Could she be something of a nature lover, too? I *knew* I liked her.

She stood, retied her robe, and picked up her bag. I did not want to put down my book, but I had to determine which direction she was heading so that I could dash out to see if she was going to start calling fellow agents. She called no one. She went straight to the Southampton Suite, which was one of the smaller cottages more suited for someone on a federal employee's salary.

Not being one prone to frequent splurges, a pang of guilt swept over me for reserving the most expensive suite the resort had available. For reasons I could not explain, I felt myself wanting to make Carla's life better.

Data

Even though the text exchange had been short, the conversation with the man she had been pursuing for months had left Carla mentally exhausted. She had hundreds of things she wanted to say, but the limited means of delivery had forced her to trim those thoughts down to just a few dozen words. She had typed as fast as she could but did not say all she wanted to say.

The discussion had worn her down. Or was it simply that sitting in the sun for so long had left her dehydrated? Half the water in her water bottle was gone before she realized how thirsty she had been.

She gazed out into the forest she had explored as a college student and remembered making all kinds of discoveries in those woods with her friend. She longed for those old days again, but only for a moment before refocusing on how she was going to handle this new situation that had been thrust upon her. It was easy to become distracted by all the bird activity and the forest leaves slowly changing into autumn colors.

Carla could *not* concentrate, so she got comfortable, pulled her hat back over her eyes, and let her mind escape back to her college days and the summer vacations to her favorite hideaway.

Waking suddenly to the sound of a robin peeping nearby, she pushed back her hat, stretched herself awake, and then noticed that whoever had been in her favorite spot was now gone, so she moved out to the end of the deck. Carla loved to watch the robins and bright red cardinals dart in and out of the trees and underbrush.

If I arrange things just so, I can help this man take out some hard-core criminals and then use the evidence I gather in those cases to track him down and arrest him. But could I live with myself afterward? And what if after he is incarcerated, more sociopaths need to be taken out? Or worse, what if he were to turn on us because we turned on him? Would he use this weapon on us? Yes, no doubt. We'll simply have to appropriate the weapon first.

Federal Agent Bright had a hard time reconciling her actions and her intentions. She had sworn an oath to uphold the law, yet as a human being, she felt a burning need to do everything possible to protect the thousands of innocent people, including children, who would be victimized if she did not do enough. Those people who *would* be abused were the ones who made her lean toward helping this vigilante.

Her job was to catch and arrest criminals, but he simply killed them on the spot. When the people she had arrested got out of prison, notably harsher than they were before, even after serving a sentence that always seemed too short, how many more children would have the misfortune of being in their path?

With no decisions yet made, it was not too late to recover the fuzzy images she had deleted back at the office and get back on the right side of the law. Even if she took an hour or two to prepare and organize the data she had copied onto her USB flash drive, all she had to do was *not* give it to him and she would still be okay. She could and would use that data in future investigations no matter what she decided tomorrow, so she headed to her room to organize the files and data to make it easier to read and understand.

Border

Five o'clock in the morning, on a *Sunday* morning, is just too early to get out of bed, especially when you're on vacation. Yet there was my alarm clock blaring a horrific mixture of eighties music and static. I slapped the big red "OFF" button and rolled out of bed for a few morning rituals.

An old pair of jeans and a sweatshirt were all I needed, despite the cooler weather chasing out the warm front that had produced all the heavy storms for the past week. I walked through the tiny hamlet in heavy boots with my hands in my pockets, as it was somewhat cooler than I had anticipated.

My sunrise walk took a route that allowed me to see the front of Carla's suite first, and then the back. No lights appeared to be burning. Retrieving a pair of binoculars from the trunk of my car, I glanced around but didn't see anyone, presumably because they had the good sense to still be in bed. Then I ventured out into the surrounding forest.

Autumn leaves in the forest were stunning. And distracting. The golden yellow and blazing orange foliage seemed to glow on its own with the sunrise behind them. As moisture on the leaves warmed, tiny droplets formed and dripped down into bright red, deep purple, and dark green undergrowth. If an artist captured this scene, only an abstract watercolor could do the scene justice.

Staying within earshot of the parking lot so that I could hear any cars coming or going, I walked back under the changing black walnut, red maple, and sugar maple leaves overhead and tried to push my way through some of the heavier buckthorn and arrowwood underbrush.

An occasional stop just to enjoy a quick look around paid off. I heard the cardinals first, then spotted the bright red male. He was so brightly colored that he would be hard to miss. When I slowly approached, he flew away, but only a short distance. I stood still for a while, listening intently and searching the underbrush in the opposite direction that the cardinal had flown.

Soon, my patience paid off. I caught a slight movement in a thick pokeberry bush beneath a small maple tree dressed in brilliant golden orange attire. I knew not to approach the nest. If she felt threatened, she could easily abandon the eggs, only to lay more elsewhere in a couple of weeks, despite the cooling weather.

Peering through the foliage, I could see her quick but infrequent movements as she patiently waited for her eggs to hatch. Then, straight out of nowhere, I wished Carla could be with me to see the nesting cardinal. I felt sure that this was exactly what she was looking for in the woods yesterday.

Just as I was about to stir and be on my way, the male flew back in with something in its beak. He hopped through the tangle of branches, came to rest on the edge of the nest, and fed the female what looked like a huckleberry.

This seemingly mindless creature not only had enough sense to try to lead me away from his mate and their eggs, but he also knew to feed her (after he determined I was not a threat) so she wouldn't have to leave their eggs unattended.

I let them share the meal in peace and then returned to my task. As I stood from the squat I'd been in for a while, my knee popped relatively loudly and the male cardinal took flight.

He flew past me and away from the nest again. I heard his little wings beating furiously as he attempted to draw me away from the eggs, however, he changed direction abruptly, appearing to be in a bit of a panic as his mode of flight visibly changed from feigned weakness to a flight of fright.

The cardinal flew up and out of sight quickly as a huge owl soared silently into view, banking left and right to navigate between the trees. As the owl's body pitched and leaned gracefully during turns, its head remained level so that its eyes stayed parallel to the ground at all times.

The beautiful raptor flew by me without a care, and I was amazed at the enormous wingspan, which had to be close to five feet. The eerie silence in which it flew was mesmerizing. Wings powerful enough to pilot this large bird swiftly through the forest flapped strongly, yet were perfectly silent.

I had heard the much smaller cardinal's wings from thirty or forty feet away loud and clear, yet this sizeable owl flew within ten or fifteen feet of me, and I heard nothing.

What a treat! The great horned owl weaved its way through the colorful foliage and disappeared as other, lesser birds retreated and hid from this formidable forest predator.

Okay, back to the task at hand. No more stops.

Or so I thought.

Another couple hundred feet back into the woods revealed what appeared to be a manmade clearing. I simply had to investigate. I found that the northeast corner of the land belonging to the village touched the southwest corner of a farmer's freshly harvested field.

On the other easternmost side of the property was a poorly paved road with what looked like a checkpoint between the lanes. There was a small structure where a guard might sit and two small gates attached to the north and south side of the shack, but the tiny guardhouse was empty and both gates were up.

While I stood and watched, two cars drove through the gates, one going north, and another going south. The southbound car hesitated at the gate, waiting a moment despite the checkpoint being unmanned, but went on ahead. Into the United States! This was the Canadian border. The fence on the north side of the hamlet where I was staying marked the northern border of America, and the "checkpoint" gate was what *used* to be a manned border crossing. But unlike other crossings, which were barricaded, some for many years, this one was open, allowing free traffic flow in both directions.

As I stared in disbelief, recalling the empty promises made by those fancying themselves as politicians, I noticed a path along the outside of the farmer's fence, far enough away from the cleared field to take advantage of the cover of the trees. The trail was worn enough to make it obvious that it must have existed for quite a long time, although partially covered by fall leaves. The trail went north and south alongside the farmer's field on the western edge, over both of the fences in the corner of the hidden village.

The path's intention was clear, but it took me by surprise. The handful of times I had driven into Canada, I was always stopped and questioned about fruit and guns. With the largest—*by far* the largest—open border between countries in the world, it should be apparent to all that there are many easy ways to get into America undetected.

This particular border crossing seemed to be *blatantly* open and free though, with the gate left up, just *taunting* people to enter America undetected. Not that the average Canadian has a burning desire to come to the United States.

I shook my head and turned back in my original intended direction. Healthy, thick foliage hindered my way in places, but I found a position in the woods where I could see the parking lot and Special Agent Bright's front door, well within the cover of the forest but near the pool where we had been sitting the day before. There were no new cars in the parking lot.

I'm not the type to bore easily, but I had to find ways to entertain myself while keeping an eye out for new visitors to the resort. The wildlife in the immediate area provided relief from the monotony, especially when a doe and her fawn walked slowly by, nibbling on only the most tender of green shoots and the ripest of wild berries.

Carla only left her room once when she sat by the pool for a short while. She stared out into the woods daydreaming for a moment before opening her book. She read a few pages but then fell fast asleep. I had to smile. Who doesn't love a good vacation?

When she woke up, a lazy glance at her phone made her jump out of her lounge chair and hurry off to her room. I thought maybe I would watch her emerge from her room to see how she was dressed.

If she appeared to be wearing her vest under her clothes, I would interpret that as her anticipating trouble, and I would bail. Otherwise, I would approach her and introduce myself.

I made my way back to my room to take a quick shower, get dressed, and find an inconspicuous place to watch the door to her room.

Confidence

Carla woke up and found herself still in the lounge chair on the deck by the pool. After a moment of orientation, she turned on her phone to check the time and realized she needed to go back to her room to prepare for the strangest lunch date she could remember, despite her past dealings with too many bad boys.

She wasn't sure how to dress. Casual? Business? Then she reminded herself that this was *not* a date so it would be best to dress professionally, but after looking in the mirror, she changed her mind. Taking off her business attire, she slipped back into her comfortable vacation clothes. Her phone vibrated with a text message from "Imagine."

```
Are we still on for lunch?
```

```
yes! Running a min late tho
```

She did not allow herself to notice it was eight past noon.

```
(-`,  No worries!
```

She found the silly little smiley face a bit infectious and caught herself smiling as she hurried over to the Cottageshire Café where the maître d' asked, "Ms. Bright?"

"Yes?" Carla answered cautiously.

"Right this way, ma'am."

Following, she felt uncomfortable, but not as uneasy as she probably should be feeling, knowing so little about the individual she was meeting. Although every step she took seemed to change a little of the uneasiness into a building excitement. She scolded herself again by the time they reached a cozy booth near the fireplace, but when the maître d' motioned for her to sit at an *empty* booth, she didn't even try to hide her disappointment.

"Your guest will be here momentarily."

Before she could even get comfortable or have a second nervous sip of water, a man in jeans and a sports jacket walked in and approached her. He was wearing dark sunglasses but had a reassuring smile and a kind voice as he extended his hand, not as a handshake, but to hand her something. Carla knew she should be terrified, but she was not. He projected confidence and trust.

Not a bad way to start.

Meeting

"Hello!" I held out a book of matches from the Jazzmen club to make sure she knew I was who I claimed to be, however, she did not immediately react or reach for the token of a message, but instead tried hard to see through my dark sunglasses.

"Um, hello," was all she said as she studied my face.

"Sorry for appearing to be late. I imagined this introduction would be awkward enough without the maître d' hovering over us, enjoying the discomfort."

"You're right, this is a little awkward." In a hushed voice, she added, "It's not every day you have lunch with the serial killer you've been chasing for months. But please, do sit down." She waved me into the seat across the booth from her and continued. "How do I know you are who you say you are? The man with the new state-of-the-art weapon?"

Admittedly, her use of the term "serial killer" took me by surprise. I had not thought of myself in that way, but from her perspective, that might be the case. She appeared to be trying to look into my eyes through my sunglasses and either missed or ignored the matches, so I tossed them onto the table between us and asked, "Is that convincing enough?"

One glance at the matches on the table was all she needed. "Hmm. Yes, I think so. Tell me…" She still did not know what to call me, and I wanted it to remain that way for now. It was my turn to ignore her prompt. She went on undeterred after a short pause of expectation. "How does this work? How do we trust each other? What's keeping you from turning your weapon on me, and what's to stop me from arresting you right now and bringing you in? Are you armed right now?"

"All good questions!" I smiled my best disarming smile and tried to build some trust. "I'm not sure where to start. I think maybe you need to understand the nature of this weapon before we can continue to work on trusting each other. Can we first have a— I don't know, a leap of faith, if you will, and commit to trusting each other to achieve a common goal? After all, we are both, quite literally, trusting each other with our lives right now."

"Are you armed right now?" She repeated herself, irritated.

I was thankful for the authentic-sounding period music playing. She spoke in a tone loud enough for others to hear had there been no music. The worried look on her face told me I needed to reassure her and let her know I intended no harm. "I am not carrying any weapons. I assured you that I would not be, and I am not. I am trusting you completely. Hopefully, you can do the same for me, as I'm betting you *are* armed." I'm sure she could see me looking at the hand in her jacket despite the dark sunglasses.

Special Agent Bright looked at me sideways, not yet sure if she could believe me, but moved her hand from her weapon to the table.

I rephrased my question. "Can we agree to trust each other until one of us gives the other a reason not to?"

"Mmmm…"

"How about this, if it gets to the point where you and I have a conflict we cannot seem to resolve, I will simply disappear. I will take my venture elsewhere and do my best to pass on a better world to the next generation on my own."

"Seriously?"

Raising a questioning eyebrow, I stopped myself from saying, "Huh?"

"That's why you do what you do? You want to pass on a better world to future generations?"

"Well, yeah. Why wouldn't I? Isn't that what you want, too? Isn't that why you do what you do?"

She took her eyes off my face for the first time since she glanced at the matches on the table and looked at her hands. "Well, yeah." Carla smiled a contagious smile and my heart raced.

Peeking through my sunglasses and into my eyes, she asked half-jokingly, "And what makes you think I'd let you disappear?"

My heart raced even faster. Her words were threatening, but her slight smile and demeanor suggested she might be feeling exactly what I was feeling. Is that possible? I was just about to ask what she meant, exactly, when the waitress walked up and asked what we wanted to drink, speaking in an authentic-sounding, old English accent. Carla answered, "Earl Grey, please,"

I looked at her, smiled, and did my best to imitate her inflection from a few moments ago, "Seriously?"

Her face became a question. "What?"

"I'll have Earl Grey, too, please."

Our waitress hurried off while Carla and I admired each other, both of us trying to figure the other out. I could tell my dark shades were bothering her, so I said, "Tell you what, I'll start with the trust," and removed them.

She had a look of recognition on her face, which quickly changed to anger and distrust. "You're a guest here! You were here yesterday, weren't you? Before we even agreed to meet here! You were here as we were texting each other, weren't you?"

"Yes to all those questions. That was why I suggested we meet here. We were both already here." The uncomfortable feelings were back and she glared at me. "Hey! What can I say? I'm just a regular guy. I like vacations, too."

Maybe her expression softened a little, but not much.

"Agent Bright, I had no idea you were going to be here, or that you were going to text me after a month of silence. Imagine how *I* felt when I realized you were sitting right next to me, texting me."

Nothing. Stoic.

"It is kind of *freaky*, really. I mean, what are the chances?" I acted out "freaky" with my hands and a weird expression on my face for more effect. The simple attempt at humor did not help. She was not amused. "You know, I was here *two days* before you showed up. How could I have possibly known you were coming here on the same weekend as me?"

She leaned back in her seat and seemed to consider this point, but I noticed her hand had stealthily slipped back into her jacket. As she placed her hand back onto the table, she said, "Well, okay. I can believe that. It's not like I made reservations well in advance."

"Very good! Very nice, now we're getting somewhere. I have put myself out here for you in a show of trust. You know what I look like now. You could easily ruin my life and disrupt my dreams of taking out the worst of the worst. My entire *life* just changed, hopefully for the better, but that's entirely up to you."

Thankfully, a moment later the waitress showed up with our tea, and we steeped and sipped in silence for a short while. It was not an awkward silence, but more of a moment reserved for thought, and we both seemed to understand that.

Long before the silence became uncomfortable, Carla asked, "What is it that you want from me? And why me?"

Focusing on what I wanted from her so that maybe I would not have to address the fact that I literally stalked her so I could recruit her, I offered, "I need someone to supply me with good information about abusive people, so I can take them out without taking out innocent people or, more importantly, without hurting an infiltrator working undercover. That's my worst nightmare, by the way, and the only reason they're not *all* dead."

184

"Why? *Why* are you doing this? What gives you the right to bypass the justice system? Who the *hell* do you think you are?"

"Okay, that's fair. I'd ask that, too." I was stalling. I wasn't prepared to answer that and wanted to be clear and honest, but did not want to reveal my unique talents just yet. I wanted her on board first. I thought it best to let her believe some weapon was in use. "I'm doing this because the justice system is completely overwhelmed. Outmanned, outgunned, underfunded, and, by no fault of its own, inadequate for the task at hand."

"That is bullshit."

"No, no, it's really not. If the FBI and the DEA were serious about stopping the flow of drugs into the United States, they would be using satellite photography technology to keep a flow of digital data feeding into computer systems capable of doing a detailed spectral analysis of foliage in suspect areas. Or simply checking for plants in remote locations growing in rows or too evenly spaced to have happened naturally."

Carla was obviously still skeptical so I went on. "It's not like they—or *you*— would be searching for individual plants or trees in a photograph, or anything like that, but rather large patches of the same kind of foliage about the size of a tennis court or a football field."

Maybe her glazed-over expression was not skepticism. Instead, she could have easily been tuning me out, not wanting to hear how decades-old technology could be used by law enforcement. "Okay! Enough of that. Still, while I agree that our justice system is easily the best in human history, it is simply not up to the daunting task of keeping up with the overload of crimes being committed."

"Well, *I* think we're doing a terrific job of putting people behind bars." Carla went on for a few minutes about all the people they had arrested and the crime rings they had broken up.

"I get it. And again, I agree! You *are* doing a terrific job. And if there were a hundred *more* people, just like you, banging away at it as hard as you do, we would still be falling behind." She seemed to understand what I was saying although she didn't like it. "I know you can't solve every crime and bring everyone who commits an offense to justice. I get that, too, but as a society, we can't even bring the worst of the offenders in for questioning."

"That *is* frustrating. Beyond my ability to fully describe."

I leaned over the table, closer to her, hoping to drive home my point and recruit her. "You and I, however, have the opportunity to change that. All we have to do is work together."

"Hmmm, tell me, what makes this weapon of yours so special? I mean, why it and not something conventional, like a gun or a, I don't know, well, like a gun?"

I thought for a second before answering. Maybe a teaser would be beneficial. "Well, as you know, this weapon cannot be detected by anyone, in any way. It leaves no trace whatsoever when used, or at least none I'm aware of. It's perfectly accurate and does not require fuel or reloading, nor is any kind of maintenance required."

She looked horrified but said nothing.

"Yeah, pretty scary, right?"

"How many of these weapons have you made? Where are they?"

"As far as I know, only one exists."

"As far as you know? What did you do, steal it from someone?"

"I discovered it."

"It's not even yours?!?"

"Oh yes, it's mine. Without a doubt. Maybe I should clarify." I gathered my thoughts for a moment before going on. "I discovered the *process*, so to speak, that makes this weapon work, so it's conceivable that once people know about it, someone else could discover this process as well, so we *have* to keep this between you and me."

"No one else knows about this?"

"Wow. I hope not. I haven't told anyone. I'm about to trust you, though, if you can assure me that *I* can trust *you*. Otherwise, if you're not on board, my life changes drastically. The Canadian border is a very short walk away."

We both instinctively stopped talking as the waitress approached. "Are you two rea'y to order, or wo' you like another moment?"

Without taking her eyes from mine, Carla absentmindedly ordered the lunch special of the day.

I knew exactly what I wanted. "I'll have the Shepherd's Pie, please." The server walked off without wasting another accented syllable.

"You know, there's something significant going on right now, right *here*." I needed this woman to recognize the potential we had as a team, and to be on board with me. I appeared to have her attention at the moment. "The decisions you and I make during lunch today won't just decide the fate of the criminals we encounter in the future, but all their future victims as well."

Carla's eyes left mine for the first time in a few long minutes. She tilted her head and gazed through the window behind me. She said nothing, but her faraway expression spoke volumes.

Speaking quietly so I could accentuate her thoughtful moment, I added, "The fate of thousands, maybe even *tens* of thousands of people could be decided today, over Shepherd's Pie and Toad in the Hole."

For some reason, that snapped her back into the moment. "Over what? Over Shepherd's Pie and *what?*"

I pointed to the daily specials chalkboard. "The special you ordered. Toad in the Hole."

"*That's* the special for today?"

"I'm afraid so."

Carla smiled an embarrassed little smile and my day warmed. Then she asked, "*Toad* in the *Hole!?*" and burst into the most beautiful, infectious laughter I have ever heard, and my entire *life* warmed. Between bouts of laughter, she managed to ask, "...the hell *is* that?"

We laughed away the tension, both of us somehow knowing that we'd be working closely together for quite some time, despite never really agreeing to anything. After a while, she tried to hide her smile behind her cup of Earl Grey, but not too hard. She sipped her tea and watched my eyes again as though she were trying to read my mind or figure me out.

Taking a deep breath, Carla summarized. "So, you have some kind of new weaponry that allows you to take the life of anyone you choose, virtually undetected, right? And it never needs reloading or maintenance of any kind? *And* it's one-hundred percent accurate?"

"Hmmm, yeah. Something like that." I was nodding absentmindedly, too.

"And you do not use it for self-gain, even though you put yourself at risk. Why? For the good of the whole?"

"Well, again, yeah, something like that."

"Why would I believe that?"

For *this* unanticipated question, I had an answer. "You are used to dealing with the extremes. You pursue criminals for a living and work with people who are typically— *typically*, mind you, not always—driven to be the best of the best, which usually leads to narcissism. I am neither. I am a middle-of-the-road kind of guy, decent and, well, I like to think of myself as a good American who simply happened across something that changed the perspective and expectations of my entire life. I feel like I *have* to do positive things with these po—this powerful weapon."

I nearly slipped before I was ready. Her expression changed slightly. I knew *she* knew I had corrected myself. I was beginning to think that showing her what I was capable of doing was a higher priority than I had previously thought.

"Middle of the road, huh?"

"Well, I used to be. This is all fairly new to me, too."

"While before you were a nine-to-five kind of guy, working for a living like the rest of us?"

"Absolutely. Well, except for the part about nine-to-five. If I pulled in to work at nine it was because I was stuck in traffic for two or three hours."

"Now *that* I get."

"No doubt."

We chatted about former lives and jobs until our lunch was served. We shared things off each other's plates like best friends and continued to talk and build the bonds that would need to be strong. And, her Toad in the Hole wasn't bad. I planned to look into how Yorkshire pudding with sausage acquired such an off-putting name.

At one point, the server brought us a fresh pot of hot water and dropped a hand-wrapped bag of loose-leaf Earl Grey in it for us. The aroma was pleasing and satisfying, and I could tell she loved it, too. As I poured our tea, she offered some knowledge of her own.

"This tea has to be the highest quality I've ever had, but, you know," She hesitated a moment while she glanced around. "This hamlet is meant to represent the eighteenth century, and they do very well with nearly everything. However, Earl Charles Grey, British Prime Minister to King William the IV, I think, didn't come up with the recipe until the eighteen-twenties."

My turn to be impressed. Our eyes met and lingered, and we seemed to connect. "Interesting. I won't tell if you don't."

"Deal!" She sipped her tea again to hide her smile.

Before we realized it, two and a half hours had passed, so I asked Carla if she was ready to help or if she wanted me to move on.

"Help? Or do things *your* way?"

"Agent Bright, I—"

"Please! *Carla.* My name is Carla."

"Very good! Thank you. Well, Carla, I really would like to do things *our* way. What I've been doing can't go on forever. I *can* continue to do this on my own, and you can, too, but we could do *so* much more together. I'm willing to work with you in any way I can that will accomplish *our* goals. I think we can meet in the middle somewhere. You?"

"Hmmm. Remains to be seen. I'll need to see this weapon of yours first, and understand its nature."

"'Hmmm' is right. Would you be happy with seeing it without understanding it?"

"What? What do you mean?" Her demeanor turned a little untrusting. Couldn't blame her for that, either.

"Well, as I mentioned earlier, *I* don't understand it either."

"That's not very reassuring."

"No, no it's not. However, once you see this, I think you'll understand what I mean."

"Mmm-hmm. I'm sure." A little sarcasm never hurt anyone.

"We need someplace a little more private." I waved the server over for the bill.

"Why, do you have it on you? You said you weren't armed."

"I am carrying no weapon, I promise you. If you strip-searched me right now, you wouldn't find anything that would hurt anyone in any way." She laughed and showed considerable strength and restraint in not making another sarcastic remark, possibly about my anatomy. I appreciated that.

"Where is the weapon?"

"Just follow me, I'll show you," I said as I handed the waitress my plastic instead of asking for the bill. Carla strained to see the name on the card so I satisfied her curiosity by explaining, "Don't bother, it's a disposable Visa cash gift card, paid for with cash weeks ago."

Carla smiled another embarrassed smile. "It's my nature."

"No problem. I'm registered here at the resort under a bogus name, too, by the way, that will trace back to a dead drug addict. Just in case you're wondering about that, too."

Disclosure

I led Carla out of the café, around the corner to the pool, and out to the part of the deck we both considered to be our favorite spot. Pulling one of the lounge chairs close to one of the others, I motioned for her to have a seat. "Get comfy!"

"Get comfy?"

"Yep."

She looked out into the forest, no doubt wondering if I had hidden a gadget out in the underbrush, but then shrugged and stretched out on the chair. I tried to get comfortable as well and asked out of curiosity, and on a whim, "If I were a freak of nature of some kind, would you still be willing to work with me?"

"Come again?" My new friend had a bit of irritation in her voice, so I got right to the point.

"Okay, I'm going to tell you the whole truth about this 'weapon.'" I did the annoying air-quote thing. Not sure why. "I was going to try to pull off a bullshit story about the weapon being in orbit and needing commands that I would enter with my phone or something, but you'd see right through that even if I could keep a straight face, *and* you probably wouldn't think it was anywhere near as funny as me."

"I hope you're going to explain yourself."

"Trying." I briefly considered backing out and getting out of the situation immediately.

"Well?"

"Patience, Grasshopper!" I focused on her ankles. "Can you move your toes right now?"

Panic-stricken, she raised her voice, "No! Holy…" I had released her and she was frantically moving her toes and feet around as she massaged them.

"I caused that."

"You did not!"

"I did."

With a mixture of skepticism and amazement, she demanded, "Do it again."

I laughed, "Come on! Really?"

"Yes, I'm not sure I believe what just happened."

"Okay, you ready?"

"Yes!"

I focused on her upper thighs. "Can you move your legs at all?"

"No! This is unbelievable!"

"Yes it is."

"Do my arm!" She held her arm out expectantly.

Okay, she was enjoying this way too much, but I obliged and focused on her shoulder momentarily. Her arm went limp and plopped down on the armrest.

"Incredible."

"Yeah."

"Ummm, how do you do that?"

"As I said, I simply do not understand *how* it works. I only understand how to *use* it."

"How did you learn to do this? Did someone teach you? Or have you had this all your life? What happens when you do it to yourself?"

I laughed. "Wait, slow down! One question at a time here. I just recently discovered I could do this, not long ago. No one taught me, I just realized what I could do, and, Carla…" I looked into her eyes, "you're the only other person I've shared this with."

"No one else knows?"

"No, no one else knows."

She considered this for a moment. As she contemplated, I could tell her mind processed and considered the possibilities. I found myself with a deep desire to know more about what was going on behind those beautiful eyes.

"Forgive me, but I have to ask, how does the whole, ummm, well," she tilted her head and raised her eyebrows for a split second, "*death* thing work? What do you do, prevent them from breathing long enough for them to suffocate? Surely not. What a horrible way to die!"

"No, no, it's not like that. When I focus this—whatever it is, on someone's mind, they drop dead immediately. Their brain functions seem to be instantly scrambled beyond repair. It's instantaneous. They are literally dead before they hit the ground."

"That's pretty horrible, too."

"Can't argue with that, but there is no suffering at all. Death is instantaneous. But maybe with us working together, I'll never have to do that again."

"Let's hope not. You are *not* judge, jury, and executioner. No one person is or can be."

"Carla, that is *one* of the reasons I sought out someone like you. Do you understand that?"

After a thoughtful nod and a moment of silence, Carla said more to herself than to me, "And this is why we haven't been able to find any evidence at all or cause of death." She appeared to fade deep into thought again, so I gave her a few moments to let her process. After a while she asked, "What if, this *thing*, I don't know, goes off by accident or something and you killed an innocent bystander?"

A tilt of my head revealed that I hadn't anticipated this question. "That's not really how it works. You have to focus a certain way, like, well, like firing a gun. You have to intentionally take off the safety, aim, and fire in a manner that won't harm innocent bystanders. Even an accidental discharge means the trigger was pulled. When you react out of pure instinct, you still control your weapon. What I do, I have to do intentionally. It doesn't just *happen*."

"Teach me how!"

I had to laugh again. "Well, I'm not even sure how *I* do it. I wouldn't know where to begin to try to teach this to someone else."

Carla asked question after question, most of which I could answer and explain, but it was obvious to me that she was also casually pumping me for personal information as well, so I was careful not to reveal anything she could use to track me down later if our newfound friendship went sour. I did not yet want her to know my true identity. She needed to earn that trust.

Neither did I tell her the circumstances in which I realized my new talents, for she could easily trace those experiments back to ERL, and then to me. I did not tell her where I grew up or that I later moved into a cozy log cabin in the Rocky Mountains. At one point, I even mentioned cold Chicago winters just to throw her off track.

I had to put my interests first, which, in my humble opinion, had also become the best interest of decent people everywhere. This colossal responsibility had been thrust into my custody uninvited, but I was not about to abuse my fellow humans or let the opportunity waste away.

Mid-sunset kindled a wide sky of dark blues, beautiful reds, and brilliant oranges. Dropping temperatures caused Carla to shiver. We had talked all afternoon and half the evening.

I offered her my jacket but she refused and made a warmer suggestion instead. "I have the makings for sandwiches back in my room. Would you like me to make you one? We could get a fire going in the fireplace and warm up."

"Okay, that sounds nice, Carla. I hadn't realized it was getting so late."

She stood, stretched again with her trademark squeaky growl, and said simply, "Come!" with a wave of her hand.

I stood and followed her, and, oh, my, gosh. She walked *so good.* I had it bad.

Her room was surprisingly clean and organized, although there were three different outfits of clothes laying on her bed that she scooped up quickly, as soon as we walked in the door. She folded them in half and hastily stuffed them in her suitcase with a bit of a sheepish grin. I'm not sure what the fuss was about, but I had the impression that I was missing something.

She did indeed have the makings for good sandwiches, which she constructed as though they were works of art. I *knew* I liked her! Herbal tea and one small chocolate and mint morsel apiece for dessert, then she was all business again. She pulled a USB flash drive from her pocket and held it up between our faces so that it was right between each other's eyes. "This contains some of the data you've been asking for."

Floored, I imitated her again. "Seriously?"

"Yes. The data is about as raw as it can get, so don't get too excited, but I think the two of us working together can extract enough information from it all to allow us to get close to some of the 'big dogs,' as they say."

"Excellent!"

"You have to understand that this could get us *close* to the otherwise untouchables at the top. I doubt we have any intelligence on the bastards actually in power. I'd be willing to bet that we can get to people high up on the food chain, though," and with a shrug she added, "but then what?"

"I've been working on a plan that might help us with that."

"Yeah?"

"Yeah. I've been thinking about this for a long time. We might be able to use their religious beliefs against them."

"Interesting. Tell me more?"

"It depends upon their belief system, of course, and how entrenched or brainwashed they are, but essentially, we convince them that their god wants them to come clean, and if they don't, parts of their bodies will stop working."

I glanced at her leg, indicating they would feel the same sensation she felt earlier when she realized I was making her foot numb.

"As they are living through it, they won't know the condition isn't permanent and this new experience will be beyond their capacity to understand, so they will likely believe and comply."

Carla appeared to be in deep thought again, so I assured her that as far as I knew, there were no lasting side effects. Unless, of course, I focused on their minds.

"I tried this on myself many times when I was first learning. The process seems to be the same as an arm or leg going numb from a lack of circulation. Few complications have resulted from that happening repeatedly to someone, except for an occasional blood clot, but that was because of a lack of blood flow. As far as I could tell, this only affected the nervous system and did not stop the flow of blood."

One piece was still unclear to me. "The question I have is, what do we do once we find the worst of these guys? What do we do with them? How do we—you—how do *you* take them in and put them away? How do you explain their confession?"

"That will be challenging." Mostly to herself, Carla mused aloud, "Maybe we only go after people who are already wanted?"

"And the first thing they will do is tell everyone that someone got their god to torture them into confessing. You could get away with that once by claiming they are lying, but when others tell similar stories, all of them will be set free by our wonderful judicial system."

"Mmm, yeah." She paused a moment to reflect and added, "I can see how easy it would be to—I think I understand now why you are okay with being judge, jury, and executioner."

"If only I could get to the root of the problem. The top of the food chain, as *you* say."

"Well, it all starts here." Carla held the USB flash drive up again. "We have to find them before we can do anything." She plugged the USB drive into her laptop, and we started digging through files. The data had been gathered with the idea of building cases to present to prosecutors and had not been intended to use as a tool to *track* criminals. Still, we managed to uncover several people in the New York City area that fit the bill and might be located relatively easily.

At nearly three in the morning, we took a break. She got up from the desk chair and moved to her bed, which was the only other place to sit in her small room with me in the easy chair.

Carla stacked her pillows against the headboard and leaned against them while we continued talking, although we didn't talk long. She fell asleep sitting up. Smiling, I stood and quietly covered her with a spare blanket I found in the closet. I was very happy she had already taken off her shoes. I would have had to try to remove those, which could have caused problems.

What now? Slip out?

I didn't want to leave because I wasn't sure how I might get back in touch with her again. Using the restroom didn't even wake her. Her laptop screen had already timed out and locked, so I couldn't continue researching. If I had a USB cable or adapter with me, I could have copied the data to my phone.

I might as well get some sleep, too.

Even a man as inexperienced with women as me knew that the chair in which I sat was a far better option than risking getting my butt kicked by an FBI agent because I crawled into bed with her. I turned off all the lights except the one in the bathroom so there would be enough indirect lighting for her to see me in the morning, and hopefully wouldn't be startled by my presence and shoot me or something. Because that would suck.

When I finally fell asleep, minutes later her alarm clock woke us both. Carla slapped it off as fast as lightning, and gasped when she rolled back over and saw me in her chair. After a moment she recognized me and flashed me her mean face, then she lifted her blanket and did a clothing check.

"Why are you still here!?"

"Umm, well, I guess we both fell asleep. Are we finished? Do you want me to leave?" I was trying hard not to smile after seeing her do a nudity check.

"Oh, no, it's okay." She laughed a pleasant laugh and asked, "What time did we fall asleep?"

"I don't know, three or so."

"I need to get ready for work. It's a long drive in from here."

"Okay, what about the work *we* did? Can I get a copy of that?"

"Yes, but first can we agree on something?"

"Probably, yes. I'm willing to work with you any way I can, but what did you have in mind?"

"Feel free to use this data to find a way to get to the people at the top, but take no action against them without me. The ones at the top need to be put away by the judicial system, flawed as it is. Those are the conditions in which I will freely share this data with you, and more in the future if this arrangement works out. Good?"

"Good. I can easily agree to those terms."

Carla swung her legs out of bed, yawned so big and for so long I thought her face might pop inside out, and then went over to sit at her laptop. When she logged back on, the moment she moved her mouse out of the upper right corner of her screen, the computer produced a loud beep. She smiled and said, "Thanks for being trustworthy."

Woo! This girl is sneaky.

I knew at that moment I'd have to watch her closely, but I was glad I had treated her in the manner in which she deserved, and had acted honorably. Trust is often difficult to earn, but it is always easy to lose.

Alliance

FBI Special Agent Carla Bright and I worked together fairly well. We only experienced a few minor disagreements that were easy enough to resolve, and within a few weeks, we had a routine that produced the desired results. She did a phenomenal amount of work, often enlisting the help of several junior agents to get specific intelligence on suspects.

One of the things we both despised was when people recruited children into the harsh world of gang violence. Those suspected of abusing kids in any way were invariably given a higher priority, although most of our targets were in the illegal drug trade.

Every few days, we met at some new place to exchange USB drives, on which she provided new data with details on where I might find potential targets. Included were tips on where I might likely find them alone. I returned the drive to her with my findings, which she added to the FBI's database.

Dozens of encounters were made possible with Carla's input, several of which led to arrests. Occasionally, when criminals seemed too hard to catch, or were particularly nasty, I made on-the-spot, rogue decisions to end the suffering of their victims. There were a few people I frightened enough to get them to turn themselves in by scaring them with their own religious beliefs. Those tactics did not always work though. One such encounter could have easily gone bad for me.

Acting on Carla's intel about a man responsible for arranging much of the cocaine distribution into The Bronx and part of Yonkers, I brazenly knocked on his flat door. He answered in a robe, expecting a "masseuse" for their weekly Thursday massage, but I intercepted her and parted with $500 to get her to skip the appointment, and keep her mouth shut. When he saw I was no "therapist" he tried to slam the door in my face. I focused on his torso and watched him collapse.

He was blocking the door, so I stepped into the flat to pull him out of the way. The door swung shut and slammed when his legs were out of the way, and out of my peripheral vision I saw something large moving in my direction. Still bent over the owner of the flat, I jerked my head around just in time to see another man rushing toward me, a knife in his right hand and a lust for blood in his eyes.

I tried to focus on his mind, but he moved too quickly. His chest caught it and he spilled halfway onto his boss, and half on the hardwood floor, but knocked me back against the door. The man with the knife didn't stop. He recovered quickly and took a vicious swipe at me. The blade was so sharp it sliced my jacket wide open, barely missing flesh. I focused on his neck and took the knife from his hand. The owner had scrambled to his feet by then, so I had to let go of my second newest "friend" and put the first one down again.

And so it went until I had them tied back-to-back, sitting on the floor, gagged with belts that held wadded-up pieces of junk mail stuffed in their mouths. Then I had to take a breather. I plopped down on their couch and began talking to them like they were old buddies.

"Whew! I *have* to start working out more!"

They both tried to yell through their gags, cursing me no doubt. I checked the clean cut in my jacket. "Oh, maaaan! I just bought this, too." The slice had also passed through the zipper like it was butter. I examined the exceptionally sharp knife. It was well-balanced, fit my hand perfectly, and was as sharp as a razor because of a precision edge.

"Hey!" I continued talking as though we were all buddies. "This is nice!" I picked up several more pieces of junk mail from the coffee table and sliced through them all at the same time. "Do you sharpen your own knives or have them done somewhere?"

More muffled cursing.

"Hmm?" I asked absentmindedly, studying the carved artwork on the handle. "What was that?" As they both continued their rage, I turned my attention to the small but lavishly decorated flat and noticed quite a few religious appurtenances at one end of the living room. "Is that some kind of shrine? Don't tell me you guys are religious. You sell death, essentially, to children. Slow, agonizing deaths. Then you come home and, what? Thank your gods for your good fortune?"

Hanging his head in shame, the guy who had come at me with a knife fell silent. The flat owner had the opposite reaction. He became so furious his face turned red and beads of sweat formed on his forehead as he screamed louder into his gag. I patiently waited for him to run out of steam, but he went on and on, so I focused on both of their necks. Right before the hysterical one passed out, I released them and let them catch their breath. Using their religion to my advantage would likely get them to cooperate.

Doing my best to keep a grin in check, I stood and threw my arms and face up dramatically. After a moment, when I was sure I had their attention, I nodded a short, quick, jerky nod. Turning my attention to the flat owner, I gave him a wild-eyed, intense stare and changed my voice to a raspy whisper.

"I'm to find out, from *you*, everything I need to know to put an end to your evil ways. Your future depends on how well you cooperate, and *someone* knows you understand." When I whispered the word "someone" I glanced up and added a menacing inflection.

I could barely stifle my laughter, but he could *not* hide his fear.

"Aa? Ah uw e eu!" I had no idea what he was saying and didn't care, yet.

I hit him in the neck again with a paralyzing focus, letting him suffer a moment while I held his head up with his hair and stared hard into his eyes. With the same raspy whisper, I assured him, "You need to give this some serious thought. You know what will happen if you don't. Do you think it's *me* paralyzing you?"

Both of them spilled their guts. I caught it all on a digital recorder so I wouldn't have to take notes or attempt to remember details. I didn't even have to kill them when I was finished. The man with the knife kindly offered a solution in the form of a compromise. He had enough heroin on him to put them both away for a while. I gladly dispersed the drugs evenly into both of their pockets and in obvious places in the flat.

Using an electrical cord from a lamp, I tied them even more securely and texted the address to Carla.

```
Just a suggestion, maybe get people here quickly before they
work themselves loose from their bonds? I will prop the door
open so that you can clearly see them tied together in the
floor. No warrant needed. Look in the freezer for more drugs.
```

```
on it!
```

Taking their mobile phones so that I would have their contacts, I propped their door open with a pillow from the couch. When no one else was in the hall, I hurried away.

While the beginning of that experience was disturbing, it was a walk in the park compared to another encounter I had. The day started strangely, too. I was acting on another lead provided by Carla one rainy morning, waiting across the street from a seedy hotel where the thugs were recently reported staying.

I should have guessed it was going to be an interesting day the moment I saw a large dog dragging a small picnic table behind him. Someone had tied the dog's leash to the table and left him unattended. The light rain allowed the table legs to slide along the oily street and the dog bolted as if he were on a mission.

A couple of minutes later an old man passed by in the same direction. He was yelling and carrying a plastic shopping bag. When he got a little closer, I thought I could understand what he was yelling, "Deeooohhgee!"

"DeeOOOOHHgee!"

He was looking for his best friend, apparently. Our eyes met for a moment, so I pointed down the street. He spotted the moving picnic table and got a horrible look of disbelief on his face, with maybe a touch of relief mixed in as well.

"Dee*OOH*gee! Come *here*, boy! *Where* is he *going?*"

Tossing a wave of thanks and a single, appreciative up-nod my way, the old man hurried off. I watched him for a moment to see if I could witness the reunion, but as I watched him make his way through the busy street, the sprinkling turned to rain, so I ducked under a nearby awning with a handful of others.

The refreshing shower reminded me of the Rocky Mountains, and for a moment I missed my old life. I longed for my back porch and the calmness of the forest in the back yard. I wondered what I would be doing right now if I hadn't moved to New York. Still miserable at my old job, I'm sure, and most likely still completely unaware of my potential. Yet that didn't change how much I wished I was on that back porch.

Several people huddled under the old awning with me, trying to avoid the dirty water rolling over the edges. As I watched for the thugs, the old Beatles tune "Rain" popped into my head and humored me for a while, but when I burst out laughing the guy next to me gave me a disgusted eye. I couldn't help saying to the New Yorker, "Oh! 'Dee-oh-gee'! D, O, G! Funny! Clever name for a dog, no?"

He obviously hadn't witnessed the dog spectacle, or the owner looking for him, and simply muttered, "Freak" in a cracked, dry voice that contrasted peculiarly with the moisture of the downpour.

"Oh, you have no idea," I muttered under my breath.

Gusty winds picked up, blowing the drenching rain around and up into the faces of passersby. Those who weren't huddled under the sparse awnings pushed umbrellas into the wind, or held makeshift umbrellas over their heads, except one guy in a plain black suit, bright white shirt, and a thin black tie who didn't seem to be bothered much. The song "Rain" continued to echo through my mind as I watched the guy continue on the sidewalk without a care in the world.

Then he began acting even more strangely. When the wind increased, he spun around on a heel of his loafers and walked backward against the blowing rain, not even watching where he was going. After a few steps, he spun around and walked forward again, only to snap back around and walk backward a short while again. People moved out of his way, but no one else even acknowledged his odd behavior. He whirled back around and soon faded into the crowd.

Still, the song "Rain" played in my head.

When the shower let up, a bright rainbow appeared between two buildings. As I marveled at its brilliance and clarity, I noticed it was a double rainbow. Nice! Out of curiosity, I moved out into the street between two parked cars to see if, by chance, there was a third one, and sure enough, there was. A triple rainbow! How often does that happen? The third one was faint, but it was there without a doubt.

Only one other woman noticed the rainbows. Odd. Something this rare should be attracting more attention. Several people lit cigarettes and dozens more moved along the sidewalks again.

A clean-shaven man in what appeared to be brand-new camouflaged fatigues carried two large, sagging duffle bags. His attire resembled that of a soldier, but his hair was way too long and shaggy for him to be in the military. The camo pants were the kind that bunched at the ankles, but all his clothes were so new they still had creases in them from when they were folded on a shelf in some store.

The man also had an odd expression on his face that was hard to ignore or forget. His back was to the triple rainbow, so I doubted that's what caused the unusual expression.

He stopped, looked into the trash can on the corner, and reached in with his bare hands. Removing trash piece by piece, he organized it all into piles on the damp sidewalk but set aside some of the cups and bottles. When most of the trash had been removed, he began stuffing paper into one duffle bag and plastic and glass into another.

Okay, now that's taking recycling to the extreme. At least put on some gloves.

I watched him absentmindedly while still being mindful of the thugs for which I waited. I wished they would return to their hotel so I could take care of business and move on.

When the recycling guy worked his way over to the cups and bottles he had set aside, he meticulously removed the lids or tops from them and poured the remaining contents of all coffee cups into one cup. All the liquids in bottles into one large water bottle that still had a lid he could screw on. The empties then went into the correct duffle bags, according to the material.

People walked by and barely noticed him as he replaced all the remaining garbage into the trashcan. When the traffic light changed, he walked across the street quickly, but stopped at the other corner trashcan and repeated the same process. I shook my head and tried to pay closer attention to the occasional visitors entering and exiting the hotel, however, I kept finding myself watching the recycling camo guy, but I think it was more the odd look on his face than his activities that kept drawing my attention. He seemed distant, or maybe even detached from reality.

Rainbows faded and the day quickly warmed. I tried to ignore all the distractions and focused on finding the men on Carla's list, but then I noticed the camo guy sitting on a low windowsill, sipping the coffee cup he had retrieved from the trash.

He was drinking from the very cup he had used to accumulate the discarded coffee and tea, and who knows what else, from all the other paper cups in the trash. I was shocked. I gagged. He turned the cup up and downed the contents, then looked into the cup with disgust and spit coffee grinds, or *some*thing, back into the cup. When he began unscrewing the lid on the plastic bottle, with the murky soda, tea, and juice mess sloshing around inside, I had to turn away.

It made me wonder what might drive one to engage in such senseless, risky behavior. If he was thirsty, he could walk right over to Central Park and drink all the free water he wanted. How does someone become so out of touch with reality that he would behave in a way that would make most people sick?

I don't know. Heartbreaking.

Errors

As odd of a day as it was, my waiting finally paid off. Four guys in a massive SUV drove up to the hotel's canopy. Three got out and the other drove away, carelessly cutting off other drivers. When the three went inside, I waited a couple of seconds and hurried across the street.

They were waiting for the elevator, but the doors opened as I approached, so I hurried over and slipped in with them before the doors closed. I pushed the top floor button. When they got off at six, they turned to the right. Once they were out of sight, I pushed the button for the seventh floor. As soon as the doors opened up again, I rushed to the stairs and hurried down them, hoping to see which room they were entering. Carelessly swinging open the door, I stepped into the hall and found myself face-to-face with the people I was trying to follow.

Not good.

One of them recognized me from the elevator and was immediately suspicious. My reaction of freezing when I saw them confirmed his suspicions. He jerked his gun out of his jacket and pointed it at my chest. The other two followed his lead. Collectively, they escorted me back into the stairwell, closing the door behind us.

"Who the hell are you?"

"Why, whatever do you mean?" Usually, the one being the smartass is the only one who enjoys smartass remarks.

The man on my left looked over the edge of the staircase and said, "Just throw him over."

There was no hesitation as the man on his right raised his gun, intending to hit me on the head first, I guessed, so I dropped all three of them before the situation got any more out of control.

As they all collapsed, one of them fell into me and pushed me down the stairs. I stumbled backward trying to catch myself, as two of their guns clanged loudly down the metal and concrete steps. I managed to get one hand on the railing, trying to steady myself, but just as I caught my balance, I stepped on one of the weapons. The movement of the action on the gun caused me to slip and stumble down the remaining stairs.

I'm lucky I didn't twist an ankle, wrench my back, or break my neck slamming into the wall at the bottom of the flight of stairs. Or get hit in the head by the butt of a thug's gun. Or get flung down the stairwell. Or get shot.

Lucky.

Shaking my head yet again, I picked up their guns, went through their pockets, and took anything that might prove useful later, including two more pistols, several spare clips, their phones, some papers, and the access card to their room.

Before I could finish going through their pockets, I heard a door open a couple of floors below me, and then footsteps. Which way were they going? Down, most likely, but I couldn't chance it.

Slipping out of the stairwell, I headed in the same direction the thugs had been going, intending to search their room. However, the access card had no number on it. I was considering trying all the rooms when the elevator door down the hall opened. Someone stepped out and headed in my direction. Was it the driver for the three *resting peacefully* in the stairwell?

I walked up to one of the vending machines at the end of the hall and tried to appear interested in finding a refreshing beverage. Whoever was behind me in the hall approached far too closely as I fed two one-dollar bills from my wallet into the cold drink machine.

While turning around, I unscrewed the top and upended the bottle of water. The man knocked on the last door on his left but no one answered. He looked at me while he waited for someone to answer, but no one did. I had no way of knowing if he was with the men in the stairwell, so I couldn't just drop him, and I couldn't just stand there drinking water, so I took off.

As I walked past him, he reached into his pocket and pulled out his phone. His phone!

Aw, hell.

If he was their driver, he was likely calling one of the phones that were now in my pocket. I walked quickly, making my way to the elevator as fast as possible without drawing attention to myself. It was best to get away from him, and as far away from the hotel as possible before the bodies were found.

Sure enough, one of the phones in my pocket began vibrating. I was relieved it was on vibrate and not set up to blare some funky ring tune that could easily be recognized.

After punching the down arrow, the few moments waiting for the doors to open seemed like an eternity. The guy at the end of the hall gave up and was hurrying toward the elevators, too. When the doors finally opened, he shouted, "Hold the door!" I did. I didn't want to, but I *sure* didn't want him to take the stairs. He tried to call again once he was in the elevator, but had no bars. I crossed the street, made a block, and hailed a cab.

"Can you just drop me at a subway entrance?"

Once on the subway, I tried to access their phones, but they were all password protected. I would just have to give them to Carla, who I knew couldn't meet until later in the day, so I decided to check with Jeanna to make sure the business was operating smoothly. It was, although she had one complaint about working too many hours again, so I reminded her to *please* try and hire people *before* it gets to that point in the future. I also told her to give herself another raise. A *good* raise. Twenty percent or so.

"But you just gave me a raise a couple months ago."

Okay, she had *two* complaints.

Spending someone else's money is almost always rewarding, especially when you know you are spending it in a way that helps the economy instead of hurting it. The money was now being spent on a profitable business, making more money that flowed into the economy in the form of several employee salaries and payments to supporting vendors.

While we were in Jeanna's office talking, a man walked into the open area outside everyone's office, sat at the guest computer, and logged on. He thumbed through a pad of notes while his desktop loaded, and then began hammering away on the keyboard as though he had a purpose.

A minute later, two of the young women Jeanna had hired approached the man, and both of them handed him a CD. The three talked for a moment, laughing and having a good time. The girls seemed to be a bit taken by him. I tried to talk to Jeanna but kept getting distracted by the three outside her office. He took their CDs and wrote something on both of them.

"Okay, what's going on out there? What are they doing?" I wasn't irritated. They were all making me too much money for me to be worried about a little idle time. I was just curious.

Jeanna looked embarrassed, but explained. "That's the contract programmer we hired to enhance the website software. We wanted reports and the financials to be available online, remember? And you said to hire only the best software engineer."

"Yes, very good! Thanks for making that happen, but that doesn't answer my question. What are they doing? Why are they all over the poor guy?"

Still embarrassed, she said, "Well, first, he's hot as hell, but he's also something of a rock star."

"What, really?" I felt a little out of touch with the younger crowd and the newest music. I watched the girls all but throwing themselves at him and had to laugh.

"Yeah. I didn't make the connection until after I hired him."

"But he looks like he is *my* age. Not that that's old, mind you, but aren't rock stars typically all inked up with long hair and bad attitudes? He's a clean-cut guy and seems responsible and decent enough."

"Still…" Jeanna was a bit starry-eyed, too, but refrained from asking me if I was a throwback from the seventies. The guy ate up the attention, but he managed to maintain a professional demeanor the entire time. Nice, accommodating, and appreciative of his fans, yet he wasn't sleazy or suggesting they hook up later or anything like that. He just autographed their copies of his CD and made sure they saw his wedding ring.

When the girls went back to their offices, still giggling, he returned to programming, all business, as though nothing had happened, but Jeanna continued to stare at him around her computer monitor.

"Okay! I'll leave you two alone then." I didn't get a reaction. She just stared and smiled. Made me laugh. I'm not even sure if she noticed when I left.

I like having an office where people can have fun now and then.

Fountain

Another subway ride at about 4:45 p.m. took me to a random intersection where I had never sent a text to Carla's phone before. A thorough search for traffic cams gave me the confidence to safely turn on my special phone to send Carla a text message.

"I have info and hardware. Can we meet?"

More time than usual passed before she got back to me, but that kind of thing is to be expected from time to time. I understood she had to separate herself from her fellow law enforcement officers before she could contact me, which could easily take a while. However, this time was different. The moment I heard her voice, it was obvious she was angry.

"I'm here cleaning up your mess!" Her sharp whisper cut straight through to my conscience.

"What do you mean? What mess? You mean the thugs in the stairwell who were going to kill me where I stood?"

"Well, there's that mess, too, but that's a problem for later. The hotel security cameras caught you on video."

"Uh oh." My chest tightened. "But I never took off my hat or my sunglasses."

"The elevator camera got a pretty good look at your face, despite your sunglasses."

I was stunned. I might have to run. "What do I need to do?"

"Nothing. I have the file, but I'm going to have to lose it or destroy it now. I don't appreciate being put in this position."

"No, of course not. Don't do anything to risk your job! I will quietly slip out of the country and go away for good before I let that happen. It's easier to do than you might think."

"Oh, you mean don't risk my job by doing illegal things like passing on classified FBI information to a known vigilante? Or meet with a known killer and not arrest him? Or—"

"Okay! I get it. I'm just saying, if you need to turn on me, and claim it was all just part of a sting operation or something, that's alright."

Silence. I didn't know then that she was deeply touched when I offered her a way out, even after she chewed me out. I couldn't help but wonder if she was rethinking her long-term plans.

"Do I need to cut off all contact and run?"

"No, no. No! I have a better idea." Her disposition had softened a bit.

"Yeah?"

"I think now's the time to take a trip to the Middle East."

Reinforcing her position, I assured her I was on board. "Okay. I'm ready." I didn't relish the idea, but I was more than willing to take out the worst of those with hostile intentions toward anyone unlike themselves.

"Very good. Do you want to get together this evening and discuss some plans?"

"I do! Where would you like to meet?" Still wanting to lighten the mood, I added, "Your office?"

She didn't laugh out loud, but I could tell she smiled. "Several bands are playing in the first spring concert this evening in Bryant Park, so there will be quite a lot of people there. At eight o'clock I'll be sitting on the edge of the fountain near Avenue of the Americas, on the opposite side of the park from the library. Meet me there?"

"Perfect!"

All was well until I started getting ready to go that evening. The closer it got to the time I needed to leave, the more anxious I became. I felt that nervous tightness in my chest again, and it made me uncomfortable. The feeling was so prevalent that I changed into clothing more suitable for running.

My rudimentary understanding of anxiety is that it is something humans feel when they anticipate an unfavorable outcome. Was I overreacting? Being too precautious? Maybe, but I still left the house wearing loose-fitting jeans and running shoes. If I had to make a quick getaway, I could. If something *else* caused my anxiety, well, I guess I'd just be comfortable that evening.

Before heading out, I wrapped the guns I'd taken from the thugs at the hotel earlier in newspaper and put them into a large paper shopping bag with handles. Along with the weapons and ammunition, I added the phones and the updated USB drive, carefully cleaning everything with bleach and then handling them with rubber gloves only.

Arriving at the park a few minutes early, I sat beside young, potted elephant ear plants that appeared to be waving to the crowd as the cool breeze pushed the big, healthy leaves back and forth. From behind the parade of leaves, I looked over a dark green, lush bed of ivy and spotted Carla already sitting on the edge of the fountain, listening to some new band wail on about the horrific injustices of being young, broke, and ignorant. The music was fairly decent, as long as you didn't listen too closely to the lyrics.

Not quite eight o'clock, I eased over and sat on the other side of the fountain from her. I watched her for a short while, amused, as she bobbed her head to the pulsating beat of the band. Carla wore a low-cut blouse and had her hair pulled back into a ponytail. For the moment, she seemed to be more woman than FBI, and the attraction I felt for her intensified.

After just a few moments, Carla appeared to become aware of someone watching her. There was a reason she had become a professional investigator. Her instincts served her well. With her expression changing back to something more businesslike, she scanned the crowd but not for long. Her eyes locked onto the first set of eyes she saw looking at her, which were mine. Her expression softened as she returned my smile. It was a tiny gesture, but it felt good.

But then her face hardened again. I guessed she remembered how she was supposed to be mad at me over the incident at the hotel. I stood and walked around the fountain to sit beside her.

"I know," I assured her. "Everything was going so well, and I *seemingly* blew it, but I need you to know that it was either me or them. The guns that they were all pointing at me are in here." I offered her the bag with the guns and the phones as a peace offering, but she just stared into my eyes.

I went on. "All three of them had their guns drawn on me until one of them ordered the others to push me down the stairs."

Still, the staring.

"I was about to die!"

"Yeah, I know. I watched the videos." Her expression eased up a bit again. "You could have simply not put yourself, *and them*, in that situation."

"Well, that's true, but then they'd still be out there, willing to kill people on a mere whim and a hunch. I *have* to put myself out there, Carla. I can*not* let this talent I have waste away, unused."

"Yes, I get it, but think this through. What exactly am I supposed to do with these guns? Check them in as evidence? Where do I say I got them?"

"I see your point, but I couldn't just leave them in the stairwell. What if some kid found them, or some young man with aspirations of becoming a hoodlum?"

"We just should have been more careful. And someone *did* find their bodies."

She made a good point. "Yes, there's always that." I was so pleased she had said "we" that I had no desire to restate my position on the matter again. "So, what do we do now?" In my mind, I emphasized *we*.

Shaking her head, Carla pulled up a spreadsheet on her phone. "I could not believe this. Despite *three times* the number of arrests, according to this report, look, crime in New York City is up." She pointed at red-highlighted cells.

"What? How is that even possible?"

"More crimes are showing up on these reports because of all the extra arrests we've been making. Crime isn't really up. More crimes are being reported and recorded. Dozens of your encounters have led to twice as many arrests."

"So, before we started this, fewer people were reporting crimes?"

"No, not exactly." Carla's expression was thoughtful for a moment before going on. "Because of all *our* activity, more crimes are being entered into the system. Mostly because of the seriousness of the infractions."

"Surely the reporting system can distinguish between crimes solved, and crimes where no one was caught."

"Not this report. Or any of the others anyone pays attention to."

"Well, I'm not going to let these dumbass reports stop me. Somebody needs to straighten out their data and their reporting system." I cocked my head and added as a mumble, "Actually, I could help them with that, too."

We sat for a minute while the band screamed a finale to one of their more popular numbers. When the applause died down, they started another song that was more upbeat, and both of us became lost in thought.

Carla broke the silence. "As I mentioned on the phone earlier, I've gathered intelligence on terrorist locations in several places throughout the Middle East. I think that, if all goes well and we play our cards right—" she winked "—we could visit three terrorist training camps, and up to four other strongholds if we have time, while I take a week's vacation. That would give us nine days to get there, take care of business, and get back."

"Hmmm. Would we need an interpreter of some kind? How would we get there? And don't they have routes in and out of their territories sealed pretty tightly or at least watched closely?"

"There are still a few details I—we—need to work out, but I already have a plan in place, mostly. Also, as a side note," she looked at me sideways, "any suspicious deaths in the Mid-East would fall well *outside* the jurisdiction of the FBI."

"Nice. I'm glad you've been giving this some thought. I didn't even know where to start."

"We'll have to make extensive use of, well, your abilities. Are you okay with that?"

"I am *so* okay with that."

"Is it exhausting, or does it come pretty easily?"

"Honestly, I've never used it for extended periods of time, but I could see where, eventually, it might cause some mental fatigue."

"When we get to those training camps, there will be a need for mass, you know, like you did to those inmate rioters in Texas."

"I don't have a problem taking out an entire terrorist training camp."

After a few moments, Carla commented, "You know, it's a little scary that you can do all that. I should be terrified, but I'm not."

Tearing my attention away from the crime statistics spreadsheet, I noticed she was looking into my eyes, and *I* was the one who was a little bit afraid.

The band began a perfectly timed soft and smooth number that helped reset the mood. Two of the band members harmonized well together, a bit reminiscent of Simon and Garfunkel, and we both seemed to be lost in the moment. I gazed back into Carla's eyes, and after a few moments of hesitation, leaned in closer. Our arms and shoulders touched, and I noticed her warmth. Carla didn't shy away so I moved in a little closer to her perfectly beautiful face.

"Why? Why always the bad boy?" She whispered. I wasn't sure what she meant, but I could make a good guess. The scrumptious Carla Bright leaned in closer, too, and kissed me. She took my breath away with that kiss, *and* my heart. I was able to catch my breath, but she *still* has my heart, and to this day, I *swear* that while we kissed, kids were running all around us and that fountain with sparklers.

Arrangements

In the morning, while sitting at Carla's kitchen table, we discussed our plans over hot tea and fresh berries. Smiling a lot, I might note. More than either of us had in quite some time.

"As you pointed out yesterday, it's not difficult to get out of the United States undetected, but once we're out of the States, being a federal agent will mean nothing to anyone and will very likely be a disadvantage in a lot of situations. We cannot tell anyone I'm with the FBI."

"Understood. Believe me, if anyone appreciates anonymity, it's me." More smiling. If I were witnessing all this joy being experienced by others, I would roll my eyes. "So! Tell me more about these plans you've made for us."

"Okay!" She took a moment to gather her thoughts and then plunged right in. "On the Friday evening when my vacation starts in a few weeks, we meet at The Reading Room in Bar Harbor, Maine."

"Bar Harbor? When I think of terrorists, I don't think of small towns in Maine."

Undeterred, Carla went on. "We have a romantic dinner and spend the night at the Bar Harbor Inn."

"I'm in so far!"

"Saturday morning we get up early and leave behind anything that can be used to track our movements, like mobile phones and anything else that requires an I.P. address. Then at eight sharp, we board the *Katsu Maru*."

"The cat what?" Eyebrows raised. It sounded vaguely familiar.

"The *Katsu Maru*. It's a small, privately owned gambling yacht that splashes around off the northeast coast, catering to high-roller New Englanders and Canadians."

"Interesting." Inside, I groaned and thought again of that guy who had said something about gambling being entertainment for those bad at math.

"We gamble a little, enjoy the sights, *tip the crew,* and then slip off the boat when it docks in Halifax."

"We 'slip off the boat'? Just like that?"

"Yep. The crew doesn't seem to care who gets *off* the boat, especially if the tip is the right amount, and there's not a lot anyone wants to do about it. They were under surveillance for a while, but there were bigger fish to fry and they weren't really breaking any laws."

"Okay. So, we're in Halifax, broke from gambling, then what?"

She laughed her delightfully genuine laugh and went on. "Then we catch a freight plane to Belfast."

"We just *catch* a freight plane?"

"The crew regularly transports people, and other dubious cargo, for a small fee."

"Gotcha. Those Irish boys!" I mixed something of a nod and a wink.

"From Irish boys to flyboys. Next, we'll bribe some Turkish flyboys to get us into Siirt, Turkey, where we'll base our operations with some friendlies."

"Siirt?"

"Yes. It's far enough from the Syrian, Iraqi, and Iranian borders for them to be true Turks, who typically hate terrorism as much as we do. From there, we'll be within 300 miles of the three terrorist training camps I mentioned, which are in both Syria and Iran. There are more insurgent strongholds in Iraq we could visit, too, en route, *and* if we have time there are several other targets we could hit, including other training camps another couple hundred miles away."

With raised eyebrows I remarked, "Impressive. You *have* given this some thought. How do we get to these targets once we're in Siirt?"

"Those are some of the details we'll have to work out when we get there, but it depends on how much money we can get our hands on and keep hidden."

"Oh, I have money. How much will we need?"

"A lot, but we'll need to keep it in bundles stored separately. We have less than six weeks to prepare. How much money can you convert to cash in that short amount of time, without flagging my colleagues, the DEA, and Homeland Security?"

"Enough. Just give me an idea of what we'll need."

"Well, it depends. We could hire someone to cart us around, but that's not always reliable. Distant alliances can be unpredictable and deadly. We could hire some Turkish mercenaries with a chopper, but that's very expensive and not so stealthy. We could buy a desert vehicle, which might be our best bet, although I don't know how reliable that would be, either."

"Okay. I'll see how much cash I can come up with."

Carla stood to refill the tea kettle. She stretched a long, luxurious, and squeaky stretch while she was up, making it playfully obvious that the only thing she was wearing was my shirt. Life was good.

"Are you sure you want to go with me? This could be very dangerous. I'm the only one who *has* to be there."

"HellOOoo! Who are you talking to? Yes, I feel like I need to do this. I feel like I *have* to make a difference in my lifetime."

"That's something I completely understand. Just know that all you have to do to back out is say so. I won't think less of you. You already have my respect and nothing will ever change that."

"I appreciate that, but I won't be backing out."

I sincerely admired this woman. After a moment of reflection, I added, "There's one other thing I feel like I have to do before we go."

"Yeah? What's that?"

I hesitated a moment. Maybe I needed to gather my thoughts. Maybe I was second-guessing myself. Or maybe I wanted her to pay close attention to what I had to say. I don't think it was purely for drama, but whatever the reason, the hesitation worked. She finished pouring boiling water through her tea strainer and looked into my eyes, tilting her head slightly. "I feel like I need to share my story with the world."

"What? Seriously?" She appeared genuinely shocked.

"Yes. In case something goes wrong. The last several months have been extraordinary. I'd like to tell someone about what has now become *our* story, before we leave, just in case something does go wrong."

"How would that work? How could you possibly do that?"

"Well, I have an idea. I noticed that an author I met once will be in town in a few days. For a few weeks now, I've been thinking about telling him my story."

"Is that wise?"

"I don't know. He seemed…genuine. More interested in the big picture than self-gain, or profiting at the expense of others."

"Sounds like you've given this some thought and your mind's already made up."

I raised an eyebrow and tilted my head in a bit of a concession.

Carla's expression was one of acceptance as she graciously asked, "Would you like me to go with you to meet him? I could, I don't know, collaborate or something."

"That'd be nice. I would, actually, thanks." I didn't need help, of course, but the thought of spending more time with Carla was certainly appealing.

We both got up and started cleaning the minor mess we'd made for breakfast while we discussed the plans for the rest of the weekend. We didn't even think about parting ways. Throughout the rest of the day, we kept finding ourselves at all the touristy New York destinations. Museums, the top of the Empire State Building, a musical she had heard was decent, and Central Park.

Sitting on a bench near the Loeb Boathouse, we shared a black and white cookie and listened to four guys with brass play "Saturday in the Park," and whether by design or coincidence, at precisely 3:34 they began playing "25 or 6 to 4."

We did all the things I had been wanting to do since I moved to New York but did not want to do alone. *Easily*, it was one of my best weekends, but eventually, Monday morning encroached upon our fun. I left early so she could get ready for work although I secretly hoped she would call in sick.

My days were full the following week as I prepared for our trip. There were a lot of things I wanted to accomplish before going into the Middle East for over a week, such as a trial run of the gambling vessel to Halifax. I made a reservation for the cruise, but they only accepted cash at the dock. It cost a thousand dollars to board her, but that bought passage, gambling rights, and your first five hundred dollars in chips. You could also purchase more chips from the cashier after the ship was out to sea.

In case things got out of control, I thought I'd bring a couple of sets of two-thousand-dollar bundles, and I used my alternate ID to make the reservations. The ship left early enough in the morning for me to have to fly out the evening before and spend the night in Bar Harbor.

Partner

Two full days of whirlwind preparations and dinner dates with Carla left me exhausted and ready for a break. While sitting at the airport, still winded from the hustle and bustle of airport security hurdles, I slowed down for a moment and thought about the business I'd built from nothing but a website and money taken from drug dealers.

Actually, it was the business *Jeanna* built. True, she had started with a semi-solid business plan in place and quite a lot of start-up cash, but she was the one who pulled it all together and made it successful. While looking at our financials and bank accounts online, I realized that, thanks to Jeanna, there was no longer any need for the original dummy accounts to be shuffling all that money around.

At that moment, I decided to make her a partner in the business, if she wanted any part of it. My phone was to my ear in seconds.

While I waited on the phone line to connect, I marveled at how fast our new web reporting site was. Rock star programmer is right.

"Jeanna!" I interrupted her sentence-long greeting.

"Oh, hello boss!" She said, pleasantly. "I never know for sure if it's you calling because your caller ID always says 'Restricted.'"

"Sorry about that! Listen, I have good news and bad news."

"Uh oh, am I fired for hiring too many people?"

"Huh? No! No." I thought about that for a second, "Hmmm, um, how many people *have* you hired?"

"Three more, totaling eight employees," she said meekly.

"Three more!? Really? Well, do they have enough to do to stay busy?"

"Oh, yeah!"

"Are any of them attorneys?"

"Uuuhh, no."

"Well, okay then, that's fine."

"Soooo, the bad news is?" Jeanna was sounding a bit anxious.

"Bad news? Oh! Sorry, yes, the bad news. Well, we seem to have lost those original six accounts. The early contracts were not set up as well as our new ones. Live and

216

learn, I guess. Cease and desist all business with them and mark all six of those accounts closed."

"Will do, but that's no big deal," she assured me. "We weren't making a lot of profit off them anyway, and it took them forever to answer e-mails and such."

I suppressed a laugh. "Very good!"

"And the good news is?"

"Ah! Well, I was thinking. We have *all* the other accounts because of *your* hard work and worries, so it only seems right to make you a partner. How do you feel about that?"

"A partner? What, wait, what does that mean?"

"Not much, really. You'd keep doing what you've been doing, only you'd get more money doing it, and you wouldn't have to ask my permission to do things, unless it's business-changing, of course."

"Are you serious? Why would you do this?"

"Because you built our entire customer base."

"With your company and hard-earned money."

I had to bite my tongue to keep myself from telling her it wasn't my money. I managed to stay on track. "Also, because if something were to ever happen to me, you could continue to operate the business and keep our employees employed."

"Please don't say that!"

"You'll be half owner and partner, but if something *should* happen to me, or if I just retired or something, the business would be yours."

"I don't know what to say."

"You can say you're going to contact a good corporate attorney who will have the papers drawn up immediately. Just… just don't hire him, okay?"

She laughed.

"I'd like to see this happen as soon as possible. Try to set up a meeting Friday morning to get the ball rolling."

"I will! And, *thank you*, boss."

I could tell she was holding back tears, but I'll admit it. I'm a fan of happy tears.

S. L. Oliver

Sunrises in Bar Harbor are a sight to see. Fresh ocean air enticed my senses and stimulated my mind, despite the bad cup of coffee from the motel. I stood alone on a pier, leaning against the corner of the dock's railing, facing the mouth of Frenchman Bay, waiting for the *Katsu Maru* to begin boarding.

Dawn's twilight slowly brightened from a vivid orange to a brilliant, light yellow, and I patiently stood and absorbed every moment. Glad I did, too. About the time that the sun was high enough on the horizon to read by its light, several dolphins swam by, surfacing and diving, chasing a school of small fish. I swear two of them surfaced near me just to check me out. Beautiful, remarkable animals, with intensely intelligent eyes. What were they thinking? What were they saying to each other?

"Look uncle Flipper, a human!"

"That's right little buddy! Splash him with your tail or wave a fin or something at him to see if you can get him to do some tricks!"

As they swam away, I imagined their shrill squeaking and chattering was dolphin laughter.

Tired of holding an empty Styrofoam cup, I did a "near me" search for a place to get a hot cup of tea. There appeared to be a couple of promising shops around Agamont Park, just off the pier, but before I could will myself to tear my eyes from the beautiful bay, the cabin door of the *Katsu Maru* popped open and a crew member emerged to take down the chain from the gangway leading to their deck. The doors of three vehicles parked nearby all opened in unison and four people resembling gamblers stepped out, stretched, and made their way to the gangplank.

Once on deck, a woman who was obviously hired, at least in part, for her willingness to expose much of her spectacular cleavage, asked us for identification and collected a thousand dollars from each of us. The inside of the yacht was lush with art and furnishings designed to make people feel rich and powerful. An appetizing snack buffet enticed several people as they boarded.

Windows around three sides of the cabin offered beautiful views of ocean and shoreline, and skylights no doubt provided breathtaking views of star-filled nights away from the light pollution of the east coast.

Six named poker tables in the middle of the cabin were equipped with all the modern gadgets and high-tech tools like video capture for cards lying face down on the table, like they use in televised poker tournaments. The sleeping quarters were a bit lacking. Nothing more than bunk bed cots hanging from one wall, reminiscent of the sleeping quarters in wartime submarines. One gambler put it rather aptly. "If you're tryin' ta sleep on *this* boat ride, you're already a loser."

A yellow taxi skidded to a halt outside on the dock and a young man in an old cowboy hat scrambled out and ran up the gangplank. He checked in, paid his fee, and the hostess called out, "That's thirty-six!"

"Full boat!" shouted a crew member dramatically as he and a shipmate drew in the walkway and closed the cabin door. Other crew members out on deck pulled ropes from bollards and stowed them as the captain pulled away from the pier and headed toward the mouth of Frenchman Bay.

More dolphins were the star attractions for a while as they played in the wake of the *Katsu Maru*. To me they appeared as though they were having a blast swimming along with us but, as evidenced earlier, what do I know about dolphin humor? As we approached the open sea, they fell back and eventually disappeared behind the tops of two-foot swells.

I don't usually eat breakfast, but a few slices of bacon and a bowl of mixed berries hit the spot while the crew set up the room for gambling. When land was just about out of sight, the captain of the ship left the bridge to his first mate and burst into the cabin shouting, "Let the games begin!" You would think it was the Olympics, but the crew came alive and manned the exchange stations and dealer stools.

Pointing as he spoke, the captain went on. "We're offering Texas Hold 'Em on the three port tables, Robstown, Boardwalk, and 'Vegas, and Three Card Declared Fame on the three starboard tables, Reno, Blackhawk, and Biloxi!" Each of the dealers waved as he introduced their tables. "And please remember that the dealers work for free meals and tips!"

Pretty much everyone has played or at least heard of Texas Hold 'Em and three-card poker, but I had never even heard of Three Card Declared Fame, so I sat at the "Robstown" Texas Hold 'Em table to stick with what I knew. I noticed it didn't take long for the three-card poker tables to fill up, though.

When people settled in and the last comfortably warm leather chair at each table was filled, dealers began calling their games. Ours made a loud brapping sound with a deck of cards that got our attention. "One of our most popular requests is no limit, ten-twenty blinds. Is everyone comfortable starting there, with blinds going up every thirty minutes?"

Everyone at my table seemed to agree, so I shrugged, said, "Sure," and the dealer began shuffling. I started roughly, unable to place a bet for a few hands, but then won three out of the next seven small pots. I did a lot of conservative betting and folded when I had anything less than a great hand.

An hour and fifteen minutes later, two guys started winning frequently and began betting higher. I figured they had learned the tells of some of the less experienced players, like me, and would continue to win for a while. I won a fairly large pot, but then lost a little of it to the next two hands, so I announced that I was going to take a break, have a bite to eat, and try my luck at one of the other games.

After being down for the first two hours and watching my chips dwindle slowly, I managed to walk away from my first tournament game of Texas Hold 'Em a couple hundred dollars ahead.

Two hundred dollars is not a lot, I know. No one would ever get rich playing poker like that, but just knowing that I hadn't gambled away all my money to high rollers gave me a boost of confidence.

Peering over at the Three Card Declared Fame tables through the buffet glass, I determined that the variances of the game seemed to keep things interesting. From what I could see through the glass, they appeared to be playing with two different color decks.

When a seat opened up at the Blackhawk table, I set my plate down and slipped in while the dealer announced a new player. He picked up the hands lying in front of him and someone said, "Jackson Five!" He quickly picked out two jacks and a five from the red deck and set them aside, face up.

Someone else offered "Dolly Parton!" A nine, a two, and a five were set aside as well. I wondered what it was all about. "Dr. Pepper!" A ten, a two, and a four were set aside. An old man laughed, "Troubled hand!" With a dramatic devil-like laugh, the dealer picked three sixes out of the red deck and set them aside as well.

"Anything else?" No one spoke up, so he expertly spread the remaining cards from the red deck face down, so that it resembled red carpet, presumably, and neatly placed the four declared hands on the "red carpet" so everyone could see them. I must have had a questioning look on my face because the woman next to me leaned in and explained in a whisper. "Get any of those hands and you split the pot."

"Ah! Thanks!" Three Card Declared Fame. Sweet! The pots did not get as big as the ones in Texas Hold 'Em, but the game moved a little faster. After a few minutes of playing, I hadn't won a single hand, so I moved back to a Texas Hold 'Em table.

In a few moments though, I felt like I might be getting a little queasy from being on the water. I had never been seasick before, so I didn't know what it was supposed to feel like, but every now and then I felt something. Oddly, it was like experiencing mild episodes of déjà vu. Every time the dealer dealt a hand, I was struck with a déjà vu moment, like clockwork. Had I eaten something from the buffet that had not been cooked thoroughly?

One player seemed to be accumulating quite a nice percentage of everyone else's chips. The blue-eyed, blonde-headed kid in the old cowboy hat who had nearly missed the boat had one serious streak of luck.

For a while, every time he bet, he won, however, I couldn't concentrate with all the queasy ups and downs. I wasn't winning anything and had anted away most of my winnings, so I excused myself and stepped out on the deck for a few minutes of fresh ocean air. It helped. The queasiness was gone and I stopped having the weird déjà vu experiences.

I played more Texas Hold 'Em during the remainder of the nine-hour trip and found out I was pretty good at it. Or lucky, at least. More than half of everyone who had come aboard had either lost all their money or had walked away from the tables with their winnings, and I was up over eighteen hundred dollars. Okay, yes, this was chump change compared with what I had taken from criminals, but it was more of the thrill of winning a big hand that made it fun.

When enough people lost their last dollar, the dealers consolidated all the remaining players to a single Texas Hold 'Em table. Even at this Winner's Table, the kid wearing the cowboy hat seemed to be the most seasoned gambler. His jovial blue eyes darted around as he studied everyone's tells.

The kid had cleaned out nearly everyone at the three-card tables, and I was determined to get some of those chips. However, the queasiness and déjà vu started plaguing me again. Right in the middle of the hands that were getting interesting, like when someone would go all in, or when several people were raising, the queasiness and odd feelings returned.

Between hands, I massaged the back of my neck and said to the group, "Wow. I just *keep* having déjà vu. Weird, huh?" Several people glanced at me, some curious, some skeptical, but the kid in the cowboy hat glared at me sharply with eyes that were no longer jovial.

An odd man sitting next to him made a stern proclamation, "They say that when people have déjà vu it's because someone has used a time machine to alter time." Most people laughed, but the kid snapped a harsh gaze toward the odd man. The laughing died down when people realized he actually believed what he said.

After I mentioned it, the queasiness subsided and I did not experience another déjà vu, *and* I started winning again, nearly tripling my entrance fee by the time we docked in Melville Cove, right on schedule. The captain got everyone's attention while he stood in front of the door to the gangplank.

"This vessel departs at oh-eight-hundred in the morning. You can spend the night in the sleeping cabins, or you can step out and see the town, but this door closes and seals at twenty-two-hundred this evening. If you're not back by then, you'll have to make arrangements at one of the many hotels here in Halifax. Understood?"

Nods and every affirmative answer you could imagine rang out. "Remember! Twenty-two-hundred tonight, oh-eight-hundred in the morning." The captain stepped out of the way and the crew opened the door. Several people hurried out, but most people continued to lounge around. The woman who had leaned over and explained what the red deck cards had meant peeked up from her book when she noticed me looking around, appearing to be lost again. "There's not a whole lot here."

"I'm sorry, what was that?"

"In Halifax. There's not a whole lot to do. The town's okay and all, and the people are all very nice, but Halifax isn't known for its nightlife, fine dining, or shopping."

"Gotcha. Sounds like you've made this trip a time or two."

"Three or four times a year. I gamble a little, meet up with old friends, meet *new* friends—" she gave me a look "—and get caught up on some reading."

"Very nice."

"I usually sleep better when I'm on the water like this, too. My girlfriend will be joining us in the morning. She's been here in town a few days visiting family."

She marked her place and put her book aside, acting very much like she wanted to talk, so I sat in the cushy chair closest to her arm of the couch and we chatted. She told me all about several of the other gamblers, including the kid in the old cowboy hat, "Chip" Granberry, whose claim to fame is winning that old hat he wears all the time in a poker game when he was eighteen years old, from the legendary Doyle Brunson himself.

I was skeptical. "Do you believe that?"

"I don't know, but that is one lucky kid. I've seen him a few times, and he always wins a lot of money. They don't call him 'Chip' because he's a chip off the old block."

"Hmmm, well, okay. I appreciate the heads-up. I'll keep an eye out for him. If he's betting, I'm folding."

A woman plopped down on the other side of the couch and the two began chatting like old friends, so I excused myself before they started introductions and went out on the deck to watch the sun set behind the harbor.

The trip back to Bar Harbor in the morning turned out to be a heartbreaker. A few minutes after rounding the southern tip of Nova Scotia, the yacht began a sharp turn to port and red lights began blinking. Our speed increased, and the dealers ended the current hands and began putting away all evidence of gambling. A moment later the captain announced on the speaker system, "All hands on deck!" I wondered if they were having a drill or if we were being boarded or busted—or worse.

"Look!" A man pointed dead ahead to a plume of smoke and everyone stood to get a better view. A ship appeared to be burning a few miles ahead. All hands were indeed on deck, facing fore steadily, some with life preserver rings and ropes in hand. I was quite impressed.

As we approached the carnage, we could see there were two ships, both sinking. The larger of the two was bow down with the stern completely out of the water, and the other was bow up with the stern completely submerged, smoke still billowing from her aft decks.

I felt the rumble of the engines, straining from being pushed to their limit, yet our approach seemed painfully slow. People needed urgent help and could be in the water drowning or bleeding to death as the saltwater and movements necessary to remain afloat prevented their blood from clotting. Perhaps sharks or other predatory fish were circling about.

Still, our progress was steady, but slow, as the captain of our yacht held the course perfectly in line to get to the smaller of the sinking ships as quickly as possible. The wait was maddening. I couldn't even begin to imagine what the people in the water must be going through. We all stood patiently and waited to arrive, although some were more patient than others. One of the dealers stood near me and chewed her nails to the point where I thought her fingers would bleed.

One of my fellow gamblers got the attention of the first mate, who stood on the deck below the windows, ready to take charge of any rescue attempts. The gambler shouted through the glass, "I'm retired Navy. I've manned several rescues. Can I help?" The first mate put his radio to his ear and spoke words we could not hear, but within seconds the cabin door opened and a crew member motioned for him to follow. I couldn't help slapping him on the back as he brushed past me.

When we were closer to the disaster, I could read the name of the ship with the bow up. Sleek, elegant, soft green lettering read, *S. L. Oliver*.

Several hands at once pointed ahead and slightly to starboard, and everyone's face turned in unison. Hands could be seen waving above choppy white caps, and the yacht veered toward them. I thought we were going to run right over the hapless individual, but the captain reversed engines when we were within a few dozen yards. Passengers and crew alike struggled to keep their balance as the trusty *Katsu Maru* stopped quickly.

Two life preservers landed in the water next to the woman, who slipped one of the rings over her head and under her arms. Crew members and a surprisingly strong retired sailor easily pulled the woman aboard. I wanted to help, too, but it was obvious they had it under control. For every person helping there were two others already doing nothing but backing up each man who had their hands on a rope.

Shivering from the cold water, a very slender woman wearing a modest two-piece swimsuit splashed onto the deck. Between coughs and gasps, she pleaded for them to find the others quickly. Two of the crew wrapped her in towels and blankets as the captain powered up the engines again to hurry toward an area where other crew members pointed. The water behind the *Katsu Maru* churned violently, and I was surprised again by the maneuverability of the yacht. She accelerated far faster than I thought possible.

Someone who appeared as though he might double as a medic, along with the girl who had checked us in, led the rescued passenger below deck to the infirmary. The poor woman sobbed uncontrollably while reporting what had happened and continued to beg them to hasten their search.

From the southwest approached a much larger ship at quite a clip. Someone simply said, "Coast Guard." Sure enough, when they got closer, the white and semi-vertical red stripe near the bow became evident.

We stopped less than two hundred feet from the sinking *S. L. Oliver* and life preservers were tossed overboard again. They pulled a guy with a head injury out of the water who couldn't seem to take his eyes off the sinking ship. Even when the other vessel slipped under the waves rather suddenly, he watched his ship with sad eyes.

Exhausted from swimming and treading water without a life vest, he just sat on the deck while two crew members tried to stop the bleeding. He swayed back and forth slightly after he stood back up, but continued to stare after the *S. L. Oliver* and his losses.

The U.S. Coast Guard cutter roared close to the other side of the sinking ship, and four smaller boats departed and began searching for survivors. Several members of our crew tended to "our" rescues, but all other eyes scanned the waves.

Even as they guided the injured man below deck, he stared back over his shoulder at his sinking ship. When the *S. L. Oliver* gurgled and splashed her way beneath the surface, he grabbed the doorway so he could stop and watch. With one final plume of water and smoke, she was gone, but the haunting expression in his eyes looked permanent.

One other survivor from the *S. L. Oliver* was rescued by the Coast Guard, but no one from the other ship was found, alive or dead. All hands were lost. Help simply arrived too late.

Before too long, ships and helicopters filled the entire area, but the original Coast Guard cutter on the scene pulled alongside us after a while and ordered the *Katsu Maru* captain to idle the engines. The cutter expertly stayed within three or four feet off our starboard railing as the survivors were transferred to their ship. The Coast Guard crew stood tall on their port deck and saluted the *Katsu Maru* crew for their service to fellow mariners as they pulled away. Our captain and the retired sailor returned the salute with honor.

Through radio chatter, news broadcasts, and interviews of the two survivors, officials slowly pieced together a preliminary story of what had happened. A freighter had overtaken the smaller pleasure yacht and slammed into her stern, damaging both vessels significantly.

The freighter was thought to be unmanned or under the control of someone malicious. The friends and family aboard the *S. L. Oliver* had been blindsided by the freighter. Whoever was steering the yacht may have seen the freighter at the last minute and tried to maneuver away and avoid the collision, but the pleasure boat was meant more for open sea yachting than evasive style course changes.

All her passengers were at a gathering on the open front deck, and the ones who did not survive probably never knew what hit them, although they may have wondered what was going on as they turned sharply a few seconds before the collision. All the passengers tumbled from the deck into the water, but some of them were likely struck by one of the two ships. There was very little anyone could do.

A humbling experience I will never forget. The name *S. L. Oliver* will stay with me forever, like a long-lost friend I know I'll never see again. No one gambled the remainder of the trip, and every single one of the gamblers who had any money left tipped the crew generously. I also made a point to single out and shake the hand of the retired sailor and thank him for his efforts and his military service. Someone tried to tip him, too, but he refused to accept it and even seemed a little offended by the thought.

Those who take being in the military seriously are a special kind of people. Even in retirement they still serve their fellow Americans.

Redirect

"Carla."

"Yes?"

"I missed you while I was gone."

Smiling, "Good! I missed you too."

"Before we go on this trip, we have to brush up on Texas Hold 'Em, Three Card Declared Fame, and open water rescue missions."

"Okay." Carla paused and her smile turned a little crooked in confusion. "Um, what?"

She listened intently while I told her about all I had witnessed. She interrupted once to exclaim that she had heard about the disaster on the news, but had no idea it was even in the area of the route we had planned.

That weekend, in an independently owned bookstore near where Little Italy and East Village mix together, we approached the author of *The Scrapbook Lecture* at the first stop of his New York book signing tour. When we walked in, we heard a disturbance in the back of the bookstore.

We looked at each other as if to say, "How rude." We both tended to treat bookstores very much like libraries and did our best to keep quiet for those who might be reading. But the people in the back seemed to be doing their best to talk over one another, getting louder and louder. We asked an employee where the book signing might be, and she smiled, pointed over a shelf and said, "Just follow the raucous."

Carla and I eyed each other again, neither of us wanting to draw attention to ourselves, but we eased over in that direction. A small but loud crowd stood around a few taken seats and shouted at the author, who sat quietly and listened. When someone finished making his boisterous point, the author would let an off-the-cuff point escape his lips, either agreeing or offering a polite alternative that made people stop and think.

"The Secret Service *had* to be involved in the conspiracy!" shouted some overzealous enthusiast who didn't want to know the truth, but instead only wanted someone to stand up and take the blame for Kennedy's death, or at least point out those who were ultimately responsible. "No one else could have changed the route of the motorcade at the last minute!"

Nods in the audience meant a lot of people agreed and, one by one, shifted their nods and expectations back to the author, who took the opportunity to make another point. "It's true that evidence was caught on film by a Dallas news crew which suggests that at least one Secret Service agent was involved. However, the route of the motorcade was published in *two* Dallas newspapers two or three days *before* the assassination, and the motorcade followed that route precisely except for a couple of unscheduled stops that made them run a few minutes late."

Dramatic gasps and shock from the crowd sounded almost fake, or even rehearsed. "Yes, that's right. The route wasn't altered. That rumor is more 'mis/dis' in the form of a malicious exaggeration. During the initial planning, *weeks* before the trip, the route required a couple of adjustments when the planners discovered they had to turn right on Houston from Main, and left on Elm. You can't enter I-30 or I-35 from Main. You have to use Elm Street, where Kennedy was shot."

"Excuse me, 'mis/dis'?" A woman sitting in the front row was irritated at the terminology being used.

"Misinformation slash disinformation. Something at which the CIA excels, and, as a side note, more than a few times in history, this term was used in a way to make it sound as though they were referring to a person named Miss Diss."

Several of the people who were gathered to learn more about the events leading up to the assassination of JFK did not seem to want to believe the simple truth about the route. They firmly believed the mis/dis, and there was no changing their minds. The author certainly had his work cut out for him, but he did so with the confidence of someone who had studied the subject for many years.

The man fielded questions for quite some time, doing his best to teach people that the truth was far easier to believe than all the mis/dis others have tried to profit from over the years.

Finally, he announced he had time for one or two more questions before a lunch break, but wound up answering four, one being about the multiple shooter theory. A relatively calm enthusiast that had kept his hand up for a long time finally got to speak as the author pointed at him and ignored the rudest of the other people trying to speak out of turn.

"There had to be at least two shooters. Our fine president's head would not have been knocked back and to the left if the bullet had come from behind, as did the first bullet to strike Kennedy."

"And why do you believe there was more than one shooter, because of what you've seen in the Zapruder film?"

"Yes, of course," answered several people, including the patient one he had addressed.

"Yes, of course! Well, there very well could have been multiple shooters, but all the shots that *struck* Kennedy and Connally came from *behind* the presidential Lincoln, and probably from the infamous sixth floor window." Another outcry took a moment to die down. "Okay, so, you all agree we should use the Zapruder film to help determine the origin of the projectile that knocked Kennedy's head about?"

Overwhelming agreement.

"Can we also all agree that the bullet would have knocked his head in the same direction the bullet was traveling? In other words, if it came from behind, his head would have been knocked roughly forward, and if the bullet came from the grassy knoll, it would have knocked his head back and to the left, correct?"

More firm agreement rippled throughout the crowd, although a few of the brighter participants were now silent, interested in where the author was leading them. A few others were starting to become even more agitated, but there was a unified and resounding agreement that the Zapruder film should be used as evidence to help decide from which direction the shot originated. When he was sure he had buy-in from most of the crowd, the author spun his notebook around and had the Zapruder film already streaming in slow motion.

"Watch closely now," everyone waited patiently, anticipating that fateful moment, "aaaaaand, here." The author paused the film before the shot was fired. "This is frame number 312. Now watch his head as I advance to the next frame, number 313." The crowd gasped. Some were horrified by the sight of the gruesome blood, skull, and brain splatter. Others were shocked by the fact that their belief system had just been turned upside down. His head was unquestionably knocked forward.

"In fact, poor President Kennedy's head doesn't begin to move 'back and to the left' until *two* frames after the initial bullet strike, at number 315. His head was first knocked *forward* by a projectile originating from somewhere *behind* him. The "back and to the left" motion is likely caused by his chin bouncing off his chest with quite a bit of force, as it is not knocked violently as it was with the bullet strike. Or, tragically, the motion is possibly caused by the muscle spasms of a dying American president. Continue watching closely, please."

The short sequence played repeatedly, in slow motion, so that everyone could watch it repeatedly and let the truth soak in. Finally. After decades.

Two people stormed out of the discussion yelling at the top of their lungs, as though the author had somehow changed history instead of their minds. Most of the people just sat silently, stunned at how little they actually knew. Some were simply *shocked* at how so few of the facts about Kennedy's assassination made it out for public consumption. Even Ollie had *purposefully* lied to them all, just to make a few more ticket and videotape sales.

We watched the author sneak away while the crowd was quiet, excusing himself for some lunch. He walked into the bookstore's café, and we slipped in line behind him. I whispered to Carla to please order us both something for lunch and waited for just the right opportunity. When the cashier totaled the man's meal, I stepped up, reached around the credit card he had extended and handed the girl a bill. "Take this twenty instead of his card and you can keep the change."

She grinned and said simply, "Okay!"

Smiling a gracious smile, the author said, "Thank you, but you don't have to do that. I typically write this kind of thing off on my taxes."

"Then keep the receipt," I suggested, grinning as well. "I feel like I owe you lunch, at least, after you gave me a jump back at Dealey Plaza several months ago."

His face lit up. "Oh yeah! You left your headlights on. How are you?"

"I'm great, but if you don't mind, I'd appreciate a moment of your time to discuss a business proposal."

He seemed indecisive, so I added, "Unless you're opposed to discussing business over lunch."

"Not at all. Multitasking is my thing." With a motion of his head as he headed for the café, he invited us to lunch. "Join me?" I *knew* I liked this guy.

Carla ordered our lunch while I gave a quick synopsis of what I had in mind, which was me paying him to tell our story. We exchanged small talk while we settled into our lunches, but then I dove right in with more detail about what I wanted and why.

No one was within earshot, so I was brutally honest with him and spoke only the truth in a matter-of-fact way that no rational thinker could believe. I didn't think there was an easy way to tell someone about what I could do, and proof would *have* to be offered, regardless of how directly or indirectly I disclosed the disturbing truth.

Finishing his sandwich without a word while he sipped a tiny amount of coffee between each bite, he heard me out. When I finished, he offered a polite thanks, but no thanks, and appeared to be getting ready to get up and leave.

"Wait, I can prove it all easily enough."

Carla glanced around, leaned in, and whispered, "I don't think that's a good idea."

Our new friend looked at us skeptically and without a worry insisted that we, "Do so now, or I'm out of here. I don't have time for nonsense."

Leaning back and shaking her head disapprovingly, Carla motioned me to proceed with a wave of her hand and a "bad idea" expression on her face, so I proved it to him. He was afraid at first, but his reaction changed to astonishment and curiosity almost immediately.

I could tell his mind was whirring, attempting to analyze what had just happened, yet he was still not able to fully comprehend what he had experienced only moments earlier. "How?" was all he could ask.

"Write our story and find out?"

The author hesitated again, but I hoped that meant he was no longer leaning toward refusing, so I wrote a fairly large dollar amount on a café napkin, turned it around as I slid it over to him and asked him if that would be enough.

More hesitation. Suddenly inspired by the recruiters who came to see me so long ago to hire me for ERL, I took the napkin back, said with a good-natured smart-ass tone, "You're right, it's not a short story," while striking out the amount I had written before, and wrote another dollar amount quite a bit higher.

"Um, okay." He shrugged a resigned gesture and extended his hand for a handshake. The guy was all in. I knew he would be.

As I shook his hand, I couldn't help but ask, "So, does this count as one of my ten indebted deeds to pay forward?"

A snort of an upbeat laugh melded into a quick, "You betcha!"

We met three or four times a week for the next few weeks. First, he extended his stay in New York, then I stayed in Denver for a week while he interviewed me extensively, all the time making detailed notes. We talked on the phone a few times after that and he came back to New York for another week. We became fast friends.

I realized something during the process, too. Paying someone who is doing legitimate, honest work for you with what amounts to dirty money can be difficult. Especially when you're talking about a figure close to six digits. I had hundreds of thousands of dollars stashed in various places, not to mention the nice salary I was paying myself from the company I had created. Still, getting large sums of money to someone in a way that cannot be traced is difficult.

In the end, after much thought, I decided to let the problem be his and hand-delivered a wheeled travel bag full of twenty- and fifty-dollar bills to his doorstep. He had to have known where the money came from but didn't seem to mind.

For weeks, my life consisted of little else but discussing the past and making plans for the immediate future.

Carla and I wanted to make a devastating impact on as many terrorist training camps and strongholds as possible in the short six or seven days we would have. She had told a couple of her colleagues that she was going north to her favorite hideaway just outside Mooers for her vacation, so we rented a cottage for the week and both weekends, and left her phone there, plugged in, so the battery wouldn't die. It did not matter really, as we didn't dare take anything with us that could be tracked or traced back to our lives if they were to get stolen, or worse.

Late that Friday evening in Bar Harbor, we took a few minutes to answer a few more interview questions from our author friend before disabling our last mobile phone.

"No, thank *you*," I insisted as we finished a half-hour conversation. "I appreciate you taking the time to ask detailed questions."

With the speakerphone on, Carla could hear the author as well. "You guys be safe over there. That's some of the most hostile territory on Earth. Not just in the Middle East, but the entire planet. Please believe me when I tell you that any number of bad things can happen in a hurry over there, and within *every* moment exists the potential to produce something completely unpredictable." He sounded sincere and quite convincing, like he knew firsthand. I made a mental note to ask him about that when we returned.

I assured him, "We'll keep our heads down when they need to be."

"When are you leaving?"

"We board the *Katsu Maru* first thing in the morning."

"Well, again, you two have a safe trip."

"We will, thanks."

"Okay, goodbye!"

Harmonizing a bit, we both chimed in at the same time. Me: "Goo'bye!" Carla: "Bye-bye!"

"Bye now." Why is it so hard to hang up sometimes? People just go on and on, waiting for the other party to end the conversation and hang up first. In our previous telephone conversations, we just hung up when we were finished. This time, however, it was as though he felt like he might not ever see us again.

Overseas

The good ship Katsu Maru was just as I left her. I was happy to see she was still manned by the same capable crew. Their boarding routines were the same, and what could have even been the same pod of dolphins followed us out to sea again. However, there were some *mean* card sharks aboard on this trip. Carla and I both lost about half of our allotted gambling budget by the time we made it to Halifax.

We took a thirty-minute cab ride to The Inn On The Lake, near the airport where Carla called her Irish contacts and worked her magic. The inn was comfortable and the staff was top notch. I would not have minded staying a couple more days, but we didn't linger.

Early the next morning we met a delivery truck driver who smuggled us into the freight area of the airport. Money changed hands and we were ushered from the back of the truck into the cargo hold of a plane destined for Belfast. A man with a lively Irish accent and genuinely feigned compassion pointed to a corner of the hold where several burlap sacks were piled. "It gets damned cold back here once we're in the air. I suggest you make good use of the burlap. We'll fly as low as possible, but the air will still get thin."

Forty minutes later, Carla and I were pressed up against each other trying to stay warm. She looked up at me and said with a straight face, "I'm finding it d-difficult to d-d-distinguish between the p-plane's vibration and the shhhhhivering."

Temperatures in the cargo hold had dropped significantly within minutes of leveling out, as did the oxygen levels. The floor was vibrating relentlessly, making comfort an impossibility. "I'm never flying cargo class again. First class only for me."

Carla couldn't stop herself from retorting, "Exc-e-exc-except for the tr-tr-trip back, maybe?"

"Ha! Yeah. There's always th-th-that."

Turkey

Siirt was not what I expected. It's not like I was imagining a third-world shanty town or anything of that nature, but it *is* one of the oldest cities on planet Earth. I did not expect a city that had begun as a settlement on the Tigris River at least 5000 years ago to appear so modern.

Some of the locals wore traditional Turkish attire, but most were clothed very much as they dress in New York City. A lot of the younger people wore T-shirts with anything distinctly American printed on them. Large sections of the city were very old, but there were many new buildings and city sections where businesses and shops were booming. People left shopping malls carrying multiple bags or sat on the patios of trendy coffee bars and yelled into mobile phones while countless new cars zipped by on well-maintained roads.

However, our modern accommodations were built around a third-world style, open-air bazaar. The hotel lined three sides of the market with several stories of balconies overlooking the chaos. The entrance to the hotel was strategically placed so patrons would have to walk all the way through the bazaar to get to the front desk.

Hordes of Turks shouted all around us. No one spoke in the appropriate volumes for private conversations. It was as though everyone wanted to be a part of the dominant conversation in the vicinity. The abrasive chorus of loud voices mixed with the other sounds of the market and became a nearly intolerable racket. Live birds were squawking, goats were bleating, and meat was being butchered as we walked through the bazaar.

A variety of smells assaulted our senses, too. At times, the foul odor of rotting trash or animal waste made our upper lips recoil in disgust. Other times, often just a few steps away, the enticing scents of Turkish delights on an open grill made our mouths water.

Vendors accosted us from both sides and other patrons squeezed between us. Laughing and pointing, she shouted through the crowd, "I'll meet you at the front desk!"

Before we made our way to the hotel door, we had both made purchases. I bought a bag of the best roasted pistachios I had ever tasted, and when Carla showed up a few minutes later she held up a similar bag of pistachios. We laughed again about our similar tastes, but what was amazing was, in that small amount of time, she had also purchased a cheap phone, a pair of sandals, *and* a rolled-up rug she had thrown over a shoulder.

With a sheepish smile, Carla offered, "I'm just trying to gain the trust of the locals."

"Mmm-hmm. And you're doing a fine job of that, too."

Carla threw the rug over my shoulder, pressed her body against mine, and kissed me. Once again, I realized what a lucky man I am.

We spent the remainder of the day in our room while Carla made arrangements for transportation suitable for desert travel. She had obviously made several contacts before we left and had a wealth of information and intelligence on a USB drive that she slipped into her new phone. She even spoke a smattering of Turkish to some of the contacts.

Hanging up and breathing a sigh of relief, Carla summarized her findings. "Looks like we are down to two options. We either ride camels, which will take nearly three days just to reach—"

She stopped, resisted the urge to look over her shoulder, and did a volume check before continuing. The sound of hundreds of Turkish traders in the bazaar below was masking our conversation well enough, but still, she opted for fewer specifics.

"—our first destination. Or, we rent a four-by-four, get as close as we can to the camps, hide the truck, and then hike the rest of the way in, which, overall, is faster than camels, but a lot harder. We might have to walk a few miles through 120-degree temperatures."

"I'm up for a nice walk. You?"

"I'm willing to bet it'll be harder than either of us are imagining or expecting. Are you sure about this?"

"Carla, have you ever ridden a camel before?"

"Nope. You?"

"No. How about a horse? Have you ever ridden a horse?"

Shaking her head, she admitted she had not. "Never."

I had, but that was years ago. "So, it's decided then?"

Carla was on the phone again immediately.

The people who rented us the four-by-four were not like your friendly neighborhood over-the-counter rental car service. We met a man outside what might have been an office building, in a parking lot with high brick walls. He did not ask us for identification or insurance. He just counted the handful of cash we gave him, handed us the keys, and suggested that it would be wise to return the vehicle.

We loaded up, rug and all, and were on our way, however, we did not even get to the edge of town before the truck started chugging and running very roughly. Carla called the man back, but no one answered.

We had managed to get the truck over to the curb in front of some Turk's home before it died completely. People in the surrounding homes peeked through their windows as I popped the hood and tried to determine what might be wrong. Carla called the number back a few more times and between calls, we discussed whether or not we should try to ask any of the locals for help.

It became obvious we were being ripped off when three men in a brand-new truck drove up and started shouting in Turkish. Two of them got out and confronted us, and Carla did her best to translate.

"They're claiming that this is their truck, and that they reported it stolen yesterday."

One of them reached in under the hood and made some adjustment. Most likely, he reconnected the wires to an electric fuel pump or reattached a key vacuum hose that had been rigged to fall off after a few bumps in the road. Whatever he did, our rented vehicle started and began to run smoothly in a few seconds.

When I realized they intended to take it, I lunged for the tailgate as tires spun in the dirt and gravel. Reaching into the back of the truck, I managed to retrieve our backpacks but watched them drive away in a choking cloud of dust with everything else.

Stolen pistachios and souvenirs were the least of our worries at the moment though. I waited until the last possible second to let the two men in our rented truck get out of sight before focusing on the neck of the third man before he could drive away as well. He slumped over and fell against the steering wheel.

"Carla! Get in behind me and drive through some side roads. We need to get out of here *fast*," I yelled, as I tossed the backpacks into the back. Opening the driver's door, I climbed over the thief and pulled him into the center of the bench seat, out of Carla's way.

Without hesitation or question, she climbed in behind the wheel. Making the first right turn, she drove through several side streets slowly and calmly, as if she were on the way to Uncle Coskun's house. I noticed she watched the rear-view mirror closely, too. I had my hands full trying to keep the owner of the truck subdued, yet not falling over. I found a mobile phone charger in the glove box and used the coiled cord to tie his wrists together, and to the seat belt around his lap.

"Someone may be following us."

I looked behind us but didn't see anyone at the moment. "See if you can find a straight road and drive down it for a short while. If I can focus on them for just a second—"

"There! See that blue compact?" Carla was looking out of the corner of her eyes into the rearview mirror.

"Yes. Can you turn a corner and pull into a driveway or turnout?"

"I'll try."

She did not appear frightened at all. Concerned, but not frightened. For someone who was used to carrying a gun and having backup, she was handling the pressure very well. I truly admired this woman. Carla turned a corner slowly, making sure the people behind us saw where she turned. Then she stepped on the accelerator when she was out of sight again and whipped that big truck into someone's driveway.

Sure enough, after a few breathless moments, the same blue car turned the corner and nearly drove by. However, someone in the back seat pointed at the truck and the car screeched to a halt. In perfect English, our captive truck owner said simply, "My sons will kill you."

As all three of them piled out of the car, which had stopped behind the truck to block our escape, they waved handguns and AK-47s menacingly. A wild look possessed their eyes when they saw their father sitting in the middle, not in charge of his own truck. One of them leveled their weapon at Carla, so I dropped him where he stood. The other two raised their weapons immediately and they died a mercifully quick death as well.

I did not want to be killing anyone's sons or any Turks at all. The Turkish people are some of America's very best friends. But when it came down to us or them, it was an easy decision to make.

Motioning to Carla, I asked her, "Watch him?" She nodded, so I piled out of the truck, drug the bodies out of the way, and threw the weapons into the bed of the truck. Meanwhile, Carla backed out, easily pushing the car out of the way with the rear bumper as curtains and shades moved slightly in the windows of the surrounding homes. I jumped back in to find the owner of the truck gazing after his sons, wondering what had happened. Carla took off and punched buttons on the truck's dashboard GPS while driving too fast through varying types of neighborhoods.

Few words were spoken as we hurried out of town. Finally, I turned to the Turkish man, who was surprisingly devoid of emotion, and asked him, "Why did you try to rip us off? We paid good money to rent that four-by-four. We had a deal."

"You Americans. You take, take, take, like you own everything. Such arrogance. And now you've taken my truck and three of my sons."

"I've never *taken* anything from you or your family. And neither has she," I insisted, nodding at Carla. "We paid you good money for a service you offered, but you deliberately stole from us."

"You've taken my truck! *And* my sons!"

I noticed he kept referring to his truck before mentioning his sons, which helped me to realize that there was no point in arguing with someone whose point of view was based on greed and narcissistic logic. He would never admit to understanding that his dishonest actions had consequences.

"What are we going to do with this guy?" I asked Carla.

"I don't know. Still weighing our options."

"It would be hard to just drop him off somewhere, now that he knows which direction we're heading." I indicated the GPS showing our destination, which was *not* our true destination. Carla seemed to stay a step or two ahead of everyone else.

Always the optimist, Carla went on. "It's true that he just lost three of his sons and that he blames us and America for it all, but I'm guessing that the rest of his family still needs him. We can't just kill him."

I grumbled under my breath, knowing that one day this Turk could be our undoing.

Carla looked thoughtful for a moment, and asked the man, "If we let you go, how can we be sure you'll forget all about this encounter, and accept these losses as a part of the price of being a criminal?"

The owner of the truck stared off ahead of us, saying nothing.

"He's not going to let this go, Carla. When we come back to town, he'll be here waiting for us. We need to silence him."

"No, I don't think he's a threat. He merely stole money from us. We have his truck now, which is far nicer than the four-by-four we rented. We'll drop him off in the middle of the desert, with some water. That will give us time to finish and get the hell out of Siirt."

"If you think that's wise," I conceded. *I* did *not* think it was wise.

We drove about nine miles east, then went off-road for a couple of miles and made him get out of the truck. I took his phone but gave him water. As we drove away, he defiantly started running back toward the road before we were even out of sight. That could mean only one thing. He was determined to avenge the deaths of his sons. He could not see, and did not *want* to see, that he had caused this bad situation to happen.

The Turk and his remaining sons would blame and pursue us for the rest of their lives, and very likely influence others to despise Americans as well. I could not have

237

this Turkish gangster, and his sons, chasing us for the rest of our lives. While Carla was punching the correct coordinates into the GPS, I looked back and dropped the man as he ran.

Not a good way to start our trip, but not only had we survived and avoided getting ripped off, we came out ahead, financially. The truck we had taken from the thieves was far more reliable transportation than the four-by-four we had rented and we also no longer needed to return to Siirt with a rented vehicle.

While driving through the outskirts of town, Carla spotted a large parking lot with dozens of cars. She pulled in and drove around until she found a truck that resembled the one we were driving.

"Hurry! Switch plates with that truck!"

I jumped out and used the back of a blade on my pocketknife to quickly switch the license plates. To my surprise, she continued driving around until she spotted another similar truck and again said, "Hurry!" Pointing at another license plate and looking around for witnesses, "Switch plates with that truck, too!"

"Again?"

"Yes. *Hurry!*"

When I got back in the truck I said, "I'm glad you're an FBI agent, because you'd make a devious crook."

She gunned it and got out of the neighborhood as quickly as possible. When we were well out of town, she pulled over. "Let's get those weapons out of sight."

"Okay, what do you want to do, get rid of them?"

"No, let's hide them behind the seat, for now. *You* have an impressive weapon at your disposal, but I do not. I'm feeling a little naked without my nine millimeter."

"Yes, of course."

In a few moments the road cleared, so we retrieved two AK-47s and two pistols from the bed of the truck. We stashed the AK-47s behind the seat, but as we were putting the handguns in the glove box, she took one and admired it.

"Nice," she said dryly as she pulled out the magazine and gave it a once-over. "Laser sighted, fifteen round, forty caliber GLOCK twenty-two. Did you know that the casings on these weapons are manufactured to be *so* hard, they're nearly as hard as diamonds?"

Made me laugh. But no, I did not know that. "Diamonds?"

"Diamonds."

We put one of the pistols in the glove box, but the other she stuffed into the back of her pants.

In southwest Sirnak, we stopped in a town that was too small to be marked on our map. There we filled our tank, bought a couple of five-gallon gas cans, and filled them, too. While we waited for dusk, Carla found a market where we bought several large containers of bottled water, two loaves of heavy bread containing black olives, and a large bag of dried figs, which was all we could find that might last for days without refrigeration.

When the sun was near the horizon, we rolled out of town slowly and made our way further south. The border between Turkey and Syria was nothing more than a razor wire fence in places, separating Turkish farmland from Syrian. If we were on foot, we could have easily stepped through the fence in numerous places, but we would need the truck to travel the long distances between the terrorist training camps.

Near the area where Mardin and Sirnak meet and share a border with Syria, we slipped off the road and squeezed the truck into a thick cluster of Syrian Maple trees. Carla got out without a word and started digging through one of our backpacks. I stepped out to stretch my legs, too. After a few moments of fervent searching, she pulled out a large aerosol can and looked pleased.

"Uhh, whatcha have there?"

"It's a type of insulation, but it's also good for something else, too."

"Ok." I watched her shake the can for a moment and then duck down behind the truck. By the time I made it around there to see what she was doing, she already had part of the tread of the tire covered with the content of the spray can. "What the?"

Whatever she had sprayed on the tires was expanding. She finished quickly and moved to the back tire and began covering it, too. When all the exposed tread was covered, she tossed me the can. "Do the other side?"

I wasn't sure why but I granted her request. When I finished, I noticed she had dug a couple of interesting items out of her backpack. Thermal imaging night vision goggles.

"Come on! Really?"

"Yep. Let me show you how to use them while that insulation dries."

In about twenty minutes, the insulation on the tires was still tacky but hard, so she had me pull the truck up a couple of feet. We sprayed the remaining exposed portion of the tires and I used the saw blade in my pocketknife to even the rough edges that had been next to the ground, still not understanding why the thick truck tires needed any insulation at all.

By the time I got to the last tire, the insulation was so hard that the saw blade could barely cut it. Then it hit me. We could easily run over the razor wire with the thick coating on our tires. Clever.

Using my pocketknife again, I unscrewed the lenses covering the taillights and removed the bulbs from the reverse lights. I wanted to remove the brake lights, too, but they were the two-element bulbs. If I removed them, we couldn't turn on the lights when we needed them. I put on one of the pairs of night vision goggles and began poking around under the dashboard.

Looking over my shoulder and mimicking me good-naturedly, Carla asked, "Ummm, whatcha doing?"

"I'm... looking... for the... fuse box."

"Okaaaay." Carla thought about it for a moment. "Why?"

"Ah! Here it is." Thankfully, the fuses had English labels also. "I'm removing the fuse for the brake lights."

"What? Really? Oh. So we can drive in the dark with no lights showing."

"Exactly. We can make good use of these night vision goggles."

We snacked on figs while we waited for traffic on the road along the border to die down more. When no one was in sight, we strapped on our night vision goggles, started the truck and backed our way out of the grove of trees.

Carla was moving her hand around in front of her goggles. "Can you drive with these things on?"

"We'll find out!" I eased over the rolls of razor wire and headed south into Syria through dry and rocky terrain. The GPS in the truck was all but worthless except that it continuously updated our current coordinates, so we at least knew we were going in the right direction. Fortunately, the area was mostly flat, although missing the larger rocks was challenging. Driving in total darkness with night vision goggles leaves a lot to be desired, too. We could see amazingly well with only a small amount of moonlight, but it was two-dimensional, like a computer screen.

Syria

Driving mostly around the edges of crop fields, we saw and circumvented dozens of small towns. Villages, really. Most of these communities consisted entirely of just a few homes up to about two hundred dwellings. Some were built using local stone and others were made with mismatched pieces of lumber, but curiously, nearly every village had one compound that was larger and surrounded by high walls.

Some of the communities were so small they weren't even marked on the GPS, yet nearly all of them contained one home that was noticeably larger than the others and closed off with high rock walls.

Carla whispered, "The Middle East. Yet another land of a thousand kingdoms."

Lost in thought, I considered her observation for a dozen miles, wondering what life must be like having to answer to what probably equated to local gang members running the town instead of the local government. They were in charge, and most likely maintained tight control over things and people. "Lesser" men probably paid high "taxes" and women weren't allowed to drive or even go outside without a male escort.

Once again, I realized how lucky I was to be an American at this particular time in history.

We were making good time but got held up occasionally when we were forced to wait for traffic to clear on one of the few roads we had to cross. When it was possible, we drove along the darker roads with the lights out to make it harder for anyone to follow our tracks, which were painfully obvious in farmer's fields. Most of the trip was spent off-road though, bouncing over obstacles and finding ways through or around ravines. I was surprised at the number of rigs pumping oil out of the desert, and by how many new ones were being drilled.

"Okay, we're approaching the coordinates," Carla reported. "See if you can find a place to hide the truck."

A water-retaining pond for crops offered the only shelter around in the form of a depression and low water. We parked on the bank, completely hidden from anyone unless they walked up to the pond. Carla stuffed the other pistol into her waistline as well, just in case, and we took the opportunity to empty one of the five-gallon cans of gas into the tank to be more prepared for a fast getaway. We pulled desert camouflage ponchos out of our backpacks and slipped them on over our heads.

Getting lost in Syria at night would not end well, so I made a mental note of distant landmarks on the horizon and found a familiar constellation that had two stars lined up in the same general direction we were headed. Carla noted our GPS coordinates.

"How far is it?"

She lifted her goggles for a moment to see her GPS. "One point two miles."

It seemed like a lot further than that after thirty minutes of traversing through unfamiliar territory in the dark of night.

Nearing the village, we heard the shouts of a large group. At first, we thought we had been spotted, but after pressing our bodies to the ground for a few minutes we realized that the men in the village were either celebrating or training.

"Can you understand what they are yelling?" I whispered near Carla's ear.

"They're not saying anything, I don't think. Sounds like they're just yelling."

"Let's get closer."

We eased up nearer the village, but could not see anyone, and certainly couldn't see inside the high walls of the compound that seemed to house the men doing all the shouting.

"How do I know which ones are the terrorists here for training, and which ones are the villagers?"

Carla pointed her night vision goggles at me. "There are no villagers here. This is not one of those farming communities we've been driving by. Everyone here serves the single purpose of training extremists to kill innocent men, women and children."

"So, everyone dies? Even the women?"

"According to Homeland Security files, women aren't allowed here, or at any of our targets."

"So how do we do this? Wait for them to go to sleep? Take out the noisy ones first? Or start with the outlying buildings?

Carla considered her response for a moment while we watched the community for anyone moving about. "The noisy ones behind the high walls will be at it most of the night. If we sweep the exterior buildings first, we stand a better chance of taking out everyone undetected. If the trainees see each other falling, they might have time to warn others or even offer some kind of resistance."

"Sounds reasonable."

"Can you assume that every structure has people in them, asleep or otherwise, and take them out quickly, one at a time?"

"I can try, but I'd be more confident about it if I were closer."

While we were slowly making our way toward the compound, Carla put her hand on my arm, obviously wanting me to stop. She was pointing to her right, where a man with an AK-47 over his shoulder had walked around the corner of a building. A sentry! We froze as the guard approached, with nothing in the immediate area to hide behind. Carla stood directly between me and the guard, otherwise, I would have just taken him out. I whispered, "Slowly, get down," into the wind.

We had the advantage of thermal imaging tools, but there was still enough starlight to see us if he looked in our direction. Sure enough, before Carla could ease down out of the way, he spotted us and stopped. He started for his weapon, but I was faster. Before the sentry could raise his voice, I focused on his mind and he crumpled to the ground in a heap.

Quickly and quietly, we moved to the side of the nearest structure. I swept through the inside of the building but heard nothing. If anyone was inside, they had likely been asleep.

"Stay with me, but stay behind me." I needed to know where she was at all times, and I was *sure* she understood that.

"Nooooo problem."

Carla pulled on my arm as I was about to peek around the building. "We're really doing this, aren't we? We're about to take out a terrorist training camp."

"Yes. Yes we are."

She tugged on my arm again and pulled me closer for the most awkward kiss ever.

When you're wearing night vision goggles, are you still supposed to close your eyes when you kiss?

Fortunately, those kids with the sparklers didn't show up again.

I shook my head clear, took a deep breath, and peeked around the corner. No one outside the high walls of the compound seemed to be stirring, so I focused on the two nearest structures. Again, I heard nothing. If there had been any occupants, they had not been standing either, but then, it was the middle of the night. And so it went as we made our way around the perimeter until we noticed what appeared to be candlelight in a window. I felt like I needed to look inside to try to determine for myself what these people might be doing.

"Are you crazy!? Can we please just take care of this and move on?"

"I need to know." I moved closer, clearing dwellings along the way, although I could not confirm if I had yet taken out anyone but the sentry. When we were within fifteen feet of the window with the light inside, we could hear people talking, but neither of us could even determine what language they were speaking.

I tried to look in the window to see what was going on in there, but could not. I had to get closer. Carla was shaking her head, not wanting to risk being seen, but I was confident that I could react faster than they could if they were to see me. However, as I stepped out from behind the adjacent building to get closer, I was startled by the sound of automatic weapons firing. I pushed Carla back behind the wall as more gunfire shattered the quiet night in a sustained onslaught of piercing staccato.

Checking myself for holes and blood, I found none, so I checked Carla, too. She seemed fine. Still, the barrage of automatic gunfire continued and the woman with whom I had fallen in love was shaking severely. I could see the silhouette of her shoulders bouncing up and down quickly and her hand was over her mouth. Terrified, I ripped off the night vision goggles trying to see her better, but of course, that has the opposite effect.

"Are you okay? Are you hit?" The relentless gunfire seemed to intensify. I didn't think it would ever end.

"Yes," came back a choked response. She was using the thumb of one hand to point back over her shoulder while her other hand covered her mouth. She was pointing back at the high-walled compound.

"Are you... laughing?"

She nodded, but was now bent over with her hands on her knees. Trying to say something, she gave up, waving me off. She knew I had figured out that the gunfire was coming from inside the high walls.

"Seriously?"

Between stifled guffaws she managed a "Sorry! I've never seen you scared before, and you actually checked yourself for wounds!"

"Oh, yeah, great. Laugh it up there—" The gunfire stopped as abruptly as it had started and it was deathly quiet again. Whispering, I asked Carla, "Okay, are we finished here? Can we get back to work?" I always found it difficult to keep a straight face and act angry when I really ought to be.

"By all means. But, you'll know it if you get shot, okay?" She straight-faced it, too, but I could see her shoulders still bouncing up and down ever so slightly.

We both slowly peeked around opposite corners of the building we were behind. Seeing nothing, we slipped out of the shadows and knelt in the sand below the window. She removed her goggles as well, and we eased our faces up to take a look inside the dwelling.

Suicide bomb vests. Three bearded young men were making vests for suicide bombers. I watched for a few seconds as two of them crudely coated some kind of plastic explosive in what appeared to be shotgun pellets. The other terrorist was sliding the TV-remote-sized masses into pre-sewn pockets on the inside of what could have been fishermen's vests.

These men were knowingly creating tools designed to kill innocent people, including children. I waited until no one was handling explosives, and then dropped all three of them. They made quite a bit of noise when they fell, but no one else in the community seemed to notice

An hour later, I was confident that none of the trainees *or* trainers would ever kill again.

Lost in thought, Carla mused aloud. "There's no way we can leave all these weapons here for more terrorists to find."

She was right. "Well, we can't take them all with us. How do we destroy them all, blow them up?"

"If we blow it all up, that will surely attract a lot of attention we don't need."

"What we need is a timer." Carla raised an eyebrow and waited for me to explain. "Let's throw all the weapons into a room with an exterior door."

We worked quickly and moved all the weapons we could find into a well-fortified room, with the explosives from the suicide vests placed around the bottom of the pile. We wired one of the detonators to the door, which we did not shut, but left slightly ajar with a rock jammed in the doorframe to keep it from closing. The wind would pick up in the morning and set off the explosives.

Satisfied, we headed back to the truck. Along the way, Carla noticed that we could easily follow our tracks back to the pond. "Not good. We were too exposed last night."

"Yeah. See any other tracks anywhere? Did anyone else happen along while we were gone?"

"I don't see anything." Carla sounded a bit unnerved.

Slowly and cautiously, we approached the truck, taking full advantage of our night vision goggles. It occurred to me that we may have done *too* good a job of concealing our transportation. We could not see it at all until we were right up on it. If someone had found it and had decided to wait there for us to return, we would not be able to see them until we were only a few yards away. Easing up to the mound around the pond, we slowly peeked over the edge.

Both of us saw the movement at the same time and froze. Someone was down at the bank of the irrigation pond, about thirty yards to our left. He appeared to be on his hands and knees at the water's edge, looking around. In a moment he put his face right down in the water, very much like an animal getting a drink of water.

"I think that's a wolf, or maybe a dog."

Its head was too small and its neck was too big in relation to the rest of its body to be a dog or a wolf, so I offered another possibility. "I think it might be a hyena. It seems to be alone, away from its clan, so I'm betting it will run from us." I stood and moved toward the truck. The hyena scampered off but the incident reminded us that it was not just Syrians we should be watching for, but wildlife as well. There could easily be other predators lurking about. Or vipers. Scorpions, too.

Carla stayed close to me and offered, "Let's put as much distance as possible between us and that compound before it blows."

Inconvenience

A polite but semi-arrogant Middle Eastern man waited to see how severely the TSA would harass him before he showed them his Interpol credentials.

"You're traveling to Syria?"

"I am."

"And you made these plans at the last minute?" The TSA agent was eyeing him carefully.

"I did."

"Why?"

He knew the agent was just killing time while he waited on his coworker to report the results she was finding online. "I did not know I was going to Syria until this morning."

"What business do you have there?"

"International police business."

"Excuse me? Are you being a wiseass?"

Handing the TSA agent his Interpol credentials, he said politely, "Here, perhaps this will help expedite this procedure. I could win a game of chess in the time it's taking your computer system to return the results of my identity."

A few minutes later a higher-ranking officer joined them, returned his badge, and pleasantly wished him a safe trip. "Sorry for any inconveniences you may have endured. We are still on an elevated alert."

He knew all too well. "No problem at all."

Wildlife

A low rumbling woke me. The sun was bright and I was sweating in the ninety-degree morning heat. Carla woke, too. "What's that noise?"

"I don't know! We're too far away to be hearing explosions from the weapons cache we rigged to blow. We drove over a hundred miles last night."

Both our heads were snapping around frantically as the rumbling became noticeably louder. In the morning light, I realized the cover we thought we had found left a lot to be desired. We were next to a small bluff, which was on our left, along with a rugged line of hills beyond that. The trees on our right were more like large bushes with nothing but wide-open spaces on the other side of the sparse vegetation. It was the only cover we could find when the sunrise started to appear.

"Look! LOOK!! What's that cloud of dust?" Carla was on her knees in the seat with two handfuls of cocked pistols in an instant.

I watched the rolling dust for a moment. "I've seen dust storms before but there doesn't seem to be enough wind for that."

"I've seen dust storms, too, but I've never heard one *rumble*. Roll up the windows!"

I switched on the ignition and powered up the windows. "Should we take off? Or stay put?"

"I DON'T KNOW!" Carla was yelling, obviously stressed as the rumbling grew exponentially louder.

Stampeding over a hill thundered a huge herd of gazelle, bounding long distances in a frenzied flight, squeezed together in an impossibly close bunch. For a moment I wondered how they kept from trampling each other, and then they were upon us.

Thunder escalated to a deafening roar that made us feel like we were going insane as the edge of the herd bounded over the truck. A few of them rocked the truck when they used it to bound even higher and further, denting the metal as though it were made of tinfoil.

A circular crack appeared with a loud pop in the lower right part of the windshield, and then we were startled by a louder pop as another break appeared closer to the rearview mirror.

Carla's eyes were wide with bewilderment, and I'm sure mine were too. She mouthed, "What the—" but the gazelle were gone as suddenly as they had appeared. Then we saw the cause of the commotion. A cheetah was chasing the herd. A cheetah! It had singled out one of the slower animals and was closing in on it quickly.

We watched it leap onto the back of the gazelle, latch onto its neck with powerful jaws, and pull the doomed creature to the ground. We were close enough to see blood spurt from the wound. The unfortunate beast thrashed violently, trying to gouge the big cat with sharp horns, but the cheetah had obviously done this before and knew to bite the neck as close to the head as possible.

Carla was horrified, identifying more with the gazelle than the cheetah. "Oh, that poor animal."

Identifying more with the cheetah, I added, "Yeah, but that is one badass cat." The gazelle thrashed violently trying to shake the clamped predator off its neck. The violence had some dark irony to it as well. By killing the weakest and slowest of the herd, the cat was making the herd of gazelles stronger. In the future, survival would be even harder for the cat and its offspring as it continuously eliminated inferior genes from the herd.

As we calmly sat watching the cruelty and realities of nature from the safety of our truck, the gazelle kicked and thrashed for a full minute before it finally lay still. The cheetah shook its kill one last time, let go of the lifeless neck, and stretched out beside its kill to catch its breath.

Although hard to believe, we had just witnessed a kill in the wild. I didn't even know there were any large cats left anywhere in the Middle East.

Scanning around with watchful eyes for a short while, and still breathing hard, the sleek cat rose wearily, bit the gazelle's snout, and began dragging it toward an outcropping of rocks at the base of the bluff to our left. We watched until it was completely out of sight.

Dazed, Carla whispered, "Now *that* is something I will never forget."

I had to agree. "Me either. I just don't know what to expect out of life anymore."

"Life *has* been full of surprises lately. Makes me realize how lucky we are."

"Yes we are, Carla."

After a moment, she announced, "Okay! There's no getting back to sleep for me now. How about you?"

"No way. Wide awake. And we're not exactly out of sight anyway."

"Want me to drive a while?"

I could tell she did not want to drive, but I loved her even more for offering. "I'm good. I need you to navigate anyway. You handle that GPS like a pro."

With a nod, Carla added, "Getting us to Iran, through Iraq, will be a neat trick."

"Soooo, we're just going to cut across Iraq to get to Iran?"

"Yep." She sounded sure of herself.

"Well, okay then."

We drove through some rough terrain in an attempt to stay out of places Carla knew to be military hotspots, but had to stop on the west side of a fairly busy highway. We decided there were far too many vehicles whizzing by for us to safely cross the highway during the day, so we circled back around to park in the semi-shade of an old grove of date palms. The trees were planted in rows, suggesting they were once part of someone's orchard, but they looked like they had not been maintained for years.

A beautiful and peaceful landscape surrounded us. I could see why someone would want to settle here and plant a date palm orchard. Beside the straggling remnants of the orchard was a rocky hill with hundreds of wildflowers growing on it. Water filled a round pond near the hill, but a closer examination told a story that brought a tear to my eye.

The mound covered in wildflowers was not a hill at all. It had once been someone's home. Now it was a pile of rubble covered by drifting sand. The "pond" was a crater from some high explosive detonation. And if you looked closely, you could see the remnants of tree stumps where the rest of the orchard had been.

Most likely, the place had become occupied by hostile forces and American troops destroyed it. But what of the date farmers? What had become of them? Were they forced to join forces with the hostiles? Did they flee and abandon their home? Were they killed when the bombs struck?

The varying heights of singed and jagged tree stumps seemed to represent the disrupted lives of the family that once lived here.

Carla startled me back to the moment. "We should hide the truck."

Under the remaining date palms were piles of large leaves and dried fruit branches, so we began throwing them onto the truck. We didn't consider what desert dwellers might be living under those leaves though. Carla shrieked and danced as an enormous, impossibly fast tarantula scampered between her feet.

From sheer reaction, I tried to stomp the center of all the hairy legs as it ran past, but it was moving far too fast. Circling around and kicking up sand, it disappeared back into the jumble of leaves.

Carla was *freaked* out. Her face was distorted into horror-stricken fear as she backed away with her eyes still fixed on the spot where she last saw the horrendous spider. And then it was my turn to laugh.

"Okay, you face down hardened criminals with the heavy iron, navigate your way across foreign lands fraught with danger, and walk into terrorist training camps in the middle of the night, but you're deathly afraid of spiders?"

Her frightful expression changed to a piercing glare at me, even as she continued backing away. "*Afraid* of *spiders!?* That thing was big enough to throw a brick through a windshield."

"If that spider had been a full-grown man, you wouldn't be backing off right now. You'd be facing him down."

She finally stopped retreating. "Are they poisonous?"

"The infamous camel spider? No, actually, they're not. They're not even a real spider. Spiders are venomous, or at least had venomous ancestors. Camel spiders might bite you, and it'd hurt, but they're not poisonous."

"Are they everywhere?" Carla was still shaken, but she seemed to be recovering.

I lied to her face. "No, no, they are very rare." They are not so rare. I was just trying to help her cope. Besides, the chances of us seeing another one somewhere else were fairly slim. "They are somewhere between spider and scorpion, but they don't have a stinger, either."

"That's not helping."

"Sorry!" I offered, as I continued covering the truck.

"*What* are you *doing*!?"

Laughing, I told her I was going to finish covering the truck. She covered her mouth with one hand and looked quite indecisive. "Just stay over there, Carla, it's okay. I'll finish."

"Okay. Please be careful. Look out!"

"Why don't you keep an eye out for humans?"

Carla insisted on staying in the cab of the truck until nightfall. I managed to get a little sleep, but when I woke, I noticed Carla was sitting in as small a space as possible with her eyes wide open and hugging her knees to her chest.

"Are you still freaked out about that spider?"

"I couldn't sleep a wink. Can we get the hell out of here?"

"Certainly."

Iran

Getting across the rest of Iraq was remarkably uneventful, despite it taking a day and a half, but the only way to get across the Iraqi/Iranian border was to bribe the Iraqi border guards. Carla assured me that negotiating with the Iranian guards would be far more difficult, but we improvised a plan that might get us across the border.

The truck we were driving was common enough in Iraq, but in Iran it would draw too much unwanted attention. Getting believable license plates for it would prove close to impossible, too, so we decided to bribe the Iraqi guards with the truck and leave it with them. There were only two Iranian guards on duty across the border, so we could easily detain them and take their military vehicle.

We had to add what the Iraqi guards perceived to be a large sum of American currency to the bribe, but they let us pass. They also agreed to turn their backs for a few minutes by taking the truck for a test drive while we attempted to bribe the Iranian border guards. However, the predictable Iranians were nowhere near as accommodating as the Iraqis had been, so I paralyzed them with sweeps through their upper spinal cord until they were cooperative.

Their uniforms were too small for me, but we took them anyway, along with their weapons, all forms of communication, and their tank-like truck. We were hoping this would give us time to get far away from the remote crossing. With any luck, we would have a couple or more hours before the guards were due to be changed.

To help ease their humiliation and increase our chances of success, before we tied them up, I put my hand over my heart and handed them both a stack of American fifty-dollar bills. I wish I could have communicated our intentions to them, after all, we were doing it for them, too.

Our "new" military truck blended in well enough for us to travel on many of the Iranian roads. The body of the desert-camouflaged truck appeared to be a typical military Jeep-style transport, except it was completely encased by an outside shell with small windows that were possibly bullet-proof.

I doubted that anyone could see in, or would even *try* to look in if they were given the opportunity. They would not likely want to take a chance on making eye contact with who should be the occupants.

Once we were as near to our target as we dared approach in a military truck, we had to wait for darkness to fall before we could begin a trek over foothills and small mountains.

Even after the sun set there was still too much traffic on the road to chance dashing over the first few foothills. Time seemed to drag on and on while we waited for the night to get late enough for traffic to settle down.

Well after sunset, we drove off the side of the road into the darkness, until we encountered rocks too large for the truck to handle. Continued on foot, we struggled our way through ravines and over treacherous cliffs, in the middle of the night, wearing night goggles and heavy backpacks. The going was far slower than we had anticipated, but we pressed on.

Dawn reached the Persian valley just moments before we arrived. We pushed ourselves hard to get there before the sun came up, but it was already too light to try to approach our second target. We hid behind a jagged outcropping of rocks on a hillside, high enough to see what was going on within the compound. As the sun slowly seeped its light over the horizon, the scene that unfolded before our eyes took us both by surprise.

A semi-circle of snow-capped mountains surrounded a lush, green valley dotted with a few random trees. A small herd of deer ventured out away from the cover of the foothills to feast upon the healthy vegetation on the valley floor. Several flocks of colorful birds were flying about, landing together in one spot and then taking off again to pick an even better location. A lone heron slowly walked around the edges of a marshy pond and a small mammal of some kind waddled away from the water as the heron approached its position.

"Wow." I was speechless.

"Beautiful. It looks a lot like Austria."

"And a little bit like a Rocky Mountain getaway I love, too." I was having a hard time focusing on the task at hand after spotting a mountain brook splashing its way down into the valley. After a moment, I noticed Carla staring at me. She had an unidentifiable expression. "You okay?"

"That's the first time you've ever mentioned anything from your past."

"What? Seriously?"

"Yes! You know it's true."

Our eyes locked and I assured her, "We'll get there." I'm not sure if my words conveyed my heartfelt intentions when her facial expressions showed a hint of disbelief. "I promise." I kissed her sweet lips and gazed into her eyes again. A long, beautiful moment passed but was abruptly interrupted when gunfire broke the silence. Startled, we both snapped our heads toward the training camp while deer and birds vacated the area in haste. The day's training exercises had begun.

Back to work for us, too, as I spoke my mind. "The way I see it, we have two basic choices. We either find a way to get closer, or fall back and wait till nightfall, losing an entire day."

Thinking for a moment, Carla threw in her thoughts. "If we wait all day, do we really lose a whole day? If we find a way to get close enough to take them all out, what then? Do we still have to wait until nightfall to move to our next target?"

She was right. "Good point." We watched misguided apprentices repeat drill after drill, learning how to work as a team to burst into a room and kill all the occupants. As if one needed to be trained to walk into a room and kill unarmed civilians.

Searching for a way to get closer, I noticed that the creek that flowed through the valley passed fairly close to the main compound. Pointing, I asked Carla, "How tall do you think the grass is along the banks of that creek?"

Pressing her binoculars to her eyes, she said, "It's hard to tell from up here," pointing, she went on, "but I think we can get down to the valley floor near the creek undetected by staying behind that ridge."

"Let's try!"

There were a few places that might have left us exposed to the training camp below, but our light-colored, desert ponchos helped us to blend into the hillside while we made our way down the craggy foothill.

At the base of the mountain, the brook splashed into a pool with one last set of spectacular waterfalls. The day warmed in a hurry, so we stopped at one of the cascades to cool off in the falling water. With the temperature already approaching one hundred degrees and the sun in our faces, the ponchos we had over our clothes were making us hot and miserable. The water was cool and refreshing, and it felt good to get the top layer of sand off my skin.

"Don't drink the water. Just because it's cool and clear doesn't mean it's clean. No telling what's in it. Or what's in the snow at the top." Some lessons learned are well worth sharing. Carla looked thoughtful for a moment, caught a handful of water and smelled it. She shrugged but didn't drink any.

Wildflowers and prairie grass lined the pool where the falls ended and all along the creek, however, they were barely waist high. We found that if we crouched over, we could remain hidden from view, but making our way over mud and slippery rocks while bent over was very tiring. When we had made it about half of the way there, we took a break in the sparse shade of a small tree.

"How close do you need to be?"

"Honestly, I don't know." I had never had the opportunity to check maximum effective distances. The furthest distance I had successfully used my "weapon" was that day at the prison in Texas, and that had been difficult and tiring.

Carla thought about it for a few seconds. "I'd be hesitant to try if we're not sure. I don't want to tip them off to our presence."

"Agreed. Let's just see if we can get to that point nearest the camp. If we can't, we'll try it from as close as we can get."

"Works for me."

Forging ahead, but stopping frequently to peek through the prairie grass and reorient ourselves after winding through the meandering creek bed, we made our way to about three-quarters of the way to our goal. The creek became more and more shallow and the constant crouching with heavy backpacks became burdensome.

Finally, it was either start crawling to get closer, or attempt to work from a horseshoe bend that offered just enough cover, and a little shade. The choice seemed obvious.

We were close enough to smell the spent gunpowder from the training exercises that had continued throughout our approach, but we were unable to see much of the camp.

"Do you think you can focus well enough to start right and sweep left?"

I nodded, remembering that day in Huntsville again. "I'm sure of it, yes."

"If you start over there," Carla was pointing to our right, "I think any that run from what they see could easily wind up in this open area in front of us."

"Okay, stay behind me and spot me. If you see anyone running, or any I'm missing, let me know."

Carla got behind me on the opposite bank of the creek with her head barely peeking over the prairie grasses. "Ready!"

As she suggested, I began dropping terrorists as fast as I could. Carla was right. Screaming with terror, hardened radicals abandoned their training and ran from the compound, scattering in all directions, but mostly out into the open directly in front of us. I waited until most of them appeared to be exposed and took them all out.

I guessed some of them had run in the opposite direction and were still running on the other side of all the structures. "Stay with me!"

"Right behind you!" Carla put her hand on my shoulder so I'd know exactly where she was at all times.

We scrambled out of the creek and ran to the edge of the building closest to us. I did my best to clear the space on the other side of all the structures, but before we reached any of the buildings, I heard trucks starting and taking off. Unfortunately, by the time we made it to the southeast corner of the nearest structure, four vehicles were heading roughly north.

I focused on the fleeing trucks intensely, and one by one they turned into slow arcs, with two of them crashing into each other and becoming tangled into a pile of wreckage.

Carla pointed northwest where several people were running. I swept over them and watched them all drop. The only thing moving was one truck that was still swinging in a wide arc, but slowing somewhat. I focused through every structure in the area. We heard one crashing noise that probably meant someone had been hiding within.

"How do we know I got them all?"

"I don't know, but maybe we need to stick to doing this at night."

"Yeah."

Carla said exactly what I was thinking. "I don't like being out in the open like this."

"Me either. Do we have time to destroy their weapons?"

"I don't think we have a choice."

"I wish your colleagues at the FBI could just call in an air strike or something."

Compared to our first target, this training camp was very poorly stocked. Still, there were dozens of AK-47s and many thousands of rounds of ammunition. We parked one of their trucks on top of them, punched a hole in the fuel tank, and lit it all on fire. Before the ammunition had time to become hot enough to go off, we drove away in one of their other trucks. Quickly.

Even though we chose an old, Soviet-era surplus six-by-six, it barely made it up a hundred feet of the rugged foothill. The ground was just too rocky. We torched the junk and set out on foot again.

Near the top of the pass, as we scrambled over the rough terrain, I noticed someone in the hills quite a distance away from us who appeared to be watching the training camp burn. We had no way of knowing if he had seen us yet, but his gaze was fixed upon the carnage in the valley.

"Can you take him out from here?"

"Maybe, but what if he's not one of them? What if it was just the smoke that attracted his attention?"

"There's little chance of that. All the people in this area work to support this terrorist organization in some capacity. Feeding them, supplying them with the heroin hydrochloride that they trade for the weapons we just destroyed."

Taking turns with the binoculars, it was difficult to tell if he was friend or foe. He was wearing a heavy black vest over a white shirt that matched his long, full beard. On his head he wore a knitted toboggan that anyone's aunt could have made.

"Okay." Carla conceded after reconsidering, "He could easily have been forced into supporting this terror organization."

"Let's just move on then and let him be." I doubted if the man had seen us, and he was too old to be a terrorist in training.

"Agreed." Carla wasted no words or time. She just moved off silently, staying low enough behind the tumble of boulders to remain hidden from the Iranian.

We both glanced back occasionally, keeping an eye out behind us, and every now and then one of us would swear we saw what might have been the man we had seen earlier following us.

"We can't allow anyone, friend or foe, to follow us or identify us. And if his intentions were honest, he'd be trying to get our attention instead of sneaking around behind our backs, closing in on us. I think you should sweep the area and clear out anyone following us."

"Okay. I'm not happy about it, but I think you're right. I'll try." I swept the rugged terrain above us several times but had no way of knowing if my efforts were successful. "Should we go back up and check?"

"*I'm* not going back up there. I'm exhausted. Going downhill only."

I had to agree. "Let's just keep a watchful eye behind us then, alright?"

Over her shoulder, as she did a semi-controlled slide down the side of a boulder, Carla simply said, "Without a doubt."

Influences

Roughly five hundred miles east was our next target, in the very heart of Iran. The intel Carla had retrieved from Homeland Security indicated that this heavily fortified compound was more of a weapons cache than a terrorist training facility. The site included a military-grade targeting facility where many young terrorists learned to fire automatic weapons into simulated crowds. It had to be destroyed.

Making good time on a busy highway, we drove through several towns that were as modern as any cities you would find in America. I was surprised to see a large number of signs in English, too. Maybe even more than we had seen in Turkey.

Dozens of buildings featured designs with such architectural grace and beauty they could easily have been in New York or San Francisco, and very few of the thousands of people we saw were wearing traditional Iranian attire. Almost everyone wore western style clothing. There were even occasional glimpses of advertisements with the familiar red Coca-Cola logo.

Again, westernized cityscapes were *not* what I expected, but we soon found ourselves back in typical farmland, approaching our final target. A wheat field ended abruptly when jagged, rocky hills began pushing their way up through the fertile farmland. The harsh terrain we encountered made us appreciate the durability of our transportation, but our progress was eventually impeded by small cliffs and steep hills, so we gathered our backpacks and took off at a trot.

Witnesses

An angry group of young men chatted excitedly atop their camels and pointed at an Iranian military vehicle making its way over rocky terrain in the general direction of their terrorist cell's weapons warehouse. They were dressed in anciently traditional Arab garb, riding single-hump camels with a lineage that could be traced back nearly as long as their own family lines. But they used high-tech binoculars to watch the intruders and carried satellite phones and fully automatic assault rifles.

One of the individuals in the group had the good fortune of being the first-born son of a wealthy oil man from Saudi Arabia. Minimal efforts on his part were enough to maintain a large following of other like-minded, idealistic young men.

Speaking in Arabic—not Farsi, but Arabic, the well-spoken leader demanded answers from his followers. Roughly translated into English and rich with arrogance, he asked as though he thought all the Iranian soil around him was his simply because he was standing on it, "Why is the Iranian military invading our land?"

The others stammered around, with no real answers until the arrogant one interrupted them again. "We will follow them. Omar, can I count on you to ride back to camp and have couriers fetch every weapon and able body in camp?"

"Yes, Mohammed."

"Make sure they remain out of sight. I don't want to tip off these Iranian pigs."

"Yes, Mohammed."

An arrogant glance inspired the weaker man to prod his camel.

Tracks

We didn't trot long. Rocky and broken landscapes challenged us for two solid hours, but the rough terrain gradually changed into loose soil and then dunes that were even harder to traverse. Shifting sand slowed our pace, but we forged on knowing our target was reachable by nightfall. We were so focused on getting to our destination that we did not notice the billowing black smoke about ten or twelve miles behind us.

Sweating profusely in the midday sun had caused a layer of sand to settle in our perspiration. As Carla was mumbling something about needing a shower in the worst way possible, we cleared the pass between two dunes and spotted the training camp between two more slopes.

Seeing our target made us more aware of our situation. Despite our desert-camo attire, we were clearly visible because of the dark shadows we were casting on the light sand. Also impossible to hide were the miles of tracks we were leaving.

Keeping the tallest of the dunes between us and the camp, we moved in as close as we dared in the daylight.

Vehicle

Four remaining angry young Arabs followed tire tracks until they found the military vehicle stopped before a ravine with walls too steep for it to navigate. They dismounted their camels and carefully surveyed the truck and the surrounding area using binoculars capable of taking digital images.

"I see two sets of footprints on the other side of the chasm."

"Did anyone stay with the vehicle?" Mohammed had a way of asking questions that would be impossible to answer without great personal risk.

"I am unable to see within. The windows are small and darkened."

"You will need to get closer then. Take Abeeb. Kill any of the remaining Iranian soldiers and burn the bodies with the vehicle."

Thermite

Before the sun went down, several people lazily rode into camp on the backs of two-hump camels. A few minutes later several departed, heading in the same direction from which the first riders appeared.

"Do you think you can take out those riders without hurting the camels?"

"I can try." Focusing as narrowly as I could, I took them out one by one, starting with the ones in the rear and working my way forward. I had them all in the sand before anyone realized anything was wrong.

"You are getting very good at this."

For a moment I considered how incredibly insensitive we had become. Killing people should not be so easy. I should be feeling remorse or regret. Guilt. I tried to force myself to feel something, which is a little like forcing yourself to go to sleep. It just doesn't work that way. I felt nothing.

Why should I care?

These people would rather doom all future generations of Americans to stone-aged living than grant a single woman basic human rights. They would completely undermine freedom *everywhere*, if they could, or kill us where we stood if they had half a chance, along with any children who happened to be nearby.

I found it hard to feel anything but relief when considering the deaths of a group of terrorists. Callous? Or survival?

In a few minutes, the camels all wandered off toward the desert sunset together.

"Hopefully, I can take out the remaining extremists without hurting any of their camels, too. I sure would like to try to ride a couple back to the truck."

"Not a bad idea." Her words did not fully connect with her facial expression as she eyed the camels warily.

With an orange and black sky looming over a sandy horizon, we hydrated thoroughly, secured our backpacks, and moved in closer. I dropped the sentries quickly and then several men sitting around a large campfire.

This "heavily fortified compound" was far too easy to approach and disable. We both looked around cautiously in disbelief and agreed to hold back and wait a few minutes to see if we missed anyone. One last sentry made his way back to camp about a half hour later, but no one else seemed to be around.

We made our way down a sand dune and into camp, which consisted of two crudely built structures. One was a small building that served as sleeping quarters and the other was a long, windowless building packed tightly with hundreds of crates, which were full of weapons and ammunition.

"This was just *way* too easy," I mused. Carla instinctively moved closer to me as we stood back-to-back in the doorway of the elongated building. We peered into the darkness of the weapons warehouse while keeping a watchful eye on the surrounding area. She had pulled out her flashlight and was looking at the crates. There was a mixture of English, Russian and Chinese writing that made it hard to know at a glance what was in all the crates, but her light landed on a crate and she stared at it for a moment.

"There."

"What?" I had no idea what she meant.

"That's how we'll destroy these weapons."

Her light was centered on the word THERMITE. "Thermite? Some kind of incendiary weapon, I'm guessing."

"Uh, YE-ah! Simple, but very effective. It's nothing but one part aluminum and three parts iron oxide, but it'll burn through a foot of steel in seconds."

Nodding as if I believed her, I said simply, "That'll work."

"We just need something to ignite it, like a hand grenade, or maybe some C4."

We stepped in and searched the warehouse. Moments later, Carla lit up. "Oh! Look at this! Help me!" She was dragging a heavy crate out from under a shelf. We pulled it out and used one of the Bowie-like knives she had so thoughtfully packed in our backpacks to open it. "RPGs, baby! I always wanted to fire one of these."

I had to laugh a little because, admittedly, I always wanted to fire one, too. The crate contained one launcher and four rockets so I looked at her, grinning, and asked, "Two apiece?"

Working quickly through the last few minutes of the sunset, we poured the thermite under the crates of ammunition that would best serve to help destroy the other weapons in the warehouse. I threw the RPG crate atop one shoulder and we hustled off into the cooling nightfall.

Rage

"There!" The young Arab man looked through his binoculars and pointed at two people hurrying out of their warehouse carrying a large wooden crate. "They are stealing our weapons!" Two of his companions and at least half the couriers that had joined them raised their rifles and began to take aim, but the leader among them calmly stopped them.

"No. Wait. Let us see what they are doing. If they were stealing weapons, they would be carrying a lot more than that. We will continue to follow these Iranian military thugs so that we may learn exactly what they are doing in our lands."

The two intruders stopped at the base of a dune. In a few moments, a flashlight lit their faces and the contents of the crate. The man with the binoculars reported what he saw, "Those two are not Iranian. They appear to be Americans or Brits."

Taking the binoculars, the leader simply said, "Hmmm," as he watched them. Suddenly, a rocket blasted from the launcher and violently slammed into the warehouse with an extremely loud explosion. Other detonations, large and small, followed in a chain reaction as the Arabs lay in the sand, stunned.

"They are destroying our weapons!" The young Arabs were distraught at the loss and could not understand why Mohammed had not intervened. They collectively pointed their weapons back at their two enemies.

"Wait," commanded Mohammed. He wasn't worried. He could easily replace the destroyed weapons. Spending his father's money was something at which he excelled. "Let us observe and learn about these intruders." He stood with the binoculars to his eyes and continued to watch.

However, when he saw a *woman* firing the rocket launcher, his calm demeanor quickly morphed into fury. His face became contorted and the veins in his forehead and neck glistened in the yellow, fiery glow. More explosions fueled more rage.

Windstorm

"Give me that thing!" Carla shouted over the explosions. "There won't be anything left in a minute."

I handed her the launcher, still grinning. "Fire all three rounds as fast as you can and let's get the hell out of here." She took a knee and placed the launcher on her shoulder. I loaded a grenade and patted her arm. "Hit it!"

"Want, to, be sure." Carla drew in a breath and held it before aiming one last time and pulling the trigger. The RPG flung itself across the camp, illuminating a trail of sand through the darkness as it traveled a mere three feet off the ground. She was dead on, hitting the distant warehouse within a couple of feet of the center.

Another huge fireball mushroomed into the night air and we stared in awe for a few moments. Snapping out of it, I loaded the remaining RPGs for her as she fired them and knocked holes in each end of the warehouse. The brilliant light coming from the inferno was too intense to view directly, or even indirectly. I turned my back and noticed that the light was bright enough to wash out the starlight completely.

"That's the thermite burning. Our job here is done." With that, she dropped the launcher back into the crate, whipped out a GLOCK, and emptied her clip firing at the launcher. "No one will ever use *that* again."

"I guess not," I mused. "*Now* our job here is done."

We began the trek back to our stolen vehicle by following our own footprints, which were still obvious even in the dark away from the burning weapons cache. A nighttime wind steadily increased though, and obliterated all our tracks, so we relied on our GPS to get us back to our vehicle. We were both relieved that our footprints had been blown away.

When we were partially through the rocky area of our return trek, the wind and the chill became too much for us to bear. The temperature had dropped considerably and the wind was blowing sand into our eyes and mouths. We decided to stop and try to get out of the elements for a while. The downwind side of a rock outcropping seemed like a good place to get out of the wind. My poncho became a makeshift tent under which we spooned for warmth, wrapped in her poncho.

As we lay there cuddling in our cozy, improvised tent, her face aglow from the indirect beam of a flashlight, the thought of romance crossed my mind. I leaned over to kiss her and felt the grinding of the sand in my clothes next to my skin. The uncomfortable reminder changed my romantic kiss into a goodnight kiss. I closed my eyes, but instead of going to sleep, I began to wonder how humans managed to survive in desert regions like this.

Command

Speaking loudly so that his voice could be heard through the high winds, the group's leader set his plan in motion. "Omar, stay here with half the couriers. Continue to follow them when they awaken. And do not let them retreat should they attempt such a futile maneuver."

"Yes, Mohammed."

Addressing half the mounted couriers, Mohammed commanded with confidence, "Omar is in charge in my absence."

Omar swelled with pride at being left in charge. Less than a week ago he had arrived back home after dropping out of a university in France. His parents knew nothing of this radical change and would not understand his feelings of *needing* to join his childhood friends' Jihad.

Mohammed urged his camel forward with several others in tow while Omar watched them leave.

"Prepare yourselves, my friends." His inflated ego getting the best of his judgment, Omar issued his first command decision. "At dawn, we will approach and kill the infidels for destroying the means of protecting ourselves."

Threat

Something had wrested me from a fitful, unsatisfying sleep. The remnants of a dream clouded my mind and I was not sure if the sounds I remembered from seconds earlier were part of my dream, or were what woke me. I lifted the edge of the poncho we had draped over us and could see the beginnings of sunrise. I moved slowly in case the desert-colored camouflage was indeed hiding us. The wild wind had died down but a cool, gentle breeze continued.

A shuffling sound nearby caused me to freeze for a few moments.

Carla stirred as I began pulling the poncho back again. I put my finger to her lips and softly shushed her, trying very hard not to sound like Elmer Fudd. "Shhh… Be very, very quiet." Her eyes popped open and she went from groggy to full alert in less than a second.

We both listened intently, lying perfectly still except for the poncho I was slowly moving so that we could see. An unidentifiable sound caused us to look at each other for answers that neither of us seemed to have. The sound was becoming less noticeable, as if it were moving away from us, so I began uncovering us faster so we could face this new challenge. In a moment, the source of the sound came into view. A lone, saddled camel trotted off in the distance.

"That couldn't be good," I whispered into Carla's ear. We both turned in the direction where the camel tracks originated, but could see nothing because of the rocks and hills.

Carla put her lips near my ear and whispered, "Someone followed us."

"Looks like it."

"Can you sweep the entire area?"

Hesitant, I asked, "I could, but what if they are not hostile?"

"Then they wouldn't be following us, and they wouldn't be quietly moving around at dawn."

She was probably right, but I could not stop myself from investigating first. I sat up slowly, scanning the area and trying to see over the boulders we had camped beside. Carla did the same, with both of us paying particularly close attention to the direction from which the camel had appeared. Seeing nothing, we stood and expanded our search. There did not seem to be anyone in the area.

Still whispering, I asked Carla, "Should we follow the camel's tracks, or hightail it out of here?"

"If we don't take out whoever is out there, they will easily be able to follow our tracks. We'll be sitting ducks out in the sand."

"Ok," again, she was right. "We'd be heading in the wrong direction though, so how far should we go? A mile? Ten miles?"

"I don't know. As far as we need to?"

Keeping the rising sun to our backs, we paralleled the tracks, easing over each hill and even using a mirror she produced from her backpack to peer over dunes and around rock outcroppings. We did not have to go far. We heard other camels bleating and nuzzling, so we approached the source of the noise cautiously. Peeking over a hilltop, between a rock and a rare clump of bushes, we saw what appeared to be a camp of Iranians, still asleep.

Carla speculated in a hushed whisper as she tried to get a better view with the binoculars, "If they were asleep, *surely* the noise from the camels would have woken them up by now."

"Maybe they're in a drunken stupor," I offered.

"While following us? What are the chances that a traveling group of Iranians just happened to camp near us, here in the middle of nowhere?" Handing me her binoculars, she added, "See what you think."

I focused on a couple of them and could see that they appeared to have fallen where they stood. I had seen people fall like that far too often not to recognize it. No longer whispering, I said, "Those people aren't sleeping. They are dead."

"Dead? Are you sure?" She took the binoculars and refocused the lenses. "I don't see any blood."

While Carla tried to verify my claims, I watched for any other movement. I thought I saw something that did not quite look like rock or sand about a hundred yards northwest. I tapped my companion on the arm, pointed, and returned to whispering. "Over there,"

In a moment, Carla said, "Could be another one of their camels."

"See any tracks going in that direction?"

She paused. "No. No, I don't. Could be a turban we're seeing, too."

"Do we investigate, or get the hell out of here?" I was leaning toward investigating, but did not have a plan. "Like you said, we'll be very easy to follow in this sand."

"Yeah. And if that is a turban, and it belongs to the people who killed this bunch, they are very likely watching us right now."

In agreement, I added, "Yeah, and I'm guessing they are about as fond of witnesses as we are."

As we discussed options, and traded the binoculars back and forth, a camel partially walked out from behind the rocks where we thought we had seen a turban. We both breathed a sigh of relief. Without the element of surprise, our party of two would not stand a chance against a large group.

We wanted to believe that what we saw was simply a camel, although deep down I think we both knew that there was more to the story. Not wanting to risk being seen, we chose not to investigate the dead bodies we had found.

Dissent

"We cannot wait for Omar; the infidels are awake and up now. We must reach their vehicle before they do, for I want to witness their reaction when they see it has been destroyed."

Abeeb wondered why the intruders had been allowed to destroy their entire weapons cache. He felt that, had the armament been *his* responsibility, he would not have allowed anyone near it. The young Arab had doubts about the effectiveness of Mohammed's leadership from the beginning, but his father was the source of their funding, so he continued to follow.

They hurried through the sand and rocky terrain so they would have time to set up an ambush for the two infidels when they came back to their burned truck.

Safety

Walking backwards through the dry ravine to keep watch behind us, I asked over my shoulder, "This is exhausting, are we close?"

"Yes, we have to keep moving."

My legs were burning, my feet hurt and my lungs ached from breathing hot, dry air. I walked normally for a while. "We're not close, are we?"

"Well, we have another three miles to go." She stopped and gulped her water until every drop was gone.

"Here, I have plenty left." I offered her my last water bottle but she did not take it.

"Drink," she insisted.

I obliged, but only drank about a third of it and put it away. We powered through the last few miles but slowed as we approached "our" vehicle. We wanted to scout the area to make sure no one had happened along and found it.

When we were close, Carla peeked over the edge of a ravine with her binoculars and immediately made a discouraging sound. She turned around with a somewhat defeated expression as she slid down the ravine wall a couple of feet.

"What? What do you see?"

She handed me the binoculars and I focused them on the burned-out shell of our stolen Iranian military vehicle.

"All our supplies." Hesitating, she added, "Our *water!*" Carla was shaking her head.

I scanned the area looking for signs of anyone left in the area.

Carla continued to lament, "Our means to get back! *Why* didn't we take a couple of those camels?"

"Should we see if we can salvage anything?" I was hoping some of the water survived.

"I'm sure we'd be ambushed." Having said that, she took back the binoculars and began frantically searching all around us, whispering, "And I'm sure that whoever did this is watching us right now." She scrambled to the top of the ravine again for a visual scan. The wind blowing across her ears prevented her from hearing any signs of anyone approaching, so she slipped in her earplugs to see if that helped. It didn't, so she slid back down into the ravine.

I could see nothing but desert. No signs of any other life. I noticed that it was close to high noon, so it was not like they would predictably have their backs to the sun. They could be anywhere in the rocks or in the same network of canyons and ravines as us.

Searching the area with binoculars was proving to be a waste of time, and the wind whistling through the ravine covered any sounds they made, so I made a couple of suggestions. "Do we find high ground and stand guard till they show themselves, or do we get on the move now?"

Carla had taken the binoculars away from her eyes and was standing very still, staring up the ravine over my shoulder. She pulled the gun from her belt and switched off the safety.

Suffering

"I was not able to see their faces!" Anger seemed to ooze from the pores in Mohammed's face. Pointing to four of his followers, he commanded, "You two, and you two. Flank them on either side of the small canyon they are in and fill the infidels with lead."

"Yes, Mohammed," they all agreed.

"Remember your training! Aim for the belly only and allow them to die a long and difficult, *suffering* death."

Chase

"Shhh! Listen!" Carla was still looking over my shoulder up the ravine. Suddenly, bad things started happening fast. The moment I heard something behind me, she leaned around my body and opened fire while yelling "Get down!"

Hers was not the only firearm I heard. Whoever was behind me opened fire, too. As I turned to sweep them dead, a hail of lead implanted itself into the ravine wall beside me and something burned my arm. I could hear the whir of bullets whizzing by me over the extremely loud pops of high-powered cartridges.

Carla dove into the rocks, still firing her GLOCK.

I saw movement coming from the other end of the ravine. A rifle barrel came into view and pointed straight at Carla so I swept that entire area with the most vicious focus I could muster and the barrel fell into the rocks. Carla was already changing clips as I turned and dropped the remaining attacker, who was already bleeding from at least three wounds but still shooting erratically. She had one other already on the ground, quite still, but I focused on him, too, just to be sure.

And then all was quiet. The desert was silent again except for the sound of the wind. And a loud ringing in my ears.

Irritated with me, Carla demanded, "What the hell are you doing? Why didn't you get down?"

I pointed down the ravine at the fallen man. I may have had a bit of a sarcastic expression on my face, too.

"Oh."

"Listen! There are more!" We could hear shouting, then silence. Something flew into the ravine with us and bounced off the rocks with a metallic sound. Carla and I both shouted, "GET DOWN!" in unison. I was face first into the rocks as the grenade exploded. Fortunately, it had taken a favorable bounce and landed in rocks large enough to shelter us.

Again, in unison, "You ok? Uh huh."

"Follow me!" Running down the ravine, I swept the area in front of me thoroughly. She picked up the AK-47 lying in the rocks as we ran by. I could hear Carla yelling something about me bleeding badly. It didn't register at first. I was in a fog, or maybe in survival mode. She tugged on my arm as I ran, urging me to stop. When we came to a bend in the ravine that was fairly open and allowed us to see in both directions at the same time, I stopped. She had ripped a sleeve off her shirt.

My hand was wet. It was bloody. I twisted my right arm around and saw a hunk of flesh torn away a few inches from my wrist. Bone was exposed, and some of it had been shot away, too.

"Huh. Seems like it would hurt more."

Carla wrapped my arm and tied the sleeve around the wound tight enough to help stop the bleeding, and we were off again. Between breaths, Carla muttered, "Fortunately, it grazed you. We don't have what it takes to remove a slug."

"I'm fine!" Trying to relieve some stress, I added, "John Wayne would say, 'It's just a flesh wound.'" When she didn't laugh, I added, "Tough crowd."

"Knock it off, will you? This is serious. Let's regroup. We should attack these people instead of running from them. They have all the advantages if we are on the run."

We could hear them shouting in what could have been Arabic. "Alright, can you tell where they are?" The ringing in my ears prevented me from pinpointing where they were.

"No, but if you'll keep watch, I'll take a peek"

"Yeah, I don't know about that, Carla. I don't like the idea of you poking your head up into view."

Too late. She was already scooting her back up the side of the ravine, inching her way toward ground level. I had a bad feeling about it, and sure enough, we both saw an object coming at about the same time. Another hand grenade! There was no way she could take cover in time. We both knew it. Before I could react in any way, she jerked up the AK-47 she had recovered and opened fire at the grenade, which exploded in mid-air far enough away to spare us.

She shot the grenade out of the air.

NASA could not have calculated those trajectories with enough accuracy to succeed even if they had months to prepare, but Carla had reacted with pure instinct and shot a fast-moving target the size of an apple with an unfamiliar weapon she had never even fired before.

We looked at each other in amazement. She busted out laughing suddenly, and then said, "Uh, they're over there," pointing in the direction from which the grenade had come.

Over the worsening ringing in my ears, I agreed with more sarcasm. "Uh, yeah." I focused where she pointed, but still heard loud voices. Apparently, their ears were ringing, too. I focused more intently but still heard shouting, which continued to get closer. "The rocks must be interfering. We may need to flank them so that I can see them, or at least have less rock between us."

An assault rifle poked around the corner and began firing wildly. We dodged another volley of automatic gunfire and began running down the ravine with me sweeping the area in front of us again. We nearly stumbled over a fallen attacker I had dropped but kept moving.

Another explosion behind us told me that we were staying ahead of them, but the ravine was getting wider and wider, offering fewer places to hide. As bullets ricocheted off the rocks around us, the ravine came to an end and dropped off into a dry riverbed that offered even fewer places to hide.

Bullets rained in and whizzed by in multiple directions as we wedged ourselves into a small crevice in the ravine wall, our bodies pressed together, but we were still dangerously exposed. I continued to focus in the general directions of the shooters, but they were all around us.

Their shouts rose to a crescendo and I felt sure they had spotted us as even more gunfire erupted. However, the voices became quiet one at a time until no one was shouting or shooting. We waited for the ambush we felt sure was coming, her with a GLOCK in one hand and an AK-47 in another, and me ready to focus on anything that moved.

Nothing.

We waited and waited. Occasionally, we heard a camel nuzzing, so we knew they didn't just give up and leave.

"What the hell?" After what must have been twenty minutes, I began to grow impatient. "Are they just waiting for us to poke up a head or something?"

"I don't know, but I think we might try to take a look using that mirror." Carla squirmed around so I could get inside her backpack. I retrieved it and peered over the ravine wall behind us. Examining the entire area was excruciatingly slow, but I saw nothing. She took a turn and searched thoroughly, as well. Neither of us saw any sign of our attackers, or any movement other than a camel strolling by.

I shrugged. "I have an idea."

"Yeah?"

"Let's move back up the ravine."

"Well, we can't stay here," she conceded. "And we can't go out into the open out there." She waved her GLOCK out toward the open riverbed.

Glancing up, I chipped in, "And I'm *not* poking my head up there."

We slowly made our way back up the ravine, listening intently, but hearing nothing but the occasional, low-pitched camel nuzz.

"They already retrieved their dead." Carla was pointing to the spot where one of our attackers had fallen.

"What does that mean? Did they just give up and leave?"

"I don't know." She was using the mirror to see around corners before proceeding while I kept a watchful eye behind and above us.

When we reached the spot near where we left our truck, Carla noticed a cache of supplies left on the edge of the ravine and pointed them out.

"Oh, that is too good to be true." I could see canteens and medical supplies. "They are rigged to explode, for sure."

Slowly, we climbed out of the ravine, avoiding the supplies altogether. A closer inspection of the burned vehicle assured us that nothing was salvageable. As we inspected the truck, three riderless camels walked up together and stood near us as if they expected something. We looked at each other, both of us knowing that they were our way out.

The camels did not fear us when we approached. With only a small amount of urging, two of them knelt so that we could mount them. They seemed to respond to the same kinds of movement commands that horses understand. Soon, we were on our way, but high atop the camels we could see a lot more of the area.

"Look!" I could see what appeared to be our attackers lying in the rocks and sand with their weapons piled nearby. As we approached, I swept them repeatedly with a deadly focus, just to be sure.

"There are a lot of footprints in the area, and only a few led away from the bodies." Carla had her binoculars to her eyes again.

"Someone saved our asses." I was sure of it.

"I think you're right, but who? And why would they run away?"

Cessation

We followed the tracks of our rescuers for a short distance, but it soon became obvious they were going in nearly the opposite direction we needed to go.

"We should be going northwest." Carla seemed like she was finished here and wanted to go home. As tough as she is, a harrowing shootout could take its toll on anyone. My knees were still feeling a little wobbly, too.

Although I would have liked to thank these people personally, we couldn't just chase them down. They could easily misinterpret our approach as hostile and attack us the way they did the people who ambushed us.

"I think that if they wanted contact with us, they would have stayed around and introduced themselves back there."

Carla nodded and looked back northwest. "We really should try to get back to Turkey, which is at least six hundred miles away. Or maybe Afghanistan, which is a little closer. It's already Friday. And we are riding camels."

"Wait, whaaa?" I counted off the days in my head. Sure enough, Friday. "Well, okay. I need clean bandages, too."

We headed back northwest, hurrying the camels along. Before we had traveled two miles, however, Carla noticed someone off to our right, waving both hands over his head, obviously trying to attract our attention. "He's pointing to a pile of supplies on the ground in front of him."

"Offering it to us?"

"I think so." Carla tried to hold her camel perfectly still while she refocused the binoculars. "Now he's pouring water from one of the canteens into his mouth."

"He's showing us it's safe to drink," I added.

"Or sacrificing himself to kill us. He is well out of gunshot range. Can you focus on him?"

"Probably not, but I wouldn't be comfortable taking any of them out after they saved us and offered us water."

Still peering through the binoculars, Carla reported, "Now he's gesturing to us to come get the supplies."

After much discussion, we decided to move on without accepting the stranger's offer. I put my hand over my heart as a sign of thanks and we continued northwest. The man gathered the supplies, turned, and hurriedly walked roughly east and disappeared over a dune.

In a few minutes, we noticed a group of men riding camels that were running fast, paralleling our direction. When they were well ahead of us, they turned left and positioned themselves directly in our path. We stopped and both of us retrieved our binoculars this time. They all had their hands over their hearts returning my gesture.

One of them dismounted his camel, placed the supplies back onto the ground, and took another drink from one of the canteens. He was pouring the water from a couple of inches above his mouth to make it obvious that he was drinking the water. This time, they abandoned the supplies and rode off about a quarter of a mile to the east.

We rode to the supplies and checked them out. There was a modern first aid kit, including alcohol and fresh bandages. We went ahead and took advantage of that and cleaned my wound, which looked far worse than it felt until we poured the alcohol over it. I think maybe our new friends heard me yelling from a quarter mile away.

With our thirsts quenched and the supplies stowed away, we were about to continue northwest but the men were gesturing for us to follow them. The only dismounted man pointed to another small pile of supplies on the ground. This time he picked up a large phone that looked like it was from the early nineties.

"Oh!" Carla sounded excited.

"What? There's no way we could get a signal out here."

"No, that's a satellite phone."

I repeated Carla's sentiment. "Oh. Okay. Should we follow them then, or move on?"

Our new friends rode off roughly east again, leaving the supplies on a flat rock.

"Let's go get that phone." Without waiting for confirmation, Carla hurried her camel away. Upon reaching the supplies, we could see our new friends off in the distance again. This time they had a large tent erected and a campfire started with something roasting over the fire.

Then the satellite phone rang. We exchanged glances with each other and at the people around the tent. Carla suggested that I answer the phone, as they might not even talk to a woman.

I picked it up and answered. "Hello?"

A bouncing Middle Eastern accent came across the line clearly after a moment's pause. "Hello, and thank you for trusting us."

"Extending that trust was difficult, seeing how you're making it painfully obvious that you don't trust us."

"We are sorry for that," the stranger assured me, "but we know what you are capable of doing."

"Actually, my companion was the one who shot that grenade out of the sky."

After a moment's hesitation, the Middle Eastern voice continued. "While that sounds like a marvelous feat, I meant you. We know what *you* are capable of accomplishing with your mind."

I was stunned. How could a complete stranger know this? I decided to play dumb to try to find out more. "What do you mean?"

"We are aware. In fact, there is someone here with us who you know, and who very much wishes to speak to you, although you probably will not want to talk to him at first. Please trust me once again when I say that your perceptions about him are all wrong."

Who could I possibly know in the middle of an Iranian desert?

When the voice came over the phone, I recognized him immediately. I felt a wave of loathing sweep across my face and I was glad I did not have the device on speakerphone, for he called me by name. The loathing turned to dread as I realized my two worlds were colliding. I still did not want Carla to know anything about my "other" life. I was simply not ready for that yet. She was still an FBI agent, despite the growing love I felt for her.

"Please hear me out," begged Abu Azmi Adham Asrar ibn Ibrahim Al-shamrani El-qaatil… a.k.a. Al, The Killer.

"You better make this good you son of a bitch."

"I am Detective Kemal, a Turkish special investigator. I was working undercover for Interpol while I was with you back at the lab."

This is my life. A serial killer vigilante surrounded by feds.

Al, a.k.a. Kemal, went on, speaking quickly. "I am the one who tipped off your Homeland Security about the impending attack. I then had to leave the US immediately to retain my cover, no matter how bad it seemed to my American coworkers and friends. I infiltrated that terrorist cell *years* earlier, dedicating my life to finding their leaders. Foiling terrorists' plans to destroy the building where you and I worked did not mean my job was over. In fact, the arrests made by my colleagues that day meant I would rise in the ranks of the cell I had infiltrated by attrition. I *had* to pursue that opportunity."

Not yet sure what to think or say, I looked out toward the distant group standing in the shade of one of their tents. "So, you also saved all our asses that day back at the lab." I noticed that Carla's ears appeared to perk up at the mention of something from my past, but I had to admit that I was glad Kemal was not the monster I had thought him to be. I *had* trusted him with a nascent friendship, after all.

"Many lives were saved by nearly as many people, but American technology ultimately suffered an enormous setback. That attack was designed to disrupt the development of new technologies, so even though the bombing was a failure, the closure of Elucidate Research Laboratories made the terrorists feel victorious. Now they are even more emboldened. Or, they were until you two wiped out a large number of them."

Through binoculars, Kemal could see Carla's growing impatience about being left out of the conversation, so he went on. "However, all that is a different story for another time. Right now, we have other tasks to which we need to attend."

"What exactly do you mean?"

He told us that word had traveled through the terrorist cell networks and all other weapons caches and training camps were now on high alert and the chances of us taking out another facility were very low. I didn't bother to tell him that we were out of time and heading home. Either way, extremists all over the Middle East were on the lookout for us. Getting home through hostile territory would be close to impossible without help.

"Also, there is a group of people east of here that I am *sure* you will want to meet."

"Ok, why would I want to meet them? We don't exactly have a lot of time for socializing."

Kemal was insistent. "I am sure you will want to meet these people. Besides, if you decide you want to go home after you meet them, we have the means to fly you wherever you want to go."

"I'll need to discuss this with my companion."

"Of course, I understand. If you decide to come with us, we will all form a perimeter a good distance from this tent to stand guard for you."

"No need for that. I think we have established some trust here."

"You do not understand, they have a–if you will pardon the pun–a deathly fear of you and your abilities."

"I see."

"And do not worry, I will not use your name or speak of the past in front of the FBI agent."

Kemal, the Turkish detective, sure seemed to know a lot about me. Disturbing.

Carla listened to me explain the situation and warily agreed to sleep in their camp. We made ourselves at home as the sun began setting and enjoyed some of the fire-roasted fowl they had left for us.

She fell asleep inside the tent, but despite my exhaustion, I was too restless for slumber. I had too much on my mind and decided to stay up and keep watch, just in case. To help pass the time, I used the satellite phone to call our author friend and summarize the events of the past few days. We talked until the battery died.

Afterword

A note from the author…

Okay, sorry for the abrupt ending, but it imitates real life. My friend's battery died while we were talking and I didn't hear from them again for many months. Honestly, I thought he and Carla had been killed in that hostile desert, but obviously not. It's no secret that their story is a trilogy now.

When I didn't hear from him for weeks, I began putting their story into the form of a novel, although I changed enough of the circumstances, locations and names to protect them in case they were hiding, and not captured, or worse. Writing *The Attunement* took several months, and just *days* after the first edition was released, he contacted me. Too late to "stop the press," as they say.

I urge you to read *The Attuned* and *The Attunist*, if you haven't already, to learn about the adventures of two of my favorite people.